ALSO BY

SANTIAGO GAMBOA

Necropolis
Night Prayers

RETURN TO THE DARK VALLEY

Santiago Gamboa

RETURN TO THE
DARK VALLEY

*Translated from the Spanish
by Howard Curtis*

Europa
editions

Europa Editions
214 West 29th Street
New York, N.Y. 10001
www.europaeditions.com
info@europaeditions.com

Copyright © Santiago Gamboa c/o Schavelzon Graham Agencia Literaria
www.schavelzongraham.com
First Publication 2017 by Europa Editions

Translation by Howard Curtis
Original title: *Volver al oscuro valle*
Translation copyright © 2017 by Europa Editions

Library of Congress Cataloging in Publication Data is available
ISBN 978-1-60945-425-8

Gamboa, Santiago
Return to the Dark Valley

Book design by Emanuele Ragnisco
www.mekkanografici.com

Cover photo © fcscafeine/iStock

Prepress by Grafica Punto Print – Rome

Printed in the USA

CONTENTS

PART I
THEORY OF SUFFERING BODIES
(OR FIGURES EMERGING FROM THE WRECKAGE) - 15

PART II
HEADING FOR THE 5TH PARALLEL
(OR THE REPUBLIC OF GOODNESS) - 295

EPILOGUE
(RETURNING WHERE RIMBAUD
WANTED TO RETURN) - 443

ABOUT THE AUTHOR - 463

To Analía and Alejandro, riding to Golgonooza

That Man should labour & sorrow,
& learn & forget, & return
To the dark valley whence he came,
to begin his labours anew.
—WILLIAM BLAKE

Because even though the abyss swallowed them the song
continued in the air of the valley, the mist of the valley . . .
—ROBERTO BOLAÑO

RETURN TO THE
DARK VALLEY

PART I
THEORY OF SUFFERING BODIES
(OR FIGURES EMERGING
FROM THE WRECKAGE)

1

These were still the difficult years. I was very tired and wanted to write a book about cheerful, silent, active people. That was my intention. I had spent time in India, about two years, and when I got back to Italy I found everything had changed. Sadness was everywhere now. An unexpected storm cloud hovered in the skies of Europe, and nothing was the way it had been. From the doors of the old Roman buildings hung overlapping "For Sale" notices, a kind of collage that dramatized the anguish of owners having to leave or at least to withstand the blows. The highways and byways of the city swarmed with people who hid their eyes or looked at each other with guilty expressions.

Being there, just hanging about, with nothing specific to do on a working day, wasn't the best letter of introduction. Nor did it demonstrate much social usefulness. Especially if you spent the hours in some corner café observing the transformation of the city and taking brief notes, making incoherent doodles, or drawing little men scaling mountains. That's why it was best to change places frequently, in order not to attract attention and immediately be classified as a slacker or a piece of riffraff. When faced with a crisis, people are obsessed with respectability.

It's understandable. When masses of people seek work without the least hope of finding it, when businesses reduce their personnel and the fashion stores announce sales out of season, the best thing to do is become a man without a face. The Invisible Man, the Man of the Crowd.

I was that man. Always observing, attentive to the slightest vibration, perhaps waiting for something, with a cup of tea or coffee in my hand, letting myself be swept along by the frantic activity of the passersby, the way active humans come and go and fill squares and avenues, like shoals of fish driven by the tides. A movement that allows cities to go on living and produce wealth. To be healthy and respectable conurbations.

Exemplary conurbations.

This story begins the day my quiet life as an observer was shaken by a small earthquake. It was something very simple. I was sitting on a café terrace on Corso Trieste, watching the stream of pedestrians pass by in the direction of the African quarter, when my cell phone vibrated on the table.

A new message, I told myself. An e-mail.

"Please go to Madrid, Consul, to the Hotel de las Letras. Book into Room 711 and wait for me. Will be in touch. Juana."

That was the whole message, not a word more. Enough to unleash a modest storm inside me, like galleries collapsing. Juana. That apparently harmless combination of letters that had occupied my life for a brief time. My mouth still open, uttering her name. It had all happened some years before.

I looked at my watch, it was eleven in the morning. I reread the message and felt an even greater sense of sadness, as if a current of air or a tornado were lifting me from my chair, above the avenue and its tall pines. I had to hurry. To run.

"I'll be there today, await instructions," I replied immediately, signaling to the waiter for my check.

Before long, I, too, was in movement, energetic and active, heading for the airport.

2

It was drizzling, it was hot. Sitting in a Roman taxi, I watched Via Nomentana pass by, as far as Stazione Termini, then Merulana and, eventually, Cristoforo Colombo. The longest and perhaps most beautiful route to the airport. *Arrivederci Roma*, I thought—remembering an old song— as I looked out at the beloved city. Something told me it would be a while before I returned, as the name Juana, with its incredible power of evocation, kept coming back, ever more distinctly, insistently, violently.

How long had it been? Seven years? Yes, seven years since I'd met her, when I was a consul in India and had to deal with the case of her brother, who had been arrested in Bangkok. In all this time, I hadn't had any news of her or her son, even though I had written to consulates in many countries, who in turn had asked for information from the respective immigration authorities.

"Juana Manrique. Pas d'information liée à ce nom."

That was the response from the French Ministry of Foreign Affairs in Paris, the last place from which Juana had been in touch with me. There were similar responses from a further twenty foreign ministries.

It was a mystery: a woman and a child who had vanished into the congested air of the world. One more disease of our dizzying era. I had never quite understood her during the few days I had spent with her in Delhi, which might have been why her image had come back to me frequently over the years, always in the form of a question: what strange things was she fleeing so stubbornly? When I finished my consular mission, I returned from Asia to my previous life, a life of writing and reading and watching. The same life I was now about to abandon because of a brief message from her.

The taxi made its way through the traffic jams of the EUR district until it reached the freeway leading to Fiumicino. Now I too was leaving, like that breathless multitude I had spent so much time observing and had always thought so remote from my own life.

Rome was struggling manfully to continue as an active, energetic city, but it wasn't an easy battle. A strange economic indicator called "spread," which was not supposed to go above 300, was approaching 500. Greece and Spain had already broken through that limit and were close to ruin. The Italian news bulletins began with the daily spread figure flashing up on the screen, its rise referred to in anguished tones: "470!", "478!" Terrified people raised their hands and exclaimed: "What will become of us?" "Will we reach 500?" The most absurd hypotheses were heard in the cafés. It was said that the Mafia wanted to bankrupt the country in order to remove it from the Eurozone and continue to exploit it free of the control of Brussels.

The newspaper La Repubblica reported that fifty-two entrepreneurs had committed suicide in less than a year. The Italian banks, setting a fine example of solidarity and compassion, preferred to capitalize their money in fixed-limit European funds instead of lending it to their long-term customers, thus preventing them from working. And the average business needs credit the way plants need light.

But the world crisis had first arrived in symbolic form, with a major shipwreck just off the Tuscan coast, opposite the island of Giglio. It was an omen of what was about to happen to the whole country, like some ancient oracle saying:

"Something serious is coming. Run to your houses."

What exactly happened? A poor devil named Francesco Schettino, captain of a luxury cruise ship belonging to a company called Costa Crociere, thought to send a nautical greeting to the island of Giglio, something known in Italy as "the bow"—a custom practiced by ship's captains, consisting of passing very close to a harbor and sounding the siren—but he got too close and hit a reef. It was the company's largest ship, with 1,500 double cabins, five swimming pools, a casino, discotheques and restaurants, a theatre on three floors, and 6000 square meters of gymnasiums and spa.

Like running a five-star hotel at high speed into a mountain of stones!

Crippled and taking in water, the ship remained afloat for three hours before tipping over onto its side and half sinking. Thirty-two passengers died, trapped in the elevators or in their own cabins. Only three of the bodies were recovered, a year later, when the rusted carcass of the ship was raised from the water. Captain Schettino, who according to witnesses was drunk, had been the first person to abandon ship.

The Italians followed the shipwreck live, with bated breath, and once again the voice of the oracle echoed through the air:

"Oh, Death terrible in misfortune! Oh, house fecund in disasters!"

Soon afterwards, like a plane smashing into a skyscraper, the crisis began. A violent economic storm struck the fragile peninsula and left it to drift, with half its body sunk in the water. What to do? Some threw themselves into the sea and tried to swim to other coasts, but where? Young Italians, most of them unemployed, did not hesitate. They packed their bags and headed north to work as dishwashers and waiters in Germany, Norway, Holland, or Switzerland.

Fleeing north, ever north.

There they found welfare states with social security and

generous benefits. After all, they were part of the community, children of the same Europe! The taxpayers of these generous, hyperactive, and responsible countries scratched their chins a little and looked suspiciously at this unexpected white migration. Before long, without making too much of a fuss, they asked if the entry of their poor cousins from the south might be restricted slightly, or if these people could at least search in their own wallets.

But if the youth of Italy was fleeing the shipwreck by going to Berlin or Copenhagen to wash dishes, what could be said of that other wave of servants who had come from farther away to wash the Italians' dishes? Those tens of thousands of Peruvians, Filipinos, Bangladeshis, Colombians, and Ecuadorians, where could they go? There were too many hands wanting to grab a scouring pad or a broom and too few hours of work available in the houses of Rome or the trattorias of Trastevere. Some undertook the pilgrimage northward, in the wake of their former bosses, but got there without help or subsidy. They were the lowest class of working immigrants. Some had arrived in Italy fleeing the collapse in Spain, which came first. The young had time and spirit, they could wait a while longer, but those who had been there since the mid-nineties or before had no strength left.

"It's time to go back," they said.

And so began the long return: reunions, disillusion, a homecoming without glory, empty-handed.

Arrivederci Roma!

As my taxi plowed on through the rain, I registered, as if for the last time, the fields on either side of the freeway, vast sheds containing discount supermarkets, industrial parks. I felt a strange sensation of farewell or defeat in the atmosphere, but I alone was anxious.

When I got to the airport, I had to make my way through noisy crowds. The numbers of people who were leaving! Up until that moment, I had preferred to stay, since in my case emigrating to another country would not have meant the slightest change. I don't know if I've mentioned the fact that I'm a writer, and it's good to write in the middle of a storm, although that may not sound very sympathetic to the country in which I live. It may even be immoral, despicable, but it's genuine. Literature is also written when the streets are running with blood, when the last hero is about to fall, riddled by a hail of bullets, or a child smashes its little head on the asphalt. What is good for writing doesn't always benefit the defenseless population around it. That at least is what I thought, not knowing what was to happen later. That's why in my most recent notebooks I hadn't been writing about fugitives or shipwrecks, but about another time, a time not so distant. A journey into the life of one of the greatest fugitives of both East and West. The life of the poet Arthur Rimbaud, my most constant companion in all those years of traveling between Asia and Europe. All the rest had remained in the past, linked to other periods of my life. But Juana, coming from that same disturbing place in my memory, had upset that precarious balance. It was her voice that had made me leave Rome in a hurry for something new that, I sensed, might even be seen as a slow return.

3

DR. CAYETANO FRÍAS TELLERT, PSYCHOLOGIST
PATIENT: MANUELA BELTRÁN

Strange as it may seem to anyone who knows me, Doctor, I'm a very ordinary person. I may be tired or badly dressed, my hair may be sweaty from just getting up, my T-shirt may be creased, my shorts threadbare or stained with strange liquids, those damn stains! But if you let me tidy myself at the mirror for a while and then take a closer look at me, a really close, affectionate look, I might surprise you. Sorry, Doctor, if I'm talking to you like a typical girl from Cali, and in such familiar language, could it be I'm falling in love? why should I have wanted to start by saying these things, things that, when it comes down to it, have nothing to do with me? Anyway, I'm going to repeat it just once: I'm one of those girls that any of you disgusting alpha males, with five whiskeys inside you, maybe even fewer, would already be itching to take into the back room, without even knowing or caring what I have inside me. I'm like those zombies you see sitting early in the morning on the first buses or in subway cars, who keep yawning because they were working until late the night before, waiting on tables or looking after children or cleaning houses. Not like the rich girls who only yawn if they've been out on the town or fucking their rich boyfriends.

Unfortunately, I wasn't lucky enough to be one of those.

Nor am I like the Caribbean girls you see in bad movies or read about in bad novels, with their red lips and their bodies vibrating in rhythm, of course not, but if you talk to me for a while (not strictly about my appearance!) you'll realize, to your surprise, that I'm interested in indie movies, world politics, and the debate on the end of history. Sociology, too, and especially literature, because as it happens, I'm a student of letters in Madrid, and that's why it isn't a man's tan, or his convertible, that turns me on the most, but novels and poetry collections and anything that's printed and is halfway decent, you know what I mean? I'm a lousy intellectual, Doctor, although I wasn't always. Plus, I lost it all. Let's get this over with, once and for all.

I must be crazy.

Really crazy.

I say this not for you to like me, let alone pity me, Doctor, not even for you to understand what I've been through and that terrible thing that happened to me that until now I've never dared tell anybody. I'm writing this to give myself courage.

It's just a sad, wretched declaration of principles.

I'm going to tell a story. One of the many stories I could tell, though this one's the story of my life. I'll skip over my childhood, which is the most boring part of all lives and the memories that interest me. People get all symbolic when it comes to childhood, and who can stand that? There's no symbolism, but sometimes childhood produces a lyric tone that doesn't sit well with the prose of confession and life.

All right, now, Doctor. Let's go there.

After my Dad left home and deserted us, over there in Cali, and my mother wept a while for her life and her daughter, but above all because she hadn't done anything to keep him, anyway, after that, tired of waiting, upset and very lonely, my Mom shrugged her shoulders and went out on the street with a kind of neon sign on her forehead saying "Female Available," or if you prefer, "Desperately Seeking Man," I don't know, what's certain is that, as often happens to single mothers, she thought of it as a lottery, someone would turn to look at her, and that's how it was that, very quickly and without the slightest quality control, she brought a guy home to live with her, a foul-smelling man who came clumping into the house, creating all the obvious problems you can imagine for me, her preadolescent twelve-year-old daughter, which is why as soon as I saw him come in and then unpack some horrible cardboard boxes containing his clothes, I said to myself, something nasty's going to happen, this isn't good, be careful, and I knew that sooner or later I had to get out of that hellhole.

But I was still very young, Doctor, and I delayed leaving for about two years. What could I do? That was my one mistake, not getting out of there soon enough.

As was to be supposed, Mother's boyfriend was a coarse, violent, ignorant son of a bitch, a drunk and a popper of pills and whatever they put in front of him, a cokehead, a crack smoker. He even sniffed glue. I got tired of him spying on me in the bathroom and hearing him fucking Mother, screaming and cursing. Once I caught him jerking off with his hand wrapped in a pair of my panties, can you get your head around something like that, Doctor?

The man made me nauseous.

After something very nasty happened—I'm planning to tell you about it later, when I'm strong enough, although you can already imagine it, can't you?—driven crazy with pain and humiliation, I made up a story that God had called me and that I wanted to go to a convent school to pray for the sins of the world. Obviously I didn't believe in anything, no way! What I wanted was to get out of that fucking house.

There was a convent near Palmira called Santa Águeda, run by nuns from the Order of St. Clare, and Mother agreed to take me. So did her disgusting boyfriend, who thought he'd be safe that way. The guy was a partner in a motorcycle dealership in district three, and in Cali that's a more lucrative business than selling coke, so he had money and that was the source of his power over Mother. She boasted that we were in the middle class now. Middle class, forget it, she was still working as a waitress in a chicken rotisserie in La Flora. The man didn't trust me because I could denounce him and so for him it was a relief to know I was going. He even gave money to the nuns so that they'd take me quickly before I could change my mind. And so it was.

But in Santa Águeda the life I'd been hoping to get away from was still there, Doctor, only even crazier than outside. The place was like a volcano of raging hormones. The novices, who'd all been forced there by their families, apparently to get them away from the vices of the world, were fucking perverts and drug addicts. Adolescence in total eruption. The fourth night I was there, a girl from my dormitory asked me if I was a virgin and I didn't know what to reply. She said that if I didn't know, that meant I was, because you know these things, and then she asked if at least I'd had sex with another woman or if I'd like to eat a girl's pussy. I told her I wouldn't. It's really great, she said, don't you want me to teach you? Seeing my surprise, she lifted the sheet, put in her hand, and stroked me. Then she stuck her head in and started sucking me and I kept very still, embarrassed but also happy because I felt things and it was nice. When she took her head out from under the blankets she was very red in the face, and then she said to me, now it's your turn to suck me, come on, and she opened her legs, but I couldn't do it and I told her that it disgusted me, that I was too young for that kind of thing, but she insisted, what do you mean, young? didn't you say you were fourteen? I told her I owed her one and pulled the sheet up over me.

Then I dreamed that I was a rabbit running across a meadow. Something like a shadow was pursuing me, carrying a club in its hand to hit me on the back of my head and throw me in a pan. Sometimes my pursuer was my mother's boyfriend and sometimes the girl from the dormitory, whose name was Vanessa, and suddenly she lifted her uniform and you could see her red pussy, and hear her saying, you owe me one, bitch! but I kept running until they trapped me and when they were about to deliver the blow a gap appeared in the grass and I escaped through it.

I woke up screaming and the nun keeping night watch switched on the light and asked, what's going on?

Nothing, Mother, nothing. A bad dream.

In the convent, they had a Chevrolet van for running errands, shopping at the market, and transporting the choir. I joined the choir on my very first day because I always liked singing, and after a few months they took us to an event in Palmira. I think it was for a religious festival, I can't remember which one. And what a surprise I got! When we changed into our elegant uniforms, I saw that some of my companions had G-strings on under their smocks, which were like nuns' habits. Then, in the van, a tall bitch who was called Sister Concepción and we called Conche told me that they'd put them on because there were going to be men there, and even though they were novices and students, men were men and when they looked at us they could tell we were wearing G-strings.

That struck me as strange because I felt nothing, and even wore gray underwear that went from the navel almost down to the knee. Passion killers! Conche called them, and I didn't argue, although our only passion was supposed to be God and praying for the vices and sins of the world, or perhaps something even more concrete, which was to make this little shithouse or quadrilateral of excrement we call Planet Earth a little less foul (if you think that's too vulgar, Doctor, we can delete it).

I'd also noticed that the novices shaved themselves.

One evening I went into the bathroom and found several of them sitting in a circle, with their habits raised to their waists and their panties around their ankles. They were holding razors and had bowls with water and soap between their legs.

Conche, who knew everything, was telling them: first use the scissors to reduce the bush, girls, and then move the razor up and down in the direction of the hair so as not to irritate the follicles, gently but firmly, okay? so that you can feel it cutting, and when I asked them what was so bad about having hair they said, so as not to look like natives, bitch, and to stop lumps forming, and they laughed. They thought it was funny how little I knew of life even though I was fourteen. According to them, I should already know how the world was and why lumps formed in the pubic hairs.

Oh, if I'd told them the truth as I'm thinking to tell you, Doctor, those bitches would have been amazed, and some would even have cried. But let's take it a bit at a time, and we'll see if I can summon up the courage as I go along.

The day arrived and we went to Palmira to sing with other religious schools. Then the city council provided a buffet in a big hall upstairs, with a view of a very pretty shaded square and park. Palmira is near Cali but I'd never been there, and I liked it. In my modest way, I felt that I was getting to know the world, because Palmira might be backward and hot and even ugly, but it's still the world, isn't it?

At the buffet, I ate French fries and ham appetizers. My classmates were talking with a group of boys from another school, young men in white shirts and gray pants, all with spotty faces, all tongue-tied, very ugly but very beautiful, you know what I mean? You could see their innocence and their desire to believe in something and that's why they were beautiful, although they tried to act tough, even though they were just a bunch of ordinary young guys.

Learners.

That's what I thought when I saw them.

I stayed close to the window, looking out at the park, and for a moment I forgot what was around me, engrossed in the shapes of the clouds, which looked like roosters' crests, and

the wind shaking the palm trees. The sun was going down
slowly behind the mountains and I said to myself, when it
comes down to it life is beautiful, Manuelita, don't make such
a fuss, the world is overflowing with peace and beauty, look at
the mountains in the distance and that little brown village all
the way over there, isn't it beautiful? Keep going, I said to
myself again, and I filled my lungs with that air that brought so
many things that did me good, and closed my eyes and convinced myself that life and even God had seen me and were
about to give me a second chance.

I ate some fried bread with onions and tomatoes and took
a sip of my Coca-Cola, waiting for them to call us to go down
to the Chevrolet. The reverend mother was still talking with
officials from the town council and the choir mistress, planning more excursions and concerts. One of the officials
showed her some papers and told her dates, and the reverend
mother took out her diary and drew red circles around particular dates.

I went to the bathroom and there I found Vanessa,
Estéfany, and Lady, who were the worst. They were already
smoking, blowing the smoke out through the window. We
weren't allowed to smoke and I was scared of being caught
with them, but I couldn't get out of the damned bathroom
without being called a nerd or God knows what, so I went into
a cubicle to take a leak. That's when it struck me that the
smoke smelled different, it wasn't cigarettes they were smoking
but marijuana. I knew that fucking smell well because of
Mother's boyfriend, where did they get it from?

I asked them and they said that the guys from the boys'
boarding school had given them three joints to get them in the
mood. In addition they had half a bottle of Domecq brandy
and they were mixing it with soda in a plastic bottle. This is a
private party, Vanessa told me, but you can stay if you want.
And there's going to be a surprise.

No sooner had she said this than I heard a noise at the window and saw one of the tongue-tied young guys in gray uniforms come in. He had come from the men's bathroom, balancing on the ledge, which was pretty dangerous. He jumped down from the windowsill with his little angel face and pimples on his forehead and started smoking a joint with them, sucking greedily, almost desperately, taking deep breaths. It was obvious they already knew each other because Vanessa and Lady started kissing him on the mouth and in no time at all they took down his pants. I looked at the door of the bathroom and felt panic, what if someone came in? They took a huge cock out of his underpants and Estéfany, already high as a kite, stuck it in her mouth. I thought about the mother superior, who was only a few yards away. I wasn't doing anything but I was there. The young guy lay down on the bench, shifting so that Estéfany could suck him off more comfortably, and all the while he was sticking his hand under Vanessa's and Lady's skirts.

Suddenly, another young guy fell through the window and joined the party. He opened an envelope of silver paper and took out a powder that they started putting in their noses. They offered it to me and I said again, no, thanks, I'm too young for that, and they all laughed, too young? you're fourteen, aren't you? and I said, yes, I'm too young for vices like that. Then the newcomer knelt in front of me and said, you're not too young and it's not a vice, it'll be great, let me teach you something, and then the other girls said, yes, yes, deflower her, come on, deflower her! They grabbed me by the shoulders until I was lying down and they pulled down my panties, laughing and joking about my pubic hair, look at that bush! it's like a jungle! I kicked, I was choking with anger but I couldn't scream. Seeing that I couldn't escape, I took a puff at a newly lit joint, but it turned out to have a sweet taste that wasn't marijuana and in no time at all it was if a cannon had shot me through the window, I was flying with my eyes closed, my muscles loose. It made me cough and I felt like throwing up, and I managed to say, this isn't weed, and the boy said, no, sweetheart, it's crack, do you want some more? When he parted my legs I stopped struggling. He put his head down and I felt his tongue and his teeth biting me. I liked it. It was cool that this young guy who was so handsome should notice me, because for a while now my body had been asking me something, as if the scars had disappeared. Then the boy took down his pants and slowly put it into me, and it didn't hurt. I was so high from the crack that it took my fear away. When the three girls saw that I wasn't bleeding they said, didn't she tell us she was a virgin? look at her, the bitch, the hypocrite!

I didn't give a fuck. I closed my eyes and enjoyed it.

When I opened them again I felt as if years had passed, but my boy was still there, on top of me. Although he was also kissing Estéfany, the bastard. Lady was fucking the first boy on the other bench and Vanessa, sprawled on the floor, was greedily smoking one crack joint after another, as if clinging to that tube of smoke was her only chance of survival.

Suddenly I felt a tremor, my muscles tensed, preparing for something, and I gave out a soft cry. Estéfany heard it and said to the guy:

"Don't get her pregnant, come on her belly button."

He quickly took it out and spilled himself over me, a hot drool that trickled slowly down my sides. I gave a stupid smile because my head was out of it, and just then I heard knocking on the door. My heart beat faster. It was the mother superior saying, girls? are you ready? We're going! Fortunately she didn't ask us to open the door. We washed our faces with cold water and straightened our uniforms. The boys got out through the same window they'd come in by.

On the ride back in the Chevrolet the chafing of the cushion made me come every time the van braked or accelerated.

Vanessa noticed. She had purple circles around her eyes, which were swollen from the crack. She looked at me and said, well, hypocrite, did you like it? Fucking's great.

When we got back to Santa Águeda we were sent to the chapel to pray until dinnertime, fortunately, because all three of us were still high. It's awesome, praying like that, Doctor. That's when you understand religion and the appearances of the Lord, who that day wasn't on the cross but sitting beside me, looking at me tenderly, and so I took advantage to ask him, or rather, I said to him, now that I can I want to ask you a question, just one, why wasn't I given a normal life? why was it my fate, when I'm so fragile, such a crybaby? Christ heard my question and smiled but didn't answer, as if the answer wasn't important, and so I insisted: why have you abandoned me in the middle of so many bad people? and he kept looking without looking, in a way that his presence didn't seem to contradict, it was strange, until I couldn't stand it anymore and said to him, inside my mind, why don't you or anybody ever hear me when I scream?

Silence, nothing but silence.

What that party in Palmira did was to gradually open the gates of hell, because from that day on not a week went by when we didn't do drugs or get it on with anyone that showed up at the convent, whether man, woman, or priest. And we did it with enormous joy, as if something religious was being manifested in all that apparent chaos. Isn't there a certain spirituality in excess? Between the extremes of sorrow and the extremes of escape, why do we have to prefer sorrow? I was born to sorrow, but what do judges know of the sorrows of life?

This seems like fiction, but it was true.

It even seems like literature, but before that it was true.

One of those stories whose aim is to forge beauty out of the ugliest and dirtiest things in life.

After two months, I was given the task of going with the

sister in charge of the kitchen to do the weekly shopping, and when she wasn't looking I slipped away and bought myself a beautiful collection of G-strings in the colors of the flag. I felt patriotic and jubilant, a good pupil who wears tricolor G-strings so that the men of the country, our heroes, should die wrapped in the flag. I wanted to swallow the world whole, to burn my adolescence like someone throwing gallons of gasoline over a stand of dry trees and setting fire to it. I couldn't wait to do that.

I had with me money from the other girls in my dormitory to buy them their special orders. From the drugstore, Canesten for a newcomer named Lucy, who had really bad thrush and stank. Aspirin for hangovers, Lúa fruit salts, Ibuprofen, condoms, KY jelly. In another place to which they had directed me, a bit scared, I bought drugs. They'd told me the prices, so I got some bags of crack for Vanessa, five grams of coke, and a quarter kilo of marijuana, which was what we all did most of. I hid it all in the fruit sack. I also bought three bottles of aguardiente from Cauca, which was great to mix with the juices they gave us at meals.

4

When I got to Madrid, I learned the extraordinary news that an Islamist cell had just seized the Irish embassy on Paseo de la Castellana. Seeing the images on the screens in the airport, I couldn't believe my eyes.

BREAKING NEWS! BREAKING NEWS!

Groups of soldiers were patrolling the corridors of the terminal, nervous and aggressive, asking for papers and frisking anyone they thought looked suspicious, especially those with dark skin or of Arab appearance. People crowded around the monitors with expressions of fear on their faces, as if saying, what else is going to happen now?

I hadn't known anything about it when I left Rome, and the flight had lasted barely two hours, which meant it was all very recent, but everything that happens in the world is unexpected seconds before it happens, except to those who plan and execute it. A red news ticker at the bottom of the screens presented a permanent flash:

TERRORISTS SEIZE IRISH EMBASSY IN MADRID!

Distant sirens and the clatter of a helicopter engine mingled with the deafening announcements from the loudspeakers. Iberia flight to Palma de Mallorca . . . !!! To make matters worse, the airport employees increased the volume of the monitors with every new bulletin. Perhaps worst of all was the din of the crowd. The cries of people yelling to each other, people talking and gesticulating, in person or on their cell phones, the shouts and the laughter, the protests, the comments and explanations. Some travelers were sleeping on the rows of seats or even on the floor, beside the machines dispensing drinks and candy, using them to lean their backs against because they were empty. A number of mothers were breastfeeding their babies on the escalators, which were out of service.

I went into the bathroom. The smell knocked me back. There was no toilet paper in the cubicles and the bowls were overflowing with shit and urine. I waited in line to pee in one of the urinals, which was oozing a dark liquid. As for washing your hands, forget it.

Outside, very close to the entrance, I saw a family sitting in a circle on the tiled floor of the arrivals lounge. They were eating from a pan, on plastic plates. What was happening in Madrid? What were all these people doing? They were leaving. They were waiting their turn to leave Spain on charter flights to Northern Europe or Latin America. Just as in Italy, here, too, many people had decided to leave, or simply to return home.

I walked out of the terminal and found a taxi amid the crowds. The driver had the radio tuned to a news program, although he preferred to tell me himself what was happening, looking in the rearview mirror, putting both of us at risk. He was nervous, slapping the wheel and waving his hands as he talked.

"What they've said so far is that first three black guys walked into the embassy, quite casually, and then two more, acting as if they were coming to apply for something. And nobody knows how, those five sons of bitches killed the guards and opened the door to the others to come in with weapons and bombs. Apparently they even drove a car into the garage.

On the radio they're saying some of these guys are Spanish, but how can they be Spanish? They must be blacks with Spanish passports, which isn't the same thing. They're holding thirty people hostage, and they say they're going to cut their throats and blow up the building if they don't give them God knows how much money. How can those bastards be Spanish? They're screwing us."

Blacks? I thought. Black terrorists? That's what the taxi driver said. They must be Africans. Let's wait and see.

I was nervous by the time I got to the hotel, but when I registered there was no message from Juana. When would I see her? I felt worried and reread the message on my phone: "Please go to Madrid, Consul, to the Hotel de las Letras. Book into Room 711 and wait for me. Will be in touch. Juana."

"Is Room 711 free?" I asked at reception.

The girl looked on her screen.

"Yes, sir, but there's a small supplement."

"I'll take it."

When I entered the room, I understood why Juana had chosen it. It had a big picture window looking out on the corner of the Gran Vía, with the Telefónica building almost opposite. Thanks to the isolation, the sounds were vague and distant, even though the avenue was clearly visible. Would I see her that night? I was nervous.

I switched on the TV.

Channel One was broadcasting developments live. Twenty heavily armed and apparently well trained men were still inside. Three people had died, the two guards at the entrance and one in the garage.

The latest news was that the terrorists had just issued a first press release. The taxi driver had been right to say they were black. Well, Africans. But they didn't want money. They said they belonged to Boko Haram, the Nigerian Islamist group, and they demanded an immediate stop to the bombing of ISIS targets in Iraq and Syria. They were prepared to die "for their brothers in the caliphate" and if there was no response they would cut the throat of one of the hostages after six hours, in front of the cameras, and put it out on social media. That was their fearsome threat: one every six hours, available on the Internet. How much time was left? It was already starting to get dark. The images showed the police operation, with hundreds of men deployed around Paseo de la Castellana, armored cars blocking the adjacent streets, and helicopters circling with floodlights. Somewhere in the shadows there were probably special forces and snipers lurking.

Next came footage from a security camera in a nearby building, footage that showed the exact moment when the terrorists entered the embassy. According to one of the pundits, there was a logic to the seizure, since of all the Anglo-Saxon embassies the Irish was the least closely guarded. At this point, the program was interrupted and they went over to Moncloa Palace, where the emergency committee was meeting.

A senator from the Popular Party said the following:

"This is an unprecedented disaster, but the public can be confident that we are taking all necessary measures to deal with this attack and to make sure that such unprecedented disasters do not happen again in the future."

Questioned about the security measures being put in place, Madrid's chief of police told the interviewer, a woman:

"I can hardly tell you about the operation, can I, my dear? Not if the terrorists in there are also watching television. Not even with my hand over my mouth, like the soccer people."

The Irish prime minister expressed his gratitude for the actions of the Spanish police, and said that democracies had to remain united against terrorism. He ended his speech with a strange slogan:

"We'll win and they won't!"

From Washington, the president of the United States made

it clear that he was in direct contact with Moncloa Palace, looking for the best way to bring the crisis to an end and safeguard the lives of the hostages. He offered all the logistical and material help that might be necessary.

Jordan and Egypt expressed their solidarity with Spain. King Abdullah II said:

"The fight against Islamic State and its Jihadist offshoots around the world is World War III."

I lay down on the bed and watched the endlessly repeated images go by. To be honest, in the security footage showing the attack on the embassy they didn't all look like Africans, although since it was in black and white and had been taken from a distance it was difficult to be sure of anything. Then TVE aired a segment on Boko Haram, who they were and what their best known acts in the past were, like the abduction of 219 schoolgirls in Nigeria. I learned that they had been in existence since 1979 and that their strange name is translated literally as "Western education is a sin." Its leader, Abubakar Shekau, majored in Islamic Studies in the city of Maidaguri, capital of the province of Borno in the north of Nigeria.

Suddenly the news ticker appeared again at the bottom of the screen, flashing:

BREAKING NEWS! BREAKING NEWS!

From somewhere in Iraq, the grand caliph of the Islamic State, Abu Bakr al-Baghdadi, had sent an online message welcoming the Madrid attack and calling for a worldwide revolt against the power of the West. He praised the "brothers" of Boko Haram in Spain and called for more actions not just in Europe but around the world. At the end of his speech he quoted, or rather paraphrased, a famous phrase by Che Guevara: "We have to create not one but many Vietnams against the West." The European fronts of Islamic State—also known as direct action cells—were ready to go into action and were almost invisible to the police. In London and Paris there were highly organized structures; in Berlin and Madrid, too, although smaller. Boko Haram had reached Europe not long before, but was already strong in the black *banlieues* of Paris and especially in Belgium, in the Matongé district of Brussels, which had become a headache for the police. In its violent way, it was participating in globalization and making it its own.

In addition, the recruitment of white Europeans was making progress. Marginalized young people with histories of failure and problems of adaptation. Jihadism was an outlet for their resentment and desire for revenge. In this way, those who were the system's losers were coming together, some of them, although not all, aware of, and feeling guilt at, the historical responsibility their respective countries bore in the humiliation of vast areas of the globe. They identified with this struggle not because they were religious, but because of the worldwide rebellion against a power that had excluded them in their own countries. The war was no longer between Christians and Muslims, or even between white Europeans and their African or Middle Eastern fringes, but between winners and losers.

That seemed to be the new paradigm.

A section of those who weren't with the Christian far right opted for Jihadism. And so, little by little, ISIS was spreading to high schools and social clubs, winning over people with more balanced profiles and even academic backgrounds. In France there were believed to be 20,000 followers, men and women, although not all of them were fighters.

Most joined the various Muslim Brotherhoods—so, too, in Britain, Belgium, and Holland—which already had a significant number of members.

I tried to close my eyes, what time was it? Around ten. Getting to sleep in the middle of such chaos, and anxious for Juana to arrive, seemed like an impossible task. I thought about taking a stroll, because there were many memories for me in Madrid, where I had spent an important period of my life. It was here that I had followed a university course in Hispanic Philology and taken my first steps in the literary world. As a young man I had walked a thousand times down these streets in the center of the city, although everything was different now. The streets that glittered today, in spite of the crisis, were dark alleys in those years. An icy wind blew along the Gran Vía that made the bones ache in winter. It drizzled frequently, and in the doorways were gaunt figures straight out of Goya's darkest paintings. They were junkies. Prostitutes with rotting teeth walked up and down in front of the Telefónica building hoping for someone desperate to approach them, and there were robbers and people with knives, just like in any Third World city.

There weren't many Latin Americans in the university, but in the squares and parks it was common to meet Argentinians selling leather masks and something they called *billuta*, which as far as I could see were necklaces and bracelets. Other Argentinians read tarot cards in Retiro Park. I remember one of them, perhaps the best known. He would hand out a card saying: "Professor Julio Canteros. Contemporary Argentinian Poet." Practically all the tarot readers were poets or writers, which at times made me harbor serious doubts about my aspiration to become a writer.

Madrid, Madrid.

Every corner of the city awaited me with some memory or other of a time I had thought was over. That human reflex that leads us to take the same old route, to retrace our steps and seek out certain streets, was I ready for that? Better to wait for a while in the hotel. Juana might be there soon.

I called room service and ordered something to eat. Nothing special, just a chicken sandwich and a Diet Coke. And I again concentrated on the news on TVE.

What was happening with the ultimatum? The terrorists were asking for new things. Not only a stop to the bombing, but that the United Nations recognize the borders of Islamic State, including an exit to the Mediterranean in the north of Lebanon. Plus a condemnation of Israel and a restoration of Palestine to the 1967 borders. All highly unlikely things that they would never be able to obtain and Spain couldn't give them. Maybe that's what they were after: to force an intervention and die killing the hostages, going out in a blaze of glory. They were Jihadists and they didn't mind dying in combat.

Four hours had already passed. If the threats were serious, somebody would soon be having his throat cut. The history of mankind is also the history of its throat cuttings and public sacrifices. People like to witness executions. The multitudes get up early to make sure of a good place near the hangman. Aztecs, Romans, Persians, revolutionaries, and intellectuals. Today, through the social networks, Jihadism reminds us that we have always been spectators of death.

After eating, I fell asleep on top of the bed, tired and anxious, in an uncomfortable position.

By the time I woke, morning had already broken.

The noise of the Gran Vía reached me from a long way away, muted by the window's double glazing. The sun was flooding in, it was a glorious morning. After remembering where I was and why, the silence of the telephone started to seriously worry me.

Juana, Juana, where are you?

On the way to the shower, I had a banal thought: how would it be to stay in a hotel forever, without ever going out on the streets?

It's what happens in Stanley Kubrick's movie *The Shining*. But the true theme of that film is how bad hotels are for writers who don't write, as happens to the unfortunate main character, who goes crazy and tries to kill his wife and son with an axe (there are worse forms of madness). But basically the hotel is innocent. Any writer who doesn't write is a socially aggressive being, whether in a comfortable harem or on a beach.

There is a piece of performance art by Joseph Beuys that consisted of his staying in New York for three days without leaving his hotel room, which he shared with a coyote. The piece was called *I Like America and America Likes Me*, and the performance took place in 1974, during Beuys's first show in the United States. Arriving in New York, he was driven in an ambulance to the art gallery, lying on a stretcher and wrapped in a felt blanket. Then he was taken to the hotel by the same means and spent three days there with the coyote, still covered in felt and carrying a shepherd's staff. He performed a number of symbolic gestures and the coyote chewed at the blanket. At the end, Beuys and the coyote embraced. The day he left, he was taken to the airport in his ambulance and returned to Europe without touching American soil. His explanation for such a bizarre and pointless gesture was this:

"I wanted to isolate myself and see nothing of the United States apart from the coyote."

My coyote was a telephone and the longed-for voice that couldn't make up its mind to arrive.

Thirty years earlier, when I was scraping a living in Paris, I was also waiting for a call from a woman that, of course, never came. Such are the strange symmetries of life. My lodging in those days was an attic room, less than a hundred square feet in area, without a bath, and with a skylight looking out on the roof of the building. I was twenty-four and had everything to prove. I would buy books for ten francs from the *bouquinistes* on the banks of the Seine and choose the thickest so that they lasted, because I could only afford to buy one every three days. I had too much free time and had to ration it out. Never more than a hundred pages a day. I would read and look at the telephone, hating its silence. Some evenings I would sit down with the phone in my lap and fall asleep, but it never rang. I would sometimes dream of it ringing and wake with a start, but there was still only silence. Sometimes, when I was out, I would imagine the telephone ringing in my absence, again and again. I could almost hear it. As I entered my street, Rue Dulud, the sound would grow louder. I'd start running desperately, open the front door, and run up the six floors. But when I opened my door, there was nothing.

The arrival of automatic answering machines was, as far as I was concerned, a therapy to counter insanity. I bought a second-hand one after I started hearing the telephone when I was downtown, miles from where I was living. My heart would skip a beat and a voice would say to me: now it's ringing, now. And I'd hear it. I'm talking about that distant era when we humans didn't have cell phones. But the answering machine changed everything.

Now I really liked going out, being on the streets, breathing. When I got back to my little room I'd glance at the green light on the phone that indicated the number of calls.

Generally, the number was zero.

What a strange symmetry. When was Juana planning to come?

Tocotocotocoto!!!

The noise of a helicopter brought me back to the present. I ran to the window and sensed its presence just above the hotel. Had something new happened? I switched on the TV again.

Oh, my God, the first man had had his throat cut.

His name was Kevin McPhee, he was fifty-two, and the embassy's political advisor. In the video he was on his knees. His executioner was behind him, with a black hood, and in the background, on a cloth, was some writing in Arabic. They had dressed him in that same orange tunic ISIS uses in its executions. At this point the recording stopped abruptly, although you could see it complete on the Internet. They weren't going to show the moment his throat was cut on TVE, of course, but

it was described as "barbaric," with the traditional blunt knife
that prolongs the suffering and adds a macabre sense of spec-
tacle. Then they showed photographs of the victim with his
wife and children in Kilkenny, near Dublin, about to be wel-
comed by the prime minister. In one of the photographs, he
was in a tie and a tweed suit. There was another in a jeep, perhaps on vacation, and a third at a Christmas party. His privacy
was exposed. As if death justified displaying his life to all and
sundry. These photographs, except to those close to him,
already seemed posthumous.

Now they were negotiating to have his body handed over.
The terrorists were threatening to throw it out the window
onto the street.

Tocotoco!!!

Again, the helicopter. I leaned over the small balcony and
thought I saw its shadow behind the Telefónica building opposite, but immediately afterwards it seemed to be coming from
behind me. Cries and insults rose from the street. Someone
was insistently sounding a car horn.

Beeeeep!!!

"I'll show you, you dickhead!"

I went back to the TV.

A German pundit was saying that with this attack the group
Boko Haram was making official its entry into the Islamic war
with the West. If many young people in Islamic counties in
Africa such as Niger, Mauritania, Somalia, Chad, Mali, Sudan,
and even Kenya were joining at the rate of several thousand a
month, it was because they interpreted it as an uprising against
the former colonizers. Others, he went on, see it as a way of
venting their anger at this paradise on the northern shore of
the Mediterranean that rejects them. As far as this pundit was
concerned, the prospects were grim: on the one hand, the fugitives in their rafts, bringing poverty and Ebola with them; on
the other, the Jihadists with their historical revenge.

And he concluded by saying:

"Both movements are born out of twentieth-century colonization and the greed with which whole nations were exploited and their resources plundered, leaving the population in poverty, ignorance, and neglect. This may be the first payment due on what was done in the twentieth century."

The helicopter passed again, although this time a little farther away. I ran to the window and opened it, but the fight was still going on down there, so I went back to the desk and took out my notebooks. I was about to go through them when the Spanish prime minister appeared on the screen.

"We continue to count on the determination of our police forces and our elite groups, who have the situation under control, and above all on the help of all the free and democratic nations of the world," he said, sitting in his office. "What we are dealing with here is a new form of transcontinental terrorism. We are doing all that can possibly be done to protect the lives of the hostages."

When his speech was over, they went back to the TVE studios, where a political correspondent implied that SWAT teams from the United States had arrived in Madrid, as well as the intelligence services of Ireland and Great Britain, Israel's Mossad, and of course police officers from Nigeria, probably from Abuya and Lagos, who were well acquainted with Boko Haram. Only Russia, which was waging a second cold war with the West, had not offered to send its special forces. In fact, as another panelist pointed out, no clear statement had been received yet from Moscow, not even after the Irish official had had his throat cut. This in spite of the fact that they themselves were still facing a threat from insurgent offshoots of the Chechen guerrillas, also defined as Islamic militants.

I was tired of checking my messages in the hope of news of Juana. Like a jealous lover, I analyzed her e-mail, the time she had sent it, looking for some clue. Was she in Spain? I became convinced that she wasn't, since it had said, "Go to Madrid," not "Come to Madrid." Better to work on something, focus my brain in another direction.

So I sat down at the desk with my notebooks.

5

For quite some time now I had been making notes about Rimbaud, reading and rereading his poems and letters, collecting editions of his books in various languages, and above all, thinking about him, trying to imagine his voice when he said:

Allez tous vous faire foutre!

That's what little Arthur yelled at his classmates in the school in Charleville when they came and pestered him while he was in the library, reading. He would later yell it at Charleville itself, when he left for Paris, and finally at all of Europe, when he decided to abandon it forever.

Allez tous vous faire foutre!

Those who knew him say that as a boy he had ice-cold eyes, even though his appearance was that of a frail, helpless child. A strange combination. When he sat in the front row of the class, the teacher would feel uncomfortable, as if he were being judged. It wasn't long before they all realized that he wasn't like everybody else. At the age of thirteen, he composed a poem in Latin of sixty hexameters and sent it as a birthday gift to the Prince Imperial, Louis Napoleon, who congratulated the school and ordered his letter of gratitude to be published.

Arthur's father, Frédéric Rimbaud, was a strict and somewhat melancholy military man who rose to the rank of captain and spent his life in garrisons in North Africa. Especially in Algeria, in a town named Sebdou, which barely figured on the maps, not far from Oran, the city where Albert Camus's *The Plague* is set.

In Sebdou, France was fighting the sultan of Morocco and various rebel tribes led by Muslim ascetics known as marabouts. To combat them, Rimbaud's father proposed calling on the services of the magician Robert-Houdin, who challenged the marabouts to a conjuring show in which he used hypnotic suggestion and his famous trick of "the light and heavy chest." First he asked one of the marabouts to lift a very light cardboard box, which the man did with one finger. Then Robert-Houdin performed hypnosis and asked him to lift it again, but this time he couldn't do so, even using both hands and all his strength. This impressed the tribes so much that the revolts died down for a while in the region.

Lieutenant Rimbaud was a key figure in the colonial authorities, with the post of *chef du bureau arabe*, and had a more than respectable military career: he was awarded the Crimea medal and the Sardinia medal, and a little earlier, in 1854—the year his son Arthur was born—he was made Chevalier of the Legion of Honor. In other words, the young poet was born into the household of a hero of the fatherland, a hero of France! And as often happens, in such a place there is no room for anybody else. Even more so in the case of Frédéric, who in addition to being a soldier was a literary man. Two of his works were entitled *Military Eloquence* and *Book of War* and, to cap it all, he even translated the Quran into French!

Frédéric had learned Arabic in those slow afternoons in barracks. This suggests that he did not sit in his office swatting flies and watching the ceiling fan turn, as most officers may have done. He was an intellectual and a lone wolf. And as a good soldier, he was severe and very strict. Useful qualities when it came to performing laborious tasks.

In 1853, Frédéric the Hero of France married a woman

who by the standards of the time was already quite old. Her name was Marie Catherine Félicité Vitalie Cuif and she was twenty-eight. She was the daughter of rich peasants from the Ardennes, implacable and straitlaced, and above all very Catholic. Their first child was born that same year, as was traditional, and was given his father's name: Jean-Nicolas-Frédéric. The second—the hero of this story—arrived on October 20, 1854, and was christened Jean-Nicolas-Arthur.

After those two years, the father returned to North Africa, moving from garrison to garrison, and on his visits home regularly made his wife pregnant. She was to give birth to three more children, all daughters. The first died young; the two survivors were christened Vitalie and Isabelle. Once Lieutenant Rimbaud decided that his procreative labors were over, he simply disappeared. The Arabian deserts sucked him in. They threw a fine layer of sand over him that blurred the lines of his face, except in the memory of his second son. Arthur was six years old at the time. And when Frédéric finally returned to France, he didn't go to live with them. These were harsh times. Things as simple as compassion, filial love, or fidelity to a woman had no place in a soul forged in steel. They were attributes excluded from military life. That distance, those dreams of the absent father would perhaps—no, almost certainly—have something to do with the young poet's future quest.

In the meantime, what was the boy doing? At the age of nine, Arthur wrote a composition that begins with the following words:

Le soleil était encore chaud; cependant il n'éclairait presque plus la terre; comme un flambeau placé devant les voûtes gigantesques ne les éclaire plus que par une faible lueur, ainsi le soleil, flambeau terrestre . . .

His favorite expression in those days was *saperlipotte de saperlipopette!* which meant something like "boring old nonsense." He said it about his studies of Latin and Greek, which he would later master, and about history, geography, and even spelling.

Saperlipotte de saperlipopette!

He read adventure novels and admired the king of the genre, James Fenimore Cooper, as well as a very curious French imitator of Cooper named Gustave Aimard, who traveled all over America—North and South—where he lived with indigenous tribes, and who then, on his return, spent time in Turkey and the Caucasus. Among other things, Aimard was one of the pioneers in the art of plagiarism, making a word-for-word copy in French of the novella *Amalia*, by the Argentinian José Mármol, under the strange title *La Mas-Horca*. Arthur was drawn to the fact that Aimard was a fugitive: an orphaned child, he had fled his adoptive family and set sail for South America. Fugitives, adventurers, writers. The budding young writer does not know that right from the start, in his reading, he is sowing the seeds, not only of his future work, but of his whole life. But who lives with hindsight?

At the age of twelve, Arthur wrote a historical text about Babylon and Egypt. "He's a prodigy!" exclaimed the principal of the school in Charleville-Méziers. Vitalie sighed, full of pride. This son would bring the family what people in the provinces long for: respectability and social status.

The gods of poetry know how to arrange things, so in 1870, when the young man was fifteen, a new teacher arrived at the school. His name was Georges Izambard, and he also wrote verses. He had heard the legend of the genius and was curious, but when he saw him for the first time he found it hard to believe this shy, bright-eyed young boy could possibly be the monster of erudition he had been told about. Arthur was won over by Izambard, immediately recognizing him as a kindred spirit. They began meeting outside school to talk about poetry, literature, and life.

It is easy to imagine them walking along some path on the outskirts of Charleville, perhaps following the waters of the Meuse. Arthur with his hands in his pockets, shy, occasionally throwing a stone into the current, and by his side, Izambard, telling him of past literary adventures or quoting lines of verse. Two young men casually discussing literature and reinventing the world. Judging by the letters he later wrote, Izambard was one of the people he loved most in the world. These walks allowed him to assert his identity as a poet, which is the most difficult thing of all at the start: to follow your intuition, to believe in something that cannot be seen or touched because it has not yet taken shape, and to do so with intensity, in the same way that others believe in and even love gods that they have never seen either.

Izambard had a good library containing books by famous rebels, who would show him where to direct those flames that were devouring Arthur. He gave him François Villon, Rabelais, Montesquieu, Voltaire, Rousseau. He gave him the Parnassian poets, who at the time were holding the torch of poetry in Paris. He also gave him Victor Hugo, the great seer, who in spite of his fame was much vilified by respectable society. In fact, when Vitalie found him reading Hugo, she tore the book from his hands. She did not look kindly on this enthusiasm of Arthur's. Basically, she tried to do what any responsible mother would have done: get him away from poetry! But that was impossible. She merely produced the opposite effect, which was to strengthen him in the idea that this was the life he wanted to lead. This and no other. A touching decision, and a risky one too, since it would give him access to the most beautiful but also the most brutal aspects of experience.

The encounter with Izambard was the final step in his education, and in 1870 he began writing poems that would remain part of his definitive oeuvre: "Sensation," "Le Forgeron," "Credo in unam," "Ophélie," "Le bal des pendus," and so on.

Such was his self-belief that he dared to send a couple of his poems to the review produced by the Parnassians in Paris, the *Parnasse Contemporain*. Rimbaud's *Complete Works* in the Pléiade edition include this letter addressed to Théodore de Banville, editor of the review. It is his second letter, dating from May 24, 1870. What he writes in it are not so much statements as outbursts, such is the young man's overwhelming elation at having taken the decision to dive unprotected into the shark tank, where the wildest, fiercest poetry is to be found. I imagine him scarcely able to breathe. And then, rereading them, amazed and fearful at what he is about to do: send two of his poems to the most important review in France!

What temerity!

With the letter, he enclosed handwritten copies of "Credo in unam" and "Ophélie."

In the letter he says:

> *I love all poets and all good Parnassians, since every poet is a Parnassian, in love with ideal beauty.*

And later he adds:

> *In two years, or perhaps even one, I'll be in Paris. I, too, gentlemen, will be a Parnassian. I don't know what I have in me, something longing to come out. I swear to you, dear master, that I will always worship the two goddesses: the Muse and Freedom.*

And he ends with a postscript that is almost a plea:

> *I am not well known, but what does that matter? All poets are brothers. These verses believe, love, hope. That is*

all. Dear master: Help me, I am young. Hold out your hand to me.

I can imagine him a few weeks later, prowling about the newsstand, waiting for the latest publications to arrive from Paris, until finally he sees it, and then the nervous way he must have leafed through the pages looking for his poems, his name . . . in vain.

The poems had not been published.

It is the first and hardest lesson for any writer starting out on his career: an editor's rejection. A door abruptly closing, taking with it what he believes will be his only opportunity. It isn't, of course, but he is not to know that. The clamor of the moment generates bewilderment, frustration, anger. Arthur tells Izambard, who tries to console him.

"They're rejecting me because I'm from the provinces," Arthur says.

As far as he is concerned, he is already a full-fledged poet, and he can't wait to reach the salons of Paris and conquer what he believes already belongs to him. He alone knows it, but he's right: they are already his. The poems the *Parnasse Contemporain* refused to publish are still read today, unlike those of Théodore de Banville, the man who rejected them. That's literature. These first poems may lack the bitter stamp characteristic of the mature Rimbaud, but he is already head and shoulders above most of his contemporaries.

When the school year came to an end in 1870, Arthur won the annual competition of the Academy, on the following subject: a speech in Latin verse that Sancho Panza might have addressed to his donkey—what young student today could do something like that? The jury was astonished by the young man's talent, but any joy he may have felt was spoiled by an unwelcome piece of news: that his beloved teacher and friend Izambard was leaving. That same month the Franco-Prussian War had started and, his situation being uncertain, he preferred to be closer to his family home in Douai, near the Belgian border.

For Arthur it was a catastrophe. He felt abandoned, as if he had lost a father for the second time. When he found out, he wrote that as far as he was concerned, the idea of spending a single day in Charleville without Izambard was "simply unbearable," and he threatened to run away to Paris as soon as he received the prize medal. The day Izambard left, Arthur went with him to the station. It was a warm morning. Before Izambard got on the train, they embraced desperately. When the locomotive began to move, Arthur felt his soul fall to his feet, and there he stood, motionless, until the train was no more than a thin line on the horizon. Now his friend was gone. He may have thought that this was what life was like: a series of desertions and a great deal of loneliness. Or he may have told himself that attachments make us weak. In any case, there he stood for some time, until the platform was empty.

A few days later he received his prize from the Academy with contempt. Vitalie and his sisters were proud. His brother was not very effusive, but congratulated him. To Arthur, such pompous honors seemed empty, laughable, contemptible. He was furious. What is a medal? A piece of tin. Nothing in comparison with what he had lost.

The patriotic fervor aroused by the war with Germany was strong in Charleville, which was close to one of the fronts. In his first letter to Izambard, Arthur writes: "My native town is the stupidest of provincial towns." He says that all the retired shopkeepers have put on uniforms and now march beside the shoemakers and fruit vendors.

Saperlipotte de saperlipopette!

His old battle cry echoed again. He was about to strike his first menacing, well-aimed blow.

On August 28, less than two weeks later, Arthur escaped his mother's vigilance and boarded a train for Paris. I imagine him once again sitting in a railroad car, alone, his nose glued to the window, watching the meadows along the Meuse grow ever more distant, until he has left his hometown far behind. Paris is 145 miles from Charleville. A modern express covers the distance in two and a half hours, but at that time it must have been closer to seven.

Final stop: Paris, Gare de l'Est!

There he was, his mind about to explode with what he was doing. I imagine his emotion on seeing the first rooftops of the city, the streets alive with trade meandering around the railroad tracks. It was already so close. The capital of poetry. Paris, at last.

There was a problem, though: as he had been unable to carry out his original escape plan—which involved selling some medals before setting off—he didn't have a centime on him to pay for his journey. And so, when he got off the train, the ticket collectors took him to a police station, and after a brief, fruitless interrogation, he was transferred to Mazas Prison, where he spent a week, since he had no papers on him and had refused to give his name.

What did Vitalie think? In the middle of a war, his poor mother must have imagined the worst: that her son had joined the army and was facing God alone knew what dangers. So many things could happen to an adolescent!

When he saw there was no way out, Arthur turned to the man he considered his father, Georges Izambard, begging him to come to Paris. Izambard sent money and a letter to the public prosecutor, enough to get him released. But instead of returning to Charleville, Rimbaud took a train to Douai and showed up unannounced at Izambard's house.

According to his best biographer, the Irish critic and scholar Enid Starkie, the poem "The Seekers of Lice" alludes to this period in Douai, when Izambard's aunts set about washing his beautiful curly blond hair, and above all removing from his scalp the elusive lice and nits he had picked up during his time in a Paris prison.

6

The days at Santa Águeda went by calmly, with a lot of delirious praying as well as a great deal of what might be thought of "lower activities." It was an explosion of hormones, the final holocaust of the hymen. We were young, we were discovering freedom and the power that came from our bodies. If we had been outside, in a public school, we would have done the same, which is why there are so many teenage pregnancies.

My group of rebel novices established itself and became my new tribe. Time passed and I turned sixteen, and we celebrated it with a big party, held in secret, of course, at the bottom of the garden and in the middle of the night, fucking two young social studies teachers on loan from the Esculapian community, and a couple of police officers, too. All drinking and doing coke out of cans. Well, I was doing coke, being the most concerned about my health among us, while Vanessa and Estéfany each smoked at least half a dozen pipes of crack from a huge bag that the police officers brought them as a gift, in return for what I don't know but I can imagine. That was the beginning of the end, because after the party there was some left over and Vanessa started selling it to other girls in the convent. She gave it to them to try and then sold it.

Soon afterwards, one day when we were in the gym, the nuns went to the dormitory and searched it. They looked in suitcases, trunks, and overnight bags, and that's how they found Vanessa's rucksack filled with small bags of crack, along with coke, condoms, and anal lubricant. In another case they found a whole lot of money in cash and half a bottle of aguardiente.

All hell broke loose.

The first thing the mother superior did was call the police, and since they knew we were a group they immediately separated us, each of us alone in an office while they went through all our things with a fine-tooth comb. Then the police sniffer dogs arrived, and one of them practically swallowed one of Vanessa's G-strings. In Estéfany's things they found six boxes of contraceptive pills and in Lady's overnight bag some condoms, but nothing serious. In mine they didn't find a thing, because I didn't have anything. I never kept anything with me.

Vanessa's parents, wealthy people from Cauca who owned land rich in sugarcane, which they rented out to sugar manufacturers, came to take charge of the situation, because the mother superior had made an official complaint. Heads would have to roll, and the convent was determined to impose a severe punishment in order to avoid scandal. After a long meeting, the lawyer for Vanessa's parents asked to speak with me in private, so I was taken to another office where her mother was. The poor woman's face was distorted with anger and frustration, but when I went in she greeted me in a very friendly manner and took off her dark glasses to speak. The lawyer explained the situation. He said that Vanessa's family was prepared to give me a huge reward.

"Look, Manuela, if you help us out with Vanessa, we'll remunerate you very well in the future. We hear you've had problems with your mother . . . "

Vanessa must have told them that, I thought, but what was the deal? what did they want from me?

"We want you to say those drugs were yours and that Vanessa knew nothing about them," the lawyer said. "That you asked her as a favor to keep that package for you without telling her what it was."

It took my breath away, how could they ask that of me? The woman saw the look of distress on my face and made a sign to the lawyer.

"You'll spend a maximum of two years in a reform school," he said. "I'll deal with your case personally to make sure you come out as early as possible. The Cáceres family will pay for you to go to university in Bogotá or wherever you like, inside Colombia, with a monthly maintenance equivalent to at least three salaries and accommodation paid while you study. When you come of age, you can go out into the world, with a bright future ahead of you, what do you think? Consider it carefully. In two days there'll be a preliminary hearing that you'll attend with your classmates. That's the right moment for you to speak up. It's your big opportunity."

That night I fell asleep thinking about my life, about how hard it had all been because of being the daughter of a feckless man and a vain and crazy woman. In what way was I to blame for what was happening around me? They didn't call my mother, and she hadn't been to see me in a while. She only talked to me on the telephone every now and again. My life belonged to me, and me alone.

Plus, there was "the thing."

My great tragedy, which I plan to tell you about in a while, Doctor, when I've finally summoned up the strength. Now I had an opportunity to start over, from scratch, with a new pack of cards. Reform school would be hell, but I was already used to various kinds of hell. I doubted it was worse or more savage than the hell I carried inside me, so I made up my mind. On the day of the hearing, the convent van picked the six of us up. As punishment, we had been separated. We hadn't been able to talk and now, in the Chevrolet, with the mother superior in front, there was no way to find out anything. We parked outside the juvenile court and with each step I took up the stairs, my heart sank. Would I be able to go through with it? We entered the courtroom where Vanessa's family was and every-thing seemed unreal. Soon afterwards they brought her in, pale and shaking. Everyone thought it was from fear, but I knew it was because she'd been deprived of crack. Her parents knew that, too. The hearing started and the charge against her from the school was read out. Then the juvenile judge said that if nobody had any comment to make, we could proceed.

It was then that the lawyer looked at me, as if to say: "Now!"

So I stood up and raised my hand, very determined, and an usher led me to a microphone installed on the left-hand side of the courtroom. My voice came out sounding strong. When I reached the point of what I had to say there was a big *ohhh!* from those who were there. I sneaked a glance at Vanessa's mother and she made a friendly gesture. Then two officials took me to an office and the judge spoke to me on my own and asked me if I confirmed what I had said in court.

"Yes," I said, "I deceived Vanessa Cáceres. Those drugs were mine, I persuaded some of the novices to try the stuff and then starting selling it to them to pay for my own habit."

We went back to the courtroom and the judge asked me to repeat my confession. I did it without blinking. I didn't even look at Vanessa for fear that something would give us away. The judge asked why I had waited until now and I said, because it wasn't until now that I'd understood the seriousness of what I had done and the consequences for my innocent friend, Señorita Vanessa Cáceres. And I concluded by saying:

"It is the Lord who is resolving this, separating the innocent from the guilty, and putting lies in the horrible place reserved for lies."

As I was speaking I had a hallucination: the courtroom had turned into an abandoned church. And I saw myself on my knees, begging forgiveness. In the semidarkness, I recognized the figure of the judge, but now he was a priest. He stood look-ing at me in silence and I withdrew in fear along the aisle, at first on my knees and then with slow, clumsy steps, one by one, to get away from that terrible silence accusing me from the altar, at the far end of the church, and I was almost at the front door when the priest or judge spoke, or rather cried out, and when I heard him it seemed as if the sound was coming from the darkest part of the sky, as if the air had filled with sparks and fires and the whole of mankind, defenseless, was getting ready to surrender. That's what I thought when I heard the judge's voice.

"Manuela Beltrán! Do you repent?"

I again fell to my knees, as enraptured with guilt as the first man sentenced in court, in the name of God or of something greater than God, before the innocent.

At this point, the eyes of all those present in that wretched courtroom became visible again in my dream, and I felt that their looks were knives about to tear my flesh, because that ceremony was no longer about forgiveness or guilt, but a human sacrifice, and then I saw the judge approach with a very thin knife while the guards, giving way to each other and bowing, very politely, almost lovingly, asked me to lie down on the table; then one of them opened my dress down the middle while the other arranged my head on a bundle of papers to make me more comfortable, and from there I again met the eyes of Vanessa's mother, who seemed to be whispering in my ear, goodbye . . . goodbye . . . goodbye . . . while the mother superior lifted a finger to her lips, silence, don't speak or think, silence and more silence, and beyond her, beyond the backs of the seats and the railing, the eyes of my depraved friends, who were closing their mouths with two fingers in order not to laugh, and all the others, the public in the courtroom, started to chant hallelujahs and prayers, until the judge raised his arms and brought them down hard, sinking the knife in my chest, up to the hilt, making a first clean cut and a second in the shape of a cross, and then, separating tissue and muscle, pulled out my heart with his hand and raised it so that everyone could see it, and I saw it, a horrible, throbbing mass, full of little side hearts that were also swelling, and the blood gushed down the judge's forearms and into the sleeves of his robe, and then he asked aloud:

"How is the blood and how the heart of the guilty?"

He paused and responded:

"Black like this blood and black like this heart!"

I managed to see it throbbing and felt sorry for myself, but I didn't feel any pain, quite the contrary, rather a strange kind of relief since in there, in that muscle that already seemed to be dying, all the horrible things I had experienced were kept, and now at last they were separated from me, far away from me, and I realized it was better to keep going without a heart in my chest.

I woke up in the hospital. It was already dark. Seeing me open my eyes, a nurse looked at me contemptuously and called a guard. Come in, I heard her say. A doctor told me that I would stay there until I recovered, but in detention. That was why my arms were tied to the tubing of the bed. It's strange to be tied to a bed in a clinic.

"You fainted in the courtroom," the doctor said, "but the blow on the head isn't serious. You hit the edge of the step."

Then came a horrible scene, Doctor, which I wouldn't tell you about if I didn't like you: my mother's visit to the hospital. She came with her disgusting boyfriend and asked what had happened. Without letting me answer she screamed that she couldn't believe I would have done that, but I looked at her and said, look, Mother, it's best if you go, what I confessed is true, get out of here with your man and never come to see me again, let me get on with my life.

They had torn out my heart and nobody could hurt me. I insisted on her leaving and she slapped me in the face.

"You spoiled brat!" she said. "The same bad blood as your father."

The guy had spent the whole time to one side, without looking at me, but before going out he glanced at me over his shoulder and I could see his eyes. The son of a bitch was laughing. Maybe he thought he'd won once and for all, getting rid of this stupid teenager who was grown up now and was strong and could tell so many bad things about him. He was right to laugh, the bastard. I also laughed, but about something else, because in a sudden daydream I saw him lying on a camp bed, writhing with pain and humiliation, screaming in fear. Hate, humiliation, and pain. That's what I wanted with all my heart for the two of them, the two scumbags.

My time in reform school was quieter than my days at the convent. There were drugs, violence and punishment, survival, and a few deep friendships. Life in all its splendor. The advantage is that we were all more or less equal and all of us had had our hearts ripped out. That's why if they punished us it was with deep respect. Among the many things I saw, Doctor, I'll tell you one: some of the women guards had a lucrative little business going that consisted of selling the girls for sex. They told the youngest ones they were being punished for indiscipline and this was the punishment. They made them pass through the infirmary and there, in a soundproofed room, they handed them over to their clients for an hour or two. I don't know how much they charged, but the men could do whatever they wanted to them, as long as they didn't beat them. But those girls came back from the punishment covered in bruises and with their eyes fixed on the ground. I knew what they were doing to them and thought, sooner or later one of these girls will go crazy in there.

And that's what happened.

There was a girl of about thirteen, a peasant girl, who, as far as I was able to find out, was really liked by a regular client. It was something like the third time she had been handed over to the same man and when she left the cell block I saw her eyes and said to myself, there's going to be blood, because she had that placid but also nervous look in her eyes, the kind you see in people who are about to explode. The girl had no weapons but she did have teeth, and that's what she did: she bit the client's testicles off, and he bled to death in the ambulance. With that scandal, the guards' business came to an end. They were replaced and for a few months everything was quiet, until another business was set up: hiring the girls out to restaurants near the reform school. But that left you with money, so I put myself forward for one of these jobs. I ended up washing dishes in a fried chicken joint called El Pollo Madrugador, maybe my mother's influence. I made good money to buy things. No drugs, no booze. A radio, a hairbrush, a little mirror. Things for me.

One day, I saw one of the guards reading a book. Sitting alone on a bench at the end of the corridor, she was reading and reading, and to me it seemed that the expression on her face and even the position of her body was like someone who wasn't there, in the middle of that pigsty, smelling the damp and the shit. I was so surprised that I asked her, why are you reading? and the woman answered, because it helps me to pass the time and takes me out of here a little. That made me even more curious and I said to her, can you lend it to me afterwards? Three days later she handed it over to me, with the covers wrapped in newspaper. You may be wondering, Doctor, how it is that a single book can awaken a love of literature, and I'll give you a Biblical answer, "the spirit blows where it wants," or where you want it to blow, which is almost the same thing, and it blew on me that day, because as soon as I read the first page I was confined in a prison of words, a world I never wanted to leave, and that's why that night, when they switched out the lights, I continued reading in secret with just the distant yellowish light from a lamppost out in the yard.

When I finished, I raised my eyes and looked at the world,

and I swear it wasn't the same anymore. So at the end of the month, when the Cáceres family's lawyer came and brought me things, I asked him if he could send me books, novels. Five days later a box with five books in it arrived and a note from Vanessa's mother saying, "How good that you are reading, Manuelita, my daughter is fine and sends you greetings." And that became the new routine. Every two weeks a box arrived with more books, so I must have read something like half the catalog of the Book of the Month Club, which is what they had, probably decorating the study that nobody used.

Time went on, like a ball rolling down a slope, and then suddenly came to a stop, slowed down by something, and when I looked at the calendar there was already only a month left before I would leave the reform school. I was going to come of age. Plus, I'd be graduating at a distance, because while we were locked up we still followed the state educational program. It was time to be born again, and Vanessa's family did their duty.

The lawyer came to pick me up. He carried my small overnight bag along the corridor to the exit and when we got into the car he asked, where shall I take you? I didn't know what to say and he asked again, what's your mother's address? I told him I didn't have a mother. He looked at me and nodded, laughing, and took me to a restaurant to have lunch. From there he called Vanessa's mother and they talked for a while. Finally we went to a furnished apartment. I would live there until I decided what I wanted to do. That sounded fine to me, I had nothing to lose because I had absolutely nothing. If they had decided to leave me on the streets I wouldn't have been able to do anything either, it all depended on them, but also on me.

The apartment had two bedrooms and a living room, it was nice. The window looked out on a school and on the roofs of the houses of the Vipasa neighborhood. I didn't know Cali well and wasn't sure where I was, but that didn't bother me. For the first time I was going to sleep alone and that was a bit scary, but I also felt happy. At last, nobody could see me.

The lawyer came back the next day and we had breakfast together in a corner shop: coffee with milk, cheese bread, orange juice, and scrambled eggs with onion and tomato. He was a pleasant guy. His name was Antonio Castillejo and he must have been about forty. He gave off a sense of self-confidence, but the effort he made to appear more elegant than he was was obvious. With his neatly knotted tie and his already old but very well ironed shirt. If they had offered him some super-power he would have chosen to be invisible rather than to fly or read minds. That's how I saw him. After breakfast we went to a branch of Bancolombia and he helped me to open a savings account. Then he transferred into it all the money the Cáceres family had promised me two years earlier, plus the eleven percent interest. I said yes to everything. Then we went to buy a cell phone and set up an account. Which they paid for. He kept saying, is that okay? do you like it? I said yes to everything, without thinking. Because if you don't agree with anything, you'll tell me, won't you? And I said, yes, counselor, yes, everything's fine. I felt too lazy to talk, I had to wait a little. I needed time.

After two weeks—I hardly left the apartment—Vanessa's mother came to see me. She asked if I was comfortable, if there was anything I needed. I told her everything was fine, I didn't need anything. Then she remembered her promise to pay for my university studies, and asked if I had any ideas. It was only when we got to that point that something came into my head and I said, what's Vanessa studying? The woman fell silent, her face twisted and her eyes watered. She said they had taken Vanessa to a specialist clinic, but that before finishing the treatment she'd run away with two of the girls. They'd spent three months looking for her and finally found her in Bogotá, in a horrible crack house. She was half unconscious. After that, they'd put her in various clinics and other places, some of them run by former addicts, but the same thing always happened: the running away, the anguish, the months lost on the streets, and then starting all over again.

"So she wasn't able to graduate," she said. "Right now she's in a medical center in Cuba that they say is the best. The one Maradona went to. And we keep praying for her, what a burden that girl has been!"

It was only then that I saw the tears behind the dark glasses she never took off, like an old movie star. I felt sorry for her. That woman and I weren't so different. I had lost a mother and she had lost a daughter, and we were alone. The husband—I later found out—preferred to look elsewhere, toward an area of life and the world that was distant from that sad face and those glasses that hid even sadder eyes. And what did Señor Cáceres find? Young, lively students, on one hand, or languid thirtysomething divorcées on the other, who probably admired him or pretended to admire him. He was a successful lawyer with his own practice, taught history of law at the Javeriana, was a member of at least three clubs, and looked good for a man of fifty. He had friends in every circle and knew his way around a list of Chilean or French wines. He was a supporter of both América de Cali and Real Madrid, with a solid balance on his credit card and plenty of journeys and appointments lined up that took him away from his home, where his wife was, and that uncomfortable shadow over his life: the memory of his daughter.

That's what men always do, Doctor, sorry to say this: they take life easy. He never completely left her, but by leaving the problem of Vanessa to her it was as if he was saying to her: it's your fault for bringing her up badly, mothers bring up their daughters badly and when they in turn become mothers they also bring up their daughters badly, it's a story that never ends.

That's what all those whims, those nail stylists at home, those tons of Barbie dolls and those princess costumes led to, there's your little princess, the twentieth-century Cinderella who needs sedatives to exist for an hour without doing a bag of crack.

Suddenly she gave me a hug and said:

"I'll never forget what you did for her, Manuelita. You're a good girl and we're going to help you. I owe you a debt."

I felt like telling her that I had done it for me, to wash away a little of my past life. But I said nothing.

"Why don't you choose a good major and enroll in a university in Bogotá? Wouldn't you like to study there?"

I told her I liked to read.

"I know that, sweetheart, I emptied the library for you. Why don't we go and see if it can be studied? I guess it can."

I searched on the Internet and found a literature course at the Javeriana in Bogotá. I told the woman, whose name by the way was Gloria Isabel and she was forty-eight. In her sad biography, as she put it, she had three times been Queen of the Cali Fair and had taken part in the Miss Cauca contest for the municipality of Candelaria, where her parents had a ranch.

The next day, Gloria Isabel came to me early and we went to the airport to go to Bogotá. It was my first time on a plane and it made me so happy that I almost screamed. We spent the day filling out registration forms at the university, and getting an idea of the surroundings. Do you like it? she asked me, and I said, yes, everything's very nice, I couldn't believe this was really happening.

I had to return to take the exam and with my grades, which incredibly enough were high, they gave me a place in the Javeriana. Gloria Isabel let out a cry of joy, and when the date grew near we again went together to Bogotá. We looked for a room to rent and found a very good one in a house in Chapinero Alto, opposite the Portugal Park, at the bottom of those dark mountains that had impressed me so much the first time. I could feel the cold, but what joy it was to be able at last to start a new life. Then we bought some good sets of clothes to go to class in, exercise books, and a satchel.

"You're going to look really beautiful, Manuelita," Gloria Isabel, said, looking at me in one of those outfits in the fitting room on a department store on Thirteenth Street, "the boys will go crazy for you."

A few days later, with everything ready to begin classes, Gloria Isabel said she was going back to Cali. I thanked her for everything and went with her to the airport where she was going to catch a plane.

"How proud you make me, my girl," she said.

When we said goodbye, she gave me a hug and I felt her anxious breathing. Then she kissed me on the forehead and walked off toward departures. I didn't see her eyes, but I knew she was crying. After a while, she stopped and turned. We waved goodbye again and when I lost sight of her I went back out on the street and took the Transmilenio. It had started raining. The drops ran through my hair and down my cheeks, but there was something more. I, too, was crying. It was the first time I'd cried, but I didn't hide my face. It isn't the same crying in the rain in a city where nobody knows you. I felt strong. At that precise moment, my cell phone rang and I answered immediately, thinking it was Gloria Isabel calling me from the plane.

It was Castillejo, the lawyer from Cali.

"Manuela?" he said. "I know you're in Bogotá, but I have some very bad news for you."

My muscles tensed, like an animal that senses danger or is about to be attacked.

"It's your mother. She's been taken to hospital urgently. The best thing you can do is go to the airport and get on a flight."

"I'm already at the airport," I said, "what happened?"

Castillejo was silent for a few seconds.

"She had acid thrown in her face."

7

Waiting is something I'm very good at, wherever I am, so I spent the evening in the hotel, reading and making notes, in spite of the fact that my anxiety just kept growing. Why wasn't the telephone ringing? Where was Juana?

The explanations that occurred to me were these:

Less than twenty-four hours had passed since her call, and she hadn't imagined I would respond so quickly.

She would come that night.

She had no idea I was so close to Madrid. Maybe she had assumed I was still in India.

The seizure of the Irish embassy had blocked the access routes to the city and she was trapped or delayed somewhere.

But all these hypotheses came crashing down if I asked myself the most banal of questions: Why hadn't she called the hotel and asked for me? Hadn't she seen my message?

There was a lot of hubbub around the hotel, as if a whole crowd was trying to cross the avenue and those on the other side were stopping them for some reason. I opened the window and again heard cries.

"Move out of the way, for fuck's sake!"

"Go fuck yourself!"

Tocotocococo!!!!!

This time I saw the helicopter rise between the rooftops and hang for a few seconds above the Gran Vía. An open-sided Augusta Bell, with soldiers on the sides and mounted Gatling guns. Spain was at war. Then, like a noisy insect, it again took flight.

I couldn't do anything but stay there, observing the bustle of the street, so I sat down beside the window. It was a good place to contemplate what was happening in the city.

Spain was caught in an incessant human movement that stretched to the fringes. A great collective mutation and a return journey. I had seen them in the airport, but they were also here, in the packed subway entrances or waiting for buses that were unlikely to come. Southern Europe had split into rich and poor, workers and unemployed. There was even another classification starting up: between useful people and marginals.

Just as in the Protestant world, morality tended to favor those who could resist, the respectable, while the dispossessed met with silent disapproval. The old Hispanic vice of confusing genius with appearance was reaching new heights. The cult of the superficial, inherited from the end of the last century, was now triumphant. Dolce & Gabbana sunglasses, 450 euros plus VAT, I'll take a pair! Abercrombie underpants, 45 euros plus VAT, I want half a dozen! What's the latest tablet? I'll take it! Are you sure it isn't Chinese? Look at my long eyelashes, look at my decorated nails, look at the muscles of my abdomen, appreciate my vulva shaved with pink laser, like Darth Vader's light saber; admire my body, tanned in the middle of winter, isn't it all lovely? Life is beautiful, very beautiful. That's why I want to show it, why I want the world to see me and know! I want lots of likes on my Facebook page.

You, on the other hand, are poor, ugly, and unhappy.

In the middle of the crisis, the fortunate minority practiced a combination of every form of luxury and frivolity, including laughter. Are these difficult days we're living through? The best thing is to be laughing most of the time. Television was full of comedy shows, humorists, talk shows, stand-up comedians, impersonators, con men. They came out like ants! Everybody wanted to tell a joke because it was necessary to roar with laughter. What antidote against reality is better than laughter? None! You have to enjoy yourself. Movies and television, music and literature have to be entertaining. What else are they for if not that? Forget Kafka. He's boring. Watch an American series instead, they're very good! Have you seen *Breaking Bad*? But before that, take a photo of me on the beach, another on the balcony of my bungalow, and another at the gluten-free buffet in the Marriott. Then let's quickly upload them on the Internet. We want to tell the universe that we're happy and we're in the Seychelles!

Beautiful and happy, yes. Of course.

They say we're individualistic and superficial? That's pure envy. The world is unfair and it's not my fault, just imagine, even the OECD says that in thirty-four of its countries, the income of the richest ten percent is ten times greater than that of the poorest. How is that my fault? If it wasn't so long, I'd read Thomas Piketty's book *Capital in the Twenty-First Century*, though of course I have bought it. From what I hear, it points out that the real problem is inequality, or rather: when the dividends from the assets of a national economy are greater than the cash flow of the wage-earning masses. Do you understand that? I do, more or less.

Come on, another selfie!

On the other side, steeped in sadness, are those who observe that happy life but are unable to reach it. It's the low-definition world of those who are outside the party, hearing the music from the street. They would like to be active and energetic, but they can't. Their fashionable underpants are torn, their glasses scratched, their smartphones can't take the latest apps. They're already not very fast and they break down all the time. You have to buy something new to feel better!

Don't worry, reality says to them. The fact that you're

unemployed and pretty much screwed doesn't mean you can't be happy. There are discount stores for people like you, people affected by the new trends of the global economy, low-cost universal hypermarkets intended for you, the neo-poor of the West; plus, they're very close to where you live, you just have to cross the street to buy sunglasses, very similar to the good ones, that only cost fifteen euros and some underpants for seven, try them. You'll see it doesn't even show. It's not so bad. Look at these Korean tablets, they're identical. You just have to get used to it and the truth is, there are some very nice things available. You're screwed, nobody denies that, but don't forget that there are whole areas of the world, like Bangladesh or the Philippines, where, fortunately, people are much more screwed than you and work for a pittance, they're almost slaves and there are children working in the factories and they don't have social security or welfare. Thanks to them, we can offer you something of good quality. And at unbeatable prices! Who's going to notice?

The world is cruel, although not as cruel as all that. Above all, it's vast and multicolored and offers enormous variety.

Let me give you another example.

Many of those who still have a fixed income, social benefits, capital in the bank, and investment portfolios in shares or economically safe areas, take advantage of the inequality to go to Asia and indulge in a bit of sexual tourism, which when it comes down to it is the best therapy for the stresses of contemporary life.

With what's at stake and all the dangers that lie in wait!

There, you can get young women and even children for peanuts and drink the evenings away with a delicious mai tai. The sunset in Phuket is beautiful, indescribable. What can't be bought there, on those beaches, probably can't be bought.

European women executives, even more stressed because in addition to their obligations they have to fight the rough, exhausting battle for gender equality, prefer to relax in the Caribbean, where well-endowed black men dance salsa, smile, and don't need to take Viagra. They have it built in. Others, whose budgets don't quite stretch, go to Tunisia on low-cost flights. There are some really interesting packages! Young North African men aren't as tall as the Cubans, but they have a lot of energy, and they're cheaper. They allow you to offload a little of your postcolonial guilt and, above all, they don't ask you to take them away with you!

The risk, of course, is that a crazy Islamist will appear with an assault rifle in the exclusive area of the Hyatt Beach in Djerba and casually machine-gun two or three dozen white tourists on the beach. Fat Brits pass without logical transition from their piña coladas and their sun cream to the clouds of paradise, or perhaps to the hell of another, more arid beach. That damned Islamic State insists on ruining our vacations!

And what about those who can't travel, those who row against the current, fighting the burden of daily life? What do these souls do to find relief? How do they combat the terrible solitude, the frustration, the general feeling of malaise?

Postmodernity has thought of them, too. Among the immigrants who survived and have stayed in Europe, there is of course one job that's always available: providing sexual services. It's an activity that ignores crises and is always there, when the sun goes down, on the access roads and squares of the city. The need to relieve yourself is not governed by spread or the Euribor indices or the share prices in Milan! You feel heat between your legs whatever the share price is; all social classes feel irrepressible desires, that's modern promiscuity for you, and everyone wants a piece of the action. Viagra and Cialis are the most widely sold pills in a world filled with anxious men. We are sick, but the greatest sin is feeling discouraged. There's always masturbation for when it's too expensive or you're really screwed.

That's why the roads out of many cities continue to be populated, from sunset to sunrise, with half-naked young girls from the former Second and Third Worlds who are there, however unwillingly, to give hand jobs and blow jobs to the men of the extinct First.

Offering the fleeting relief of fornication.

The man tortured by stress invites the girl to get in and heads for a nearby alley, which at that hour is already covered in used condoms and dirty Kleenex. He parks, switches off the engine, and pulls his pants down to his knees. Depending on what he's after, he reclines the seat or simply lies back. She starts sucking and tries to persuade him to broaden the service. She offers him greater consumption. She would like to obtain more income from an already agreed transaction by offering little extras at low cost, just like the display racks beside the checkouts in supermarkets. Pure capitalism.

"Don't you like my body?" she cries, moving her hips. Then she continues her work, moving her head up and down between the client's legs. Finally, the man makes up his mind and takes out another twenty euros. She climbs on top of him and his erection doesn't last even though he took Cialis three hours ago. Fucking generic medicines! It's late. Now the man is a bit scared and looks in the rearview mirror. The truth is that this dark spot would be ideal for a robbery. He imagines the girl's partner already approaching, crouching with something in his hand, and that idea makes his Cialis-induced erection disappear completely. He keeps his eye on the rearview mirror. He thinks about the questions the police will ask, the explanation he will have to give his wife.

"What's going on?" the nymphet asks, pleased because she knows she's already earned her money and the man won't be able to do anything. "Let's go," he says anxiously. She pulls up her panties, smooths her skirt, and gets out, very close to where the man picked her up. No sooner is she out on the street than she takes a bottle of antibacterial liquid soap from her bag and rubs between her legs. She washes her hands and mouth. She swallows a Halls mint, touches up her makeup, and goes back to the freeway and the position she's worked so hard to defend.

Transvestites, too, are all the rage in periods of deflation. Although they are a greater risk, since their services are more complex and are addressed to psyches that not only are tormented by modern times but also ask themselves questions and cannot resolve their ambiguity. In this profession, Brazilians lead the way, but there are Colombians and Dominicans, too. Some have had their front teeth taken out in order to do a special kind of blow job known as a "tiger cub's bite" or a "baby's bite," one of the most expensive products in their catalog. They all carry Viagra pills in their wallets, since what the majority of their clients are looking for is an engorged penis in a woman's body: once again the extinct Third World embedding itself in the extinct First, although not by force and in this case with a lot of Vaseline. Innovative and unconventional forms of the old North-South dialogue.

I switched the TV on again to the news channel. Now the siege had entered a different phase. The secretary-general of NATO had arrived in Madrid and right now was meeting behind closed doors with the emergency committee at the Moncloa.

What was happening out there?

After the first throat cutting, the terrorists had decided to postpone further executions for twenty-four hours, giving the negotiators time to prepare their proposal. When it came down to it, Boko Haram must have known that Ireland and Spain were neither strong nor decisive—they didn't tilt the balance—in international coalitions, so that it wouldn't be easy for them to stop or even reduce the tactical bombardment of Islamic State's military infrastructure and their leaders' "safe" houses, which was the biggest impediment to Al-Baghdadi's plans right now.

I imagined Juana desperately trying to get to Madrid from some provincial Spanish airport or from some city in the south of France. Flights must have been delayed, trains at a standstill. There were police checkpoints everywhere. Why arrange to meet me in Madrid if she didn't live here?

Darkness had long since fallen, and I again thought to go out on the street. Take a walk, maybe go as far as Plaza de Santa Ana. I hadn't heard the helicopter for a while and opened the window. The noise of the Gran Vía entered like a hurricane. The car horns, the din of people yelling into their phones, the squeal of brakes.

I looked toward Calle Clavel and saw a drug addict urinating behind a trash can.

"I can't fuck, but look how I can piss!" he cried.

8
I, Tertullian, and my Universal Republic

I approach the microphone, take it off its base, and stick it to my mouth. I look up and take a deep breath through my nose. From here, the lights of the hall are like stars in a modest private firmament. Then I trace an arc with my hand and cry:

"Are you with me or against me?"

The roar of the response makes the walls and floors shake. It's like a strong wind that whips my face.

"With you!!!" they cry.

That's how I usually start my meetings, and then, when that first ovation dies down, I fix my eyes on some spectator and address him. I regulate my breathing and begin my speech:

"Because the time has come to take a stand, to take risks for intelligent and sacred life on Earth, not to be soft! We can't be soft in today's world!"

And the audience repeats with me: "We can't, we can't!"

At this point the people yell, there are whistles and snorts, and I know I already have them in my hand. Now I can take them where I like.

And I say to them: "We have to look at the sky, the farthest and deepest part of the sky, behind the clouds, behind the silent storms and the dark spaces, behind the rings of the last and most solitary of planets, and repeat this simple human prayer:

"'I won't be soft, Masters and Ancestors of the Earth, I won't let your property be turned into a foul dungeon. I won't allow it to become a dung heap filled with worms eating dead flesh. I won't let your kingdom be an infected and sick house of whores, or of amnesiac drug addicts.

I won't allow your enemies to swarm in the pipes and continue destroying our one refuge.

I will fight for the good, the children of the ancient ancestors of the world, we don't have to hide in our own houses. The planet is ours, with all its rivers and waterfalls of pure water and green meadows, with its air and its hills, with its trees, which are its soft fingers; ours are the clean, fertile lands, the transparent waters, and the seas, the oceans filled with fish and plankton that this dark enemy, whoever he may be, wants to destroy and pollute; they don't care about converting the sea into a liquid graveyard, into a repository for corpses, but I will fight because I want it to continue to be the origin of life and the water our second blood.

Because I want clean air that goes into the lungs and gives us breath that feeds what is living and allows it to continue. We won't let the enemies destroy our citadel.

We've already lost Europe, we still have America. North and South America. Central America, too, and the Caribbean.

America, America.

The true and only city of the ancient Masters.

Our Universal Republic.

We have weapons and faith in the truth. We are willing to die. What an honor and a joy it is to fall protecting this republic.

We are a group that defends itself from the virus infesting the earth. We are not political, but we have a policy. The world is suffering a grave immunological problem and we are its antibodies.

We have to attack the infectious spirit. To confront this new wave of psychic and neuronal violence. We will protect this kingdom on behalf of our old Masters.'"

This is what I say in my lectures, and just imagine, at first there were . . . how many? ten, fifteen of us? And today, you wouldn't believe it! Thousands come to hear me, and of course, how can they not come? I am what I am, like the fellow in the Bible, but with something more. I am someone whom nobody expects to exist.

There you have me, Consul. I'm Argentinian, as you've already realized. And something else that very few people know, a great secret that I'm going to tell you because I like you and you're a friend of Juana's. Close your eyes a moment and listen to what I'm going to tell you.

That's it, close them, are you ready? All right:

I'm the son of the Pope.

No, man, don't laugh, I'm quite serious.

You don't know the things I know, and have no reason to know them. My name is Carlitos, I'm from Córdoba, Argentina, although many years in Spain have taken away that strange, rather dirty accent I had. The left-hand side of my brain, the one that controls language, hasn't been much affected, even though I've received electric shocks and my spine was crushed several times by a heavy truck called "a passion for rugby." I've had beatings, I have the scars to prove it. They're my war wounds and that's why I shave my skull. The passing of time is a violent thing. I embraced some people before they left this world and others I myself put in the rocket before they went off into the beyond. I have been in psychiatric detention and I don't deny I've had problems. I had a propensity for alcohol and I survived by pure force of will. Today my addictions are children's things: strawberry-flavored toothpaste, junk food, *dulce de leche*. One afternoon I ate fourteen packs of Oreos and two liters of kiwi-flavored yoghurt, and I'm still here. I'm sturdy but not hypertense. If only all the struggles in the world were so easy.

You liked that, didn't you?

That I'm not from Buenos Aires, I mean. Outside Argentina it's better not to be from Buenos Aires, because everyone thinks you're an arrogant fool and maybe in some cases that's true, but not always. The thing about being the son of the Pope, on the other hand, is one of the few certainties in my life and I can demonstrate it to you, although I don't need to. It simply is that way.

What's particularly curious is that I'm not a Catholic. I only believe in the bones that can be extracted from the earth and in the fruits of those bones. They are my older brothers, my ancestors, my masters. I could call this *Theory of the Origins*.

I'm going to tell you how it was.

A long time ago, when he was the provincial superior of the Society of Jesus in Santa Fe and Buenos Aires, Bergoglio had to make a trip to Córdoba for a matter that was a little bit convoluted and secret. Wait! It was only a weekend, an insignificant weekend, but I think that in those three days he experienced the most profound moment of his life before he was elected Pope.

I'll tell you everything, let's take it slowly.

Do you remember the taking of La Calera by the Montoneros? Why should you remember, it's Argentinian history! It was the first act by which the Montoneros, if I can put it like this, made their entrance into society. *Bonjour tout le monde!* Bang, bang, bang. They were riddled with bullets, and there were mistakes, but in the end it came out well. So the following year, 1974, they carried out a major kidnapping: two bigwigs of the cereal industry, the Born brothers. They were grabbed by a cell of about forty guys, disguised and well-armed, when they were driving along a road. Boys, shall we go for a walk in the woods? It was a crazy thing! The incredible thing is that it worked out well for them again, because six months later they let the first one go and nine months later the other one, after a modest payment of sixty million dollars, of course.

Sixty million! It was huge.

That kidnapping was the origin of my life, my modest life. I'm quite serious. Wait!

My mother, who's a crazy dreamer and of course quite irresponsible, was a left-wing militant in Córdoba in those years, the daughter of a steel worker and union leader, of German descent to be more precise, anyway, you get the picture. That's how she ended up involved in a group supporting the Montoneros. She had military training, right? It was quite something. When the Born kidnapping took place, everyone was tearing their hair out and the people who were militant had to tread carefully, because there were informers everywhere and the police had a thousand eyes, don't forget that López Rega and the Triple A were around in those days. Every day the Borns were kept was a victory for the guerillas, they really scared the people they captured!

In the middle of all that, negotiations were continuing with the company, Bunge & Born, and of course there were tense moments, very difficult moments. That's only natural, right? The boys got nervous over nothing and made themselves scarce, nobody trusted anybody.

In the middle of all this mess, in this terrible climate of fear, the people from Bunge & Born asked Bergoglio to travel in secret to Córdoba and meet with a representative from the Montoneros. To take a message asking for a truce, in other words. Those were times of war, and everyone respected the Society of Jesus and its provincial superior!

Bergoglio spoke with Bunge in his office in Mar del Plata and finally accepted the assignment. He thought he could help to free those two people, and of course he did help! A few days later he traveled to Córdoba as a civilian, in camouflage, so to speak. No cassocks or dog collars, and he stayed at a hotel downtown, the Contemporáneo. There he had to wait for instructions, but when he went to reception he was surprised to find there was no message for him. So he decided to wait, to stay there without leaving his room, because where could he go? What would he gain by doing that? Time was passing and the poor man was still there, not knowing what was going on. Why did nobody call him? He had arrived at the hotel at noon and it was already seven in the evening, and I think Bergoglio must have had a moment of doubt, he must have thought, "I'm getting out of here," but in the end he didn't leave, he stayed where he was, calling reception every now and again to find out if there was any message or any news. I don't know if he registered under his real name, though I doubt it. If he was on a secret mission he wouldn't have been so stupid, but what do I know? The Hotel Contemporáneo disappeared at the end of the eighties and God knows what happened to its registers. They must have disappeared. This happened many decades ago!

Anyway, to continue with the story.

As Bergoglio looked out the window at the street, he imagined that he heard footsteps in the corridor, near his door, but there was nothing. Only silence. He wanted to leave, to get out of there, but something held him back and he waited a little longer. He felt that he couldn't get away from that hotel until something happened, until someone showed himself, and so the night went by and the morning of the next day. Nor did he dare to call the people from Bunge & Born, because he thought the telephone might be tapped. When someone's on a secret mission anything's possible.

After lunch, which just like dinner the night before he had ordered to his room—nothing special, just a chicken sandwich and a regular Coke, remember in those years they didn't yet have diet drinks—at about three in the afternoon, he finally heard someone knocking at the door, and then a voice:

"Laundry service."

Bergoglio got up from the couch and went to look through

the peephole in the door. Outside there was a chambermaid, but he said to her without opening the door that he hadn't asked for any service. The woman crossed herself and pointed to the door, so he opened it and she came in very quickly. That chambermaid, as I'm sure you've already guessed, was my mother! They greeted one another shyly and exchanged a few words in low voices: he gave her the message she had to transmit to the organization and she gave him hers for the people from Bunge & Born. That was it. Mission accomplished.

Before leaving the room, my mother looked Bergoglio in the eyes and asked permission to ask him a question, and he said yes, of course, and so she asked if it was true about eternal life, if it was known for certain that after death you were moved into another dimension and continued being yourself, then how did they know, how they had been able to find out without actually being dead. She asked this with absolute simplicity and a certain urgency in the way she looked at him. Of course, my mother was an atheist and a communist, as you can imagine, but she had never had a religious authority so close to her, which is why she dared to ask this, it was obviously something that had been bothering her for a long time, but according to what she told me, Bergoglio didn't answer her directly, saying yes or no, but began a story that she later passed on to me and which, of course, I've used a lot in my meetings.

It's a story about a procession of hooded men going through the center of a ruined city, in silence and single file, all following a leader along a road that goes up to the top of the mountain, a long way up, where a cross can be seen, and it's as if on that mountain was the last temple and the last cross in the world, and that's why that group of men was going there, in the middle of collapsed and ruined buildings, burned-out buses, and decomposed bodies, cutting though the fetid air, avoiding bodies of men and animals already stiff on the asphalt.

It was strange, in the middle of that weird apocalypse, to see a column of hooded men walking in silence, but there they were, going strong, there couldn't have been more than twenty of them and, as they went up the road, their pace grew slower, God knows where these poor devils had come from, abandoned by all gods and all creative words, but they continued believing against all hope in that symbol there, that cross that was still standing, maybe the last intact temple remaining on the face of the earth. When the procession entered a kind of trench one of the walkers fell to the ground, simply fell, nothing more than that, making the noise that a package makes on hitting a solid surface, plop, nothing more, but none of the walkers stopped, lives come to an end and others continue is what they seemed to say with their silence, and so, little by little, they faced the final slope up a flight of steps, a very hard climb, but the hooded men managed not to decrease the pace, one, two, one, two, there was something military in their rhythm, or as if in that marching there was a kind of balance, something more fragile and precarious than themselves, something that surpassed them in time and in memory, and so they went on, one, two, one, two. Soon afterwards the same noise sounded again of someone passing out and falling, plop, and then plop, plop, two more bodies, one of them rolled down the steps and ended up with his head in the ditch of a garden where there were already other corpses and the skeleton of a horse, and there he stayed, in a strange posture, and the others, as happened with the first, continued on their way, it's possible they didn't even turn to see who it was, who had fallen by the wayside, not at all, just kept advancing. The man who was leading them held in his right hand a long staff, not like the jeweled staffs of the popes, like the one my father must have today, but a very simple staff of unpolished wood, almost a tree branch, that's what it looked like from a distance, anyway, this man was marking the rhythm and continued moving forward without turning, and seeing him from the back, it was obvious that he was blind, because of the way he walked and the way he gripped the staff, it seemed obvious to everyone that he was blind, but he knew the way better than the others, he had spent his life climbing to the temple, he had to take that path every day to sit on the steps, maybe to ask for alms or receive some food, what's certain is that the man was blind and was leading the others upwards, and maybe the fact that he was blind explained his frenetic rhythm, it's a known fact that few things distract the blind: not the images of corpses nor the blood-stained asphalt nor the imploring or surprised poses of the life-less bodies, and so he went on, step after step, one, two, one, two, until there was another plop and then another, and when they realized they were already halfway up the final slope there were only half a dozen walkers left, who suddenly increased their pace, walked more quickly, as if the fallen were the bal-last of a globe that was now receiving a sudden impetus, they were already close, almost there, half of the temple building could already be seen, a soaking wet wall of a resplendent white that was starting to turn gray because of the late hour, and on top the beautiful cross, the sign that they all bore in their hearts, presumably, and toward which, naturally, they had come, because the ruined and burning city down below was for them the world outside, a cold, lawless place, and at last they reached the top and hurried to the building, and then something weird happens which is that the story has two pos-sible endings, it's a bit strange, Bergoglio tells my mother, strange but that's how it is, there are two endings and you have to choose one, and he told her them . . .

In the first, the group is already a few yards from the main door, shrouded in shadow, when out of the darkness there emerges a terrible din and the air fills with tracer bullets that light up the gloom and cut them down one by one, amid choked cries; the bullets come from out of the pitch dark, nobody knows who's firing them, but they hit everyone, including the blind man who, although wounded, supports himself on his staff and manages to take a series of steps in a circle, like a spinning top, until a second volley goes off and the air again fills with smoke; two projectiles hit him in the head and adorn the wall with fragments of his cranium. The destruction has come from the darkest part of the night and that brave group, perhaps the last men on earth to believe or bear a word, do not reach their objective: they are cut down a few yards from the temple.

That's the first ending, Bergoglio told my mother, and she made a distressed face and asked, with a touch of melancholy, what about the second? is it just as sad? and then Bergoglio said to her, it's for you to decide which of the two is sadder, I'm going to tell it to you, the second one is this:

The group reaches the summit and approaches the door of the temple, night falls, the first shadows arrive; one of the walkers turns and thinks about the long walk and the many plops made by his companions' bodies, and then the blind man says to them, go in, all of you, I can only come as far as this, I have guided you; he sits down on the steps, and although it's illogical and doesn't correspond to reality he takes out a plastic plate and puts it in front of himself to receive alms, a gesture so devoid of meaning as to be useless, since who can give him anything in a dead city, in an abandoned and lonely world? But there he sat, just like every day, and the others, pulling down the hoods of their tunics, entered an enormous nave in which there was nothing other than pure emptiness, a vault in which the steps of these tired and hungry men echoed; the echo sent back to them the noise of their breathing, the throbbing of their chests, and as it did so their fragile condition of men on their own, creatures lost or abandoned in a world of shadows, seemed more intense, and suddenly one of them, perhaps the youngest or the strongest, stepped forward and went to the apse, where the altar should have been, but on arriving there, amid the shadows of night, he realized that there was nothing there, absolutely nothing, just a strange mirror embedded in a stone, there was no altar, no image of any god, only his own image reflected in the mirror, so they went one by one through that strange sanctum that was nothing but an empty space that made them think of themselves, of course, but also of an abyss and of all the solitude that man has felt, from the first man who stood up on his two feet and walked; an altar where the only thing they could worship, the only thing they could bow down to, was their own image, because in some way their solitude and their terrible effort had converted them into gods, the gods of themselves, and at that moment Bergoglio said, this is the end of the second ending, and when he finished speaking he noticed that my mother, who at that time was a young woman, was crying, her face was bathed in tears even though she was a hardened militant, and then she said to Bergoglio, and what does it mean, in your opinion? why is there so much solitude and so much sadness in this story? and he said, I don't know, you asked me if I believed in life after death and I tell you this, I myself don't understand it perfectly but this is how it should be told, and they both felt very alone and they embraced, because with all the talking they had done time had passed and night had fallen, they hadn't realized and they were wrapped in darkness themselves, in that solitary hotel room into which the weight of night had suddenly fallen, and the embrace they gave each other was many things: two strangers who keep each other company and encourage one another in the midst of secrecy, the beginning of a response to the story of the hooded men climbing to the temple, of course, or perhaps the story of all men, or a particular man who finds himself alone and naked, without chants or rituals, metaphors or protective words, and my mother wanted to stay like that, embracing that priest forever, trying not to arouse the demons of the night.

The next day they said goodbye.

They never saw each other again and it's possible that he never even knew her name, and when a few months later she discovered she was pregnant, instead of worrying, as the other militants did, she felt very happy, her face shone like a moon, because that thing, so new and strange, that was now growing inside her had been engendered the same night Bergoglio told her that strange story, there in Cordoba, in the now-defunct Hotel Contemporáneo, a story she never managed fully to understand but which she kept with her all her life, and that's why when Bergoglio was made Pope she said to me, I always knew your father wasn't of this world, and now you see, I was right, and anyway, that's the story, nine months later I landed on this planet, I was brought up modestly and affectionately until, in my adolescence, I also began to hear strange communications, voices that arrived from afar, as if from other worlds, as if they had traveled through long and exhausting spaces, from a distance in which the past or the memory of the Earth may still be observing us and trying to warn us.

That's where I come from, Consul. And it's why I talk to my people from dark and deserted roads that nobody ever goes down. Words travel and have to be transmitted, and these words speak of rescue, of protection, of care. The planet is sick.

Much has already been lost in the world. My father and I are fighting for something similar, but from different trenches. He can't do what I do, because he is defending a god who speaks to me not as a god, but as a man. The difference between my father and me, Consul, is that in the story of the hooded men he chooses the second ending and I choose the first. Mine are the bullets and his the mirrors. I'll tell you what I'm going to do when I'm ready to go into action, it's very simple: acquire the means and the theoretical and practical training for a fighter to be born inside every person. That appears banal and simple, but it's fiendishly difficult. There's a Jewish proverb I frequently quote: "When you know the right thing to do, the hard thing is not to do it." That proverb offers us an optimistic image of man, I know, maybe too optimistic, as if his nature tended toward goodness, which isn't always true, but anyway, I prefer an unlikely but possible utopia to a depressing reality. Am I a romantic? Maybe so. Hating evil is a romantic experience because it implies being alone to face the universe. And in that solitude there are no gods or theories, only memory, only the impulse of life and the throb of the present. When you put your hand gently on the earth and leave it there for a while, you can feel it vibrate, because down there many things are gestating. This is the truth, the only one we really have. Life and the past and the very memory of the stratified world turns to liquid or stone. Like touching a child's brow to find out if he has a fever, that is how I touch the earth. In some twenty thousand years there will be a new ice age and all this that we see will go to hell, did you know that, Consul? What we are experiencing now is a thermal period in which temperatures go from 0 to 100 degrees, sometimes more, sometimes less, but I use those figures because they are what allow human life to exist, at least in the terms in which we conceive of life. But very soon everything we know will be covered by a layer of several miles of ice, and the sounds of the world will be the sounds of ice, the inner phantasmagorias of ice, because the mountains and the seas will be trampled flat by that colossal weight, and in contracting, the tectonic plates will shift, and when finally everything thaws, what will the world look like? There's no way of knowing, we don't even know if human life will reappear. Evolution will have to start over again from scratch.

That's why we must protect what we still have left, as I keep saying in my lectures. It may be a losing battle, but we must go out into the field and wage it all the same, because the life of man is shorter than the life of the planet. Inside everyone, good must triumph over evil, even after the tracer bullets finish everyone off and there is nothing to be done. To die and disappear without leaving a trace is the destiny of everything that lives, but we must continue to climb stubbornly up that road to the top of the hill, where the temple is. Sometimes being good consists only of being able to forget about death. Of course you know what free will is, don't you? The possibility for humans to choose between good and evil, which is what allows evil to exist. If it's true that man tends toward goodness, why does he turn to evil? Because evil is also human and comes from what I call "the desire to switch off the radar." It's refusing to listen to the voice telling you: don't go there, don't go out tonight, don't do that. People who ignore the nature of good switch off their radar, and they switch it off because they want to, they want to hit the rocks. You mustn't feel bad about it. Freedom consists of being able to choose evil, even knowing the consequences, do you understand me? The world is full of sons of bitches, if you'll pardon the expression, who, knowing full well what they were doing, chose to be sons of bitches. What can I tell you about the humanoid Muslims or the yellow rice eaters? They didn't choose to be born where they were born, but when you put a knife to an old lady's throat or hit a man when he's down, when you set off a bomb where there are innocent people, aren't you one big son of a bitch? If you don't realize it, it's worse, because that means that as well as being a son of a bitch you're an idiot, right? Some even celebrate it, they're filled with joy and praise already obsolete gods. All gods are obsolete.

The yellows seem quieter, the Japs, for example, but just look at them when things turn and the tide rises . . . Sword, knife, dagger, they kill with whatever's around! The other countries in Asia hate them for the things they did in the past. Islands always want to build empires, don't they? I won't even mention the Chinese. Have you seen, the police there lock you up for any little thing and then just shoot you in the back of the head. And on top of that they're Communists, which is what started all this . . . So what I say, man, is this: everyone in his own little house and everyone's happy. I'm quite serious. Because when you look at it, the world isn't as big as it seems. If we start messing up other people's houses, this is going to explode before too long and in a more violent form than has been predicted. That's why it's necessary to fight and the hour has come.

I repeat: we've already lost Europe, we still have America, and make no mistake, when I say America I'm talking about the whole of America, not just the United States, they stole the name from us and want us to just fold our arms and do nothing. America is the kingdom of our ancestors and we're going to cleanse it of scum and other scourges. I'm talking, unfortunately, about human beings. The thugs, the conspirators, the drug addicts, and the amnesiacs of religion, especially if they're Muslim or Jewish fanatics, but Christians, too. Out of our republic!

I'm not saying we have to kill them, no, that whole Hitler thing wouldn't go down well today; it's enough for them to pack their things and go; some to their cathedrals of hate, the others to pray in their deserts or their bloodstained synagogues. I don't care. And for the yellows to leave our air, to wash their hands for the last time and go back to their genetically modified rice fields and their jungles of smog and their polluted rivers. Leave us our clean America so that we can live in peace and enjoy what remains of the world, with pure water and green fields and blue seas. I'm already putting together a network of fighters. It's a new crusade, call it what you like. I'm doing it because it's necessary. The principle of this, I say to you, isn't even political or religious.

It's a bacteriological matter.

9

Ever since the international coalition led by the United States through NATO killed Fadhil Ahmad al-Hayali, Islamic State's second-in-command, the strategy of bombing targeted areas grew, with remarkable results, and so the warplanes with their enormous firepower blew up factories and arms depots, strategic roads, bridges, as well as "safe houses" or the offices of important leaders—sometimes with lodgers, colleagues, and family—which kept the Islamists of Mosul on their toes, changing shelter daily, since so many hits, with such specific targeting of what were supposedly secret locations, could only mean that someone on the inside was betraying them, a thought that plays on the nerves of any organization.

The response was a whole series of Islamist attacks on various European cities. A rifle attack on a gas station on a highway in Germany, which left two dead. A car bomb in a parking lot in Antwerp and three more explosions in Holland. According to reports, the intelligence efforts of the French police had managed to prevent nineteen attacks in just three months. The tragic events at the Bataclan in Paris were a declaration of war on the West and, incidentally, turned ISIS into the best ally of the European Far Right. But because this Madrid attack involved an embassy, it promised to be the most ambitious. That was the general view of the pundits who succeeded one another at a vertiginous rhythm on the current affairs shows on TVE, sometimes refuting, sometimes contradicting each other.

They came from all over Europe and throughout the world. It was as if an army of experts, graduates of Harvard and Oxford, specialists in war, had been waiting for this crisis, which for most of them was more than predictable.

I switched off the TV and tried to read, but it was impossible. The wait was proving to be unbearable. Then I heard knocking at the door and my heart skipped a beat. Could it be her? I went slowly to the door and looked through the peephole. I saw a chambermaid, standing by a cart filled with bags of clothes, holding a hook in her hand.

"Yes?" I said.

"Laundry service, señor, your shirt is ready."

I opened the door, what shirt? The woman checked her slip and said, oh, I'm sorry. It's for 721.

Again, night was falling, and the noise of the city had increased.

Cities, like jungles, echo when night falls. It's the moment when the animals come out of their caves and go on the prowl. They look for food and mates, which, collectively, produces a great din. That's what Madrid was like when I decided to leave the hotel, louder, noisier. People walking along yelling into their phones, fixing dates, announcing visits. I watched that hullaballoo without feeling part of it, but eventually a certain nostalgia for my life in Spain prevailed. I thought I might go to the Cervecería Alemana on Plaza de Santa Ana.

As I headed in that direction, what I'd been dreading happened: every corner from Carrera de San Jerónimo all the way to Puerta del Sol, and then Calle Espoz y Mina, which thirty years ago was a sinister place, brought with it a whole series of images, of distant memories. On Plaza del Ángel I saw the Café Central and felt a stab in the pit of my stomach. I had been living in Delhi when I read the news of the death of Antonio Vega, the singer from the group Nacha Pop, which I'd heard so many times in that Café Central, although not strictly speaking in the bar itself, but from the balcony of the building opposite, where I spent a season. A slate board on the sidewalk would announce: "Today—Nacha Pop," written in white chalk.

Then I reached Plaza de Santa Ana by the corner of the Hotel Reina Victoria, which I never entered and whose windows I was in the habit of looking at, three decades ago, when I would go with my Argentinian friends to sell leather masks on that same square. In those days, selling on the streets wasn't prohibited. I would look at the windows of the Reina Victoria and imagine scenes of sophisticated, seductive women, with long legs, in front of their mirrors, washing themselves, or stepping out of the shower wrapped in fluffy white towels and getting dressed very slowly before going out to dinner in some exclusive spot in Madrid.

Despite the crisis and the embassy siege, there were streams of people on the streets, an incredible hustle and bustle. Hadn't the pundits said that people were nervous? The Spanish tend to overdo things, and when all is said and done, Madrid is one big bar. It's many other things, of course: a huge bookstore, an enormous boxing ring. A call center, too. Everyone was carrying a cell phone glued to their ear, shouting away.

"You've got a lot of nerve, you bitch!"

"Where are you? I don't see you!!"

" . . . no, but listen, now she comes and tells me that I have to tell Lucía, and why the hell should I tell Lucía? and then she goes and dumps me . . . "

Yelling into that sacrosanct piece of equipment seemed to be the great national pastime, maybe to keep silence at bay at all costs; as if falling silent endangered their lives and was seen as a kind of surrender; as if forcing your foolish chatter on other people was a new human right. Was silence outdated, *démodé*?

Suddenly, from high up, a powerful spotlight swept quickly

over the square. It was the helicopter again. The problem hadn't gone away! But the people around me seemed absorbed in other dilemmas, in the demanding effort to have a good time and forget what didn't matter.

I was lucky to find one of the few outside tables of the Cervecería Alemana free, and I sat down and continued looking at the Hotel Reina Victoria with its purple lights. I ordered a beer, a portion of calamari, and another of tortilla. Then another beer, and a third. The food in Madrid is delicious and the body puts on a special effort to make room for it. Ah, the flavors! The adolescent who had lived here three decades ago asked, through me, for a shot of whiskey and another beer. The waiter, sweating, repeated the order:

"A beer, a shot of JB, and another portion of calamari."

Spain, Spain.

"And one of croquettes!"

This last cry seemed to come from a long time ago, from the days of the Café Comercial on Glorieta de Bilbao. Although the bar I most frequented in my youth was the Blanca Doble, on Calle Santísima Trinidad, in the Chamberí district. It was opposite that bar, at number 9 of that street, that I lived for five years, all the time I was at the university. I shared an apartment with the young poet—now dead by his own hand—Miguel Ángel Velasco.

The JB and the beer arrived. And with them, more memories. Some happy, some sad. Others simply very sad, with that strange sadness that's a mixture of nostalgia and an awareness that you can never go back. Thinking about my neighbor—and, in those years, also brother—the poet Miguel Ángel Velasco, my mind made another leap: now I was in Barcelona, in September 2011.

More than just remembering, I saw what happened that day as if on a Moviola:

I'm strolling amid the shelves of the Central Bookstore, I

stop, read the spine of one book, open another, check the alphabetical order. I'm looking for two things: the complete poems of José María Pancro, and *Zen and the Art of Motorcycle Maintenance* by Robert Pirsig. I'm doing this, skimming over titles, when something on the table where the new books are draws my attention: *La muerte una vez más*, by Miguel Ángel Velasco. I open it to look at the photograph on the flap, that face of his that was always so theatrical. Then the biographical information, but as I read it I feel dizzy and the bookshop starts to spin around me. The text begins by saying:

"The untimely death of Miguel Ángel Velasco on October 1, 2010, at the age of 47, moved both the world of poetry and . . . "

"Another beer with a shot of JB," I tell the waiter.

"Something else to eat?"

"No, just the drinks."

"Coming right up."

I was moved to tears again, and made a leap to another date: now it's September 18, 1985, when I landed for the first time in Madrid. I was nineteen. More than anything else in the world, I longed to write novels, and the only thing that would keep me close to them, or so I thought, was to study something like Hispanic Philology. Looking for a place to live, I came across an ad in the newspaper *Segunda Mano* that said: "Double room in shared apartment for rent." It was at 9, Calle Santísima Trinidad and I set off to look at it. It was a furnished apartment on the fourth floor, with two adjoining rooms and a balcony overlooking the street. No telephone. The price was good and the location was perfect, so I decided to take it. The owner, an old lady from La Rioja named Visitación Isazi, told me: "The other young man who lives here is a poet from Palma de Mallorca, you'll get along well."

That same night I met him.

He swept in like a hurricane, knocked at my door, introduced himself, and asked if I had heard his telephone ringing (he had one). I told him I had, several times. Being a native of the very provincial city of Bogotá ("a young man pure of heart, recently arrived from the provinces"), I had never seen anybody like him: long curly hair, riding boots, a pink pirate shirt open to the chest, necklaces, rings, bracelets. He entered his part of the apartment (also two adjoining rooms, larger and more comfortable than mine, with decor that looked like something from a film by Alex de la Iglesias) and immediately, through a sealed door between our respective sitting rooms, I heard him say on the telephone:

"In that case, I'm going to celebrate!"

Then, in a state of euphoria, he called various people:

"I won the Ciudad de Melilla Prize! A million pesetas!"

Later, friends started to arrive and again he knocked at my door:

"Come celebrate with us," he said, "I've just been given a prize."

I didn't dare ask him what the prize was for, but I could imagine.

From that day on, Miguel was my constant companion. He got me to read Spanish poetry. I met his entourage, above all Agustín García Calvo and the poet Isabel Escudero (I still remember a line of hers: "Death, come take away the thought of death"). I read Rilke, whom he worshipped, and Borges, whom he could recite like nobody else. With him, I confirmed my taste for Rimbaud, Baudelaire, Heine, the sonnets of Shakespeare.

Although Miguel didn't read novels, I lent him *One Hundred Years of Solitude* and he read it in a single night. The following day he said:

"It's one long poem."

Sometimes he would wake me early in the morning to read me something he had just written, or we would read aloud Edgar Allan Poe stories by candlelight, drinking vodka with coconut liqueur that his grandmother's boyfriend gave him.

When I read *Sophie's Choice* by William Styron, it seemed familiar to me: the relationship between the young southerner recently arrived in Brooklyn and the lovable madman named Nathan.

Like me, Miguel was living far from his family, so we spent Christmas and New Year together, in bars, drinking and reciting. Thanks to his aristocratic manners and his long hair, he was incredibly successful with women. We conceived a thousand crazy projects, like one to learn Latin so that we'd gain more respect in bars. We drank, we read, we visited brothels, we listened to classical music on his portable record player, we got all excited over Butragueño's goals for Real Madrid (him) and Baltazar's goals for Atlético de Madrid (me), we exhausted the city by night, the whole of it, thousands of times.

Overcoming my shyness, I read him my first stories, and much to my surprise he approved of them. And in those years I was the first to read everything he wrote. I've never again known anybody so convinced of his own genius.

Sometimes he would say:

"Listen to this, you have good taste, you'll appreciate it," and he would read me his latest poem.

A modest publication of his called *Pericoloso sporgersi* dates from those years, but I was particularly enthusiastic about his early books, especially *Las berlinas del sueño*, for which he was awarded the Adonais Prize at the age of eighteen. He was twenty-three now, and death was his great theme, his lover, his obsession.

We shared the old apartment for five years, until Visichu's grandchildren threw us out in order to refurbish it and get a higher rent. Then I went to Paris and we lost touch with each other, as people did in those days, before e-mail and social networks.

We met a few times by chance, here and there, but never with the same intensity as in our crazy youth. That was only natural. He died while I was living in India and I didn't even know. Then the poet Luis García Montero confirmed to me that he had committed suicide.

"He got out of the way," Luis said.

"Excuse me, another shot of JB, please."

"And another beer?"

"No, thanks. Just the whiskey."

In spite of everything, I told myself, Miguel achieved his goal: to leave an oeuvre behind him and to melt into death, as in that poem by Emerson that he loved and we so often repeated together:

When me they fly, I am the wings;
I am the doubter and the doubt,
And I the hymn the Brahmin sings.

Suddenly a group of quite angry young people passed by. One of them said:

"Fuck it, they cut someone else's throat!"

"Seriously? Someone else?"

"Yes, man, have a look . . . "

They walked up toward the Teatro Español. One of them was showing the others something on his smartphone, but then they laughed.

Over there on Paseo de la Castellana the siege was following its course, but the JB was having its effect and starting to take me to other places, distant in time, like a submarine that closes its hatches and dives down into the waters. But the dive stopped abruptly when at the table next to mine a woman yelled at the man who was with her:

"How can you say that, you son of a bitch?"

Reality had imposed itself again: the shouting, the brazenness of the communicating masses. It struck me that the best thing I could do was get out of here, go back to the hotel, and stay there until Juana showed up.

The man was older than the woman: maybe about forty-five, although well-preserved and athletic. I could only see him from the back. He was wearing one of those tweed jackets that lend a vaguely intellectual air, but his narcissism was evident in the kerchief around his neck. Maybe he was a bit older, fiftysomething. Seeing them together, I got the impression they were lovers.

"After all the fucking lies you've told me!"

I could see her from the front. Her beautiful dark eyes were spitting fire, and I sensed that she might start crying at any moment. I would have sworn she was Colombian. Her muscles tightened and she continued saying things to him, but in a low voice now, as if she'd suddenly realized she wasn't in her own home. But then she raised her voice again:

"You pig! You disgust me!"

The man was American, with a red neck and fair hair that was already graying a little. In his right hand he was holding a glass of something yellow that I assumed was whiskey. He was looking nervously around him, fearful of the other customers' reactions, but without losing his composure. Even from behind, I was aware of his efforts to remain calm, and I calculated that he wouldn't be able to do so for much longer.

"I thought you were a good man, not a fucking pig!"

I imagined them a little while later, making violent love in some hotel or in the backseat of his car.

There are couples for whom arguing is the only valid way to get to a certain kind of brutal, satisfying sex. Later, he would go back to his wife, and she would sleep alone and hopeful.

"You're not even ashamed of yourself . . . "

Her anger was starting to weaken. I imagined that the first night, when he seduced her at some business party and penetrated her standing up, in some empty office or in a third-floor bathroom with a view of the parking lot, he had told her he was separated, but then, a few days later, he'd had to explain that he was still living with his wife for the sake of the children.

Instead of calming down, she took a deep breath and started shouting again.

"You fucking coward! You pig!"

The man was scratching something behind his ear. He asked her to moderate her tone. His reserves of calm seemed to have reached their limit. He spoke very good Spanish and I assumed she must be a student of his, of course. Young women often confuse love with admiration. Yes. She was a girl in love with her teacher. At any second, I thought she was going to burst into tears. Suddenly she looked for something in her bag, nervously; she took out a glasses case and a pack of Kleenex. Finally she found it: a little box from which she extracted a brooch that, at least from where I was sitting, looked quite glossy and expensive. Gold, maybe, with a jewel mounted in it.

"I'm giving you back this crap, I don't want it!"

The brooch ricocheted and fell to the ground. He bent down to pick it up and put it back on the table, still without saying anything.

"You filthy fucking pig! Give it to your wife!"

His *calm* needle was already moving into the red. Then he put his glass of whiskey down on the coaster, flexed the fingers of his right hand several times, as if testing them, and gave the young woman a slap. She wasn't able to dodge it in time, and the impact propelled her against the back of the chair and the window.

"You son of a bitch! You coward!"

Once she had recovered she grabbed a glass that contained the remains of what might have been a Cuba Libre, and flung it in his face. The man grabbed a napkin, wiped his forehead and cheeks; he even took advantage to wipe behind his ears. In a flash he hit her again, this time with his fist closed. Then he grabbed her by the neck, pulled her over the table, and landed her another punch.

"That'll teach you to behave yourself!"

The man's voice was strong, his breathing heavy. When the

girl recovered and made to speak, the man's fist again collided with her jaw. Twice, three times, until she started to bleed.

"I don't want you to open that fucking mouth again, you want to go back to the jungle?"

He punched her a fifth time, on the eyebrow, and she started crying.

Nobody apart from me seemed to be following the fight. Now the man's neck was redder than ever. He hadn't finished. He loosened his tie completely, grabbed her by the dress, and resumed hitting her on her left eye, which was already starting to become inflamed.

I left my shot glass on the table and stood up. The man looked at me in surprise.

"That's enough," I said.

He looked at her and let out a laugh.

"And who's this gallant knight, come to protect the damsel? Maybe you want to fuck her? Sure, that's easy enough."

"You son of a bitch!" she cried.

He stopped looking at me and gave her another punch in the face. I would have sworn he broke a tooth or her nose.

I put a hand on his arm and said:

"Listen, at least pick on someone your own size."

He stood up like a shot, and seeing him on his feet I realized that he meant business.

He kicked me in the groin and when I doubled up in pain he landed me a punch to the jaw that made me fall backwards. When I was on the ground, he came and gave me more kicks. I tried to shield myself. At last I was able to stand, but when I turned more punches rained down on me. How many arms did he have? My nose started bleeding. I hadn't been in a fight since I was a teenager. Why had nobody come to separate us? We were out on the street! Instead, people were just watching. Maybe there was an unwritten rule to avoid sticking your nose into other people's business.

I launched a punch, but it fell short and I felt a yanking in my collarbone. Then I received another couple of blows that opened my left eyebrow. I also noticed that something didn't feel right between my ribs and I thought, okay, that's it, it's time to stop this, but when I tried to move away the guy grabbed me by the neck and knocked my head against the wooden buffet that the waiters took the cutlery and napkins from.

Then came more blows to the face.

My nose made a sharp noise, but I didn't have time to analyze it because more blows hit my eyebrows. My mouth filled with blood. My cheeks were bruised, my left eye practically closed, and the right wasn't too good. The eyelid was broken.

I thought it was going to end there, but the man hadn't finished. Far from it. Like a tiger, he leapt on me and tried with all his strength to choke me, as if determined to finish the job. I attempted to push him off, but he was strong and he was beside himself with anger. I was finding it difficult to breathe, since the blood was running into my broken septum. Desperately, I held out my arms. A reflex gesture, I suppose, caused by the asphyxia, until I touched and grabbed something solid: it was a big glass ashtray. I lifted it and, with my last strength, brought it down behind me, more or less blindly. Once, twice. Suddenly the pressure on my neck stopped and the man rolled to one side, lifeless. Falling to the ground, I was able to see him: he had a huge gash on his forehead and his eyes were blank. I heard screams. A siren.

I got up as best I could, gushing blood, and groped my way to my table. Before reaching it, a shadowy figure moved toward me. It was the girl who was with him. I didn't even see that she had picked up a stool and was aiming it with all her strength at my head.

10

I got to Cali an hour later. My beloved Gloria Isabel had landed much earlier but stayed there with her chauffeur, waiting for me, because I'd managed to tell her what had happened, and so from Palmaseca Airport we went straight to Imbanaco Hospital. The city awaited me with a somewhat grim and threatening expression, as if the Glorieta de Cencar, the Poker beer factory, the River Cali, and Fifth Street held me responsible for what had happened and were blaming me for my neglect. It was hot, more than hot, it was sweltering. It had rained all morning.

What I felt at that moment, Doctor, was that somehow my mother had burst back aggressively into my life in order to harm me. As if the acid had been thrown in my face, not hers. When we arrived, Gloria Isabel went with me to the Intensive Care waiting room and there she stayed, while I went in with a nurse. As soon as I saw her from the door my legs started shaking. Her face was bandaged, with holes for the nose, eyes, and mouth. I took her hand and stroked it. She could hardly speak, but I went close to her mouth and she said in what was not much more than a sigh: at last you came, my girl, at last, look what that bastard did to me, it was him, my girl, don't forget it was him . . .

The attacker had been Freddy, her boyfriend. I later found out the whole story. When he did too much crack or drank aguardiente, a disgusting drink that people get drunk on in Colombia, he would come back home and start to beat her. He would get the typical paranoia of the jealous drunk and drug addict. My mother didn't know what he was talking about and of course, he'd get even angrier, and this went on until the day of the tragedy. Apparently, that night there was a Colombia soccer match and the team lost, and so Freddy, who couldn't keep away from those things, like a calf with an udder, got home very drunk and very frustrated and came out with the usual crap, except that this time Mother told him to shut up and get out. Of course he started hitting her and throwing lamps and plates at her. He really let her have it, but fortunately the neighbors came to the door, which he had left open, and she was able to get out of the house and escape.

For a week she was hidden at the house of a friend from work until they saw Freddy going around the block on his motorcycle and asking people questions. So that same night, toward morning, she ran off to the house of another friend, and then to a third. This last one convinced her to go to the police and report him, and I think that was the big mistake, because the police there are really dangerous. One night she and her friend were washing the dishes when there was a knock at the door. When they opened it, two armed men came in, pushed the friend onto the couch, and said to her, keep quiet, woman, this is nothing to do with you, and they went for my mother, who had run to lock herself in her room but the door didn't have even a lock. The two of them grabbed her and then Freddy came in, high as a kite, with his eyes red from drinking for God knows how many days in a row, and then he said to the guys, put her on her back to keep her still, and when she was like that he took out the bottle of acid and poured it over her face, head, and chest, and then, frightened by her screams, they ran out.

The police had been looking for him ever since, but Freddy must already have gone to Ecuador or Venezuela, which is where all the drug traffickers, bastards, and killers in this country go to hide. Mother tried to tell me all this in her thin voice, and then she said to me, girl, if you ever find him kill him for all the harm he's done us, but then I said to her, Mother, that guy burned you on the outside, but me he burned on the inside and you know what I'm talking about, that's what I said to her, Doctor, and now, yes, here comes the most painful part of my life, I don't have any alternative, I must tell it to you, but I'm going to tell it as I'd tell it to a girlfriend if I had one or a lover if I had one, or even to my mother, if she was still alive and was my friend.

This is what happened.

A few months after Freddy moved in with us, Mother called to say she was coming home late and told me to warm up the food. I obeyed her, but the guy spent the whole meal drinking aguardiente and when he finished he went to the door and locked it, and then he came to me and said, we're going to have a little private party, just you and me, that's what he said, and right then and there he grabbed me by force and took down my panties, a child's panties, Doctor, because I'd only just turned twelve, and he told me not to scream, that we were going to do something that was perfectly natural between people who live together, and that if I screamed he was going to squeeze my throat very hard, he already had his hand around it. I could barely breathe because with the fear I was gasping for breath, because I already knew what it was the guy wanted, oh, yes, though I couldn't believe he wanted it from me, because I was still a child. I believed, in my innocence, that God wouldn't allow something so terrible to happen, that He was going to defend me, but God did nothing, He didn't give a damn and left me alone for the guy to abuse me in the most humiliating manner: first he stuck a disgusting finger in me, hurting me, and moved it back and forth for a while, digging it into me, while he drank sips of aguardiente with the other hand; then, when he got bored with what was hurting me so

much, he tore off the skirt of my uniform and dragged me to
the bed, and when we were there, oh, God, he took out his
filthy cock and brought it close to my face, and forced me to
touch it first, with my hand, and then to suck it, can you imagine, I couldn't stop crying but the guy didn't care about that,
and I remember that I thought, this is pure wickedness, there
can't be anything beyond this, anything worse than this, how
innocent I was, believing that this was the filthiest thing of all,
but I had to be prepared to go deeper into the wickedness
because the guy said, we have all the time in the world, darling,
your mother won't be back until late because she's gone out for
a night on the town with some of her workmates and left us
alone, but we're going to have a better time than she's having,
aren't we? That's what he said while he continued taking sips
from that bottle of aguardiente and suddenly he grabbed my
mouth and said, open your mouth, darling, take a sip of this,
it's really good, and he forced me to drink from that nauseating brew, and said as if he was talking to himself, you like it,
don't you? it makes you feel good, it makes parties go with a
swing, and in this way he was taking me deeper and deeper
into his wickedness, and I tried to put up with it, I knew that
if I screamed really loudly the neighbors would come, I could
hear them, but Freddy had locked the door and would have
time to do something even worse to me, something more
painful, and I was scared of the pain because I was still a child,
and in addition he told me that he'd asked my mother's permission to do what he was doing to me, and according to him,
she'd said, of course, the girl's already big and it's good for her
to learn about life, that's what the son of a bitch told me and I
believed him, or rather, I can't remember if I believed him or
if my brain was paralyzed and those words weren't really going
into my head anymore, I was so mixed up, and so I felt guilty
even though I didn't quite understand why, in all this there was
something bigger that my poor little head couldn't figure out,

something very . . . How can I explain it to you? A man will never be able to understand a rape even if he knows all the details, even if he hears a meticulous description. He'll never be able to understand.

It terrifies me to remember it, which is why I'm scared of sleeping. I've often dreamed about the rape and each time it's been more blurred. Sometimes, while I was being raped, I would see Mother sitting beside the bed, knitting; other times she was listening to the radio, humming along to the music, while putting something on the stove to boil. And the worst of it was that the guy didn't rape me once but six times, and I couldn't say anything because he threatened to kill me and kill her. I didn't open my mouth, but I'm sure that at least one of those times, Mother realized and did nothing. Instead of protecting her daughter, she kept quiet and was an accomplice, can you imagine what I feel, Doctor? Neither God nor my mother protected me, so I said to myself, I must be a monster, there must be something horrible inside me and that's why I'm being punished. The two people I loved most in the world, my mother and God, did nothing to protect me, left me alone while I was begging for help.

I'd been ripped apart for life, with my body dirty and broken. So when I saw Mother in the hospital I felt a strong desire to tell her, this is your punishment, it happened to you because you were to blame, because you let something so bad happen to your daughter. I was only a girl, nobody respected me or cared for me.

I swear to you I'm going to kill that man one day, Doctor, not because Mother asked me, but because it's the only thing that can cleanse me a little. Of course, that afternoon in the hospital I kept silent and told Mother she shouldn't try to speak anymore, because her lips and part of her tongue were burned, and she could barely move it inside her mouth, which was full of ulcers. The acid had penetrated her cheeks and dissolved the bone and the mucous membranes. She was breathing through a tube, the poor woman, how she was suffering! But I couldn't stand any more sorrow, so I said, or rather, I thought, I hope she dies soon, I hope she gets a blood clot to the heart and goes from this world where she did so little, and will go without leaving anything good behind her, I hope she dies and stops suffering because it's a completely futile and pointless kind of suffering, and I swear, Doctor, that I even felt like tearing out the breathing tube, but I didn't do it, and I thought that now that she was dying I ought to forgive her, but I thought, I can't, I'm not going to forgive her for being an accomplice, because when I was in hell she didn't once turn to look at me . . .

I went down to the waiting room and Gloria Isabel stood up to greet me. How is she? Is it serious? I nodded and started crying on her shoulder.

"My poor girl," she said, pressing me to her chest, and I wept so many tears, I hadn't even known I had them inside me, old tears that had to come out. That had probably been there since that lost and stolen childhood.

Then three Secret Service officers came and asked me questions. That's how I found out that the friend who'd been hiding her, a woman named Claudia Ramos, had had an arm, two ribs, and at least half her teeth broken. They didn't rape the poor woman, but one of the guys did stick a finger in while the others were burning Mother, and they threatened to kill her if she said anything.

I was just signing a statement when the head doctor from Intensive Care came out, looking very nervous, and said, are you Manuela Beltrán? Yes, I replied, holding onto Gloria Isabel's hand and in the presence of the lawyer, Castillejo, who had just arrived.

"Your mother has just died," he said, "her breathing stopped and we couldn't do anything. Please accept my condolences."

At last, I thought, that cruel God had listened to me.

Gloria Isabel and the lawyer hugged me, condolences, Manuelita, but I didn't feel any sadness, but something new. I felt free. Her wounds weren't going to hurt anybody anymore and now only mine remained, those she gave me and those she allowed me to be given. Now everything was different, there was just me and my cruel, stubborn, sometimes dictatorial memory, and I told myself, Freddy is the only remaining witness to all that pain, but not for long, because one day I'm going to track him down and kill him, and I'll do it in the cruelest way I can think of, he deserves to go to hell howling with pain, shitting himself with fear. That's how I want him and that's how I'll have him one day, I swear it by that god who at last is granting my wishes, a cynical, twisted god, cold-blooded and vengeful, the kind of god I need, the kind I believe in.

I think it was that same savage god who, after Mother's funeral, put a pencil and a notebook in my hand and whispered in my ear: "Invent another world for yourself, because this one isn't any good." And I understood him, and that same night, staying in Gloria Isabel's house, I wrote the first poem in the book *Asuntos pendientes*. Although it would be more accurate to say: I vomited or spat and almost shat out my first poem, because I wrote it with hate. After that episode I went back to my new life feeling lighter. As if some conflagration of the air had given me the gift of invisibility. Yes, that's how I felt and that's what I wanted to be: the invisible woman.

In Bogotá I got into a really healthy, really cool routine. I would go to classes at the university and when they were over I would stay in the library, reading, until closing time. Then I would go back to my little room. I was allowed to cook and the landlady, Doña Tránsito, was a fantastic old woman. She would give me salt, a spoonful of oil, sometimes even an egg. I liked her. At night I felt cold and I would put on two pairs of stockings and two T-shirts and listen to the rain. The amount of rain in that dark city! I was scared to go out on the street at night. The combination of darkness, cold, and rain was something I was unfamiliar with and it made me feel as if I was in danger. As if there was something unhealthy in the air. That's why I always stayed in my room, which I gradually made my own. It had a carpet, heavy curtains, and two old beds that, when I first saw them, made me wonder how many people had slept in them. They creaked. People in a cold climate are quiet, there's no noise. They don't put on music and they close their doors. They don't use the street either, or rather, they use it only to go from one side to the other, never to stay on it or listen to music or pay each other visits. At least that's what it was like in that neighborhood. There was a store nearby and sometimes I'd venture there at night to buy something, almost always a bar of chocolate, because sweet things warm you up. Those deserted streets scared me. By ten at night, there wasn't a soul about and no sound came from the houses, as if everyone was dead. People in Bogotá are strange, but also friendly in their way. I read and read. The first poem I wrote in Bogotá is about a city inhabited by ghosts where it rains all the time and the sun is like a lightbulb, giving out light but no heat.

One day, I took a bus to the elegant neighborhoods in the north of the city, and it struck me as incredible that people lived like that in a country like ours, where most people were so poor and suffered so much violence. The bright shopping malls, the people in their sweaters and coats. They all carried umbrellas, and it occurred to me that I should buy myself one. I missed the hustle and bustle of Cali, the climate, the people in shorts and sandals. You don't see anything like that in Bogotá. At least not in the Bogotá I lived in, because I later discovered that Bogotá was like a harlequin's costume, a patchwork quilt of the country, and in the south of the city, that sinister south where the most tragic things happened and the poor people lived, there were neighborhoods full of blacks from Chocó and displaced people from Los Llanos, and there you'd find noise and music, but if you went there bad things could happen to you.

Señora Tránsito always said to me, you see, my girl, you're not from here and I'm going to tell you something, from the Javeriana southward you can only go by day, very early, because if you get caught there after dark, they'll mug you, they'll steal your cell phone, they'll kidnap you and put you in a brothel or sell your organs, so don't even think about it, and I was terrified and took notice of what she said, going just from the university to the library and then back home. Another day she told me that if I went out at night even the police would rob me, they raped women in their patrol cars and took their corneas out to sell to foreigners. Something must have happened to the old woman, because although the city was dangerous, it wasn't as dangerous as all that.

In the university I was getting to know people. They were such children! In order not to waste money in the cafeteria I would take a sandwich and a thermos of juice, and go sit on the lawn way above the university, because I didn't want anybody to see me. The Javeriana is an expensive university and almost all the students are rich. There were some very beautiful girls who would hang about the walkways, getting the boys hot under the collar, know what I mean? I started to hear gossip about some of these princesses, especially those doing Media Studies. There was a girl from the Caribbean coast they called Puntilla, who always went around in tight pants or very short miniskirts. All they thought about was fucking her. She didn't seem such a bimbo to me. Showing your body is natural in a hot country, and I thought: these Bogotá guys see a bare navel and immediately think a girl's a whore.

Time passed and at the end of the semester the students were invited to submit poems for the department magazine. I sent three of the nine I had written in Bogotá, and much to my surprise they were all chosen. One of the girls in my class who kept reading her things to her classmates and telling the teachers that she was a poet didn't have a single one of her poems chosen and she almost had a nervous breakdown. Her name was Mónica. Her poems were sentimental, magnifying things that when it came down to it were just trifles. That's the problem with people who haven't suffered, Doctor, who only know life from the sidelines. What to her seemed a drama of universal proportions was nothing more than a rich girl's tantrum: my boyfriend has left me, I want to sleep with a boy but he doesn't love me, I've fallen in love with my friend's boyfriend. Oh, what terrible tragedies! That's what the poems of most of my classmates were like. The most tragic thing that had happened to them in their poor young lives was losing their cell phones or finding out their boyfriends were fucking other girls. If those were the problems of the world there would be no poetry, and anyway, who said that poetry should be a confessional for their poor childish dramas?

I didn't tell anyone that my poems had been accepted, and when the magazine came out they caused something of a stir. One of the sentimental female poets came and congratulated me; she said the poems were sad and beautiful. I thanked her. Another asked me if they were really mine. So nice of her. The head of the department, a very nice guy from the Caribbean coast named Cristo Rafael Figueroa, congratulated me in front of everyone and that made me very happy. A cool guy, that Cristo.

It was the first happy day of my life.

Soon afterwards I received a surprising request. The magazine of the University of Antioquia asked me for permission to publish my poems and wanted to know if I had more. I sent another three and they were published in the next issue, and as a result of that I started to receive mail from readers. What a surprise! I never thought that my poems could appeal to people who didn't know me and hadn't experienced similar things; just the fact that they understood them surprised me. How strange, I told myself.

Poetry was something I built up little by little, alone. If it wasn't a bit corny I'd even say that I suffered it, and that's why I always wrote in silence, without making it a celebration of myself or my life. But now they had seen me. The bad thing about publishing is that you're out there in the light of day, once and for all, and there's no turning back.

All this gave me a certain fame and very soon my classmates invited me to a reading at the house of one of them, a young man named Saúl Pérez who always dressed in black and in class had a preference for horror fiction.

He lived in Santa Ana Alta, a very ritzy neighborhood, almost impossible to get to by bus. When I finally rang the doorbell, they greeted me warmly, although they pointed out that I was late and they could have come and picked me up. They were in a lounge that looked out on the garden. On the table were beers, a bottle of whiskey and one of Néctar aguardiente. Being the host, Saúl was the first to read. His story wasn't badly written, in my opinion, but was completely crazy: after an earthquake, Bogotá fell through a fault into underground caves beneath the mountains and the only humans who were able to survive were some strange inhabitants of the sewers who had to fight giant rats that had grown fat from eating dead bodies.

When Saúl finished there was loud applause and his girl-friend, who also dressed in black, leapt on him and kissed him on the mouth, in front of everyone, the two of them moving about as if they were naked and in bed. The next person to read was Daniela, the oldest of the group. This time it was an erotic poem of which I only remember one line: "Uncover the fruit tree of my breasts." There was more applause and toasts. Then Verónica read. She was the romantic of the group. Hers was a long poem about the death of her grandmother, whom she had loved a lot, and of course when she read the last two verses she was in tears and her voice cracked. She read nine more poems. The last one was about the death of a strange character who climbed walls and walked on the roofs in the early hours of the morning. It took me a while to realize she was talking about her cat. Then Saúl said, Manuela, will you read? I stepped forward and began with my first poem, then the second. I read five of them, and when I'd finished Saúl said, please repeat the one about the night in the orphanage. I read it again and he said, solemnly, with a glass of whiskey in his hand:

"That's the best poem we've heard tonight."

His girlfriend looked nervous, which I managed to catch, even though it was a fraction of a second. Then he smiled and gave me a big hug and congratulated me. I thought that was strange. I felt obliged to say something about their work, but nothing came to mind, so I thanked them. Verónica passed me a glass of aguardiente, but just smelling it made me nauseous. No, thanks, I said. Saúl took out a small bag of coke and laid out a few lines on a glass tray. When they passed it to me I again said, no, because I had experienced all that at the age of fourteen. They laughed and Cayetano, another of our classmates, said that maybe I was a poet nun, like Sister Juana or Saint Teresa, so they started calling me Sister Manuela. Another boy, Lucas I think it was, said that maybe I was like the nun of Monza, because of an Italian movie that has a famous sex scene, specifically a blow job. They all laughed, then drank lots of booze and sniffed all the coke their smooth, straight nostrils could take. That was my second nickname after Hypocrite. The theme was the same.

But even though they were rich kids, they treated me very well. They could have asked me tiresome questions about who I was and where I came from, uncomfortable things, but they didn't do that. They limited themselves to recognizing me for my poetry, which I thought was nice. I wasn't like them, but they admired me, especially Saúl. They did say I was the most unusual person from Cali they had met because I didn't dance, and I just laughed and said, yes, I do dance but only when I'm alone.

One day I got an email from a very well-known woman poet in Bogotá called Araceli Cielo, which is a pen name. She said she had read my poems and wanted to meet me. But it gave me a fright and I didn't reply, because I said to myself, where did she get my e-mail address? who gave it to her? It might be a practical joke by my classmates on their mysterious Nun of Monza, so I didn't reply. I deleted the e-mail. A week later I received another one in which she asked if I had received the first one, but I deleted that, too, without replying.

Imagine my surprise one afternoon when Cristo himself, the cool dean of the faculty, came looking for me in class and handed me a package. What was it?

"Araceli Cielo, the poet, came to my office and left you this," Cristo said. "She asked me to make sure I got it to you."

Then he whispered in my ear, you know what this means for you? Congratulations!

Two of my classmates realized what was going on and their eyes opened like hard-boiled eggs. But I grabbed the package, put it in my satchel, and ran to Seventh to catch a bus home. I held my breath as I opened it and found her two latest books, dedicated to me, and a long letter. "To Manuela, a talented young poet, with all my admiration . . . " She had read my poems and wanted to know more about me. She gave me her cell phone number and asked me to call her. I hesitated, I felt uncomfortable with such a well-known and elegant lady from Bogotá. I kept the number on my telephone and several times I had it on the screen, ready to call it, but at the last moment changed my mind. I couldn't summon up the strength.

The following Tuesday I got a call from Gloria Isabel in Cali, wishing me a happy birthday, and I said, oh, thanks. I'd completely forgotten! That's how remote from my own life I was in those days. To celebrate, I went to the local store and bought three cans of beer. I drank them in my room, thinking about how solitary and happy my life was and at about nine that night I took out my cell phone and dialed Araceli's number. Each ring tore at my stomach, but there was no reply, so I left a message.

"I'm the girl who wrote those poems."

Three minutes later, the phone rang and it was her.

"Hi," I said, very calmly, although inside I was dying.

"It's a good thing you decided to call," she said, "I was going to look for you in your classroom."

"Today is my birthday, and I've drunk three beers. I was feeling a bit nervous. I'm sorry."

"Many happy returns. Can I buy you a coffee tomorrow?"

We met the following day in a Juan Valdez café near the university. She struck me as very youthful, with her jeans and T-shirt and brightly colored Wayuu shoulder bag. She continued talking to me about my poems, she said she had heard a new voice in them, saying important things and saying them well. She also asked what I thought of her books. I'm no good at lying, so I told her that they had a good rhythm but that there were things in them I didn't understand. Also that they were cold poems and I had to get used to them. I hadn't read much and I had everything to learn.

Instead of taking offense at this, Araceli, said she thought the same and, to be honest, couldn't understand why they were so successful. I told her that people in Bogotá liked the cold, maybe that was why, and anyway that didn't mean they were bad. They were good, but cold. Just that.

We continued talking and she invited me to lunch at a really nice place near there called Andante, opposite the university. I had a class at three, and since we couldn't stop talking we decided to continue the following day. So we started seeing each other every day. Araceli was married and had a daughter of fifteen from her first husband. Her current husband was something big in advertising and, from what I gathered, very rich. We always met at Andante, it became a routine. I showed her my new poems and she gave me advice. She said she would help me to put together a book. I wasn't sure it was what I wanted, but I let her. I liked the fact that she never asked me anything, not who I was or where I came from. We only talked about poetry. And she gave me books. She got me to read a whole lot of poets.

Thanks to that, I understood her poetry better. It was poetry that grew out of things she had read, not experienced. The only thing I had, on the other hand, were the lyrics of songs, and everybody knows, my dear Doctor, that music can make any text go down, however corny or stupid it is. That was my small, or rather, nonexistent education, and that's why I liked Araceli so much. She was generous not only in a material sense—she always paid—but generous with words, books, and advice. She was interested in me without expecting anything in return.

For quite a while, all she knew was that I was from Cali and lived in a rented room in Chapinero, nothing more, but that seemed to be enough for her, as if she understood that any day now I would start to tell her things about my life, at my own pace, of course, since I felt intimidated. Even though she used a shoulder bag and wore torn jeans, Araceli was a rich lady from the north of Bogotá, famous and respected, and I was a poor young immigrant, fleeing a rough past that I preferred to hide.

After two months, she invited me to her home and that's when I really did feel embarrassed, because she lived in a huge house in Santa Ana, like my classmate Saúl. But her house was nicer and more elegant, with a kind of turret where her study was, a circular space with wood paneling, lined with books, and with a large window leading out onto a terrace with a view of the whole of Bogotá and the mountains. Even Gloria Isabel's house, which was really nice, seemed like a ranch house compared with this.

Her husband and daughter were away. He was in Cartagena, in an apartment they had there, and the girl was visiting her father.

"We can be nice and quiet here," Araceli said, "nobody will interrupt us, and so we can talk about a thousand things."

I showed her some more of my work. She read it with great concentration and suddenly said, don't you think that this word is too big? or, don't you think this verse is too long? She could concentrate for hours. We ate right there, in the study, and then she offered me a drink. I said yes. She confessed that she was a big whiskey drinker but that I could choose something else, and she opened the bar, which was enormous, full of bottles and glasses, and I said, whiskey's fine, I've never tried it but I'm sure I'll like it, so she filled two glasses with ice and we continued talking until very late, drinking more and more, until suddenly, about midnight, she said, can I confess something to you? She went to a drawer and took out a small wooden box. She opened it and . . . What do I see? A small bag of coke and a complete kit for snorting it, with a silver tube and a mirror, all very professional. She asked me if I'd tried it and I said yes, so she laid out several lines and offered me some. I didn't know what to do and finally I accepted, I was happy, I felt good with her. Araceli put some in each nostril and we continued drinking and talking until I saw the clock and said, shit! It's three in the morning, but she said, what's the hurry? Sleep here, the house is enormous. I accepted and we continued talking and reading poetry.

The next day my head was spinning and when I got back to my little room I had to go back to bed. I slept almost until the day after. In the afternoon, Araceli sent me a number of messages. "Thank you, thank you." I thought I should ask her why she was so kind to me. What a headache! But I felt happy. Someone appreciated me for my poetry.

The next time I went to her house we started drinking whiskey earlier and she told me about an Argentinian poet named Alejandra Pizarnik. We read a few of her poems aloud and she told me about her life: that she had committed suicide when she was still young, that she was depressive and took pills. Then, already a little bit drunk, I asked Araceli, do you think that poetry is the refuge of the saddest people in the world? Araceli looked at me and, without saying anything, gave me a kiss on the mouth. I felt her lips on mine and quite naturally I opened them and explored them slowly with my tongue. Then we kissed with sudden violence and frenzy, as if we had been waiting a long time, and by the time I realized what was happening, Araceli was already running her hand up my thigh. It struck me that I hadn't shaved my legs, but she stroked me in a way that only women can do, because they know where everything is and how to do things in the correct order. As she touched me, I kissed her neck and back and breasts, which sagged a little but were beautiful. Then she herself put my hand on her waist and moved it inside her jeans.

This continued for a while, until she took her clothes off and led me to a bedroom. We threw ourselves on the bed and started having some pretty strong sex, with a lot of licking and biting. I liked it. Araceli had a body that was quite loose although beautiful, it was obvious she went to the gym. It was strange after all that excitement that there was no penis involved, I confess, but we both came and it was great and then we continued drinking and sniffing coke in bed, naked, until we fell asleep in each other's arms.

Obviously, a new phase of my life had started.

11

T he same day that young Arthur was taken to Mazas Prison, September 1, 1870, the French armies of Napoleon III fell on the battlefield of Sedan, routed by the forces of King Wilhelm of Prussia and his general Helmut von Moltke, with the modest participation of a twenty-six-year-old soldier and nurse born in Röcken named Friedrich Wilhelm Nietzsche. So it was that Napoleon III handed over his sword to spare the lives of his soldiers, and on September 2 agreed to surrender.

But that defeated France wasn't the only one, and so, taking advantage of the chaos and confusion, the Republicans proclaimed the Third Republic and issued a decree ousting Napoleon III. And to defend the Republic, the Committee of National Defense was created. The French Empire might have lost the war, but there was another France able to rise up and carry the torch.

Faced with this, King Wilhelm I sent troops to encircle Paris. He wasn't going to have his military triumph spoiled by a handful of romantic Republicans. The recurring problem of struggles between weak Davids and powerful Goliaths is that the Davids usually win, but in this case German foresight, as well as their relentless superiority, managed to overturn the biblical tradition, and in spite of the fact that the Republican Minister of Defense, León Gambetta, was able to break the siege of Paris and organize guerrillas to attack the Prussians from the rear, in the end it was all futile. It merely served to inspire the hearts of men for a time.

Georges Izambard, Rimbaud's putative father, was one of those men who threw himself into the fight. And even Rimbaud himself, who despite being a minor (he was still only fifteen!) presented himself to the National Guard and took part in training with broomsticks, since there were no weapons available. Who was this young man, ready to give his life for the same France that very soon afterwards he would hate and would leave in a state of bitterness, spitting on its soil before leaving? Let us not forget that in this young man's story, the army of France represents his absent father, who is still alive in his memory. Arthur longs for the hero to look at him and acknowledge him, perhaps even say a few affectionate words to him. What would art and literature be without absent fathers? What serves literature does not always serve life. But the young Rimbaud does not know that. It is, quite simply, something that is inside him.

At the beginning of the siege of Paris, Arthur returned to Charleville, taken there by Izambard. When Vitalie saw them arrive, she hit her son and confined him to his room, and of course insulted Izambard. As far as she was concerned, the teacher was responsible for everything bad that had happened. She knew that the demon of poetry was inside her son and she wanted to exorcise it. But to no avail, since two weeks later Rimbaud again disappeared. Now he was heading north. Izambard, like a hunting dog, followed him from Charleroi to Brussels, with all the towns in between. The fugitive poet was traveling on foot, like prehistoric men. He himself was his own cart and horse, and he was living . . . on what? According to what he said later in a letter, "on the delicious smells from kitchens." At each stop he made, Izambard was given information about his pupil, although he was unable to track him down, even in Brussels, so he returned to Douai, and on reaching his house, what a surprise! Arthur opened the door to him.

Izambard hated him, but everyone succumbed to his wicked

smile. The world falls in love with certain angels and devils. The poems he had been writing during his wanderings show the impulsive freedom that he felt being alone on the road, sleeping in ditches, perhaps seeking shelter from the rain or the cold or the wind—it was already October—in some abandoned barn.

My shelter was the Great Bear
The stars in the sky emitted soft sighs
And I heard them as I sat by the roadside.

Two weeks of daydreaming, solitude, and travel. It is hard to image a young man of sixteen wandering alone through a country at war. Enid Starkie, his biographer, says that on the way he encountered a dead soldier, who inspired one of the poems he brought with him when he returned, "Le Dormeur du val."

A young soldier, his mouth open, his head bare,
His neck bathing in cool blue cress,
Sleeps stretched out on the grass, under the sky,
Pale on his green bed where the light pours down.

It is impossible not to think of another, much later poem, written by someone from another world. The scene is almost the same: a dead soldier in a field, perhaps in a ditch. The poet observes the lifeless body and speaks to it. He begs it to come back to life. The poet is César Vallejo, who must have read Rimbaud. There is a kind of music that echoes behind their poems. This is how Vallejo's vision of a dead soldier begins:

At the end of the battle, with the fighter dead,
a man came to him and said:
"Do not die, I love you so much!"
But alas, the corpse continued to die.

I think Rimbaud would have approved of these lines.

Let us return to his story. Young Arthur is already back home. Vitalie can breathe a little and stop worrying for the moment. Her little genius had always been her biggest headache!

Separated from his idol Izambard (who was at the front), Arthur resumed his old childhood friendship with Ernest Delahaye, with whom he went for walks in the countryside and woods around Charleville and Méziers. It must have been very strange to wander amid beautiful bucolic landscapes while France was heading inexorably toward the abyss. Beauty and horror in the same plowed fields. Two young men strolling, talking endlessly, reading anything they could get from a besieged Paris.

According to a later account by Delahaye, it was on one of these afternoon walks that Rimbaud mentioned his admiration for the poet Paul Verlaine. They read each other poems from two books that could still be obtained, *Poèmes saturniens* and *Fêtes galantes*. Verlaine's work showed Arthur new possibilities of playing games with form. He realized that poetry could be more flexible and sensed that his desire was to blow things up, to destroy the rigid molds in which poetry was traditionally cast. And not just poetry. Life, too, which seemed even more rigid and fixed.

Everything has to be demolished for the world to bloom again, perhaps from the new seeds of poetry! Poets are fiery, arrogant gods who aspire to recreate the universe and elevate the human soul. In a letter to Izambard, Rimbaud talks of "necessary destructions" and claims that in the new free nation (perhaps in its new Republic) luxury and pride will have disappeared.

Rimbaud's first heroic, death-defying act was on behalf of his friend Delahaye, when the Prussians bombed and burned Méziers in December 1870. Vitalie confined her children to the house, but Arthur got out through a window and went to Méziers to look for Delahaye. I imagine Rimbaud running up a deserted, rubble-strewn street that leads to the hill, between buildings with smoking roofs and walls laid flat by cannon fire. There is a strange smell, like that of damp, rotting vegetables. Where is this young man going, alone amid so much desolation? Couldn't another burst of gunfire come from some dark corner and finish off anything still alive? We do not know if the young man had these thoughts, but he went on anyway.

The Prussians had taken the city. Seeing a young Frenchman in these parts might upset them, some still nervous soldier might open fire or decide to arrest him. But none of these things happened. Arthur's childlike appearance, which had made the French army reject him as being too young, even though he was now sixteen, now protected him.

Delahaye and his family had taken refuge in a house in the country and it was there that Rimbaud now arrived. Why was he so determined? He was eager to have his friend read two books he had recently gotten hold of: Edgar Allan Poe's *Tales of Mystery and Imagination*, translated by Baudelaire, and *Le petit chose* by Alphonse Daudet.

The siege of Paris lasted 135 days, until the lack of food became unbearable, and at the end of January 1871 the armistice and surrender were signed, although the chaos continued. The National Guard refused to withdraw, but the city filled with thieves who came to plunder it, under the pretext of defending it. There were rich pickings to be had! In the rest of France, life returned to a degree of normality. Arthur, though, refused to go back to school. Vitalie tried to force him, but he maintained his position: the country was in danger and he had to take action, join the National Guard, and serve in the defense. On February 25 he returned to Paris, but it was a squalid sojourn. He spent two weeks eating out of trash cans, begging, and sleeping under bridges in the middle of the winter.

The cold of February is the worst, but this young man had an unusual ability to bear adversity when he himself had sought it out. When it comes down to it, this is quite natural. When pain depends on you, it is easier for you to bear. Arthur had to coexist with rats and cockroaches, remove strange putrid liquids from the leftover food he put in his mouth. He was training himself to withstand whatever he might have to face. In *A Season in Hell* he talks of rain-sodden bread that he had to fight the pigeons for.

On March 3, the Germans finally entered Paris with their army, did an about-turn, and left again. Then the Parisians lit fires in the streets they had walked down in order to purify them, but in the end nothing of what had been feared happened. With the setting up of the Commune, France now had two governments: one in Paris and one in Versailles. It is uncertain whether or not Rimbaud was there at this time. Delahaye says yes and that he fought with the Commune until the troops from Versailles overran the city. His biographer Starkie says no, basing her assertion on the dates of some of his letters. What is certain is that his rapidly growing awareness of life, the way he left each stage behind him, and the avalanche of experiences that he incorporated into his poetry in those few months were really remarkable. Given his rebellious spirit, it would be logical to think that he fought with the Commune, but at the same time he was already starting to be a strange Attila leaving devastated fields behind him. It is odd that the biographers cannot agree about this, since in those days something happened that was to leave its mark on his life and even his soul forever. It was the moment when reality decided to lift him up into the air and abruptly let him fall to the ground with a resounding thud. It was as if the tide of life in all its cruelty trapped him, struck him a savage blow, and in doing so, in leaving him hurt and humiliated, awoke completely the poet who was already within him.

What happened?

A group of drunken soldiers raped him in the toilets of the military barracks on Rue Babylone, in Paris. Was it in April or June 1871? It hardly matters. It was a dark, gloomy place, and the rebellious youth had disguised himself as an older man in order to be accepted by them. His political passion was strong and perhaps sincere, and being a barracks it provided food and shelter. The young man had traveled to Paris without a sou, as was his custom, and the barracks was a good solution, given that his ardent desire was to join the Guard. Many of the soldiers who were there had been involved in trench warfare against the Germans and had witnessed their comrades' bodies rotting beside them or beneath their boots. They were hardened men. The smell of death in those fields was fresh in their memory. Ten thousand bodies lie fallen in the mud, while above them, another twenty or thirty thousand are still fighting, still alive. The bodies become deformed. Blood accumulates in the lower parts of the body and suddenly something bursts. A foul-smelling stream gushes out on top of the mud. The birds circle, pulling out eyes, the worms rise to the surface. That's what the soldier sees in battle: the bare bones of his friend, the amputations, the perforated skulls. What he has seen remains on his retina. Nobody who has contemplated such horror can ever be the same again. Anyone who survives a war, even unscathed, bears a war wound. He is someone who not only has looked death in the eyes but has lain down with death and kissed it on the mouth, has held it in his arms and sung it lullabies.

These damaged men were sleeping on camp beds in the barracks on Rue Babylone. I imagine that on closing their eyes these scenes of horror came back into their minds, so the best thing to do was to fill up with wine or moonshine until you fell into a stupor. A lot of alcohol in those stomachs that, by some miracle, were still connected to their bodies. And suddenly a kind of hallucination, what is this, shining forth amid the camp beds? An angelic youth, with curly fair hair tumbling over his shoulders. He has blue eyes and a soft innocent look that, to these other eyes, polluted with horror and evil, represents life in the bud. This adolescent looks like a young nymph. The soldiers see him come in and lie down on a straw mattress at the far end. The following day he is given a crust of bread, a cup of coffee, and a spoonful of lard. There are already eyes following him, watching him, and, gradually, desiring him. On one side, bodies sated with war; on the other, this asexual angel. On the third night, they have already been talking and because of all the wine they've drunk they start to ogle him. They make up their minds, although they'll still drink a little more. Then something happens, which is that the curly-haired young man approaches them and asks to drink with them. They give him a few sips. Time passes, it's bedtime, so they go to the dormitory. But the young poet wants to smoke one last pipe and he heads for the toilet. Many pairs of eyes watch him, on the alert like wild beasts.

Il est là bas! Allons-y . . . !

Arthur sees them coming, with their alcoholic laughter, and offers them his pipe. The men look at each other, puzzled, until one of them, the shortest one, approaches the young man, takes his hand and twists it, grabs him by the neck, and forces him to his knees. Arthur struggles, but the man, toothless, wild-eyed, hits him in the face with his open hand, just as he would do to his wife. That makes them laugh. A trickle of blood emerges from his nose and he jumps back, but two others grab him by the legs, lift him, and pull down his pants. There is a murmur when they see that pink backside, although it's a little dirty. This, too, makes them laugh. They clean it from a bowl of water and he feels them digging into his flesh. Someone puts a finger in his anus and says, it's dry! Gobs of spittle rain down on him. Filled with revulsion, Arthur starts shaking, not from fear but from anger. Another finger pushes that disgusting spittle inside him. The soldiers pass each other a jug of bitter, perhaps diluted wine. He feels something tearing and sees a few drops of blood roll down his legs.

Il est vierge, bravo!

They pour a little wine over his buttocks and he feels the burning of it, but in all this humiliation he hasn't gifted them a single moan or groan. Rather, he insults them, but a hand of steel presses on the back of his neck, making it hard for him to breathe. Already, a first soldier has put his cock in and is about to finish; then comes a second, brandishing something enormous that curves to the left. *Quel petit sabre!* they say, laughing their heads off. Again they fill him with wine-flavored spittle and the man replies: *Petit sabre? C'est une bayonette! Vous allez voir.*

Putting it in abruptly, the soldier cries, *Jocelyn, c'est moi!* or something like that, and Arthur feels the blood still running from his torn anus and the men still spitting saliva and wine at him, and another of them takes his turn and then another, there are lots of them, someone wants a repeat go and they fight, he hears a punch and someone falls to the floor, then the man who'd already his turn goes back to the dormitory muttering insults, he's very drunk, just like the others, and yells at them as he goes out, *J'en ai marre de partouzer des gonzesses avec vous, je vous emmerde!*

And so they get to the last one, who holds him down by the neck, he thinks, because suddenly he releases him, but the young man can no longer move. A small stream of blood and wine with nauseating white lumps in it flows to the drain. To finish off, they hit him, and when he falls to the floor they say to him, see you tomorrow, *petite pute*, and leave him.

Arthur crawls until he finds his pants. He tries to stand and falls, twice, three times. At last he manages to support himself on a water tank and with great effort regains his balance. He walks toward the door. In place of a mirror there is just a broken sheet of glass, a fragment that reflects him for a second and Arthur sees a strange gleam in his eyes. He recognizes something overpowering, perhaps the most intense feeling he has ever had: hate.

For now he holds back, although he wants to kill.

He leaves the toilet with effort and walks toward the door of the dormitory. A guard is smoking pensively and on seeing him makes a gesture, as if to say, what's the matter? Nothing, Arthur says with his hand. He waits for dawn crouching in the yard and by the time first light comes he is already leaving the barracks, walking along Rue Babylone toward Saint-Denis. By noon he has already walked two and a half miles in a northerly direction. He is returning to Charleville, to his hated mother's house. He has no other refuge and the world is brimming with wickedness. His young body will recover as he advances, but nothing will be the same again.

Before, he had played with words whose meaning life had barely had time to reveal to him, but now they had become real: he had been beaten, humiliated. Out of that pain he heard a strange rhythm, a crazy tom-tom beat that he had never known before. When night fell, still hurting and very hungry, he took notebook and pencil from his bag and began to write, his eyes glowing with that new light he had seen in the broken mirror, and these lines poured out:

Mon triste coeur bave a la poupe
Mon coeur couvert de caporal.
Ils y lancent des jets de soupe.

Life and its strange gods had seen him, had followed his childhood rituals and his dangerous games. And they had decided to strike him. By his third day of walking, he had realized that he was no longer a child, not even an adolescent. It was the moment of destruction and truth. Life might have decided to strike him, but he knew how to return the blow. The young angel had to crouch to give way to the Lucifer they had caused to grow in him.

He reached Charleville and his mother greeted him without the slightest show of affection, but with reproaches and questions. Did she think she had given birth to a devil? The only thing she did, apart from feeding him and helping him to wash, was to ask him about Paris.

"Is it true it's about to fall?"

He looked at her contemptuously and said:

"No, no. It's a cursed city but it's my city."

Then he wrote Izambard a long letter and included the poem about the rape. Everything was new in these verses, starting with the strange music, but Izambard did not understand it. He thought Arthur was making fun of him and by way of response parodied the poem, making him see that these games were within anybody's reach.

"Anybody's?" Arthur asked himself, once again wounded to the core. The only person who could evaluate that disturbing melody that human barbarity had left him with . . . wasn't capable of appreciating it! Not just that, he made fun of it. Arthur's response was silence.

The savage poet was digging his claws into the soil of France with all the cruelty and intolerance of youth. Ready to spit, vomit, ejaculate his verses of destruction.

From that moment on, he stopped washing or cutting his hair, and was to be seen begging on the streets of Charleville. People muttered, isn't that the young genius from high school? *C'est lui, c'est lui!* That's him, but he's gone crazy now! And his mother, the proud mother of the previous year, had been reduced to a shadow, who went out as little as possible, tired of hearing stories about her son.

Vitalie knelt before him and begged him to go back to school, but Arthur stood firm. He had nothing to learn in that mediocre place. Instead he went to the library every morning to read and make notes. At least there was that! But in the afternoons he would sit on the café terraces, drinking, smoking his pipe, and arguing on any subject under the sun with whoever he had in front of him. He hated the idea of God, hated the Church and priests. How could anyone believe, faced with the wickedness and barbarity of the world? If there was a god, even just a small god, he should be able to protect the frail.

At other times Rimbaud would adopt the voice of that cruel god, curse death, challenge it, and laugh uproariously at the sufferings of others. He was hurt in the deepest part of himself and in his tortured heart (*coeur supplicié*) there was no room for anybody. Perhaps not even for himself.

12

Tertullian here, with the voice of reason and the future, emerging into the ether from the caves of hyperconsciousness to bring you the words of the ancient masters and sages, broadcasting from obscure and forgotten highways." Do you like that? It's how I begin my radio show, and you have no idea the audience it gets! We don't have much money and that's why, if you ask around, they'll tell you it's an underground thing, something that's classified as "garage radio," but how can it be, when our advertisers are delighted with us.

Of course, you asked me why I call myself Tertullian. Well, I liked that name ever since I first read it. I know he's a father of the Church and that's a subject that, as I told you, isn't really me. But I read some phrases of his that I later copied and which I use frequently in my speeches. Referring to the fact that man had murdered Jesus, Tertullian says the following: "The son of God was crucified, that is not shameful because it is shameful. And the son of God died, that is even more credible because it is incredible. And after he died he rose again, that is certain because it is impossible." These words, Consul, are among the most profound that any human being has ever spoken in the whole history of human life on this planet. I took away the Catholic aspect and kept only what you might call the political part. "It is certain because it is impossible" is an image you could found a world with, don't you think? That's what I'm doing. I have thousands of followers, take a look at my

Facebook page, Twitter too. I've been making what they call a *community*, to which I give a wider meaning. As I told you, at first nobody took any notice of me. Now thousands of people come to my talks, Latin Americans especially: many Ecuadorians and Peruvians; the Bolivians are a little harder but they come; Paraguayans, Argentinians and Chileans, people from Puerto Rico and the Dominican Republic. Also Colombians like you, and Mexicans, even Venezuelans!

And there's something else that I don't think I told you before: from the start I realized that this was something I had to do with our cousins in the North, otherwise it won't work; there, most people, whether white or black, respect their territory. Do you understand me when I tell you that this struggle isn't racist? You have to look at the present with the eyes of the present! Present-day diseases can't be treated with the obsolete medicine of the twentieth century, let alone that of other periods. You have to start by understanding what's going on, sometimes it's enough to open your eyes and look in front of your nose every day, as soon as you get up, open your eyes! Look here in Spain; I understand that in Spanish blood there are all bloods, including Arab and Jewish, and I have no problem with that; but you've already seen what Boko Haram have done in Madrid or ISIS in France, tried to blow us up!

The Europeans, with their left-wing laws and their sense of historical guilt, have already given up and are lost, and I don't know if you've read this, but in Europe it won't be long now, in a country like France, for example, before an Islamic government comes to power. I'd like to see you when that happens: goodbye *l'amour à la française*, goodbye to free sex and the pill and pink Viagra, that whole slow and painful acquiring of civilization that's led us to be increasingly complex and free. Don't you think I've read Nietzsche? Of course, I know that religion has been attacked intelligently. If religion wasn't a solid edifice, presided over today by my father, it wouldn't have withstood those devastating criticisms from the most lucid minds in history. Nietzsche says that the only point of religion is to help man to solve the problems it itself has created for him, and do you think it's easy to respond to that? Or when Lev Shestov, who was a Catholic, says that man is forced to sleep while the deity is dying, do you think it's easy to swallow something like that? These are major questions that mankind as it grew decided to overlook, because philosophies move and advance and the Church doesn't always produce ideas capable of responding, of building defenses against such powerful attacks.

Excuse me if I again talk about myself.

I don't claim or believe that it has any meaning to answer all these criticisms, although there is one incontrovertible fact, demonstrated by science and by Stephen Hawking: the scientific explanation of the creation of the universe makes the idea of God unnecessary and obsolete. That's pretty strong, isn't it? It's why I'm not a believer, although I respect the theoretical and philosophical framework behind the idea of God, and it's that work that I'm rescuing and in which I believe, because when it comes down to it, it's human. Here, nobody is the son of any god. We are all equally stupid or wise because we are real, solid people. Even life and the existence of love in the world or profound experiences like generosity or goodness can be questioned, which doesn't mean that they don't exist. Sometimes reason is so bedeviled that it obscures your own life, and then you start to doubt the things your fingers can touch and even what you can bite with your teeth. There's a whole philosophy that says that the world disappears with you! It's a beautiful idea, of course, but completely far-fetched.

The problem of the human being, and this you know from having read and written, is that he can doubt everything, even himself. Plato says that reality is a reflection, how can you respond to that? And we're talking about the beginnings, the dawn of thought! Even the Church: if you follow its doctrine it turns out that it was God himself who gave man the tools to doubt Him. That's brilliant, isn't it? I'd like to discuss it one day with my father. In a way, it's quite democratic. My fight is not at that level, because we'd be bound to lose. If the ignorant masses read more Nietzsche than the Bible we'd be in another dimension. But I suspect that even there, in that cold and somewhat psychotic world, the idea of God would exist, because it's such a complex intuition that it can only be human. It's born out of the lack of knowledge we have of death, which when it comes down to it is pure forgetfulness. We already knew what death is, but we've forgotten. Before birth, we were dead.

I can't explain this to you rationally, I simply know.

I know because I know.

That's what thought is in religion and in faith, either you believe or you don't. And that's it. It consists of making stories that explain human affairs. Have you heard of the Kanas? They're an indigenous Peruvian tribe living in the valley of Vilcanota, near Lake Titicaca. One of their ancient stories relates that the man who's ambitious and wants to get rich without working can go to the house of the demon, but before that he has to undergo a series of tests: undress and enter a pool of green water and another of red water, light lights in the four corners of the room, open a pan of mud where there's a snake, kiss it on the mouth, hit it on the nose, and allow it to drink his blood. On leaving the room he has to take hold of some lighted candles, put one in each nostril, another in his anus, and the last one in his mouth. With that, he'll grow wings and a wind will carry him to the house of the demon. When he gets there, he has to kneel before the deity, who is lying on his back. And this is the really incredible part, because if he genuinely wants to be rich the ambitious man has to kiss the demon's anus, but when he does that the demon will let out a huge fart, an unbearably foul-smelling gas. The ambitious man will have to inhale it and even make gestures of pleasure. If he manages that, the demon will shit through that same anus a huge quantity of gold and silver, but if he can't stand it he'll have to go to hell as a slave for the rest of his life, or his death. Do you understand, Consul? It's the native version of Faust!

But that's not my game. I'm a bit more advanced, or maybe a bit behind. My struggle is in the real world, not in the immaterial and contradictory space of ideas. My space is strength and defense. I'm a soldier. My duty is to convince others that their lives, which fade with time like all lives, can have a meaning. To escape biology and enter culture, isn't that right? It's a cyclical idea of the world, do you know the poet Rimbaud? It's what he called "necessary destructions"—necessary if we want to create new worlds.

That's my work.

Just imagine, my father, being Pope, has to confront the problems of man today with the obsolete weapons of the old Church. It's like defending yourself against Jedi light sabers or assault drones with bows and arrows. Robin Hood versus Darth Vader, you know what I mean? That's my father's courage and that's why he doesn't mind leaving the plush surroundings of the Vatican, going out into the world, and stopping on the street to talk about the rights of women and homosexuals and divorced people, and to fight for the planet, which we have to protect and keep clean. He's obsessed with cleanliness because he knows it's something that will settle on the spirit. You'll have seen him during Holy Week, washing the feet of Muslim drug addicts, and prostitutes. I think he overdoes it a little, but anyway. The old man is fighting a monster that has two thousand years of history behind it, and he has to take changes on board. Basically, I understand him. The Church has committed crimes and that's why I criticize it, but it has to be admitted that thanks to it the vast mass of Catholics are able to experience and practice some kind of spirituality, and that's no small thing, is it? It's a very strong need, like feeding ourselves or procreating.

You on the other hand, Consul, have culture, but how many people are like you? how many experience and practice what they've learned, if they've learned anything at all? Not many. A select minority, and I tell you this right now: what I do, in principle, is not addressed to the privileged, although it doesn't exclude them either. To use the language of marketing, I would say they aren't my target audience. The masses are my most urgent raw material, not those who have access, through their professions or their advantages, to other regions of the spirit. You say that today the world has lost its gods and that man is left to his own devices, but I tell you something else: those who follow me aren't alone. The citizens of my Republic can depend on the word of the elder brothers of the Earth and the water which I pass on to them, because I have ears for all that echoes from a long time ago.

I've always known who I was and what my path was. I grew up in the mystery of life, but I grew up alone; don't go believing that just because I was an only child I was privileged. Not a bit of it. I always had the barest minimum. My mother is a proud woman and she would have died before asking for anything from Bergoglio, who in those years was still provincial superior. I still respect him and even love him, in his distant way. He doesn't know about my existence, I can assure you of that. But perhaps he will know of me soon. Old Bergoglio will find out and say, I'm proud of him, he's my son and he's fighting at my side, as sons should do, except that his is a fight I can't wage openly.

When I think about that, I feel moved, but it'll pass. I'm talking about my life, wait and I'll tell you exactly how it was. My mother brought me up by herself, which I think saved her life, because her desire to look after me took her away from her militant activities. I wasn't born yet and already I'd saved someone's life! But my mother, what a fighter she was! She wasn't poor, she was middle class. The daughter of a German immigrant, her name was Susana Melinger.

My real name is Carlitos Melinger. The son of Susana.

I was born strong, it may be my father's Piedmontese inheritance, who knows? My mother filled my feeding bottle with calcium and soy milk. That's why I've never broken a bone, though God knows I've taken plenty of blows. Once, when I was eighteen, I was knocked down by a motorcycle. Nothing happened to me. I got up from the ground and went to assist the motorcyclist, who'd broken three ribs, can you imagine? The motorcycle was completely ruined.

My mother saw my potential and from when I was a child she had me playing rugby. In Argentina only the rich play rugby, it's a prestigious game. I was allowed to join in because my mother was respected among the Germans and my grandfather had a decent farm and sowed soya and cereals. I studied medicine to understand real men and their physical pains. I read philosophy and history.

My grandparents had money, though not much.

Once, after a match, a hulk named Casciari insulted me. I let it pass, but the guy just went on and on, as if he was looking to pick a fight. For a while I didn't take any notice, but he was really angry because I'd tackled him about twenty times during the match. I told him to leave me alone, that what you did on the field was something else, and he should go home quietly. But he just kept on bothering me and even mentioned my mother. I felt as if a bolt of lightning was going down my spine and lodging in my balls. I grabbed him by the shoulder and said, do you want to repeat that? The guy smiled and spat in my face.

Poor guy, the least of his worries was the punch I gave him on his nose. He was flung backwards and hit the lockers, and two of them fell on top of him. Nobody said anything because they'd all seen him provoking me, and what I learned that day was how fast my arm was. The guy didn't even see the punch coming and when I hit him I felt several teeth being knocked loose from his gums. When I helped him to his feet, he spat them out and I said to him, don't talk about my mother again, because the next time I hit you I'll knock your nose inside your face, would you like that? He was already starting to bruise when he limped over to the sink and threw cold water over his face. He apologized and I said to him, come on, let's hug, I forgive you and I'd like you to forgive me, too. You hit yourself by being so stupid, you took my fist out of my pocket. It was you and nobody else.

That day I earned everybody's respect, or fear. And that helped me. When I got back home I lay down on the bed and moved my arm about. It really was fast. What if I became a boxer? I thought about it, then told myself that maybe I'd been given that strength for something else. And I was right.

I won't bore you with details. I'll be brief. I grew up in Córdoba, partly at home, with my mother, and partly on my grandfather's farm. I learned to love that land as if it was my own. I'm not like so many Argentinians who want to get hold of a European passport and leave, not be Latin Americans anymore. I understand them, but I think they're wrong. The future of the planet is here, in America. Europe is the past. It's worth coming to Europe to understand and see it with your own eyes, nothing more. I did it myself: at the age of nineteen I went to Germany to continue my medical studies, I was a fool! There for the first time I found out about the movements whose aim was the cleansing of the territory. I got to know the skinhead world in Berlin. They were incredibly angry people, but in many cases they didn't even know why. They'd been humiliated, they came from working-class families, they thought their conflicts had something to do with the humiliation of

Germany after the war. They weren't completely wrong. They were nostalgic for a greatness they hadn't experienced and they blamed neoliberal politics and democracy, which, according to them, gave power to the ignorant masses. The thing about the Jews was something I never shared. Wasn't Jesus Christ a Jew? He was an amazing guy, even if he wasn't the son of God. What happened in Germany, as I'm sure you know, was an economic problem. The Jews had money when the country was in a mess and people didn't have anything to eat. Yes, the bourgeoisie were sons of bitches, but not because they were Jews! They were like that because they were rich and selfish. The rich are like that in every country.

These skinheads had good intentions and no culture. They didn't even understand the things that were important to them, which really drew my attention. I started reading history. I devoured books on the wars of the nineteenth and twentieth centuries. I studied them all the way back, I think, until the Trojan war. And I understood why they'd happened. It's nothing to do with morality. They all start from the same things: money, land, or religion. Call it politics, call it independence, call it holy war. Call it what you want, it comes to the same thing in the end. It's always for one of those reasons. Do you know one that wasn't?

I realized that these guys were nostalgics, and that what they hated was their own situation. Their own lives. Deep down, they hated themselves. It's always more comfortable to go out and beat up a Jew than look at yourself in the mirror and accept that you aren't worth shit, isn't it? They're losers. They're wrong because they don't have a plan that might be viable or have any chance of victory. It's just gut feeling, pure emotion. They cling to violence because it makes them feel important. They're such losers that they get their struggle mixed up with soccer. That's how confused they are.

I spent time with them in the Lichtenberg area, in the bars

near the S-Bahn station, drinking beer, looking at their black jackets and their tattoos and that kind of thing, and to be honest I learned a lot. Things that were useful to me later. I never got involved in their wars. Only once did I go with them to scare away a group of Arabs who were selling drugs. I threw a few punches and I don't deny I enjoyed it, but I didn't stay to the end. It helped me to understand how the mechanism of hatred worked and to what extent it was important in life and in political activism.

I left Lichtenberg for good after they grabbed a couple of Vietnamese and beat them up for no reason. They were left on the street, bleeding and with broken bones. One of them lost an eye. It was a scandal. Their soccer team had lost by three goals and they just wanted an outlet for their anger. It's true I did nothing to protect the Vietnamese, I didn't do anything, but I decided to get out of there for good. I realized they would never get anywhere, wasting their strength like that.

I came across other better structured and more interesting groups, although they were small. The first was the Old School Society, in Berlin, which attacked mosques, shelters for Arabs, and hard-line Salafists. With them, there was more of a method. They knew what they wanted and they started with modest objectives. I had already realized something, which was that the world could no longer continue on the same path. Don't get me wrong, I'm no Nazi. The fact that I approve of certain things doesn't make me a murderer or a defender of genocide. No, words have to mean something. I was with the skinheads, yes. I met people who were violent because their ideas were very poor. But what made them rough people wasn't ideology: they were and are that way because they're people, because they have feelings and the world hurts them in a way that it doesn't hurt anybody else, and there are certain kinds of pain, man, that can only be relieved by blows, something that today's reality forbids you. Because history and ideas and human collectives have messed everything up.

That's the way it is.

We have animal impulses that seek relief.

The people you see on the streets, who do you think they are? Not everybody is a recognized and respected bourgeois. No, man, for most people, life is a terrible struggle. This is the African jungle! While some live in air-conditioned homes others have their feet buried in shit, but it's precisely there, in those sordid places, that the future of the world is being defined. Who's going to survive a nuclear war? You tell me. The bourgeois who has his shoelaces tied for him or the lowlife who kills rats with his teeth? It's easy, man. I've read the Bible, too, and I know we've already lost paradise; that's why those who are down here continue to fight. The man who feels comfortable is screwed, because those who come from Arabia and Africa and India will swallow him up, you know what I mean? They're going to fuck us all up the ass, and without cream!

They have the strength that comes from hunger and humiliation and pain. What can you do against that? fight back? how? Call in a professor from the Sorbonne to explain it all to them? will anyone listen to him? In spite of everything, we have to understand that the sense of historical guilt is useless. You can't say they have the right to shit on Europe because Europe took their countries and colonized them. No, man, that's not the way it is. If you say that, you have to accept that the only morality is resentment and that we Latin Americans have the right to destroy Spain, to shit on her when we feel like it, and the gringos on England, and do they do it? Of course not! They're allies. Look at the Jews. If the logic of history was resentment, Israel would be firing missiles at Germany, not at the Palestinians! The lives of countries are like the lives of men. I'm not going to beat up my mother on the pretext that she hit me when I was a child. There are periods that should be shut down, stuck in a box, and left there. You have the memory of what happened, but you keep moving forward, right? That's why I say to you: things can't go on like this. The world can't and mustn't continue with this enforced mixing. Some here and others there. That's nature, which should be our example. Have you ever seen a hen going to live in a tree-top in order to find food, or a tree growing at the bottom of a river? No! Nature should be our example.

It was in those days, in Berlin, that it happened to me for the first time. First I felt that the sky was darkening in the middle of the day and that people were gesticulating in silence. A weird kind of eclipse. I wasn't capable of going out on the street so I stayed in bed and turned out the light. I spent three days without eating. Just water, Coca-Cola, chips, and beer. All that was left in the refrigerator.

I don't even know how to describe it.

As if a light had suddenly been switched off, but without my knowing what it was for, without knowing that damned switch was even there! Imagine a flock of crows flapping about in slow motion, completely blocking out the sunlight, and coming toward you. When I got up in my underwear to take a leak or drink a little water, my legs felt heavy, my bones hurt, I was dizzy. I was a total mess, and I didn't know why! The following Monday, I summoned up the strength to go out to the pharmacy. When the assistant saw me, she let go of what she was holding in her hand and pressed the emergency button. She thought I was a drug addict having withdrawal symptoms.

I said to her, don't worry, I'm only here to ask for help. I feel this way and that way. She took out some painkillers, put them on the counter, and advised me to see a doctor. I asked her if she knew where there was one and she said, yes, you go out of here, turn right, then right again, so I went there and when I arrived, I sat down in the waiting room; when it was almost my turn, I remembered that I didn't have any papers, or any money either.

I was incapable of moving.

When it was my turn I got up from my chair, but my legs gave way and I collapsed. A nurse helped me into the consultation room. When the doctor asked me who I was and what was wrong I could hardly speak. I didn't know anything, that's what was wrong. I was in a cold sweat. The same doctor called an ambulance and I was taken to the hospital, where I spent a couple of days. When they moved me from the detention ward I passed a mirror and saw my face. What I saw was my own corpse looking at me. After three days they ruled that I had severe depression. I had to rest and take Tofranil. When the doctors saw the chart, they shit their pants. I realized something elementary, man, which is that life doesn't have the slightest meaning, and instead of being liberating, that produced in me an anguish and a fear that paralyzed me; it even gave me hallucinations. To stop this suffering, you'd throw yourself from an eighth-floor window, wouldn't you? I thought of that several times, but the fear protected me. Did you know it's one of the best weapons of defense that we have? Fear makes you grab hold of something, fall on the ground, or duck your head when the bullet comes. Without fear we'd be dead. The doctor preferred to keep me going with Tofranil. My dear friend, he said to me, you have a biological disorder that, I'm sorry to say, will never leave you. He asked me about my family background and I said nothing. If I'd told him that my father was the provincial superior of the Society of Jesus in Argentina he'd have put me in an asylum.

I said yes to everything and thanked him.

Auf Wiedersehen!

With those psychiatric drugs, the world turned into something that was happening in the distance, on the other side of a very dirty, opaque window. They allowed me to choose between electroconvulsive therapy and taking antidepressants. The therapy seemed too mechanical to be useful. Do I look like a Peugeot? The pills would be fine. After two weeks, when they stopped feeding me intravenously, I stopped seeing birds. My relationship with drugs was only just starting, and I looked up and said, what is this? I thought about my masters and about the kingdom of voices and asked myself, isn't this part of the illness? In that case, nothing would have any meaning. What was I to understand through this illness? I started to think, there in the psychiatric hospital, until I reached various conclusions:

Someone wanted to show me pain, in order to make me understand the truth of the world.

Or he wanted my brain to abandon all logic because the task he gave me escapes human reason, and understanding might be a burden or an obstacle.

Or he wanted to tell me that my life wasn't completely mine, but belonged to something deeper and more permanent than me, which tries to communicate through the hallucinations of illness.

This was very possible, I told myself, because illness takes you out of the predictable current of the world. You're sitting on the edge, unable to move, and you see everyone else pass by. As if they were in a canoe, you know what I mean? The flow of life doesn't mix with your own time, where martyrdom and the past of man and hallucination are. Imagine you could remember all your pains and they came back to life. The anguish of birth, for example, passing through the narrow channel of delivery and coming out into the world. If someone could remember that, he wouldn't be like other people.

Nor does humanity remember when it walked the land naked, pursued by dinosaurs with sharp teeth and massive paws; that savage period has been left behind, lost in memory, because if we remembered it we would still be paralyzed in a fetal position, unable to leave our caves. Forgetting is as necessary as hope, man; only he who forgets can believe in something and keep going.

I left the hospital emaciated, with a bag of pills and the conviction that from now on my life was going to be that of a stranger. I went home, sat down in front of the TV set and observed what was happening in the world:

I saw giant waves, unleashed by underwater volcanoes, engulfing hundreds of thousands of people.

I saw nuclear explosions and the air burning from the combustion of radioactive neutrons, and scientists immolating themselves to save others from a disaster that might have been a thousand times worse.

I saw a young pilot burned alive in a cage and various others having their throats cut in macabre ceremonies on the seashore or in the desert.

I saw mutilated and decapitated bodies, corpses of men and women hanging from bridges, abandoned cars filled with heads and mutilated remains.

I saw thousands of hands cut off with machetes and a field of earth reddened by blood. Beside it passed an army of one-armed men weeping and asking strange things of their god.

I saw women with faces disfigured by acid that eats away at the skin and the mucous membranes. It was a chorus of live skulls howling with pain.

All that I saw on television, and suddenly I thought, have I forgotten to take my pill? No, what was happening in the world was much worse than my grimmest hallucinations, so I started to understand what it was all about. My sickness forced me to be clearheaded.

It was then that I started to sketch, for the first time, my idea of a Universal Republic.

Latin America wasn't a nightmare, it was hope. It wasn't the obsolete past, it was the future. Now I had to use my strength and my ideas and even my sickness to stop it falling into the same hands that made Europe a graveyard of memory, a necropolis populated by ghosts.

Still in Germany I continued my journey through the parties of virtue and the nation, and I saw that they were opposed to those others that protected the water and the air and the rivers. What do you think of that? How can you claim to save a race of people if you pollute its air and poison its water? That was my first surprise. In Europe, the green parties are on the Left, isn't that a stupid contradiction? They want clean fields, fertile land, pure air, and for what? to populate it with mutants, humanoids without culture, ghosts without identity.

Nature and culture can't be in contradiction, man, how can you say that? It's fine that at first we were all immigrants, because thirty thousand years ago man came out of Africa, but a little bit of time has passed since then, don't you think? Every human group has the bones of its dead buried in some specific place in the world, which means that you're from there and not from farther away, and that, it seems to me, was decided a long time ago, so why change it?

13

I opened my eyes in a blurry, unrecognizable world. Everything was very white, as if flooded with painful light. In that strange atmosphere, sounds seemed to move quickly and to be sharper. Where was I? I felt discomfort in several places, especially in the face. My skin stretched and swollen. A tube, stuck to my neck and my cheek with adhesive tape, went inside my mouth and burned my throat. Being conscious, I felt heartburn and the effort I used to contain it caused me more pain in the stomach. I noticed a sharp catheter pinned to my right wrist, joined to another tube that ran up my forearm, also attached with tape. But it was in my head that things were really bad, as if I had an ingot of ice in the middle of my brain. My face was covered in bandages. The pain traveled in rapid impulses between the cells until it became unbearable.

At last reality came into focus. I realized I was in a hospital. The nurses and the medical staff passed me by, ignoring me. There were police officers, and a lot of noise: telephones ringing, voices, conversations, alarms, footsteps on marble. I was starting to recognize all that when someone noticed that I had opened one eye (the other was covered with a bandage) and said, hey, come here, Rocky's waking up!

Three officers came in—they were wearing uniforms similar to nurses—and started asking me routine questions. What's your name, how do you feel, do you know why you're here?

"I was given a beating, and this is a hospital, isn't it?"

"That's one way of putting it," a black officer said with a smile, "don't you remember anything else?"

That this officer was black and spoke Spanish with a strong accent from Spain were two things that my battered brain tried to reconcile.

"A guy was strangling me and to defend myself I hit him with something," I said. "My head is going to explode."

The officer said:

"Calm down, try to relax, breathe deeply. I don't know if I should tell you this, but the person you fought with is in a coma right now, with acute cerebral contusion and an embolism, caused by a heavy blow. This is a high-security hospital, part of the Madrid prison system. Of course, you have a right to a lawyer."

My head seemed like a huge throbbing heart. I tried to figure out what was going on.

"Am I a prisoner? Is he in a coma? I went to the defense of a woman he was arguing with and the guy started hitting me. There are lots of witnesses."

The officer put his hand up in front of him.

"I'm glad to hear that, it could be crucial to your case. I'm referring to the witnesses. You may be lucky. In any case your being here is equivalent to preventive detention. It isn't a good thing to get into a fight on the streets, even in a good cause. And believe me, my friend, intervening in a couple's quarrel isn't in any way a good cause."

He took me to a room that, from what he told me, was also my cell. No television, and cold, rather dirty walls. Someone had written and drawn obscene things in pencil, as well as strange numbers. These totally unadorned walls made the idea of detention very obvious, and then, in putting me in bed, the officer put handcuffs on my arm and my ankle and then on the bars of the bed. Not that I could have gotten up by myself anyway, but I wasn't given the choice. Soon afterwards a court-appointed lawyer came in, looked at my medical chart, took some notes, and went away again without asking me any questions.

I thought about my situation, and the likely consequences. Had I really attempted murder? Theoretically, yes. Suddenly it seemed to me as if reality had escaped through a crack. My life, Madrid, Juana, and my incredible doubts about her were now very remote, almost unreal things. Thinking was very painful, so I tried to reduce the pain to short sentences.

The truth is that I was facing some very serious charges.

I remembered Manuel Manrique, Juana's brother, detained in Bangkwang Prison in Bangkok. What a strange symmetry! Then I slept for a while, sedated I assume by one of the countless substances entering my body intravenously. I had severe facial contusions, plus a fractured nose, right eyebrow, and right cheekbone; in addition, three broken fingers and two fractured ribs. The medical report mentioned bruises on my neck. A technical team came and took my fingerprints and opened a file with my details which was sent, or so they told me, to police headquarters, in the hope of confirming whether I had a criminal record. Two inspectors and a lawyer took from me a long statement that I was only able to sign with a great deal of effort. The court would give its opinion and might agree to bail, although since I was a foreigner, it was very likely that they would decide to keep me in custody, to stop me from leaving Spain. How long would depend on the ultimate condition of the man I had hit.

But was I really the one who'd hit him? All I'd done was protect a woman from danger and defend myself against an attack that looked like being fatal. There were the marks on my neck to prove it! If the man died, the lawyer on the other side could argue something called preter-intentional homicide, where death isn't the intention, but a fortuitous consequence.

"The difficult part," the lawyer continued, "is convincing a judge that you lifted a heavy glass ashtray and brought it down on that man's head without the intention of killing him; can one hit someone with an ashtray like that without having the intention to kill? Well, there is self-defense. The witnesses confirm that when you struck him you were on the ground with your back to him; we could call it a 'blind blow,' with your sole intention being to escape further aggression. Another advantage is that there's no previous connection between you and this man, which rules out intentionality. The best thing we can do is make a countercharge of aggravated bodily harm and, provided the man regains consciousness, look for what we call a restructuring: both bring charges against the other and in the end the law condemns you both for 'disturbing the peace' and fines the two of you. That would be the best thing. But the fellow has to regain consciousness, because if he kicks the bucket, as I'm sure you realize, that complicates things."

I thought about my meager savings and the expenses that might be incurred in this procedure, and what happened if the man died? My fate hung by a thread. I was also worried about the hotel, my belongings were there, my notebooks, what was going to happen to them? Not to mention that the bill was rising with every day that passed. I asked the officer.

"Don't worry. A card from the hotel was in your pocket and they've already gone to fetch your things. That's what I heard. At least here we don't charge you a cent!"

The nurse-officer was a friendly man. From the color of his skin, I assumed he was from Equatorial Guinea. A subject of Teodoro Obiang.

"Guinean?" I asked him.

"Yes, from Malabo. We aren't supposed to give our names to the prisoners, but my name is Pedro Ndongo Ndeme."

Equatorial Guinea! I remembered my friend the writer César Mba, author of *Malabo Blues*. I met him in Puerto Rico and ended up forming a curious triad with him and the Spanish writer José Carlos Somoza. I remember that when we said goodbye I told him: "Get a job in the government, but you have to promise me not to stage a coup." César, who was very quick and imaginative, retorted: "Go back to Colombia, but keep away from the drug trade."

Then I thought again about Juana. When she calls, someone from the hotel will be able to explain to her what happened.

Perhaps she'd already called.

In a sudden memory flash I recalled the scene in the bar, and the moment I raised the ashtray. I remembered the touch of the glass, its ripples and edges. By an incredible chance it had landed on the man's forehead.

The following day nothing had changed; time passes slowly when you're detained and are fed only tiny details.

Now Pedro Ndongo was pushing my gurney along the corridors. They had just given me a CAT scan.

"Pedro, how is the guy I hit today?"

"The same," Pedro said. "Stable."

"Who is he?"

Again that huge smile.

"I'm not allowed to give you that kind of information, my friend, not even to someone like you, even though I like you. Didn't your lawyer tell you? His name must be on the charge sheet. It's Francis Reading, he's American."

"And what does this man do for a living?"

"He's fifty-three, married with two children. He teaches literature at Complutense University. He's from New York."

"Literature?"

I thought it was a joke.

"And the young woman who was with him?"

"She's Colombian, like you. Perhaps she didn't know that when she hit you. You don't look as if you come from any particular place."

"Do you think so?"

"Well, I could swear you're not from Malabo!"

My face stretched with laughter, but the pain returned. We continued advancing down a long passageway.

"And what was that young woman doing with Mr. Reading? Is she his girlfriend or something like that?"

"Well, that's hard to know from reading the statement. She has a student card from the same faculty where he teaches. Maybe he's her teacher, it's quite common for a teacher to go out with a student, isn't it?"

"One last question, though I don't know if you can answer it. What's the Colombian girl's name?"

"Oh, that's impossible, friend. It's on the charge sheet. Her name's Manuela Beltrán."

"Manuela Beltrán?"

We reached my room-cell. Before Pedro left I said:

"Wait, one more thing. Has she been to see Reading?"

"The first day she was here for a few hours, but left when his wife arrived. Mrs. Reading is American."

"If Manuela Beltrán comes back and you see her, can you tell her I'd like to talk to her?"

"Of course, though I'm not allowed to."

Pedro was about to leave, but came back to check my drip.

"You're lucky considering how badly you were hurt, believe me."

"I haven't looked in a mirror yet."

"Avoid it for now. When I saw you the first time I covered my eyes. I mean it, that level of bruising is more common in the morgue. Your face was green and blood was coming out through your ears."

"Thank you, Officer Ndongo. You're most kind."

"I can't involve myself or have any kind of relations with the prisoners outside the strictly medical sphere. I only do it in extreme cases."

"Is mine as serious as that?"

"The street is full of psychopaths and drug addicts, baptized flesh but in a very bad state. Sometimes already rotten. But you're a decent person, that's obvious from miles away. Cities are bad and they lie in wait for people. The world in general is an increasingly inhospitable place. I tell you one thing: if you manage to get out of this, leave immediately and don't come back. Forget about what happened here."

"And what's happened in the Irish embassy? Are they still inside or have the police gone in?"

"That's not going to end so quickly. After the first throat cutting they changed their tune: now they want to show their good side and make the world feel sorry for them. Last night they let a cardiac patient go, in return for the woman reading a press release in which they asked all decent people in Europe to understand their struggle and not allow them to be branded as terrorists, but as fighters. They're screwing us around! But between you and me, the text was very well written. It was all about the dignity of Africa, about history and colonialism. They say that Africa only matters when there are coups, wars, epidemics, or famines, and that in doing this what they hope is to obtain a little attention without having to wait for the next tragedy."

"What about religion? What about ISIS?"

"For them, religion is a way of finding the purity of the world, and I confess, that speech was very strange. For a moment I thought they were thinking of moving away from the precepts of holy war."

Pedro went to the window and raised the blind. Light flooded into the room.

"Do you believe in any god?" he asked. "No? Make an effort anyway and pray that Professor Reading doesn't die, because everything will be longer and more complicated. The truth is, I don't wish that for either of you. You were unlucky enough to meet at a very bad moment. That's life: one small slip of fate and bang! A person can fall. Aristotle called it *hubris*, an excess that brings about the fall of the hero. Have you already thought about the millions of chances that it might not have happened? Best not to do that, you'll only torment yourself and it won't be any use. It happened, and things that happen can't be wiped out, however innocent we are, however much of a victim. Strange thing, life, don't you think?"

I looked at him appreciatively through my bandages.

"Did you study philosophy, Pedro?"

"No, not at all." He laughed again with his broad mouth. "I'm just an amateur. I'm not gifted for abstract thought and can only handle basic concepts. A small oversight on the part of the gods who created me. In every other respect, they gave me everything."

He closed the blinds, because night was falling, leaving us floating in the cold light of the low-energy lamps. With my good eye, I could see the bare walls, a rail with a plastic curtain that was drawn back because there was nobody in the other beds.

Before Pedro went out, I said to him:

"I'd like to ask you one last favor. It's a notebook with a brown cover, I had it on me when this incident happened. It's full of writings and notes. On the cover it says 'Rimbaud.'"

"Oh, what a great poet," Pedro exclaimed, and then recited in very good French:

"*Ô les enormes avenues du pays saint, les terrasses du temple! Qu'a-t-on fait du brahmane qui m'expliqua les Proverbes?*

"He's one of my favorite poets, do you recognize that passage?"

"Yes," I said, "it's from the *Illuminations*. It's the first part of *Lives*."

"That's right! Dammit, I like you more every time. The woman who works in the registration office is a good friend of mine. I'll have a word with her and see what we can do."

14

A few days later, Araceli came in her car—a elegant SUV—collected my things, and drove me to an apartment of hers on 67th Street, near Seventh. When we arrived, she introduced me to the doorman, she told him I was a niece from Cali who had come to study in Bogotá and was going to stay there for an indefinite time. This is where I lived when I was single, she said to me, here are the keys. It's all yours. Then she gave me a kiss and walked to the door. Aren't you coming up with me? I asked.

"Discover it for yourself, that way you'll feel freer. I've left a few things so that you won't be caught short for anything. Go on, I think you're going to like it."

I went up to the fourth floor and opened the door. I was dazed. It was a very nice place, small but cozy, with some incredible furniture, carpeted floors, decorations. The bed was like something out of a movie. I felt strange, like a maid pretending for a while that all this is hers but then continuing with the broom and the brush. Thinking this, I started laughing. The maid who thinks she's a lady, I told myself, and went dancing and laughing from one bedroom to the other, letting myself fall on the cushions and on the bed and into the armchairs. I laughed and laughed until I saw my face reflected in one of the mirrors in the bathroom, and then I felt ashamed, because my grandmother and my mother were maids and deep down so was I. We would always be maids, coming into houses like this. But then I told myself: I earned this by writing and having sex, so it's well earned. Others get much more doing the same, and without writing. I'm going to enjoy myself while I can.

You see, Doctor, I was really changing.

I went to the refrigerator and found it full. Meat, vegetables, eggs, drinks. I opened drawers and realized that it had everything. There were drinks in the bar, the bathroom was fully equipped, the towels looked wonderful, so I took off my poor student's clothes and got into the bath. I had a good bathe and lying there in the steam I imagined how great life would be if you had this in a normal way, because a little worm in my brain kept eating away at me, saying, wake up, Cinderella from the wrong side of the tracks, open your eyes, princess of the orphanage, you think all this comes free? what's Araceli going to ask of you in return for these luxuries?

I preferred not to think about it and fell asleep, and when I woke it was already dark, so I went to the bedroom and looked for my pajamas. On the night table there were two books, one by Pizarnik and another by a French poet, Arthur Rimbaud: *A Season in Hell*. I left them there and continued looking in drawers. When I opened the night table I again let out a cry. Cash! A wad of fifty-thousand-peso bills, which is the highest denomination in Colombia, Doctor, but which is like fifteen euros, no more than that, you see how cheap we are, but anyway, it was a whole lot of money. I closed it again without touching anything and went to sleep. How strange it all was, and how generous she was. Remembering my companions in the reform school, a voice whispered in my ear: you won the lottery, this rich old girl has the hots for you.

The next day Araceli came in the evening, we ordered a takeaway and made love until midnight. She was as affectionate as ever, talking about poets and trying to teach me what she knew. She read a poem dedicated to me, which to tell the truth I didn't like, but obviously I didn't tell her. Her husband was on their ranch. She enjoyed absolute freedom because he respected her rhythms. He knew that, as the good poet she was, she had phases, just like the moon, as she put it. I would never say something so corny, Doctor, I just looked her in the eyes, and she naturally started to tell me that her relationship with her husband was good, they made love two or even three times a week, she was insatiable and she wanted to try everything, as artists do; she made me laugh saying that she was the chair and founder of a group of veteran but rebellious wives who called themselves Blowjobs Always for the Same Man, and she also said, although I didn't believe her, that this was her first time with a woman, that before this she had fantasized about the idea but had never done it, that such desires didn't go down well with any of her friends, let alone with those who were already declared lesbians, but that when she saw me and read my poetry, when she started spending time with me she started having wet dreams and touching herself while she thought about me, and she confessed to me that when she had sex with her husband she imagined that she was her husband and I was her, and so she felt that what he was doing to her she was doing to me, which is quite strange, Doctor, but you probably understand it better than I do, and finally, that same day, before she left, I read her the first drafts of two poems I was working on. When I finished reading and looked up I saw that she was in tears.

I asked her what the matter was and she said it moved her to see that for me it was so easy, what I considered a first draft was already far above what she herself could do, and I told her no, her poems were good, don't say that, there's no reason to be sad, and we knocked back another half bottle of whiskey and snorted a little coke, and more, because this time she took some pills from her bag and said to me, look, let's try this, it's called ecstasy, half and half? We took those pills, and soon I was high as a kite, feeling as if I wanted to climb the walls, and of course, we fell on the bed and fucked like rabbits, we whipped each other to a frenzy, it was really cool; Araceli screamed so much when she came that the neighbors banged on the wall with a stick, even though the building had thick walls. Before she left, Araceli asked why I hadn't taken the money she had left on the night table. Then she took out another wad of bills and put it down under the book by Pizarnik.

I didn't know what to say, so I said nothing.

I realized that my life was going to be that of a kept woman. No nerves, no problems. My secret lover was paying for my life and giving me gifts, whims that were actually hers, because I never had whims. In those days I experienced a change, Doctor, which is that for the first time I thought about beauty. Am I beautiful? Am I sexy? Am I a good lay? Until I met Araceli beauty was something other women had, not me. In the convent I'd been with various guys, but nobody ever talked about beauty. They fucked us because we had everything in the right place, not because we were beautiful. Fat or thin, with big or skinny asses, cross-eyed, busty or flat-chested, we were women and they needed us. The only thing of value was being a virgin, but that didn't last long.

With Araceli I discovered another dimension because she kept saying to me, what beautiful legs, what a round ass, what pert breasts, what a divine belly, and so smooth; because she'd had a child, she had creases on her belly and stretch marks on her ass and thighs. That struck me as normal, but it mortified her. She would spend hours in the gym trying to get rid of them, but they wouldn't go. I told her that those stretch marks were signs of a life lived and that she shouldn't think about erasing them, but Araceli would protest, no, darling, when you're my age you'll understand, I've never been loved for my beauty, it's not about other people, it's about myself, I have an image of myself that's deteriorating, it has to do with the passing of time, an anxiety about wear and tear, it isn't vanity but fear of loss, I'm not a Barbie doll, but if I let my body destroy itself it's as if I was surrendering to the enemy, don't you understand? I said I did, but in reality I couldn't. Youth doesn't understand adulthood and even less when the precipice of the years begins, after forty and edging up to fifty, which is the age that Araceli was, and that, according to her, was why what she loved in me was the unattainable, possessing what she would never have in her own body, although the origin of her attraction, again according to her, was in something intangible that had to do with my silences and my poetry and with something strange that, according to her, emanated from me, a kind of sad beauty.

My relationship with Araceli grew stronger. She came to see me three or four times a week. But if she had an engagement with her husband and daughter, who I never saw in person, then she'd stay away; I liked these breaks, because although I loved her I still missed what I had known with men, I don't know what to call it, it's something to do with the heat of penetration and ejaculation. I longed to feel it, but I longed for it in silence. I never looked for it, and not because Araceli was jealous. She would always say to me, invite friends over, throw parties, enjoy your youth. For me, the best way to enjoy it was to feel protected between four walls, and that's why I preferred not to invite anyone, let alone throw parties. The few I went to, thrown by my classmates, made me realize that the true purpose of them was to make the hostess feel like a queen for a night, which was silly and superficial, like young people who had never experienced anything profound and believed that life was an endless laugh; I felt embarrassed by the unrestrained egos of these poor girls, and that's why I never went back.

I preferred to discover the city, to walk through all its neighborhoods, the north and the center, the west and the south. I realized that the rain and the cold were a matter of periods, since later there was lovely sunshine from the mountains, which didn't give out much heat but stung the skin and you always had the feeling of being cool; the sun came out and the city would shine in a special way, and then I would get on the Transmilenio and go here and there, watching people living, trying to get on the same wavelength as them, having lunch in ordinary eateries, watching. I was amused by the obsession with cell phones: the children carried them in their school uniforms, the assistants in department stores in the south, sitting on stools, or those in the north, behind elegant counters, spent their time texting furiously. The clerks in public offices, too, who you could see from the street, and only waiters in restaurants or bus drivers, who have their hands occupied, seemed to be outside this obsession, but the rest, including my classmates, always had their heads down, moving their thumbs frenetically, one half of humanity writing to the other half, and then waiting for the reply. I went for lots of walks and so I gradually learned about the people of each neighborhood, from Usme and Bosa to El Amparo, which was dangerous, and then El Rincón or Suba. I remember some graffiti on the wall of a school that said: "Your T-shirt says *I Love New York,* but your face says *I live in Suba.*"

In Cali I'd been a lost little girl, then a lost adolescent who didn't know anything of the world. It was when I went to Bogotá that I realized what a country is. At the traffic lights, there were displaced people from Urabá, Cauca, and El Llano. You saw peasants, people from Cali and Santander, people from the coast. Indigenous people, people from the islands, from the plains, from the Amazon. The crowd was a portrait of reality, with its injustices and crimes, sure, but also with its joy and colors. And in the center of the city, that symbolic thing called power. The capital of the country! That's why I liked going to Plaza de Bolívar. There I saw people with banners demanding things from the government or protesting about something, but also there were the inhabitants of the center, the destitute and the disposable (that's what they're called, can you imagine, Doctor), people who were very alive and searching for themselves, and also tourists and street vendors, and thieves and robbers, those that Señora Tránsito was so scared of, although I have to say that they never robbed me nor did I ever see them rob anybody, at least not up close, which doesn't mean anything either, because everyone knows Bogotá is a dangerous city; near there, on Eighth, I saw secondhand bookstores and booksellers out on the streets, and that's why I grew fond of that area in the center. So I decided to use the money Araceli had left me and most of it I spent on that, on secondhand books. And so December came and Gloria Isabel wrote to ask me if I wanted to go to Cali to spend Christmas with them.

She said that Vanessa was more stable now and they were going to let her leave the clinic for a few days, so I said yes, time's flying, it's been months since I last went to my city! I told Araceli and that prompted her, for the first time, to ask me if it was my family, but I told her no, I don't have a family, my parents are dead, this lady is a friend who's helping me, and of course, hearing me say that she got ideas and I saw her facial expression turn hard, a friend? what kind of friend? I didn't want her to get the wrong idea, so I said: she's the mother of a classmate of mine who got involved with drugs in a very bad way; I helped them and that's why they're inviting me, because my classmate is going to leave the clinic for Christmas. And I ended up saying: she's paying my university fees.

Araceli's face changed and she said, oh, good, I understand now, she's someone who helped you, I'm sorry, I'm nervous and I mix everything up, come here, my darling, and we threw ourselves naked on the bed and spent the evening having wild sex, because by now I'd stopped being afraid of Araceli and really liked her, in fact I was even a bit in love with her, although it sounds stupid.

Before I left for Cali, Araceli said she wanted to give me a Christmas present. She came to the apartment, we opened a bottle of wine, we toasted, and I gave her two books I had bought for her, two very beautiful editions of Colombian poetry, Aurelio Arturo and an anthology of Nadaism, which she thanked me for with lots of kisses. But I could see she was nervous and I asked her what was up. She cried a little and finally said, it's really stupid, just imagine, I suspect my husband has a girlfriend. I looked at her and said, in all innocence, well, you have one, too. Araceli gave a laugh and said, yes, I do! We opened another bottle of white wine, she took out some pills, and we took them. We spent the evening together. Finally I asked her why she thought her husband was cheating on her and she said he'd been acting strange and so she'd looked at his cell phone while he was sleeping. There were some strange messages, from someone without a name, just initials, RM. There had been calls, too, and she saw that they spoke constantly, even when he was traveling. But during the past weekend when he had been at a convention in Lima, there were no calls to RM and that struck her as strange; so she got into his bank account and saw that he had paid for two tickets and a stay at a hotel, the same one, and she realized there hadn't been any convention, so I said to her, are you sure it isn't someone from work? And she said, no, wait, there's more, in his account I saw a series of payments to restaurants, so I said to her, it's strange to go traveling with a girlfriend to Lima, don't you think? Generally, guys go to Cancún or Panama, and she said, I know, but here there were payments in bars, and then, terrified by what she was doing, she went to a public phone and dialed the mysterious number, several times, but there was no answer. The recorded message was personalized, and there was a young woman's voice saying hi, this is Rafaela, leave me a message, bye, a girl's voice, although she wasn't a hundred percent sure so she had gone further: taking a risk, she had gotten into his email and there she saw that one of the tickets was for someone named Rafaela Montero, so she searched for her on Facebook and saw her, a young girl, a really good-looking bitch, that's how Araceli put it, a journalism student at the Javeriana, can you imagine? and I thought, maybe I know her.

I asked her how she felt and she said, I feel insecure and you know something? it isn't the same, I'm not cheating on him with a man, we're in a territory that isn't his anyway and can never be his. I said nothing but I thought that it was the same, two students from the Javeriana, one for each of them. In the end, Araceli got dressed, a little sad, but before leaving she said, oh, how stupid, I almost forgot to give you your gift, here, and she took out a very well-wrapped little box. When I opened it I saw it was a cell phone, a beautiful white BlackBerry, the latest model, that way we'll be able to keep in touch because I'm going to miss you a lot, she said, and she kissed me on the mouth with a ferocity and a desperation that struck me as strange. I told her I was going to miss her, too, and that I was immediately going to learn to use the cell phone so that we could send each other messages all the time.

The next day I flew to Cali, and when I got to the airport that sensation of fragility came back to me, that feeling of being in danger. It was the city of my childhood, of course, but also of my sorrows. Terrible memories hung in that lovely warm wind, and although Gloria Isabel and Vanessa greeted me with hugs I couldn't rid myself of the nerves, the hole in the pit of my stomach. On the ride to the house, I recognized buildings, avenues, streets. A certain smell of dampness or chlorophyll. There were the samans, those trees that seemed like the true guardians of the city. And in the middle of the street and the traffic, the motorcyclists zigzagging, and when I saw them I couldn't help thinking of Freddy and wondering, is he one of them? My anxiety started to grow. Sitting beside me,

Vanessa was like a zombie. She smiled all the time, and kept giving a disturbing little laugh that didn't correspond to anything funny. She was stuffed full of tranquilizers. When we got to the house and I settled into the guest room, Gloria Isabel explained to me that Vanessa was very sedated, because that was the only way she could come home. It was what the doctors recommended.

"Seeing you here makes me incredibly happy, Manuelita," Gloria Isabel said, "it's as if you were the recovered half of my daughter."

I tried to ask Vanessa things, to find out how she was, but she always answered in the same way, I'm fine, it's all cool, thanks, and you? I asked her about the clinic, if she had friends there. And she replied, yes, lots of friends, it's really cool, why don't you come see me one day? I told her of course I would, and suddenly she asked me, and what about you, why are you here? I told her that Gloria Isabel had invited me to spend Christmas, and she said, oh, right, I forgot, that's cool, and how are you? That night, before switching off the light, I sent Araceli a couple of messages. She was still very bad: she had found a gift hidden in the garage; she opened it carefully, it was a beautiful gold chain. There was the receipt, three million and something pesos that her husband must have kept. Araceli left everything as it was, but now she was getting worried that this gift wasn't for her or her daughter, but for the girlfriend, and that's why she saw Christmas coming like a mule walking to the abyss.

I tried to calm her. I'm sure it's for you, stop thinking about it, I told her, think about other things, other periods of your life with him, for example. It's a long relationship and it's not going to be destroyed over something like that. Araceli replied, saying: oh, my darling, how it pains me that you're so far away, I'd give anything to have you here in my arms.

The holidays were very lively, although I hardly dared leave the house. Every time I saw a man drive by on a motorcycle, I said to myself, that's him, that's Freddy, and I broke out in a cold sweat, what'll happen if he recognizes me? I realized that while that man was still alive I couldn't go back to Cali. He'd also stolen my city from me, and I thought: if someday I see him and I'm able to, I'll kill him. I swear it.

With Vanessa being the way she was, everything was very healthy, with fruit juices and soft drinks. No alcohol. Gloria Isabel told me that if I wanted a glass of wine I should go to the kitchen and ask the maid; she had given instructions to keep the alcohol hidden and serve it only to particular people and in cups, as if it was coffee or tea.

I preferred not to drink anything, out of solidarity, and because after only a few drinks I would get even more paranoid, so it was better to stick with juice. I told Gloria Isabel that everything was going fine at the university and I'd brought her copies of my grades, so that she could see that I was using her money well. I told her I was writing poems and that some had been published in magazines. She asked to read them and I showed them to her. Her eyes watered and she said, they're lovely!

The poor woman didn't know the slightest thing about poetry, but she was a kind person.

The New Year came, and to be honest I couldn't wait to get back to Bogotá, where I didn't feel in danger. We took two excursions, one to the river and the other to a ranch near Lake Calima, and finally the day came to go back. Vanessa went back to her clinic and Gloria Isabel drove me to the airport. We cried when we said goodbye. She said to me: go with God, my sweet girl. Life is giving you another opportunity and what makes me happiest is that you're taking advantage and proving worthy of it. Don't change. I gave her a hug and got on the plane, again in tears.

In Bogotá the other drama was waiting for me.

Araceli was really low because, as was to be expected, the famous gold chain wasn't for either of them, so she was hysterical. She came to see me the day I got back and when I opened the door I noticed that she was already very wired on booze and coke. She almost devoured me in bed, snorting one line of coke after another, with a desperation that took me by surprise, until I said to her, calm down, Araceli, you're taking things too far, but she cried and cried, desperately.

"This has been very hard on me, darling," she said, "and you have to help me. I need you to make friends with that snotty-nosed bitch, so that you can tell me who the hell she is and what kind of fling she's having with my husband."

I swore I'd help her. She showed me a lot of photographs and I saw that the girl was indeed in the Javeriana. According to Araceli, they must have met on a course her husband taught on alternative advertising, and that's how the thing started. She was a sexy young thing, no doubt about it. At least judging by the photographs. The kind of girl who put photographs of herself in a bikini on Facebook, can you imagine, Doctor? I started looking for her at the university, and in less than two days I'd tracked her down. But Araceli kept bombarding me with messages. Did you find her? Have you spoken with her? I had to tell her I couldn't answer her in class, and begged her to be patient. It wasn't going to be easy to get close to this Rafaela. She was a real preppy and I had nothing to do with her, but I'd made a promise. Several times I found myself next to her, standing in line in the cafeteria, for example, but it was difficult because she was never alone and, as far as I could see, never studied. In a whole week, I didn't see her go into the library even once. She went here and there with her little group, all absolute preppies, and all they ever did was show each other things on their cell phones, listen to music, and parade along the walkways of the university. They only ever went to class when they got bored! I didn't think Araceli had anything to fear from an airhead like that; her husband must have been infatuated, and once the girl had gotten over the thrill of going with an older guy she admired, she'd leave him, you could see that a mile off.

But that wasn't going to be any relief to Araceli, of course, because for her the betrayal went much deeper. She'd been with him since she was young, when not only was she much prettier than Rafaela but a thousand times more interesting. The insecurity of the years and the contrast with youth turned all that into a terrible act of disloyalty. Basically, it was a question of self-esteem and beauty.

And here I'll take a little break to make a comment about myself: thanks to Araceli and her constant gifts I didn't look like a cleaner anymore, which was how I'd looked when I arrived, and which was, of course, how I really was. Because I was short, she gave me a whole lot of her daughter's clothes, which were practically new, because the girl was constantly changing her look and, like all rich teenage girls, believed that her personality and the clothes she wore were one and the same thing. So I now had a decent wardrobe of used but good clothes. I didn't have a bad body. I'm from Cali. I have good legs and wide hips, a reasonable ass, a good waist, and, out front, prominent breasts; my copper complexion was much appreciated; although I wasn't playing up any of that, I was aware that lots of guys gave me the eye, only I didn't join in the game so nobody approached me. But I was no longer the poor immigrant with her cardboard box and colored bag. Especially when I took out my BlackBerry and looked as if I was texting, when what I was doing was taking photographs of poems that I liked and rereading them anytime I felt the want or the need.

When it finally happened it was quite natural. One day Rafaelita herself spoke to me in the cafeteria. Did you write the poems in last semester's magazine? I said I did. I thought she'd realized I was stalking her, but no, quite the contrary. By some miracle, she was alone, so I said to her, do you like poetry, and she said, yes, it's my true passion, so I took advantage to say to her, well if you like let's get together one day and you can read me some, I'm studying literature, and she frowned and said, really? that's what I wanted to study, but my parents insisted that it wasn't necessary, that you could learn it by yourself, and I said to her, maybe they're right, do you read literature? and she said, yes, of course, right now I'm reading a book by Susanna Tamaro, do you know her? I told her I'd seen the name but hadn't read her, and she replied, oh, no, you have to read this, if you like I'll lend it to you when I finish, it's a bit like Ángela Becerra but Italian and more profound. As we were chatting I realized something terrible, which was that she had around her neck a big shiny gold chain, and I said to myself, that's the one, if Araceli finds out it'll kill her. Then Rafaelita said that she had to go to her class. Before leaving, she asked for my telephone number, can I call you? shall we get together another day?

I said yes.

In the evening, when Araceli came to the apartment I told her it was difficult to get close to her, because she was always surrounded by people, and I assured her I'd keep trying. I didn't want to tell her I'd already talked to her, I don't know why, or rather, I preferred to get a clearer idea of who she really was, because, to tell the truth, from that first chat, my impression wasn't bad. I felt a touch of vanity, I don't deny it: that a girl like that should talk to me was quite flattering. I decided to wait.

Then Araceli said that her husband was leaving again the following weekend for a convention in Acapulco, and that she had been astonished, Acapulco? that place where dumb people go to spend their vacations and that's full of drug traffickers and call girls? The husband said to her, yes, it's awful, but the meeting is being called by a Mexican company and I can't miss it, do you want to come? Araceli seriously considered it, but it might have set his alarm bells ringing and would also have been a flagrant contradiction. For years she'd been saying she didn't want to be the wife of the great advertising man, the consort in those congresses where they were put on a pedestal; it was his life and she preferred not to get involved in it, so she said, no, thanks, if you'd said the Mayan Riviera or Mexico City, sure, like a shot, but I wouldn't go to that place even if they paid me, thank you, and the husband said, you're right, I wouldn't go either, you see, even I have to make concessions, and Araceli thought: I'm sure he's going to take his little whore, it's the perfect plan for a sly fifty-year-old, and she said to me, help me to find out if it's true, because, with these things, I'm putting together a dossier and I swear to you I'll cause a scandal, I'll ask for a divorce and make him spit blood.

Rafaela called the next day and suggested we meet at Il Pomeriggio, a café in the Centro Andino, one of the elegant places in the north of the city. There she showed me some poems. I read them carefully and they were very bad, which was predictable; so bad that I had to make an effort not to laugh, but as I'd already learned a few tricks I commented that they had a good rhythm, that they talked about beautiful things and made you see the world with an optimistic eye. Rafaela was delighted by that, the thing about the optimistic eye, and she said to me, your stuff is more mournful, isn't it? I said yes. When we said goodbye she said something that stunned me.

"We won't be able to see each other until next week. I'm going to Mexico tomorrow and I'll be back on Tuesday. When I'm here I'll call you."

Again I felt the same contradiction. Should I tell Araceli or keep deceiving her? I walked up Eleventh as far as Avenida Chile, then went up to Seventh and caught a bus going south. Rafaela was a lousy, amateurish poet, but that didn't mean she was a bad person. She also deserved to live and to expect something from life. Was it her fault she was rich and pretty? Of course, when she was young Araceli would have done the same if she'd fallen in love with a married man. When Rafaela got bored she would leave him and Araceli could calm down. The best thing was to say nothing and keep dabbing her brow with damp cloths.

I also asked myself if I felt jealous of Araceli's jealousy, but just the idea of it, when I put it into words, made me laugh. I burst out laughing on the Avenue, surrounded by buses and Transmilenio shuttles, and people must have thought I was either crazy or on drugs. I was very fond of Araceli and I went to bed with her, but the truth is that I didn't feel love. What I felt at first was nothing more than gratitude. In fact, I didn't feel love for anyone. I didn't even know what love was. I realized that I was justifying Rafaela, that was for sure. I liked the girl, for all her superficiality and nonsense. Deep down, she was the same as me. She was sleeping with someone older out of admiration, hoping to receive some kind of help; that tradition, which is so Colombian (or is it the same everywhere, Doctor?), that the woman who gives herself to a man has to receive something in return. Although she was rich and I was poor we were doing the same thing: giving it and charging for it. Me to Araceli and Rafaela to Araceli's husband.

I didn't tell Araceli about my meeting with Rafaela. I told her I was following her and that she struck me as a frivolous, silly person. It was what Araceli wanted to hear. Since this had started she had forgotten about poetry, but I hadn't. I kept writing and from time to time I read her things, although she didn't pay any attention. Her mind was elsewhere.

When her husband left for Acapulco, Araceli came to my apartment and said, let's go, and I said, where? Anywhere. Pack a bag. I did as she said because she really didn't look well, and when we went down to her car I saw that she was ready.

There was a suitcase in the trunk. We left the car in the airport parking lot and went to look at the international departures board: Amsterdam, Paris, Buenos Aires, Lima, Panama City. I said nothing. Suddenly she cried: Let's go to Buenos Aires!

"Araceli," I said, "I don't have a passport."

She looked at me strangely and I thought: that's the way she must look at her maid.

"Oh, right," she said. "Let's go to national departures."

We looked at the schedule and stupidly, it occurred to me to say: there's a flight to Cartagena in an hour.

Araceli looked at me very strangely.

"Don't even think about it. Everyone knows me there."

Finally we flew to San Andrés, to the Hotel Decamerón. On arrival, she bought two bottles of whiskey and asked a taxi driver to get her some coke and pills. When she started drinking, she calmed down a little and that night, with both of us in the Jacuzzi, she was her old self again. We made love until she fell asleep from the drinking. I didn't like what was happening, when we got back to Bogotá I would have to start distancing myself from her, but how? I was living in her apartment and depended on her.

I decided to wait.

The following week, Rafaela called to say that she had bought a whole lot of books and had brought me a gift. A beautiful silver ring. I thanked her but I had to hide it. If Araceli saw it, I would have problems, because she continued with her questions: had I seen her at the university lately? was she tanned? I told her I wasn't sure, but something must have given me away because she said, are you sure you've seen her? I told her that I was nervous about Rafaela, that I wasn't good at spying, that I didn't like that role. Araceli gave me a hug and said: I know this isn't your problem, my darling, this doesn't hurt you.

Then it occurred to me to give her some advice, the most stupid advice of all.

"Why don't you go away with him somewhere? Maybe that way you'll be able to talk. This is doing you a lot of harm, it's taking you away from your poetry."

She was silent for a while, then said:

"Maybe, my darling, maybe. Let me think about it."

I thought he ought to pamper her, that's what she was missing.

"You can't let something like that ruin your life, don't forget you have a whole heap of readers who admire you and are waiting for your next book."

"Do you really believe that?"

"But of course, in my class there are many people who follow your work, students go around with your books in their bags. You have to think about that and protect what's important."

She said I was right, perhaps that was the best thing. Try to find some peace and quiet, not away from him but with him. Then she added:

"Would you forgive me if I go away for a while? I'll make sure you have everything."

"You don't have to give me anything," I said, "you've already been very generous and I can never pay you back."

"But you don't have to pay me back, darling. You brought me the life I no longer have."

She left looking confident and the next day thanked me for our talk. She had talked with her husband. She'd told him she felt that he'd been absent, and that she needed to spend a few days with him far from Bogotá to get back her self-confidence. Her husband, according to her, gave her lots and lots of hugs and said yes, he felt the same, and invited her to Europe, taking advantage of a business trip to London. As if it was nothing out of the ordinary, he suggested they spend two more months over there, traveling to cities they hadn't visited for a long time, and he told her she could write a collection of poetry about the most beautiful capitals in Europe.

The day before she left, she came to my apartment in the morning. We made passionate love. She was radiant. Then she took me to her bank and asked for a new debit card. She gave me a code and said, my sweet darling, you can take whatever you need from here. I've put some money in so you shouldn't be short. I refused, told her it wasn't necessary, but she insisted.

"Please accept, you dug me out of a pit. I couldn't bear the thought of being far from you if I didn't at least leave you well taken care of."

I put the card away in my purse and we said goodbye. Then she dropped me on Seventh, outside the university. Before I got out of the car she again pointed out that we were still connected, that she could keep texting me to tell me everything that happened and send me photographs, too. I was happy. At least I'd been able to give her something, I thought. A good idea.

When Araceli left, calm returned to my life and I devoted myself to reading and writing. I went to the movies, rented movies and watched them on my computer. There was a world full of art I had to find out about, bring myself up-to-date about. Once again, I was alone, which was fantastic. Nothing could harm me. My time was my own.

One day my cell phone rang. It was Rafaela. She told me she wanted to talk to me urgently, she seemed very upset. Without really knowing what I was doing I told her to come to my apartment and half an hour later she arrived, almost in tears, I offered her a coffee and she didn't want it, don't you have anything stronger? We served ourselves whiskey. I asked her about her poems and she said that she had been writing, but that now she was broken up inside. She wanted to read some and I listened to her, but suddenly she put down her tablet and said, I can't, I'm a mess.

I imagined the worst.

And the worst is what it was.

She started by saying that her friends at the university and her cousins and her sisters would kill her if they found out what she was about to tell me. I looked at her, pretending surprise.

"You're the only person who doesn't know me," she said, "in fact, you don't know anything about me and the cool thing about you is that you never ask questions. That's why I can only tell this to you, I feel as if I'm going to explode!"

I would have given my life not to have to hear what I assumed I was about to hear, but it was already happening, there was no way out.

"I got involved with a married guy and the worst of it is that I'm fucking in love with him!" Rafaela said. "I've got it really bad. We've been together six months. I can't tell you who he is because he's very famous. At first I thought it was going to be just a fling, because I already had a boyfriend, but the thing has been getting deeper and deeper, I let myself go, lowered my defenses, you know what I mean? I broke up with my boyfriend. I started to sneak out and tell lies to see him. To everyone! My parents, my sisters, my cousins, my friends. It's a really stupid thing that just kept on and now I can't stop, dammit, because I don't want to stop! We traveled together, he gave me a thousand gifts, we made plans. I know he's old enough to be my father, but he isn't my father, and it won't be the first time that's happened. Do you understand what I'm saying?"

I nodded in agreement, it was a rhetorical question. Rafaela continued talking as if she was alone.

"I'm in too deep to get out. And you know what he's just done? He's gone off to Europe for two months with his wife!!! Can you imagine that? The son of a bitch. He's a fifty-year-old son of a bitch! And I'm stuck here like an idiot."

She suddenly grabbed her tablet and said, look, I want to

read you a poem I came across the other day that expresses what I'm feeling, it's by a French poet called Paul Verlaine, do you know him?

I told her no and she started reading:

It weeps in my heart
As it rains on the city;
What is this languor
That penetrates my heart?

Oh, soft sound of the rain
On the ground and the roofs!
For a heart that is dull
Oh, the song of the rain!

It weeps without reason
In this heart that sickens.
Is it not betrayal? . . .

It is the worst pain
Not to know why
Without love or hate
My heart has such pain!

"I'm sure a woman had just left him," Rafaela said, "although he's so sensitive it sounds as if it was written by a woman."

"Yes, it's very beautiful," I said. "Where did you find it?"

"In an anthology of love poems my mother has," she said, and her eyes again watered.

I poured her another glass of whiskey, and without thinking that I was getting ever more closely involved in the very problem I wanted to avoid, I said to her, wait for things to pass, you don't know why he went, maybe what he wants is to leave her and he thought he'd tell her that while they were traveling, like a kind of honeymoon in reverse.

I'd only just said that when my cell phone vibrated. It was on the table and I saw out of the corner of my eye that it was a message from Araceli, so I grabbed the telephone and read:

"Your advice was wise, my darling. We're having a great time in London and I'm already feeling very calm. I wish I had you beside me to kiss you. I love you."

Rafaela said nothing, but I turned red with shame. What madness was this?

"What you have to do is take this time for yourself, go out, enjoy yourself, take advantage," I said to her. "When he comes back, things will be different."

She said yes, that's what she wanted to do, but there was a problem, which was that she didn't feel like going out with anybody. Suddenly she knocked back a drink in one go and said:

"Dammit, I have a brilliant idea, why don't the two of us go out tonight? Do you like dancing?"

I thought this might be a solution: maybe Rafaela would meet someone else before Araceli and her husband returned, so I said to her, look, since I arrived in Bogotá I haven't been out much, do you know any cool places?

Suddenly Rafaela seemed euphoric.

"Cool? Bogotá is full of great places. Let's go."

It struck me as strange that her mood had changed so much, but I told myself, that's what these women's tragedies are like. Araceli was exactly the same. We went out and a long night began. First she took me to El Goce Pagano. Hearing that classic salsa, the kind my mother liked, I felt something in my legs, as if they were moving by themselves. We danced for a while and she was great. She moved well and I noticed that she liked it. Several guys grabbed her, and from one of the tables they bought her drinks. I was invited onto the dance

floor by a very amusing guy from the Caribbean coast. I
enjoyed myself dancing and had a few rums. But Rafaela soon
got tired of the place—I could happily have stayed there—
and suggested going somewhere more modern and elegant,
with English music, and there she danced alone on the floor
and said hello to a whole lot of people. Half the bar were
friends of hers. After a while, she forgot all about me, which
was understandable. I felt like a fish out of water. My mood
wasn't especially friendly and nobody was in a hurry to engage
me in conversation. Nor do I think I had much to say to them,
not that I was there for that. When I saw from a distance that
Rafaela was sitting at a table and pouring herself a drink from
a bottle, I decided to go out and get a taxi. It was two in the
morning. When it came down to it, I told myself, I was there
to report back to Araceli, not to make friends. When I got
home I felt more cheerful. It was great to go out but I'd
learned my lesson: some worlds just don't mix with others.
You just have to know it.

15

The year 1871, the year of the French surrender at Versailles, saw France lose the border territories of Alsace and Lorraine, as well as being obliged to pay the Prussian Empire five thousand million francs in war reparations. Even in those days, those who lost paid. In addition, Paris experienced the defeat of the Commune, and for young Arthur it meant the brutal experience of rape in that dark barracks on Rue Babylone.

For Rimbaud it meant the end of many things: of his mimetic, celebratory poetry; of his adolescence, with its illusions of purity and consistency typical of that age, which tries at all costs to escape the pain of contradiction; and of something we might call a "nervous truce" with reality. From now on, he would attack and challenge reality, hoping to destroy it. The rape—as we have already said—was the talon that lifted him in the air and dropped him on the high seas, where the most dangerous monsters swim, where you not only have to look evil in the face, but also sustain its gaze. That was what Rimbaud did from now on: contemplate wickedness, challenge it, provoke it. Like snakes that raise their heads before attacking, so the young poet started to live, believing that life was at risk with every throw.

This was also the beginning of his hatred for the Church. Proudhon's words "God is evil" echoed loudly in his brain and he started to write it on park benches. "Merde à Dieu!" Shit to that god who had left him alone, who did not protect him when he was hurt. What else did the young genius do, apart from walking the streets of the small provincial city, unwashed, his hair tangled, scandalizing everyone?

He read and read, obsessively, to nourish both his strength and his disenchantment; he tried to work as a journalist and took up bohemianism, becoming a great drinker and smoker. Sex, which had made a violent entrance in his life, now became part of his repertory. Is it true, as some believe, that he frequented brothels and slept with women? It's quite likely. All young men do. He may have had crushes on women who probably did not understand him, but we do not know this for certain. What we know is his writings, in which there is an enormous rejection of women, almost a sense of revulsion. What would Freud have said about this? Was he rejecting his mother and seeking and idealizing his absent father?

His desire for rebellion shot off in all directions: against God and the bourgeoisie, against social rules, education, the family, politics, and the State; it involved the sexual and, of course, poetry, which he was about to transform forever.

The year 1871 was one of his most prolific.

According to Delahaye, Rimbaud spent much time in the library reading philosophy and even Satanic texts, as well as Baudelaire, whose influence would be crucial. It was during this period that he started imagining a poetic theory that would be refined over time and which he would explain in his letters. The *theory of the seer*. As far as Arthur was concerned, the poet had to recognize and anticipate the signs of the future to transmit them to the reader. Poetry is a manifestation of spirituality and must blaze a trail, no matter where it leads. The previous models, poetic or spiritual, have to disappear. There is in all this a longing for the absolute, a mystical calling that gives reality a certain symbolic radiance, since Rimbaud yearned to believe in something. His one faith was poetry, and poetry had to expand until it provided all the answers. He had already seen how it allowed him a curious alchemy: to transform the sorrows and corruption of life into the finest metal.

Oh, young Arthur, this is where things get complicated.

Whoever has poetic concerns can only resolve them with more poetry, but this, in its turn, clarifies his ideas and increases his understanding of the world. But not everything has to be understood, young Arthur. As St. Augustine suggested: on occasion, man is obliged to sleep while the deity is dying. "Beyond certain limits, human curiosity becomes inappropriate," as someone once said.

You have to know when to stop in time!

Rimbaud could not ignore the flames rising around him. Poetry was pursuing him. Filled with books and reading to the point of sickness, he took from the Kabbalah the idea that everything was a symbol of something else and that man, in his pettiness, was nothing more than a string for the deities to play their music on. Understanding this gave him a degree of arrogance, and he asserted that since the ancient Greeks, Western poetry had been nothing more than a rhymed diversion without the slightest significance. It had died with the advent of Christianity.

"Rhyme, rhyme, the insubstantial search for the beautiful word, bah!" he said, "it is just an imitative and banal art practiced by countless generations of idiots." But the truth was that Rimbaud lived at a faster pace than his contemporaries. He was an antenna that attracted the most fearful rays, increasingly charged with electricity.

And so, in Charleville, he became friendly with a strange character called Charles Bretagne. Arthur was like one of those rockets that loses parts as it rises in order to increase its speed. Izambard, his best friend from the previous year, had been eliminated. In a letter, he accused him of "walking the straight and narrow path" and writing a "horribly insipid" kind of intimist poetry.

Having dismissed Izambard, young Arthur was able to devote himself fully to his great new human influence, who was crucial to his definitive arrival in Paris.

Rimbaud was already someone else.

Je est un autre.

What interested him in Charles Bretagne was the drinking companion. Bohemia in a deeper sense. He wasn't exactly a teacher, but a friend. Bretagne laughed at the poet's ideas, but praised his verses. They drank together in the Café Dutherme in Charleville, where Arthur discovered that after enough wine and beer his shyness evaporated and the most outlandish words and ideas tumbled unhindered from his mouth. Everyone celebrated them, and he felt like the king of the world. He started to believe that through alcohol and drugs he could free himself, establishing a closer contact with the spirit.

Similarities have been sought between Rimbaud's theory and Buddhism, and some wonder how he could have known about Eastern philosophy when he only knew French, Latin, and a little Greek. According to Starkie, who presents the most striking evidence, there were already translations into French of the *Rig Veda*, the *Ramayana*, and the *Baghavad Gita*, but the knowledge that Rimbaud had of that world could also have been gained through other French writers. The Parnassians and the Romantics were strongly influenced by Eastern thought, hermetic ideas, and the occult. And of course there was also Baudelaire, whom he himself called the "king of poets." Baudelaire had incorporated into his poetry the occult theories of Swedenborg, Joseph de Maistre, and Höené-Wronski. It is quite possible that Rimbaud absorbed them through Baudelaire, since he claimed to be beginning where Baudelaire had left off.

For Baudelaire, all that exists in the world is a secret metaphor for something: the world is a forest of symbols and the poet is the person who can read in it, get to the heart of things, and make it comprehensible through his art. The poet is a *decipherer.*

When Rimbaud read this, he felt as if he was looking at himself in a mirror. His enthusiasm is clear in two famous letters, one from May 13, 1871, to Izambard and the other from May 15 to Paul Demeny, in which he outlines his theory of poetry:

> *Since examining the invisible and hearing the unheard is not the same as recapturing the spirit of dead things, Baudelaire is the first seer, the king of poets, a true God.*

He also found in Baudelaire another very important thing, something that already haunted his own experience: confirmation that, through alcohol and drugs, he could gain access to dream states in which "man communicates with the dark world that surrounds him," elevating his perception and his capacity for knowledge. I imagine him reading Baudelaire's *Les Paradis artificiels* in a state of exaltation, taking notes, struck by the force of the words, finally understanding something that he himself was ready to continue. There was everything in *Les Paradis artificiels*: "We must be drunk, drunk on virtue, poetry . . . But drunk." The only difference is that for Baudelaire these artificial paradises simply showed man what he already had inside him, that is, they were not a path toward further revelations. He also pointed out that these visions did not seem so beautiful on awakening.

Rimbaud wanted to go much further. He was ready to renounce himself, to sacrifice everything to reach that lost heart of the world. To go to heaven or hell, if necessary, as in the universe of magic and the occult, which, according to Starkie, he knew from reading Eliphas Lévi, who had said: "Work means suffering," "Every pain borne is an advance," and "Those who suffer live more."

As Rimbaud wrote:

Unspeakable torture in which he needs all his faith, all his superhuman strength, in which he becomes, among all men, the great patient, the great criminal, the great accursed one, and the supreme Sage!

Another writer who was important in his quest was Schopenhauer, who wrote: "Art, like philosophy—with which it has much in common and is intimately linked—only exists in the disinterested contemplation of things. The ability to present them in that way is the essence of genius." This confirmed to him that humanity was not yet completely awake, and that the poet had to be not only Baudelaire's *decipherer*, but someone who made a definitive spiritual liberation possible. Rimbaud wrote his theory of poetry in a matter of weeks, between March and May 1871, while he roamed Charleville dressed like a beggar, his hair tangled and dirty. It was the result of his stubborn determination not to go back to school, while poor, inconsolable Vitalie implored God to save her son and bring him back.

But Rimbaud was burning the stages of his life at great speed, constantly on the move like a butterfly in a field. He would soon set off to conquer Paris, in September 1871, although not before he had time to write one of the greatest of French poems: "Le Bateau ivre."

He was not yet seventeen.

Charleville was finished, but was he ready to return to Paris like a beggar? to live on charity and to eat scraps out of trash cans? Ready, yes, that we already know, although he had nothing to lose by trying to do things another way. That was why he sent a number of letters asking for help, including one to Izambard's friend Paul Demeny, who did not seem very enthusiastic about the young man's plans.

"Why don't you write to Paul Verlaine?" his friend Charles Bretagne said to him one day, quite casually, as if it were the most natural thing in the world to write a letter to the famous poet.

Rimbaud was stunned by the idea. Bretagne took out pen and paper and then and there wrote to Verlaine asking him to help the young man.

"You never told me he was your friend!" he said to Bretagne.

Arthur considered Verlaine the successor of Baudelaire, the new *seer*, so he could not believe what was happening. Then, with the help of Delahaye, he made fair copies of some of his poems. He put everything in an envelope and waited. He had sent a bottle out to sea, but the message reached port and was read.

Verlaine was on vacation. It was August. On his return to Paris, he found the letter with the poems and was intrigued by them. Before replying he consulted other poets among his friends and showed them Rimbaud's texts. All were surprised at their great originality. There was something there, a new voice, they all said.

One day in September the postman in Charleville handed the young man an envelope postmarked Paris. His heart skipped a beat. He opened it on the street and sat down to read the note on the steps of a house.

"Come, dear, great soul. We await you, we desire you," said Verlaine.

He enclosed money for the train fare and offered him hospitality in his own home.

Rimbaud ran like a madman through the streets of Charleville until he got to Bretagne's study. "Read this!" Then, happy like the child he still was, he crossed the town again in the opposite direction to get to Méziers and show the letter to Delahaye.

It was under the impulse of this great enthusiasm that he wrote *"Le Bateau ivre"* ("The Drunken Boat"). As Rimbaud says: "From that point on, I bathed myself in the Poem of the Sea." And who is in this drunken boat? The sailors have died and the poet is alone, trying to steer it. The dawns are depressing. The moons are terrible and the sun is bitter. The poet is on the verge of taking a great leap and, like the seer that he is, announces his future movements. Europe is already, as early as this poem, a pool of black water on which a sad child places a toy boat, "as frail as a butterfly in May."

Having finished the poem, he decided the time had come to leave.

Resigned, Vitalie let him go. At least this time Arthur was good enough to announce his departure. As he got on the train, what were his thoughts? Poetry had revolutionized his life and forced him to decipher the world. Now that same poetry was taking him away from his hated town, the town he had compared in a number of letters to hell or a penal colony. It is the secret story of a young artist who leaves home forever and, in doing so, realizes that the nets of his art are all he has. Will they be sufficiently strong to cushion a fall? The vertigo produced by life when it breaks with absolute freedom and in torrents into the brief time of youth. Like a crazed train plunging into the night and the depths of a mountain to come out, soon afterwards, on the other side. The time of adolescence is coming to an end. The inconsistency of adult life and that mysterious "other" of which he knows nothing and to which we are strangers.

Sitting on the train, Arthur thinks that his journey to solitude or to poetry must take him even farther, perhaps to those distant garrisons through which the shadow of his father roams. The eros of distance and its vertiginous drumbeat, which calls on some young people to leave. To go a long way forever. Why? Where? Perhaps there, in that territory he longs to reach, is true creation. The work of art to which he aspires.

But the journey that leaves from youth is forever and there is no turning back. The adult who returns after many years is a stranger. He no longer has the desire for purity of the young man who left, which is why he is also a traitor: like the catcher in the rye who abandoned his post and left the others alone. Poetry and the novel have revolved around this idea to the point of exhaustion. It is the endless story of art, which is why it recurs constantly. It is happening now, in any of the dawns of the world: a young artist journeying to the end of night, groping his way to the supreme solitude of writing. There is no way back, but he doesn't know that yet. The fate of his writing is his own fate and he will believe, in vain, that poetry will save him in the end.

May God have mercy on his soul.

Paris awaited him eagerly, with a sense of expectation created by Verlaine, but young Arthur surprised everyone, and not in a good way—far from it. In fact, most people went from surprise to indignation. Things went wrong from the start. As luck would have it, when the young man got off the train, he did not see anyone waiting for him, which was odd, since Verlaine and the poet Charles Cros had indeed gone to the Gare de l'Est to meet him. They must have gone to the wrong platform or arrived a little late. But Rimbaud, accustomed to walking, left the station and set off on foot for Rue Nicolet, in Montmartre, the address to which he had sent his letter. It was the Verlaine residence, although it was actually owned by his in-laws: a very bourgeois house with a garden, what the French call a "hôtel privé."

Verlaine's wife, Mathilde Mauté de Fleurville, a member of Parisian high society, was proud of her marriage to Verlaine, one of the most famous poets in France, in spite of his liking for drink and for the darker side of life. Mathilde believed firmly in the healing qualities of love, and so far, Verlaine had indeed managed to put aside his bohemian lifestyle and turn into an obedient and docile poet. In addition, they were expecting their first child.

The day Rimbaud arrived, Mathilde was burning with curiosity to meet the genius described by her husband, and she was not the only one. Her mother, too, who played the piano and was a well-known music teacher. One of her pupils was none other than Claude Debussy!

They had organized a welcome dinner for the poet with some relatives and close friends. And they were busy with this, checking the dinner service and the cutlery, when the butler announced that a very strange individual had called at the door and was asking for Monsieur Verlaine. The women looked at each other in surprise: what had happened? shouldn't Paul have come with him? Of course, they ordered the servants to bring him in. Their first sight of him was somewhat unsettling: he was not so much a man as almost a child, a dirty young provincial, with long hair and clothes that were not only far from being fashionable or from ever having been fashionable, but which in addition were too small for him, having been mended many times. They also saw that he had brought no luggage except for a bag over his shoulder. Is this Paul's genius? thought Mathilde. They greeted him politely, but Rimbaud sensed the two women's embarrassment; their false manners started to grate on him.

By the time Verlaine and Clos arrived, he was on a couch, replying in monosyllables and looking at the floor. They, too, were surprised at his appearance. He was a child! In his writings, Verlaine described him as an extraordinarily beautiful young man who was not yet fully grown, and his voice was only just changing.

The dinner was a disaster. It is considered polite in France to ask a guest many questions, as a way of expressing interest. But Rimbaud, as a provincial, hated this custom. He hated them and answered in monosyllables. Finally, says Starkie, he lit his pipe and filled the drawing room with disgusting smoke, which horrified the ladies even more: although they might have been able to live with some of the normal contradictions and eccentricities of an artist, they had their minimum social requirements. To be honest, they did not see the slightest trace of genius in this young man.

So the welcome dinner was a fiasco. It came to quite a quick end and left a sense of foreboding in the air. But not even in her worst nightmares could poor Mathilde have imagined what kind of devil had entered her house. Within a few days, the neighbors began asking troublesome questions about the guest, troubled by his appearance. On October 30, Paul and Mathilde's son Georges was born, which eased the atmosphere a little, although after just a few hours Paul went back to his old ways, going out drinking in the bars and cafés of Paris— with Rimbaud, of course. When they got back, both very drunk, Verlaine lay down next to his wife and the baby smelling of alcohol and tobacco, muttering incoherently. The next morning, Mathilde's father made up his mind to throw the intruder out, accusing him of leading his son-in-law into vice. This wasn't true. On the contrary, it was Verlaine who seemed to drive Arthur to bars, to that liquor of the poets known as absinthe, and perhaps also to drugs like hashish.

When Verlaine's father-in-law entered the guest room with the intention of kicking out the provincial poet, he discovered that Arthur had gone. Where? For a couple of weeks, Paul was unable to detemine his whereabouts. Nobody knew a thing: he did not appear in the bars they had frequented nor had he gone to any of their acquaintances to ask for help. Verlaine almost went crazy looking for him, until he met him by chance on the street. He barely recognized him.

A true beggar!

For Rimbaud, surviving in Paris by begging or doing small jobs was quite natural. Verlaine took him to see the editor of the Parnassian review, Théodore de Banville, who let him have an attic room on Rue de Buci—I assume a *chambre de bonne*—near the Odeón and Boulevard Saint Germain. He also persuaded a group of poets to provide the young genius with a daily allowance. But Arthur, like the God Shiva, had a gift for destruction, so within a few days the best thing he could think to do was to walk out naked onto the balcony and stand there touching his balls, which horrified the neighbors. Naturally, he was thrown out. After trying a number of artists' studios, Verlaine rented him a room on Rue Campagne-Première, near Boulevard Montparnasse.

Needless to say, all this solidarity on the part of the poetic and artistic world was due to their sympathy for Verlaine, because the truth of it was that Rimbaud's poetry was diametrically opposed to what was considered good at the time: in other words, classical themes, rhyme, and the celebration of beauty. To understand how far Rimbaud was from the taste of the Parisian salons, we just have to know that, among the Parnassians, the great poets of the time were Leconte de Lisle and José María de Heredia. But the urban voice, looking for alternative worlds and describing the miseries and virtues of the ego, was still unknown in French poetry in 1871.

It is worth recalling that in the novel, the abandonment of romantic themes had been happening for some time. Balzac, in about 1832, had perhaps been the first to write about what was happening in the cities, using people from the streets, ushers and vendors and judges, instead of legendary beings, pointing out in his stories how much it cost to bring a court action or the level of agricultural production of the Vendée. Victor Hugo, who was very famous, had established his fame with stories in a Romantic style, like *Notre-Dame de Paris*, set in the twelfth century, and then, influenced by Balzac—whom he watched grow, kept an eye on, and ended up assimilating—produced his masterpiece, *Les Misérables*.

This change, which had already been made by the Impressionist painters, Monet and Cézanne, then Van Gogh and Degas, was only just coming about in poetry, but when it came it was even more radical. Especially with Rimbaud and Isidore Ducasse, the other great adolescent poet who did not have time to grow and become disenchanted, since he died at the age of twenty-four in 1870.

He could almost have met young Arthur on the streets of Paris!

By the time Rimbaud was writing his first poems, Ducasse, who called himself the Comte de Lautréamont, had already published much of his work. The first of the *Chants de Maldoror* dates from 1868, but it made no impact and Arthur could not possibly have read it. In 1869, an edition of the complete works was produced but did not see the light of day because of a problem with the publisher. Then the Franco-Prussian war broke out, and in 1870 Ducasse died. Arthur could not have known his work and the curious thing is that the theory of the seer has much in common with the aesthetic credo of the Comte de Lautréamont.

All this meant that Verlaine was one of the few who admired Rimbaud at the time of his arrival, which may have been why, in poetic circles, it was said that the little devil from Charleville had bewitched him. This, of course, hardly bothered Rimbaud, whose behavior was increasingly offensive and rejectionist toward the Parisian poets. He no longer cared if he was recognized by them. Banville, Clos, even Lepelletier, who was a friend of Verlaine. He even made fun of Albert Mérat, whom he had admired before coming to Paris. The famous *Sonnet to an Asshole,* co-written with Verlaine, is a parody of Mérat's poetry.

When the painter Fantin-Latour proposed a group portrait of the most important contemporary poets, Verlaine insisted on Rimbaud being included, as a result of which Albert Mérat withdrew, saying that he didn't want to be portrayed for posterity together with such a rascal (he was referring, of course, to our young poet). In his place was a vase of flowers. The painting, *Un coin de table*, is on display at the Musée d'Orsay in Paris. The only two figures still recognizable today are Verlaine and Rimbaud.

But there was more to come before the final expulsion of Rimbaud from the literary world was decided on. The problem started at a dinner at the Café du Théatre du Bobino, where young Arthur, who was drunk, had the idea of adding the word *merde* to the end of every verse that the poet Jean Aicard read out loud, in front of the crème de la crème of Parisian poetry. Heredia, Banville, Coppée, and Clos were all present.

"*Merde*," Rimbaud said at the end of every verse. "*Merde, merde.*"

The dinner guests paid no attention, thinking he would tire of this, but the young man continued:

"*Merde, merde . . .*"

The photographer Carjat's patience had reached its limit. Furiously, he gave him two options: "Either you shut up or I'll smash your mouth in!" In response, Arthur took out Verlaine's swordstick, brandished it in the air, and, from his side of the table, flung it at the photographer, who managed to dodge the blow by a hair's breadth. This episode sealed Rimbaud's expulsion from the poetic coteries of Paris and, in a way, Verlaine's, too. In spite of all the scandals, Verlaine continued to protect him, because they were already lovers. All those nights of revelry ended with the two of them together in the room on Rue Campagne-Première. Months after the rape, and without Rimbaud having ever been with a woman, it was Verlaine, who was known to be bisexual, who showed him the path of sexual pleasure.

There is a curious fact about the events of those days: there are few images of Rimbaud, but perhaps the best known is a photograph in which he is in an oval, looking to one side with an expression that is a mixture of the seductive and the cold, wearing a suit and a thin tie. This photograph was taken by the very same Carjat he almost wounded at the dinner in the Café du Théâtre!

Verlaine's life, it goes without saying, was in ruins. His wife Mathilde, with a newborn child to attend to, did not have sufficient strength to throw him out of the house, but it was hardly necessary. Verlaine's mind was a long way away. It was as if he had already left, fascinated by the talent and the irrational force emanating from the little devil from Charleville.

The poetic establishment did not forgive Verlaine for his addiction to the poet genius, which is why in 1872 he was excluded from the annual anthology in which *Le Parnasse Contemporain* presented the year's best work. His own friends, Banville and Coppée, soiled his reputation, claiming that his way of life was licentious and his verses "disgusting and immoral." What must the selfless Mathilde have thought of this as she breastfed her little son Georges Verlaine? What must the in-laws, the Mauté de Fleurvilles, have thought?

For Rimbaud, it was time to put his theory of the seer to the test with daily binges on absinthe, in search of what he called "the long and reasoned disordering of all the senses," a prerequisite for aspiring to the most profound poetry, the sacrifice he must make to become a seer and blaze a trail for the human spirit. This is when he becomes what he called a *supplicié du vice*, a "martyr to vice." Seeing a spiritual path, a path of redemption, in excess was what, according to some scholars, allowed him to maintain his angelic expression.

16

The German guys I got to know in Berlin respected me because I was Argentinian. Argentina was a country toward which they felt enormous gratitude. And you know why? According to them, Hitler didn't die in the bunker of the Chancellery, as the official version has it, but escaped in a submarine via the Baltic, went halfway around the world, and ended up in Argentina. They're convinced that he landed in Patagonia with Eva Braun, and went to live by a lake near Bariloche, in one of the safe houses built by the Third Reich in case of defeat. He changed his name to Adolf Schütelmayor and died at the age of seventy-one. There's a documentary—I don't know if you know it, Consul—in which they show the luxurious mansion you could only reach from the lake, with watchtowers and vast rooms in the imperial style of Speer. Did you know that? Then, when Perón died in Argentina, he moved to Paraguay and changed his name again, to Kurt Bruno Kirchner. He traveled throughout Latin America, he even visited Colombia.

But let me pick up the story where I left off, in Berlin.

As I said, being Argentinian made me popular in political circles. I was still young, still a novice, so I had to bring myself up-to-date on the basics, and in spite of being in Germany I became interested in American groups. The first was a kind of great universal convention called Aryan Nation, but from there I moved on to something much more interesting called The Order, a kind of secret society founded in the United States in

1983 by two amazing guys, David Lane and Robert Jay Mathews.

Lane was a fantastic guy, a genius. He wrote something wonderful called the *88 Precepts*. Did you know that double 8 means *Heil Hitler*? H is the eighth letter of the alphabet, you see. He was a crazy guy. The son of an alcoholic and a drug addict, he was sent to an orphanage that gave him up for adoption by a Lutheran pastor. That's why he grew up with an extraordinary anger and resentment, but since he was an intelligent kid he wanted to do something with that hate and eventually founded The Order. The guys had balls, and very soon it turned into a well-structured and financed organization. They raised more than four million dollars through robberies and assaults and organized military training camps. I mean, they weren't playing with water pistols! They had a plan of defense, and then, in the end, they blew it. It always happens. Lane died in 2007 while in prison, in Indiana, from an epileptic fit. He was due for release in 2035. His most famous saying is the fourteen words: "We must secure the existence of our people and a future for white children."

There was another very crazy and very beautiful thing I learned about. It was called Wotanism, an idea that came from Jung, you know Jung, don't you? It was in an essay entitled *Wotan*, about the Norse God Odin, the Aryan God, and of course, Lane liked it because Wotanism was an ancestral vision of the world similar to the archetype of racial purity in National Socialism, and in addition it had similarities to his idea of man's natural savage condition.

He even managed to create something called the Temple of Wotan, with his *Sacred Book of the Aryan Tribes*. They're crazy when it comes to the subject of race, I agree, but they have a mysticism that I really like; out of all that, as I've said, what mattered to me were the methods. The last thing that Lane did before he died, to show the kind of guy he was, was to write a kind of short novel called *KD Rebel,* which is set in a mountain refuge where there's a colony of Wotanists who go down to the cities to persuade blonde white girls to come to the colony, and once there force them to serve as "polygamous procreators," in order to keep the production line of the Aryan race going permanently.

Anyway, I continued my education in Berlin, noting down what I saw, learning a lot about the groups I saw on the streets. To me they seemed well intentioned but very superficial. That could be seen, for example, in their dependence on something so frivolous and baseless as the craze for soccer. Let me talk a little about this. I have nothing against the game itself, which is entertaining, but how can you sustain a political ideal that depends on whether a group of men manage to put the ball into the opposite net? Do you think that demonstrates anything? Especially when the teams include blacks, Russians, Latin Americans, and even Arabs, where's your race worship then?

Look, being Argentinian, I like soccer, of course I do. I follow Messi and Di María and especially Tévez, who's a kid from the wrong side of the tracks, you can see the scars of poverty on him. Him, I do like. The boy's a gem. He comes from Fort Apache, one of the most run-down suburbs of Buenos Aires. When he was six months old his mother abandoned him, and when he was five his father was murdered, twenty-three bullet wounds. Can you imagine? When he was a baby he spilled boiling water on his face and neck, that's where he gets those horrible scars from. They are the traces of his life and I think they're beautiful. The boy is like a god.

Look at me, getting off the subject again.

As I was saying, these German guys channeled their anger badly, did superficial things with it, made violence a mere outlet for hate. You never get anywhere that way! It's good to feel anger, but you have to use it for something intelligent. How do you think nations were formed? Through anger and hate, of course, but with a plan in mind. All human wars are based on that. From hate and anger heroes are born. They are the people who succeed in leading a collective to victory. You can't fight against someone you love. Respect, yes. You can respect your enemy and honor him, but if you have him in front of you, you put a bullet in his chest. That's the law of human history. How do you think revolutions have been made? To invent the guillotine you have to have real anger, don't you think? The Bolsheviks in Moscow, too, and the English bombing Dresden and the Crusaders in the Holy Land and the Turks in Gallipoli and the Japanese in Manchuria and the Chinese in the Boxer Rebellion and the Spanish in America and the Aztecs cutting up the Toltecs and the Chichimecs with knives. Hate is everywhere, without it wars wouldn't work. How can you tell someone to go out and kill people he doesn't know, people he's never seen in his life and who've done nothing to him, if you haven't instilled hate in him? The really dangerous people are those who kill without feeling hate. That's the most inhuman thing there is!

But let me carry on with my story.

I don't even know where I was going.

One day, in Kreuzberg, at a meeting of the National Democratic Party of Germany, listening to a talk by Udo Voigt on the need to review the Nuremberg Laws, I again became aware of strange things happening. The platform on which Udo was speaking started to move, as if driven by powerful waves, everything was moving at a frantic rhythm. The wall of the stage started to fall in drops of acid onto the platform and the panelists, who didn't seem to move and just kept listening to the talk. I clutched my chair with both hands, afraid of falling to the floor, and what I saw next was even more terrifying: the sky was turning lavender and making whirlpools that swirled around Udo's words. I started to choke. I wasn't aware of falling to the floor and the next image I had was a corridor with fluorescent lights following one after another on the ceiling, like that scene from *Carlito's Way*.

When I got to the hospital I had a panic attack.

I saw flashes coming in through the windows and tried to take refuge in a surgical unit. Of course they stopped me, but it took six strong men. There was a bit of damage that, luckily, was covered by social security because I was known to be a psychiatric patient. They wired me up and started pumping drugs into my body intravenously, Chlorpromazine and other antipsychotics; I sank into something like a cauliflower heart, but made of jelly: a half-solid world where everything I touched stuck to my hand and tasted sweet.

Then I saw a knife or perhaps a surgical instrument, God knows what it was, and felt a terrible desire to pass it across my abdomen. Not to plunge it in, but to cut the skin from side to side. I rushed at the knife. I wanted to expel the wave of poison I was carrying inside. The people in the hospital thought I was going to hit the other patients or the nurses, which hadn't even crossed my mind. They grabbed hold of me and tied me to the bed with leather straps on my arms. I started to feel an itch in my nose, in my cheeks. I screamed, begging them to scratch my scalp and behind my ears, but nobody wanted to come near me. I felt a terrible rash, it was horrendous! I don't know what the hell they put in the drip, but it knocked me out.

The problem is that you can't just open the body and go in to do repairs. Everything is in its place. And at the same time it isn't, because it's as if the candles are dripping inside you. It's the worst thing there is, believe me.

I slept, as I later found out, for three days on end.

When I woke up I thought I was in the Hadamar psychiatric center on the outskirts of Koblenz, a hospital for mental patients in the Third Reich.

I felt that I was crazy and that I was going around the world covered in a sheet, stopping the lightning and fighting the fires left by the bombing.

I woke up again and realized they had moved me.

Now I was in the psychiatric prison in Beelitz-Heilstätten, in a room with broken windows and a collapsed ceiling. The rain was coming in through a hole in the roof. The wall was starting to be covered over with clinging ivy. The paint was falling to the floor in strange flakes that looked like dirty flour. The tiled floor was covered in a patina of moss that was quite slippery, so that you'd have to move very slowly.

My hallucinations all had to do with abandoned hospitals.

Especially psychiatric hospitals, which were going to be mine all my life. I also dreamed about Cane Hill Hospital, with its sinister bathtubs for washing the mad by force, today full of rotten water, lichen, and frogs. Or about the ashes of the Hellingly Asylum, which at night was home to heroin addicts and other scum who lit fires to warm themselves until someone must have fallen asleep with a lit cigarette.

I once copied out a quotation by the writer J. G. Ballard: "I'm never happier than when I can write about drained swimming pools and abandoned hotels." Well, if I was a writer, like you, my subject would be ruined hospitals. How about something called *Theory of Ruined Hospitals*? It has a good ring to it.

My sickness had no cure and I was far from my mother, though I didn't want to tell her anything either. What for? To make her suffer and feel guilty? After three months I went home, I'd lost nearly thirty pounds, which rather suited me, since in those circles everything revolves around beer and *würstel* and before you realize it you've turned into a pig. It was at this period that I started my unfortunate addiction to junk food, which led me to eat mass-produced sausages and burgers whenever I was anxious, and wash them down with gallons of soft drinks, fruit-flavored yoghurts, and that kind of thing.

I got through three or four large bottles a day.

That period coincided with a slightly crazy episode, too crazy even, which is that, as if there wasn't already enough going on, I developed an uncomfortable and fortunately passing addiction to sex that led me to the most violent and screwed-up experience of my life. Sorry to talk about something so personal, which has nothing to do with the origin of my project, but it's important if you want to get an idea of who I am.

My sex life in Argentina wasn't very interesting. I got hardly anywhere with any of the girls I liked, and only once, at the age of eighteen, did I manage to fuck a local girl. It wasn't especially memorable. Then I had a girlfriend who was a bit stupid, the cousin of one of my rugby teammates. A quiet girl who came to watch the training and who I invited to eat ice cream, and so I became her boyfriend, rather reluctantly, just to get the sex thing out of the way.

When I got to Germany things spiraled out of control. The women looked like Valkyries, powerful but unattainable. I wasn't bad-looking, I was strong and quite tall, but I had no money and that's crucial if you want to take one of those cuties out, isn't it? I barely had enough to study and attend meetings of the neo-Nazi groups, but paradoxically it was now that I had a kind of great revelation or sexual awakening.

Among the followers in Lichtenberg there was a very beautiful young woman, blonde and with a good body. She had an incredible propensity for raving it up, and one day, after a couple of beers, I made up my mind to talk to her in a noisy and very seedy bar. She already knew me, she had seen me at meetings. She told me something about her life. Her name was Saskia and she was the daughter of Russian immigrants, she was born after the fall of the wall, but her parents were still workers. One day her father let a wheelbarrow filled with bricks slip from his hands and the bricks fell down the stairwell. The problem is that it was on the eleventh floor! It was his bad luck that some workers were seriously injured: one died, another went into a coma, and a third suffered a severe head wound. Of course, Saskia's father was covered by industrial accident law, only there was a little problem, which is that when he was given a medical test they found that he was drunk. Drunk at work at nine in the morning? He was charged with aggravated negligence and homicide. He lost his job and was reduced to state aid. Saskia's mother worked in a discount supermarket and her brother was a heroin addict. Not a very stimulating family atmosphere for study, as you can see. In fact, she had tried heroin at the age of fifteen but didn't get hooked.

That same night we fucked.

She had swastikas tattooed on her buttocks and the face of Stalin under her navel. What a cutie. She had a runic *S* on each side of her pussy, making the Nazi SS sign, and hangings and piercings in her nipples and nostrils. She looked like a walking tinsmith's stand! We had a great fuck and she became an obsession with me. All day I wanted to fuck her and when I was with her, even before finishing I already felt I wanted to do it again. An amazing addiction. Saskia realized and since she was a bit crazy and I was Argentinian she was fine with it. All right, she'd say, let's go fuck, and we'd fuck in the toilet of the bar, on the stairs of the S-Bahn, in subway cars . . . We fucked everywhere! I started falling in love, just imagine, although I knew it was impossible, how was I going to introduce a girl like that to my mother? But when I'd next see Saskia and we'd fuck I'd forget all about that.

I was far from being the love of her life. She soon saw that I had no money and that I wasn't interested either in rising higher in the party, so one day she said to me, all right, darling, as of today it's over, thank you, the amusement park is closed, be a gentleman, that's what she said to me and I said goodbye with a cold, sad kiss and went home, first to drink a beer and then a bottle of cheap whiskey I'd bought. And so, as a kind of replacement I became a temporary alcoholic, while I was missing Saskia, or to be more honest and accurate, while I was dying to fuck Saskia. I thought I'd forget her by fucking other girls and went out looking for them, but it wasn't the same; and every time I saw a swastika, can you imagine, I got a hard-on.

One day I made a fatal mistake.

Wait while I pour myself a little more gin, because what I'm going to tell you isn't easy. The only way to take it in is to talk about what happened to me, although as you'll see, there's nothing natural about it.

It's a long, long way from being natural.

One night I'd been drinking on my own at home, and you know, the worst thing for a person who's lovesick is to have photographs. I grabbed my camera and started going back through them, and saw Saskia, with her white ass and her legs up, with her pussy open, holding up her tits, anyway, I went crazy, half metaphorically and half literally, because I left home like a shot to look for her; I went to Lichtenberg, to a bar called Odessa, a place that was very punk and very Nazi, but couldn't find her. They told me she was at a party on the other side of the S-Bahn. I went out with the address in my hand, hailed a taxi, and went to the place. It was on the second floor of an old abandoned warehouse.

I found a grille open on one side and went in. Then I went up a fire escape and got to the main room, and you have no idea what it was like: there they were, smoking crack and injecting heroin on a collapsed couch, listening to music at an impossible volume, in a daze, surrounded by empty vodka and schnapps bottles, it was disgusting.

I couldn't see Saskia anywhere, so I started to search for her.

From the outside gangway I passed through a window into the old offices, and I saw three men lying on a rug with their pants down and syringes in their forearms; a young guy was sucking the cock of another guy of about forty who seemed to be the leader, and a third scumbag, who was about twenty, was fucking the same guy in the ass, which is a pretty horrifying image for someone who isn't into that kind of thing, don't you think?

I continued on my way and saw that all kinds of things were happening in those half-ruined offices. It was Sodom and Gomorrah!

In another even darker place I saw some figures dancing, very drunk or very drugged, and a shaven-headed woman of about fifty in a G-string sticking the mouth of a wine bottle into another woman's ass. And all the while, a kind of emaciated faun with tattoos from head to foot was fucking her in the ass.

The music was really loud in the whole of this area and nobody heard me walking along the corridor, in spite of the amount of broken glass and rusty old iron scattered on the floor. I felt a pang in my heart imagining Saskia fucking someone in one of these offices, and I went from one room to another, scared of what I might see.

But you know how it is, if you search you find.

I saw her and almost fell on the floor. They had her tied up on a table, on her back, with a blindfold over her eyes. A kind of albino orangutan, with a neck wider than his head, had his cock in her mouth while another was dripping melted wax from a candle onto her navel.

Saskia was screaming.

It was too much for me, I went crazy.

I went in and punched the guy with his cock in her mouth, and he fell to one side and hit his head on a desk. The other one, the one with the candle, I kicked in the balls and he fell to the floor, choking. I threw the hot wax in his face and he doubled up in pain. It took Saskia a while to recognize me, but instead of being happy she started screaming hysterically, telling me to get out of there and leave them alone.

"They're my friends!" she said.

They didn't look very friendly, I thought, but on seeing what I'd done to them she slapped me across the face. She ran out into the corridor naked and a second later came back with three guys who looked like giants. One had a handkerchief tied around his head, like a Pirate of the Caribbean. The other two could have been miners or railroad workers. When I saw them, I polished up my modest German and said to them: it's all right, guys, it's all a misunderstanding, I'm going now, *Auf Wiedersehen!*, but the guys came forward and however hard I tried to punch them to the ground the only thing I managed to do was dislocate my shoulder and get my nose smashed.

"Did you come here looking for action?" said one of the chimpanzees.

They tied me to a gymnasium horse. A thin toothless guy, with the sour crack breath of onions in vinegar, approached my ear and said:

"If that's what you were looking for, princess, you've come to the right place; get ready for an unforgettable night!"

What followed was disgusting, Consul. They pulled down my pants and put half a jar of cream between my buttocks. Then they all took turns, even those I'd seen fucking each other in the first office. They took turns buggering me, begging your pardon. How many were there? More than a dozen. A chorus of ageing punk women, cadaverous and addicted, laughed and shouted. Then they opened bags of coke and stuck it in in their noses or smoked it in pipes.

They broke my ass, Consul.

Saskia turned into a devil, a kind of female Satan who took the lead in this sinister ritual and urged them to continue: come on, next one! She invited those who hadn't yet had a turn to take it, and again put cream on me.

Come for this beautiful Argentinian ass!

Today it's free!

They were all laughing shrilly, revealing gums rotted by heroin and black molars. I thought: if they don't kill me now, I'll be dead of AIDS by tomorrow afternoon. Those sons of bitches were like bags of germs.

I didn't grant them a single complaint, a single tear. Nothing. Just a resentful silence. Every time someone withdrew his cock and cleaned it with a Kleenex, I said to myself: pray for me to die, you son of a bitch, because if I get out alive my revenge will be terrible.

My masters were putting me to the test, showing me the violence of the world. All the things I had to combat. Then an idea started taking shape in my mind: don't forget them, get a good idea of who they are.

Because there will be revenge.

And so, while the guys continued laughing, I observed them out of the corner of my eye. I managed to find something in each of them that I could recognize: a tattoo, a wristwatch, a small chain, a ring. Most were Russians or Russian speakers from the former East Germany. When they got bored they forced me to take a pill that finished me off, leaving me seeing visions and unable to stand. Two of them dumped me in the back of a beat-up Opel and drove me to a truck stop on the freeway. There they left me, lying in a ditch.

What a big mistake leaving me alive, what a mistake.

I left the hospital two weeks later and didn't report them to the police. I had already understood the message loud and clear: be violent with the violent and affectionate with the affectionate. In this case, my masters demanded an exemplary revenge and I already had the profiles of seven of the attackers in a notebook. They had shown me a specific area of corruption and it was up to me to cauterize it. It was just a question of hygiene. I decided to turn into a nocturnal avenger, the immunological agent who has to attack and destroy whatever acts in a destructive manner inside the system. That had been the message. I classified it in my brain as "part of a steep learning curve leading to change."

I'd already made up my mind to leave Germany. I gave up the room I'd been renting, gave away my belongings, and said goodbye to the few friends I had. I announced that I was going back to Argentina, sent my things to Madrid, and stayed in Berlin a few days more. I took a room in a modest boarding house in Charlottensburg with the idea of passing unnoticed among tourists with backpacks. I tried not to stand out. It was very likely I was being watched.

At night, I started my search. I had images of the seven guys, so started to comb the Lichtenberg area. I had changed my appearance as much as I could, of course. I wore black clothes, hoods. I let my beard grow and lost weight. It wasn't very hard to find them. I just had to keep my eye on Saskia's brother to get to the others. I drew a series of circles on a map of the area and considered the best way to attack them. They didn't know what was in store for them! The first thing I did was go into a bar and steal the wallet of one of them when he wasn't looking. It was child's play.

The ID said Rudolf Oleg Handke, born in Innsbruck, October 21, 1981. He had a fifty-euro bill and another of ten. Another of a thousand dinars, something like a collector's item, from the Bank of Serbia. A sachet of a brown substance I assumed was heroin. An old membership card from the Association of Friends of the Tyrol in Aachen. A student card from the Ludwig Maximilian University in Munich, enrolled in educational science. Old papers with telephone numbers, which I noted down.

Once I'd finished the phase of studying my targets, which took me about a month, I went on to the second phase: the attack.

I chose a Thursday, preparing myself physically and mentally for the task. I got up early and exercised. I went out, had some fruit, at noon ate a balanced lunch. Midafternoon, I hired a van from a semi-clandestine Turkish business, using the ID I'd stolen, and started loading and installing the surgical material I needed for my task. Nobody asked any questions, they didn't even look at the photograph. At about six I took a nap and got ready for the night. At around eleven, I set off and parked the van beside an old school, in the northern area of Lichtenberg. Two of the men often passed that way, although never together.

Here I have to stop my story for a moment, Consul, because you might think that what follows isn't really mine. A story in the style of Rambo or . . . what's the other guy's name? Schwarzenegger. You may think that, but remember, I come from a hard world and was always able to deal with villains.

Anyway, let me continue.

When I saw the first one coming, I felt my blood boiling in my veins. I remembered a sentence I'd heard in a movie: "The silence that comes before disaster." But only I could hear it, not my victims. When the guy walked past the van, I got out very quickly and in no time at all had loaded him half-conscious in the back, which didn't have windows. I tied his arms with wire and struck a wedge of newspaper in his mouth, down to his throat. He opened his eyes anxiously when he saw that the floor of the van was covered in plastic, and who could blame him, it must have given him a very bad premonition. Then I put a rag soaked in ether over his face, *Gute Nacht* . . . He fell asleep like a baby.

I was forty-nine seconds behind schedule.

Soon afterwards the other one arrived and I got out. The son of a bitch must have sensed something because he hesitated, but I grabbed his arm and twisted it behind his back until it went crack. With the other hand I put a wad of newspaper down his throat. It's incredible how useful the *Frankfurter Allgemeine Zeitung* can be. I stuffed him in the van, bound him and gagged him, and gave him a good dose of ether.

With them on board I drove off, saying to myself, shall I go for more? This is easy. The original plan had been to grab two, at most three of the group of seven candidates. I felt like continuing and looked up, into the German night, but didn't receive any answer. Believing that you're strong is bad when you're going to carry out a mission, because adrenaline is a drug, did you know that?

I felt like an expert and went to another of the places circled on the map. One of them lived on the third floor of a run-down apartment block, but the entrance was on the other side, along an avenue. I knew that he always went in the back way. So that was where I parked the van.

My target was a Serb, the same one who had been fucking Saskia when I went to the warehouse that night, I was going to enjoy this one more than the others, and I thought, with a special dispensation from Odin, who was the master who calmed my muscles that night: he's going to get special treatment.

I heard a noise and looked in the rearview mirror. The bastard was coming, but he wasn't alone. He was with someone else who wasn't on my list. I tried to see if I could recognize him, but there wasn't much light. What to do? It would be too much of a hassle for everything to go belly up now, so I said to myself, what if I grab the two of them? The Serb was big but the other guy wasn't. I reckoned I could do it.

I got out of the van with a map in my hand. I played dumb and asked them for help with an address in the area. The guys turned to look at me, I'd caught them off guard and they were a bit annoyed at my intrusion. When I landed the first punch they practically didn't see it. The Serb fell against the wall, with something broken. I grabbed the thin guy by the neck and just as I was pulling his head up into the light from a streetlamp I saw that he had a wristwatch with a flame on the minute hand. That's when I recognized him. He was one of them! So I said to him out loud, I wasn't expecting you, but welcome to the party, *willkommen*.

I quickly loaded them in the van and left as cautiously as I could, I didn't want the police to stop me for an inspection or anything like that. I felt pleased with myself: I was a true professional. In less than an hour I had four of these bags of germs tied up and ready to go. My thoughts made me laugh as I took the S-Bahn. I already had a point marked, twenty-eight miles from there, where I could stop and work on them without being disturbed. I turned and looked at them, lying there one on top of the other like sacks of flour.

Now, as I drove through the night, I searched for a little inspiration. Should I give them the full treatment or just strike a blow so decisive as to transform them, through pain, into agents of change? I analyzed the situation from various points of view and came to the conclusion that the second of these options was the more appropriate: the knockout blow. Something told me that letting them go back to their germ-ridden community, but marked by their punishment, was an educational gesture that would prove interesting.

I knew that option would be more demanding physically. But when it came down to it, it was what I wanted to do, what I'd prepared for, and in addition I had all the necessary surgical equipment.

The truth is that I was dying to operate.

When I got to parking lot 49-E, near the exit from the Autobahn, I took a very narrow path through trees that led to a wood, a kind of *Schwarzwald*, as they say there. There was absolutely nothing for at least half a mile around, so I could work in peace.

I decided to call this session *Theory of Mutilated Bodies*.

I put on a white coat, latex gloves, and a surgical mask, and got ready, invoking my masters. I again gave them strong anesthetics intravenously and dedicated myself to the hard task of tying arteries and veins, sawing through bones, smoothly cutting muscles and nerves, making knots that would later allow me to assemble the stumps. I did it as best I could, although at the time, tired as I was, I couldn't be sure of the results. Last but not least, I attached drip bags filled with antibiotics and a little morphine to them, pulled them down off the van, laid them out on the plastic, and covered them with a thick sheet of asbestos. I washed the inside of the van. I put the amputated limbs in a bag for medical waste, and set off back to Berlin.

Before I left, I called emergency services from the cell phone of one of them and gave them directions. Then I sped off, leaving their cell phones on.

I was exhausted.

I drove about twenty-five miles along side roads to avoid the security cameras. My plan involved passing by an artificial lake that was part of a fish farm, because I thought it would be a good fate for the bag of amputated limbs, in which, of course, there were a number of things: four right legs, four complete arms, and sixteen fingers. A penis and a scrotum, too, guess whose? When I saw the news in the press, describing it as a "massacre carried out with macabre coolness," I felt proud of my surgical knowledge, since all of them, even the Serb whose cock I'd cut off, managed to survive. The event caused a bit of a stir, although not as much as I'd expected. The police favored the hypothesis that it had been a settling of scores between neo-Nazi groups, which wasn't completely unfounded, and thought that it wasn't worth alarming the public too much, who during that time were on their vacations.

17

I t's strange to wake up in a hospital and find yourself hand-cuffed to a bed. Where could I go in that state? Everything hurts and I'm afraid to sleep, because then the body relaxes and makes movements that revive the pain. At least there's nobody else in the room, although for how much longer I don't know. It's almost three in the morning, the grimmest hour in hospitals, churches, and prisons. The hour of pain, the hour of the devil, they say, because it is the transposed figure of the death of Christ. Its nighttime equivalent.

Three in the morning.

It's also the hour of memory, so I started remembering other prison experiences, all insignificant compared with this one. In the first I was barely seventeen and was in a small town in Colombia called Pacho, near Bogotá, where I had gone with some friends from the neighborhood to a house in the country. We were young and wanted to swallow the world, of course, and that led us to frequent all the dives in the town. In addition, we were crazy about pool, and so it was that one night, in one of those bars, the police came in and stood us up against the wall, asking for our identity cards. I didn't yet have one because I was still a minor, so they arrested me. A curious legal principle: for their protection, minors aren't allowed in pool halls, but if they're caught they're put in a cell with robbers and thugs of all descriptions.

So there I was, in a hot, unventilated room. There were fifteen of us and there was nowhere to sit. A guy who had been there for a few days was asleep on the floor on a mat. At five in the morning, a group announced that they had an escape plan and asked me if I was ready. I stalled. Just before dawn a guard came and shone his torch in our faces.

"Let's see now, my fellow townsman, you can come out . . . "

Nobody moved, because we didn't know where he was from. Until he said again:

"The young guy from Bogotá, you can come out . . . "

They took my details. A clerk filled out a form on an old typewriter. My brother and another of my friends were there, with the sergeant, waving to me.

The second time was in Madrid.

During my time at Complutense University, I was active for a while in a left-wing collective called KAI. In 1986 there was a strike against the statute for university reform promoted by the rector Gustavo Villapalos, and someone in the upper echelons of my group decided that we had to take over the headquarters of the Council of Universities, which was on the same campus. And so we did. I went in with the first group. We blocked the elevators and doors of the building and managed to get as far as the offices on the upper floors. We built barricades and took the director hostage. The police preferred not to use force, but surrounded the building and stopped us from having food sent in. Their strategy was to tire us out, but the striking students mounted a permanent demonstration outside the building and every now and again threw us bags with sandwiches, fruit, and bottles of water.

By the fourth day, the pain from my ulcer was becoming unbearable, since I had left my pills at home, and it was decided that I should go out with a female comrade and read a press release. When we passed the barricade on the second floor, a legion of uniformed arms lifted me in the air. The police nevertheless allowed us to read the press release into the microphones, then loaded us in a van and took us to the police station. On the way, I remembered that I had a scholarship from the Spanish government through the Institute for Latin American Cooperation, but it was the Spain of Felipe González, so they simply took my details and sent me home, where I was able to fill my stomach with antacid pills and doses of Mylanta.

My third imprisonment was in 1994, in Sarajevo, during the Bosnian war.

I had gone there as correspondent for the newspaper *El Tiempo*, of Bogotá, and one night I had to stay in the former headquarters of Bosnian television a little later than usual. That was where we broadcast from when the lines from the hotel weren't working. When I came out, I couldn't see any transportation that would take me to the Holiday Inn, which was the hotel where the journalists stayed, so I set off on foot, which was a pretty crazy thing to do given the situation in the city, especially as there was a strict curfew after ten at night. And so, as I was walking in the dark toward Marshal Tito Avenue—which had been renamed Sniper's Alley—a Bosnian police patrol car stopped me. I was taken to a barracks in the center of the city and the officers, who were as young as I was, put me in a cell, behind bars, but without closing the door. That night I explained to the three guards that I was Colombian and a friend to their cause, I told them I could have covered the war from Pale, on the Serbian side, but that I had decided to be in Sarajevo, with them.

"I prefer to work where the bombs fall," I said, "not where they're launched from."

They offered me a Sarajevan beer, I seem to remember it was called Sarajevo Pivo, and then an endless series of glasses of slivovitz, a spirit made from grapes and herbs that must have been about sixty proof, which came in very handy that winter night. The most dangerous moment occurred at six in the morning, when they freed me and insisted on taking me in their jeep to the hotel. A vehicle prowling through the cold, snow-covered streets of Sarajevo was an excellent target for the Serb snipers, the *chetniks*, who would have just gotten up and might be feeling like getting a few shots in before breakfast. Fortunately, that didn't happen.

But let me get back to my current desperate and uncomfortable situation.

Once again, I slept a couple of hours. Outside—in that distant and already nostalgic outside—day had already broken. Soon afterwards Pedro Ndongo arrived to check the tubes and the level of the drip. One of the bags was empty and he replaced it. As he was checking the catheter on my wrist, he noticed me moving and said:

"Good morning, my esteemed intellectual. I have a surprise for you."

"Don't tell me, Mr. Reading has woken up."

"No, not yet," Pedro said. "Yesterday I dropped by the registration office and asked for your belongings. The notebook you told me about was there, but as is only natural, they didn't let me take it out, because it's been registered. That's where Pedro Ndongo Ndeme's great ability to argue came into play and I told the woman: could you do me a favor and lend it to me so that I can make a copy? Then the original can stay here and I'll take that wretched fellow the copy and make him very happy, what do you think? The woman smiled and said she would let me do it but that I would have to take care of it myself."

He took an envelope from his jacket and there, in loose sheets, was everything I had written.

He put it by the side of the bed and added:

"I also read it."

He made a theatrical pause.

"And . . . ?" I exclaimed.

"It made me feel nostalgic for my student days, first in the

National University of Guinea and then in the Complutense. Although I was studying medicine, I spent my evenings reading poetry."

"You studied at the Complutense?" I said. "So did I."

"Really? What year?

"I graduated in philology in '90."

"Ah, no," he said, "I arrived a bit later. I started my course in 1996."

Before leaving, Pedro said to me, pointing at the photocopied sheets:

"It's good, finish it."

"Impossible," I said, "I don't have anything to write with."

"Ah, I can't help you with that. A pen is a sharp instrument, but I have a suggestion: memorize. Think and memorize, it'll be an excellent exercise. It prevents Alzheimer's. Many people have done it and good things have come out: Cervantes, Voltaire, Solzhenitsyn. They all memorized. Think of them and you won't feel alone."

Pedro came a little closer and lowered his voice.

"There's more news, which is that you're going to have company. I don't know when they're bringing him because right now he's in the operating room, I saw it on the form, he's coming here."

I spent the day reading my notes about Rimbaud. I tried to memorize some new paragraphs and corrections. During the night, they did bring in another prisoner, putting up the curtain separating the room into two spaces. I couldn't see him. The combination of the sedatives and the medication for my wounds was quite strong and that's why I barely registered his arrival.

This morning I saw him. He's a priest. He has a broken arm and a very swollen eye, as well as a deep cut on his back. He was praying and I didn't want to disturb him, I barely nodded to him. Then Pedro Ndongo came to take me for a treatment and another blood test, so I didn't see him again until the afternoon.

While we were going to one of the therapy sessions, Pedro said:

"I see your body is working well, my friend, in spite of your age: your melanocytes are responding, the Langerhans and Merkel cells . . . The treatment is working. I don't feel revulsion anymore when I look at you."

"Is it also dermatological, Pedro?"

"I'm just an intellectual of the fibers and glands."

I asked him what he knew about my cellmate.

"I can't give you much information, friend, but I do have a surprise for you: he's a compatriot of yours, a priest, are you a believer?"

"No. I already told you I'm not."

"You should consider it, not everyone has the chance to cohabit with a minister of the Church."

Images from that morning came back to me.

"And why is he so badly injured?"

"I heard he was about to be lynched. A group of demonstrators from your country. The police stepped in and saved him, but he's been arrested because he has a criminal record, there's a warrant out for him from Interpol. A priest. And it's not because he's a pedophile! Your country is very strange, my friend."

"Do you know what he's charged with?"

"Being a member of an armed criminal group."

"The paramilitaries," I said.

"The same guys who beat up blacks and Arabs here, you mean?"

"More or less, although here it's racial and there it's political."

Pedro stroked his cheeks. "The racial is always political, friend, remember Martin Luther King. Or Malcolm X, who said: 'Be obedient, be peaceful, law-abiding, but if someone attacks you send him to the cemetery.' That's more or less what you did to that poor literature teacher, isn't it?"

I grew worried again.

"Do you know anything about his condition?"

"He's still the same. He's on the third floor in the assisted prisoners' section, in a coma."

It was strange: the two of us, both accused and both victims. Both deprived of freedom.

"It would be quite stupid if we both ended up in prison."

"More stupid still if you'd both ended up dead, which is how these fights usually end up, isn't it? Don't worry, you still have an advantage over him. He can't claim victory yet. The prisons of the world are full of people who, basically, didn't want to do it. Chance and bad luck are the limits of free will. I exclude that other percentage of bastards who on the other hand did what they did in full knowledge. For them it's the opposite: prison is a way to postpone their natural death, with half a dozen bullets between their chest and their back, when ninety-three percent of their internal juices spill out onto the asphalt and happily flow into the sewers, where they'll be able to mix with the shit of the city."

I thought again about my cellmate.

"Did they put him with me because he's Colombian?"

Pedro slapped one of the sides of the bed.

"What questions you ask, friend. How should I know? Maybe some little genius said: hey, what a coincidence, these two sons of bitches are from the same country, right? Let's put them in the same room and see what happens. I'm sorry, I'm imitating, I don't know anyone who speaks like that."

"I know, Pedro. I know your style."

We got to the cell and the priest was sitting beside the bed, reading the Bible. His face really was very inflamed. His right eyelid was a purple mass and it wasn't very clear if a black, bloody thing in the middle was the eye.

Seeing me he contracted the muscles of his face, as if saying, ouch, what a thrashing they gave this one.

"I heard you're Colombian."

The priest looked up, surprised.

"Yes, and what else were you told?"

"That you were brought here because they were going to
lynch you."

"Forgive me for not standing, and were you told why they
wanted to lynch me?"

"Yes."

He showed me his arm, which was in a suspensory bandage.

"You see how far the hand of the devil reaches. And what
happened to you?"

"I had a fight in a bar, the other person was badly hurt. It
wasn't my fault."

His left eye moved up and down, examining me.

"From Bogotá?" he said.

"Yes, but I've been living outside Colombia for years."

"Almost better, although I confess something, I couldn't.
My country is the most beautiful there is in this world and if
the Lord put me there, it was for a reason."

I tried not to contradict him.

"Do you know any other countries?"

"Not many, apart from this shithole here, forgive my language. But I don't need to know any others, what for if I live
in the best? I went to the United States and look at it: in the
hands of the Jews, and with a black man as president who's a
friend to the Muslims."

Just then his male nurse came to take him away. They had
to take a statement from him.

As he went out he said to me:

"Father Ferdinand Palacios, at your service."

Soon afterwards Pedro came to take me out to the exercise
yard. Apparently my treatment required a little sun and wind.

"What do you think of your cellmate?"

"He's friendly, but strange."

"I advise you not to judge him. If you're going to have to share a room with him the best thing is to look for his good side. Everyone has a good side."

"He seems to be in a pretty bad condition," I said.

"He's hurt, that's why he's here. If they agree to extradite him, he'll serve his sentence in Colombia."

"I'd rather be in a different cell, or alone."

"That's a privilege, but don't be alarmed. This hotel has very good security. Nothing will happen to you. Your case is going through the normal channels, and while that teacher's still breathing, there won't be any changes. Ask the priest to pray for him, it might help."

18

T hat whole week, Araceli kept sending me messages. In one she said: "Experiencing this love with him has given me back the confidence I'd lost, and I feel stronger now. I think I can even understand his affair with that little bitch. I just needed confirmation about myself. Thank you, my darling."

Another day, I was in a medieval literature class—it was about *Count Lucanor*, I remember—when I received another of her messages: "Sweetheart, we just fucked three times in the Jacuzzi, I never even got that when I was his girlfriend! Forgive me for telling you. I know you understand me. I love you."

My relations with these two women, Doctor, led me to think about myself. Both were frivolous and a little crazy, but they lived with an intensity I'd never known. I felt as if I was outside the world and started to think that the way they loved was normal. Of course, poetry helped me formulate the right questions, but also told me that I didn't have any answers. Life had been needlessly cruel, expressing a wickedness that, when it came down to it, could only be in people. A wickedness that hovers in the air and suddenly chooses you at random. It's not personal, I'm just a grain of sand, but how can any kind of faith be feasible when God has gone and there's nothing to replace him? Those were the questions. I wrote and wrote, hoping to find answers. If there's nothing at the end of the road, what can give light to the heart of man?

I spent nights and nights like that.

What were my sacrifices? what rituals? I wept for no reason, standing by the window, looking at the rain. Seeking the calming effect of the rain. I stood in front of the mirror and insulted myself. I undressed and hit myself. One night the doorman knocked at my door to tell me that the neighbors had heard cries, a strange moaning. I told him everything was fine. A strange Manuela was emerging, a mutant creature with scales, capable of surviving without clean air; an animal feeding on garbage, able to perpetuate itself in a world of wild beasts. Being that way, I told myself in one of the poems, the true monster was me, and so what salvation could I aspire to? Life itself was showing it to me, with its constant trials and brutal messages. I had it in front of my nose, on the page: it was poetry itself. This is how I summed it up (in a third poem): the ruthless impulse that had torn me away from life was the very same one that now fed into my only possible salvation. Humiliation, contempt, vileness, shame, and dishonor. Meanness and derision. I knew all these things because I had lived through them all. My eyes were like the windows of a solitary rocket about to explode in space. Through them, I could look at the world and, perhaps, feel protected. Closer to something that might resemble God, but wasn't God. I could even fake a smile, a grimace that to everyone out there looked like a smile.

Days and nights passed, I don't know how many. I remained vigilant, devoted to writing. I wandered naked and dirty through the apartment. I ate out of a big pan of rice that I'd cooked and from which I scooped whole mouthfuls with my hand. I drank water by sticking my mouth up against the faucets of the dishwasher and sucking it from there. I defecated and urinated. I slept on the carpet in the corner of the living room. I masturbated with a cucumber and then ate it. I looked at the rain through the window for hours, the wet rooftops of the city, and the people down there, that noisy mass in which the demon of adversity lay hidden. I felt cold and tried to imagine how every morning would be on this cold plain. I watched flies buzzing against the windowpane before squashing them. I became cruel to the little creatures that inhabited my world. I was the great predator.

I recovered my animal strength.

I wrote and wrote until something told me: it's over, now it's ready.

You've finished. It was a strange voice.

I was exhausted and went to sleep.

The next day, which was Saturday, at six in the morning, my cell phone rang hysterically until it made me jump. Who could be calling at this hour?

Banal reality had remembered me.

Damn, I said to myself seeing her name on the screen, it's Rafaela. I felt miles away from her. What could have happened to that silly girl now? I was holding the telephone in my hand and by the time I made up my mind to answer it had already gone to voicemail, so I closed my eyes again. My pillow was still warm. The telephone rang again and I thought, should I answer? Calls at such an early hour are the devil's work. I reduced the volume to zero, but then it started vibrating.

No, I said, no and no. I'll call her later, after a good breakfast, when I'm fully awake.

That was worse, because after twenty minutes it was the entryphone that rang, again and again. I had no other remedy but to pick up. The doorman said: Señorita Rafaela is here for you. Shit, I thought, that fucks up everything. Let her up, I said. What stupid story could she have come with?

Opening the door, I found her in tears, had something happened to her the previous night? I took her over to the couch and said, breathe deeply, calm down, I'll make us some coffee and we'll talk, okay?

She hadn't stayed up all night and she hadn't taken drugs,

quite the contrary. She brought with her the smell of soap and a recent shower. I poured the coffee and grabbed some cookies. I went with them to the living room and found her still crying.

"That son of a bitch has gotten me pregnant!" she suddenly burst out.

Shit, I said to myself.

"Are you sure?" I asked.

"I'm already quite late and last night, when I looked at the calendar, I said to myself, shit, so late? Twenty days. I got scared and went this morning to buy one of those tests they sell in drugstores. I did three different tests and all three were positive."

She showed me the little plastic sticks with the red mark; I didn't know much about these things but it must have been like she said.

"What are you planning to do?" I said. "Aren't there clinics for that here in Bogotá?"

"For having an abortion?"

She said it with total contempt, as if the complete sentence was: "That's what hookers and poor women do, those who have sex when they're drunk or on drugs, not a beautiful rich girl like me."

So I corrected myself and said:

"I mean, termination of pregnancy."

She started crying again, took out her cell phone, and turned it on, angrily, nervously, as if waiting for something.

"The worst of it is that the bastard hasn't sent me a single damned message since he left for Europe, unless that old bitch confiscated it! Do you think that's possible?"

I said maybe he was somewhere without a network. Or maybe he lost it and had to buy a new one and didn't know her number.

"What, like there's no Wi-Fi in London or Paris? He hasn't gone to the fucking African jungle. And if he lost it he could have sent me an e-mail, couldn't he? or used Messenger, he doesn't need to have my number for that!"

I didn't have any other arguments, so I said:

"And why don't you write to him and tell him?"

That also annoyed her. I had the feeling she'd come to me because she needed someone to yell at.

"Me? He's the one who went away and left me stranded! I'm not writing to him no matter what he does to me, the bastard."

I looked at my watch: it was barely eight in the morning. It wasn't a good idea to offer her a drink.

"You should go to the gym and stop thinking about it," I said.

That wasn't a good idea either.

"Like it's so easy to stop thinking! I'm pregnant by a son of a bitch who's vanished into thin air, how can you think I should go to the gym?"

I'd run out of ideas.

"Would you like a drink?"

"I'm pregnant!" she cried furiously. "I can't drink alcohol."

Then she thought better of it and said, okay, what the hell, do you have rum and Coke? But have one with me.

I poured two Cuba Libres and we drank them slowly. It did her good, because after a while she stopped her yelling.

"I can't tell my mother," she said, "let alone my sisters. You'll keep it secret, won't you?"

My cell phone vibrated and I froze.

"Answer it," she said, "I don't mind."

I looked at the screen: it was another message from Araceli. A photograph from the elevator on the Eiffel Tower. The note said: "It scares me to be so happy, and I miss you, my sweet girl. ILU." There was no sign of the husband. I closed the messages and switched off the phone.

"Who's writing to you at this hour?" she asked. "Your boyfriend?"

"No," I said, "a friend from Cali. Nothing important."

We served ourselves another Cuba Libre and she asked if she could hear some music. She took off her shoes and stretched out on the couch.

"This is a nice apartment," she said, "do you rent it or is it your family's?"

"I rent it, I got it very cheap. It belongs to a relative of my mother's."

"You've never told me anything about your family or your life," she said, "do your parents live in Cali? Do you have brothers and sisters?"

"I don't like talking about it," I said. "I'm sorry, can we talk about something else?"

"Oh, sure, I'm sorry."

She took a long slug from the glass and lay there looking at the ceiling.

"It's really nice here, and very well located," she said. "No sweat, if you don't want to talk about your family I understand, I also hate to be asked certain things."

She paused, then looked up again at the ceiling.

"What do you think he's doing right now?"

"That depends," I said. "Do you know where he is?"

"I think he's still in London, he told me the conference lasts until the end of the month."

"He's probably in some meeting, bored, reading papers or taking notes. Maybe he's thinking about you, or he's in a store buying you something."

"I don't think so," she said, "with that skinny witch he won't have time for anything, unless he makes an excuse and gets away from her. But she won't let him out of her sight for even a second. If she wasn't famous too, I could tell you who she is. In fact, when you find out you're going to say . . . What?!? I wish I could tell you, believe me."

"I understand, don't worry. It's best you don't tell me anything."

Once again, she took out her cell phone and looked at it, this time with a degree of tenderness. Outside it was drizzling, the wind was making the branches of the trees knock together. It was a cold but mild morning. Somewhere not very far away, a bird sang.

"Do you really think I should tell him?" she said. "Why not? After all, he is the father. I'll have to tell him sometime."

"It's up to you," I said.

"Yes, but you gave me the idea. If you were pregnant and in love, what would you do? I mean, obviously if the same thing happened to you that happened to me."

I thought about it. The idea was so alien to my life that it had almost never entered my mind, not even as a hypothesis.

"I'd make up my mind myself whether or not to keep it, before telling him anything, because if the man's married it's most likely he'll want you to get rid of it. Especially if he already has children."

Rafaela sat up abruptly on the couch. She looked at me.

"How do you know he has children?"

"No," I said, keeping my cool, "it's just a guess. Married men have children."

"Oh, okay."

I swallowed my saliva. I had to be more careful not to put my foot in it. Fortunately she was so engrossed in her story that a moment later she'd forgotten all about it.

"Do you think I have to decide alone?" she said, caressing the screen of her cell phone. "I guess it depends, because if he's also in love, as he's told me so many times, he's bound to be happy about it. It would have been nice to receive the news together."

"Only you can know that," I said.

Still looking up at the ceiling, she took another sip of her Cuba Libre and said:

"He was the one who came looking for me and from the

start he behaved very well, like a real gentleman. Things between us happened very quickly, and I was like, really surprised to see that the weeks went by and he kept calling me, and then he started taking me with him when he had to travel. We went to Lima, Mexico, Panama. I love traveling with him."

She paused for a moment, took a sip from her glass and continued.

"I'd had a boyfriend for six years, but at that time I was very confused and had asked him for a break, time to think: that's why I was free when I met him. When my boyfriend came back and said, Rafi, darling, how much longer are you going to think? I didn't know what to do because I was already into the other guy, so I said to him: look, I don't want to continue, you're a terrific person and I love you, but no, do you understand me? He begged me, cried. He asked me if there was someone else, and of course, you never say that, especially not in a case like mine, so I said again, no, you don't understand, I'm going through a big change right now, I'm not ruling it out in the future, Jimmy, that was his name, so don't be too upset, relax for now, all right? I have to go through this alone. I prefer you not to be around because I don't want you to suffer, I love you too much for that, and I respect you too much, do you understand me? He didn't understand a damned thing obviously, but I got him off my back after three boxes of Kleenex. When he left my place, I forgot him after two minutes, and you know what the hardest part was? Changing the fucking favorites on my cell phone!"

We laughed. She wasn't as stressed now as she had been.

"Look, if you want my advice, I'd say don't keep it," I said. "Don't bring something like that into your relationship, because as far as I can see your relationship isn't about making a home together but about being boyfriend and girlfriend, traveling and having fun. He's with you because he wants to recapture his youth, and that's fine. Take it easy, take it for what it is, and if it continues you'll know. How many women end up alone and with kids because the man gets scared off? You're young, and having a child is a big burden to carry for the rest of your life."

The drizzle turned into a downpour, and there were some violent claps of thunder. The sky, at eleven in the morning, grew dark. Rafaela made a gesture of pride, but said nothing. She grabbed the telephone again, nervously.

"I don't think you've quite understood what my relationship with him is like," she said. "We go out together, we have a great time, like all couples. But the fact that he's older and married doesn't change a thing, because I'm not going with him just to pass the time. I left my long-term boyfriend and I have an idea of my future."

She stood up and went to get more ice. Then a huge amount of rum and a little Coca-Cola. Things were getting complicated.

"I'll tell you what I'm going to do," she said. "I'm going to send him a message telling him. I bet you he answers within half an hour! That way you'll see our relationship isn't just a fling."

She opened her messages and started to give rapid little taps on the screen. It seemed to me that she was demonstrating something to herself. Araceli and her husband were in Paris, and for a moment I imagined the bomb that was about to fall on them. Fortunately, Araceli had stopped asking about Rafaela.

Rafaela gave a last tap with her thumb and said, that's it, it's sent. She showed it to me. The message said: "I have to talk to you urgently. I had the test and I'm pregnant."

Then she said:

"Shall we synchronize watches? It's eleven forty. I assure you he'll answer before twelve noon. And I'm not going to look at my phone again."

"All right," I said, "but let's talk about something else because otherwise you're going to go crazy."

We spent the time drinking and watching a news bulletin. I couldn't stop thinking about Araceli and praying that the guy didn't get the message. This strange drama, that I was the only one to know all the ins and outs of, even though it wasn't mine, had finally gained the upper hand.

My other life, the real one, was in a green notebook on the table. Every now and again I looked at it. My poetry was in there, and that was the only thing that mattered, the one thing that shielded me from all this nonsense.

When twelve o'clock came, Rafaela said, "I'm going to give that idiot another ten minutes before I take a look."

She seemed uncertain. She stood up and walked a little dizzily over to pour herself another drink. I went to the kitchen and brought a plate with peanuts and potato chips. At last she made up her mind and grabbed her cell phone, but when she switched it on she turned pale. There were no messages, and what was worse, from what she said, he'd apparently already read hers. She lay back down on the couch, crying.

"The bastard! He read it and he hasn't replied?"

I tried to calm her, telling her that maybe he was in a meeting, that there could be a thousand reasons.

"If he really loves me, he should have called by now."

"Look at the calls, you did turn the volume down . . . "

She crucified me with her eyes.

I suggested we go somewhere for lunch, because I didn't have any food at home. We went down onto the street and walked as far as a hamburger joint, but she said, no, no way, let's go somewhere nice. It's on me. We took a taxi and went to a French restaurant. They gave us a table on the second floor and she asked for the wine list. To Rafaela, what was happening was inconceivable; whenever she looked at her phone her eyes filled with tears.

The food we asked for was really delicious and, in my opinion, overpriced. She seemed to need it. Suddenly her phone rang. She gave a gesture of surprise, happy and expectant, but when she looked at the screen her eyes darkened again. It was her mother. She answered and said quickly: Mother, I'm sorry, I forgot to tell you I'm not going to lunch with you, all right, bye.

By the time we finished lunch we were already very drunk, and we decided to split the check. Since I didn't have any cash, I took out Araceli's card. Rafaela took out another from Bancolombia and she confessed to me that he had given it to her in case she needed anything.

Both of us getting drunk on their accounts!

Rafaela wanted to continue the party in some bar, but I said no. I said I had to go to the library to consult some documents for an assignment, so she called another friend and left, very nervous and stressed, with the idea of continuing until nightfall. She was completely drunk. I made her promise she would call if he answered or there was any other news.

I returned home, went to bed, and practically didn't leave it again until Monday, to go to class. Rafaela didn't call again and the days passed. I felt a profound disgust with everything that had happened, but I couldn't see a way out. Why is my world so small? I asked myself, and just at that moment the TV screen showed a globe, and a voice said: "The world is in your hands, dare to enjoy it."

I started fantasizing about leaving the country. I had nothing to lose. I'd realized that I would always be alone. The one person who had looked into my heart was Araceli, but thinking about this thing with Rafaela and her fling with Araceli's husband, an intuition told me that it was going to end soon. Something was about to break.

I gave up being happy in return for a little peace and quiet. I spent hours looking at the map of the world on my computer screen, repeating the names of distant cities, considering borders and countries. Where could I be safe? Accepting that I wasn't trying to be happy or to regain my innocence, a great weight fell from my shoulders.

The day before Araceli came back, I had a call from Rafaela. She told me that the guy had finally replied, ten days later!

"And what did he tell you?"

"The bastard wants me to wait, and he'll take care of everything. But then he really stabbed me in the back. You know what the son of a bitch asked me? If I'm sure it's his! What the hell does he think I am? a call girl?"

Rafaela wasn't crying anymore, now she was offended. Her eyes vomited hatred. I asked her what she planned to do.

"He'll be here tomorrow and I'm going to make him pay, the bastard. What do you think of that, huh? I mean, like I was fucking a dozen guys."

"Did you tell him you'd left your boyfriend?"

"Of course, he knows that perfectly well!"

She took a deep breath and said, shaking with anger:

"You were right, I should have decided what I was going to do about the baby before I told him, but how was I to know he was going to be such a bastard? If you could see him when he asks me for it, he gets down on all fours and lifts his tail, like a little dog. The fucking bastard! I'm already making inquiries about terminating the pregnancy. When I do that, will you come with me?"

I said I would, and that she should inform me if there were any changes.

Araceli arrived the next day but we couldn't see each other until the end of the week. She said she and her husband were still at it like a couple of teenagers, that's why she hadn't come earlier.

"The only reason I was able to come today is that he had to

go to a ranch in El Sisga for a meeting with one of the managers of a project."

She gave me lots of hugs, squeezing me as if I were a cuddly toy.

"My darling! It's such joy to see you when I'm so happy," she said, "how have you been all this time?"

I told her about my reading and how I'd been working frantically on a book of poems.

"I've also been writing, sweetheart," she said, "sit down, I'd like to read you some of my new poems."

She read a series of odes and jolly verses that, to be honest, made me want to throw up. Hearing her, I came to a simple conclusion: anyone who's really happy had better keep away from poetry, or be very careful with it. Then she asked with great interest about what I'd done, so I went to fetch my green notebook and showed it to her. We had already served ourselves a couple of malt whiskeys that she had brought from England, plus, Doctor, I forgot to tell you that she also gave me a sweater, a summer dress, and some pairs of semitransparent panties, very erotic and elegant.

Araceli started reading my notebook, at first skimming through, and then very engrossed. Every now and again she'd raise her eyes and look at me as if to say, very good, and continue reading.

"This is wonderful," she said, "do you have a project in mind?"

I said no, it was just the result of some difficult days, things I'd written very roughly, by hand; the notebook was part of something that might be bigger, but I wasn't yet clear what it might be. I'd thought to let it mature for a while, I said, I hadn't even copied it onto the computer.

She hugged and kissed me with great tenderness. She wanted me to put on the clothes she had brought me, especially the erotic panties, and we went to bed. We fucked, and it was great, but she struck me as strange. Her body wasn't responding in the same old way.

I got up to go to the bathroom and I saw that I had a message from Rafaela saying: "I'm with him in El Sisga, on a beautiful ranch. I'm making him eat dirt, because of the way he behaved. We're talking a lot about our pregnancy. I'll tell you about it." In another message, she sent a photograph of the two of them naked on a wicker couch. Under the image, she wrote: "This one I took in secret, with the camera pointed at the mirror, while he was fucking me, you can see he really loves me, can't you? He's already told me so in every way possible."

I hid the telephone. I was scared that in a moment of carelessness Araceli might try to look at it, the way she did with her husband's phone. Although she seemed very calm. She didn't even ask me about Rafaela.

We drank, made love a while longer, and even took a few pills. Around nine o'clock she got dressed and said she had to go. I saw her to the door. Before she went out, she asked me to lend her the notebook with the poems.

"I want to read it again more carefully, darling, you've written some really beautiful things," she said. "Maybe I can help you find a structure. I have a few ideas, I think it's about time other people knew about you."

I handed it over to her and gave her a kiss.

"Take it and let me know."

The final exams arrived and I finished the semester with good grades, Doctor, and then something happened that made me reconsider the ideas I had about life and what it had in store for me.

One afternoon, the head of the department called me to his office to tell me that he had the possibility of recommending someone for a scholarship in Spain to study literature and linguistics. He had thought of me and wanted to know if I was interested.

"Good," Cristo Rafael said, "I'll put your name down as a candidate and let's keep our fingers crossed."

I left the office walking on air.

I felt so happy that I wanted to share it with someone and I sent a message to Araceli, but she didn't reply, so I continued walking along Seventh, alone, surrounded by traffic and people. I suddenly felt as if I was seeing all of this for the last time, and Bogotá, this inhospitable town that I was already starting to love, was transformed into something different. A city of prisoners.

I looked at the telephone and there was no message from Araceli. I told myself I was worse than Rafaela, obsessed with text messages, and I thought to call her. She replied immediately.

"Hi," Rafaela said, "everything okay?"

"I have to tell you something, where are you?" I said.

After a while she appeared in a taxi. She picked me up and we went to a cafe on Avenida Chile.

"They already did the scrape," she said, "in a clinic in the north; it was really very easy, it was the best thing. It's a kind of surgical abortion. It was hard, but it had to be done. You were right. Starting out in life with a child on your back is stupid. What man will want to get involved with you? We talked about it a few times and he said he'd never agree to keep it. He's reconciled with his wife and sees things differently. I thanked him for his honesty and took off after the operation."

"And what happened with him? Aren't you seeing him anymore?"

"Obviously he'd like that because he wants to fuck me, but as far as I'm concerned it's all dead and gone. I'd like to turn over a new leaf and go back to leading a normal life."

"So you're not in love with him anymore?"

"No, and it's his fault. He really made me eat shit and you don't do that to a girl like me. In the long run it was better, because I was really hooked on him. I had such withdrawal symptoms that I even considered getting back together with Jimmy! Except that . . . can I tell you something?"

"Go on."

"The poor guy took it so badly when I left him that he went downhill and started taking amphetamines and drinking. The break hit him hard but it also helped him, because one day, God knows what he was on at the time, he ended up in bed with another guy and something went click in his head. And now Jimmy's bisexual, although more gay than straight. He even has a boyfriend!"

I found it incredible that so many things could have happened in her life in such a short time. Barely three weeks!

Well, in mine, too.

Life is an incredible series of ups and downs. Now Rafaela and I were the abandoned ones, and that was fine. The sensible thing was for Araceli to be with her man, at least until the next crisis, and it occurred to me that I wouldn't be there when she experienced it. I hoped to be a long way away.

In the end I didn't tell Rafaela about the scholarship, seeing that she never even asked me why I'd called her. She took it for granted that our chats should always naturally be about her and her problems. She was young, pretty, and rich. I'd known for some time now that my life was going to be solitary. We each have our own destiny.

July came and, with it, the longed-for call from Cristo Rafael.

"Manuelita, are you holding onto something?" he said. "The papers have just arrived from Spain, they've awarded you the scholarship!"

I was struck dumb, I couldn't say a word.

"Come to my office, we'll sign and get everything ready."

I received the notification and signed that I accepted. I filled out a form with all the required information. In a few days they would e-mail me the scanned documents for requesting a visa. They gave me the tickets, the registration, a room in a university residence, and eight hundred euros a month, including the vacation months.

I left Cristo's office and started walking up Seventh. That seemed to be my therapy. The city was no longer far away, but transparent. A city of musty glass that I could see against the light. At last I was leaving.

I called Araceli and left her a message. I wanted to tell her everything and give her back the bank card. She answered at around ten at night and said, darling, that's wonderful news! You deserve it, you'll be like a shooting star!

I told her I wanted to give her back the bank card and arrange about the apartment.

"Don't worry about that, darling, that's a minor matter. Continue using it until you leave, all right? Listen, I have to go because I'm at a dinner. A big hug, darling, and congratulations. I'll call you tomorrow."

Then I called Gloria Isabel in Cali. I told her the news and she gave a cry.

"Oh, how proud and happy you've made me."

I promised to visit her before I left. I couldn't wait to leave, because I didn't actually have anything particular to do during the vacation.

Three weeks later, more or less, I bought a ticket for Cali. I chose some trifles to take Gloria Isabel as gifts, and while I was waiting to board at the airport, going for a stroll and looking at the stores, I stopped in the bookstore. I passed my eyes over the spines of the books, opened a few, and read a couple of lines, until on the table of new releases I saw a new book by Araceli.

Songs of the Equinox, Araceli Cielo.

I felt quite excited. On the back cover was a quote from someone saying that with this collection, Araceli had "taken a new, forceful, and unerring step toward a poetic understanding of life." How come she hadn't told me anything? I assumed she'd been about to call me, occupied with everything that the publication of a book entailed. They must be the poems about her journey to Europe and I thought to myself, how corny they were! If she's published them, I hope she's done some work on them.

They were just announcing boarding when I got to the gate and hurried onto the plane. Once I'd settled in my seat, I took the plastic wrapper off the book and read the first poem. Then the second and the third. I looked at the opening lines of the others and glanced through them . . .

I started crying.

I couldn't believe it.

They were my poems! My green notebook!

She'd made a few small changes: changed a few names, removed a few verses. I remembered the day she'd taken my notebook away with her. Araceli had known it was my only copy and now it would be my word, the word of an unknown provincial, against the word of a famous poet, a member of high society.

I felt as if I'd been raped for the second time. Brutally raped. But this time I was the one who'd opened the door and surrendered everything. This was the price I'd paid for all her kindness to me. What could I do now? Who was going to believe these poems were mine?

When I got to Cali I went to the bathroom in the airport, threw water over my face, and recovered. I didn't want Gloria Isabel to notice anything. Vanessa had been allowed out of the clinic, so we spent the three days together. We went and ate *cholados* in Perro Park, watched a soccer match on TV— América de Cali was playing, and although it never got out of second gear it was still the team we all loved; on Sunday, I was invited to a club called Los Farallones and stuffed myself with fried plantains washed down with lulo juice; I did what tourists do, because this was my farewell. When would I return to Cali? I thought, looking at the city.

Perhaps never.

Every now and again I'd think about Araceli's book and feel as if I'd been kicked in the stomach and couldn't breathe. They were my poems! The words with which I'd somehow managed to tame my past, that sad wretched life I'd been forced to live. Was that what she'd wanted to steal? My anger was eating away at me, and the second night things got worse, because I found a number of reviews on the Internet, all very favorable, as well as interviews with Araceli in which she spoke with great self-confidence about my poems, as if they were hers, explaining them with a faraway look in her eyes, evoking mysteries and sufferings that she had never experienced.

I cried and cried, but this time with rage. With a sense of being powerless, too, because I couldn't do anything.

I went back to Bogotá and concentrated on preparations for the journey. I already had the papers and the ticket. I just had to wait for the date. Cristo Rafael gave me the contact numbers of some friends of his and recommended some things I should see in Madrid.

The day before the journey I went to a restaurant and had dinner on my own. It was my farewell. I didn't try to call Araceli, nor did she call me, even though she knew the date. It was understandable. The following day, before closing the door on the apartment, I left the bank card on the table. I handed the key over to the doorman and asked for a taxi.

In the airport I walked nervously up and down. I checked in my bags and headed for the international departure lounge. It was full of emotional people taking photographs of each other. Families saying goodbye to their children. I, on the other hand, was alone, but my strength derived from having nothing. I passed through the middle of this tearful crowd and felt strong again, as if I were the first living being to get up and walk after a great conflagration.

Go to hell, all of you! I thought.

Drug traffickers, rapists, murderers, thieves . . . Stay here with your damned fake god, in your country of blood and shit.

I'm leaving forever.

On the plane I thought once again about Araceli and in a fit of anger I grabbed my cell phone, the same one she had given me. I looked for Rafaela's photographs and found the one from El Sisga. It had the date and the hour, plus the text saying: "I'm with him in El Sisga, on a beautiful ranch. I'm making him eat dirt, because of the way he behaved. We're talking a lot about our pregnancy. I'll tell you about it."

And then the photograph of the two of them naked on a wicker couch, with the caption:

"This one I took in secret, with the camera pointed at the mirror, while he was fucking me, you can see he really loves me, can't you? He's already told me so in every way possible."

I pressed Forward and looked for Araceli's number. Before forwarding, I wrote her a laconic farewell. "Thank you for your help. I left the bank card on the table in the apartment and the keys with the doorman. Congratulations on your new book, which I've just read. I read the reviews, too. You're a great artist. Goodbye."

The message was sent with the photographs and Rafaela's texts attached. This was my last gift to her.

That's what I thought.

Then the plane taxied along the runway and when it eventually took off I felt quite dizzy. Rising through the clouds and plunging into the dark, murky sky, away from that country that had hurt me so much, I realized that at last I was free. And that's how I ended up in Madrid, Doctor. And the rest, my life here, you already know.

Thank you for reading this.

19

A lthough this happened in Paris—modern, cosmopolitan Paris—Europe at the end of the nineteenth century was a straitlaced, intolerant world. The strange, almost marital bond between these two men, who apart from anything else were of widely different ages, was hard to swallow for everyone, even poets.

Even half a century later.

Rimbaud's principal biographer, Enid Starkie, whom I admire so much, uses terms like "sodomite" to refer to Verlaine, and describes the nights on Rue Campagne-Première as "orgies." She also says of Verlaine that he is "weak and depraved," and in mentioning the scandal in Paris speaks of "the most monstrous immorality" (the quotation marks are mine, not hers). Of course, Starkie was writing in the 1940s, not all that long after the events, and she was an Irish Catholic.

The situation is so embarrassing for some critics that, out of admiration for Rimbaud and Verlaine, they have opted to deny it. As if accepting their homosexuality would detract from their genius. But to claim that their relationship was not romantic and sexual is like trying to blot out the sun with one finger, since even among their contemporaries it was common knowledge. Starkie herself quotes a report on the first night of a play by Coppée in which another writer, Lepelletier, a friend of Verlaine's, wrote the following:

Among the men of letters present at Coppée's first night

*was the poet Paul Verlaine, on the arm of an enchanting
young lady, Mademoiselle Rimbaud.*

There is also the divorce of Mathilde and Paul, which was
dealt with expeditiously on the basis of Madame Verlaine
accusing the poet of "ill treatment," something we will examine in detail further on. Mathilde had in her possession at least
forty letters from Rimbaud to Verlaine in which everything was
so obvious that she preferred to destroy them rather than ever
let them fall into the hands of her son Georges. There is, in
addition, a curious medical test performed on Verlaine in
Brussels in 1873, after his imprisonment for the attempted
murder of Rimbaud. In the report, the doctors claim that they
"observed on his person recent signs of active and passive
sodomy." What can this be referring to? One of Verlaine's
biographers, a man named Porché, disagreed with the medical
report and wrote the following:

> *The observations that may have been made of the defor-
> mations of the* virgula viri *and the* antrum amoris *have no
> value as evidence today from a medical or legal point of view.*

The easiest thing, when it comes down to it, is to look at the
poems. Verlaine wrote in "The good disciple" the following:

> *You, the
> Jealous one who beckoned to me, here I am, here is all of me!
> Toward you I crawl, unworthy!—
> Climb on my back and plunge in!*

As for Rimbaud, there is the section of *A Season in Hell* entitled "The Foolish Virgin/The Infernal Bridegroom," the first of
the *Deliriums*, which describes the sufferings of a relationship
and which, as far as Starkie is concerned, leaves no room for

doubt. Anyway, does it matter whether or not we have conclusive proof of the kind of relationship that united them? We should be content with the poetry they left and the slight aftershock of those other poems we know existed but which have been lost, as is the case with "La Chasse spirituelle", which Rimbaud entrusted to Verlaine and which Mathilde probably destroyed along with his correspondence.

Oh, Mathilde. Posterity, which still reads Rimbaud today, understands your anger. How could you know the incredible value of what you threw on the fire? How can we blame you when in fact the history of poetry, and of all literature, is full of small incidents, manuscripts burned, lost, or stolen, or even worse: young poets or novelists who died after having a glimpse of something brilliant that would never again be seen? Literature is at once what existed and what no longer exists, what might have existed and what was has not yet been written.

By the end of 1871, Verlaine was madly in love with Rimbaud. That love was a mixture of two things: admiration, a great deal of admiration, for the young man from Charleville, but also a desire to assert his own talent and his art. Arthur considered him a great poet, but at the same time told him it was ridiculous to see him subjected to such pointless tribulations as having to think about a wife and child or leading a bourgeois life like that of any ordinary person. Poetry was a fluke of human oligarchy and the poet an aristocrat. That is why daily life is futile and the poet who surrenders to it is merely a puppet. This is what Rimbaud told Verlaine.

Before Rimbaud's arrival in Paris, Verlaine not only aspired to recognition, but above all to respectability, which is the worst enemy of any artist. Rimbaud hated all that and Verlaine let himself be won over. Talent was incompatible with the obligations of a good husband and father. Arthur, in his construction of what a poet should be, was coping with the absence of his own father, and it was Verlaine who paid for the smashed plates, since in spite of the difference in age it was the younger man who called the shots, the one who imposed the way the two of them were to live.

Is there a better or more appropriate way of life for a poet? The twentieth century would give many examples of this idea, some supporting it, others refuting it. Is the poetry of someone who lives a "poet's life," in Rimbaud's words, better? Some were obedient functionaries or submissive husbands. Kafka, who wrote the best literature of the twentieth century, was an obedient citizen. Any life can lead to literature, by the most convoluted and unexpected paths. "Literature is the sad path that takes us everywhere," wrote Breton. And not only that: in addition, it welcomes everyone, without an entrance test or letters of recommendation. Only what each person carries in his folder.

But let us return to that Paris of 1871.

Mathilde relates that when her husband came home at night, she felt terrified, and that just from hearing his steps on the stairs she already knew if he was drunk or not. Once, Paul tried to burn her hair and then slapped her. Another night, he punched her and broke her lip, but the worst episode was when he tore the child from her arms and threw him against the wall. "I'm going to put an end to this once and for all!" he cried in his drunken rage, and the baby was only saved thanks to the blankets in which he was wrapped. Then he tried to strangle her. Alerted by the screams, his father-in-law came into the room and put an end to the fight.

The next day Verlaine begged for mercy, got down on his knees before his son and implored his in-laws to forgive him, arguing that he had been out of his head on alcohol. Mathilde pardoned him once again and hoped that things might improve, but only on condition that the devil-poet leave Paris and go back to Charleville. Maddened by guilt, Paul accepted and went to beg Arthur to return to his hometown. What a scene! Rimbaud in a rage and Verlaine imploring him. What promises could he have made for the young man, unable to understand anything that did not coincide with his desires, to go back to Charleville? What could he have said for him to accept the unacceptable? Rimbaud did indeed return to Charleville. But Verlaine did not keep his promise to break with him. Quite the contrary: his love became ever more of a pressing need.

During this time, Rimbaud wrote him dozens of letters, sending them to a temporary address. Messages full of lyricism, crazy ideas, nostalgia. Verlaine asked him for time: he promised that in a couple of weeks he would settle the problem of his family and then he would be free. In a letter from May 1872, Verlaine assured him that soon they would be together and would never again be parted, and this, for the implacable young man, incapable of forgiving or being won over, had the taste of victory.

This is where we come to one of the most incredible and tragic legends concerning young Arthur, or even French poetry in general. It is the story of a poem entitled "La Chasse spirituelle" ("The Spiritual Hunt"). According to Verlaine, it was the best thing Rimbaud ever wrote, which is tantamount to saying that it was one of the greatest poems in Western literature, but unfortunately, it disappeared.

How could something like that have happened?

Rimbaud had returned to Charleville, a bitter, ignominious return. He had been expelled from that arrogant city, Paris, the very city he had planned to conquer. He was seventeen years old, and of course would have preferred to return with a medal of some kind. We see his feelings of unease in the mournful, pessimistic poems he wrote at this time, populated with images of flight and contempt, metaphors for solitude and exile.

Meanwhile, in Paris, Verlaine was in hell. Everything

seemed to him dull and meaningless. The life he had promised his wife Mathilde wounded him constantly. He felt humiliated and he missed Arthur. He loved him. In one of his letters he begs: "Write to me and tell me what my duties are and what life you think we must live." He longed for the freedom that Rimbaud inspired in him, as well as the intense pleasure of self-destruction that only the younger man could give him. He needed to see him soon. He suggested another address where Rimbaud could write to him without any risk of being discovered, and when he could no longer stand it he sent him money and begged him to come back.

Rimbaud returned in May 1872.

He settled in a room on Rue Monsieur Le Prince, and then in the Hôtel de Cluny on Rue Victor-Cousin. For both men, it was like emerging from a sarcophagus: the drinking bouts resumed, as did the poetic and philosophical discussions—and the mood swings. It is believed that it was during these frenzied days that Rimbaud wrote most of the poems that Verlaine would later publish under the title *Illuminations*. It was a prodigious summer for his poetry, and in that state of euphoria he had written "The Spiritual Hunt", which Verlaine read early in July 1872.

Rimbaud and Verlaine left for Belgium on July 7, and the poem remained in Paris, together with other papers that Verlaine had in his family home. That is why the poem disappeared. The strange thing is that Verlaine should have left it behind when he considered it so valuable. What were the circumstances of that flight to Belgium? It was somewhat improvised and almost fortuitous, like so many things in the lives of these two poor lovers. It was Rimbaud who gave Verlaine the idea on seeing him leave his in-laws' house that morning. He approached him on the street and said: "Let's get out of here now!"

Verlaine had gone out to buy some medicines for his wife,

and told him so, but Rimbaud exclaimed: "Let her go to hell!" Verlaine did not need much persuading, and so it was that they took a train north, to Arras, near the border with Belgium. Verlaine went in the clothes he was standing up in, which was unusual for him. At some point, he must have thought about the letters and poems he had left at home, and may have told Arthur. "Leave it all there, it's better not to take anything from that damned place," the younger man must have said to him. "Let's go now and forever." It may also be that when Verlaine said, "what about your poems?" Rimbaud replied: "My poems are inside me, let's go."

And so "The Spiritual Hunt", of which there was no copy, was lost forever.

This is speculation, of course. But we can still dream that one day, in a forgotten drawer somewhere in the world, the correspondence and the poems may be found, and we will be able to read "The Spiritual Hunt". The final reference to it is in a letter Verlaine sent from London in which he asks for help in recovering the papers he had left in his father-in-law's house. He indicates that "The Spiritual Hunt" was "in a separate envelope."

The story of what happened next, when Mathilde found out that her husband had fled with Rimbaud, demonstrates how far she was prepared to go to save her marriage.

Let us examine the facts.

Seeing that time was passing and Paul had not returned from the pharmacy, Mathilde started to worry. Of course a voice in her head warned her: the little devil has something to do with it! But first she thought that something serious might have happened to him, so she visited hospitals, police stations, and morgues, all to no avail. How anxious she must have felt and how afraid that the very thing she so dreaded was actually happening!

A few days later, she received a message from Paul, its tone one of guilt. He told her that he was in Brussels with Rimbaud, and he begged her not to cry. In an outburst of pride, Mathilde said to herself: "I have to free my husband from the spell of that provincial Satan." She told her mother, and the two women decided to go into action. They planned their strategy. It is not known how they discovered his whereabouts, but what is certain is that they found the hotel where the two poets were staying in Brussels, made a reservation, and set off. On arriving, Mathilde announced herself to her husband and arranged to meet him in her room. When Verlaine entered, he found her lying on the bed, naked and perfumed.

It is likely, in fact almost certain, that Verlaine was very drunk, so without thinking twice he threw himself on her. They made passionate love. In a much later poem, Verlaine describes the embraces and laughter, the many kisses. Once it was over, in a fit of remorse, Paul confessed to her the truth about his relationship with Rimbaud (which she had already assumed). Nevertheless, he swore that he would return with her to Paris.

Poor Paul Verlaine, a frail canoe caught between two hurricanes! His two lovers were breaking down his will. The spell of one dissipated somewhat under the influence of the other. Mathilde, still naked and damp with sweat, whispered in his ear that after they got back to Paris they would go on a long journey together, very far from France. She mentioned New Caledonia. Her father would give them the money and her mother would look after the baby in their absence. A second honeymoon. Verlaine, playing with her pink nipples, running his fingers through her abundant pubic hair, let himself be swayed by these images, he dreamed of remote places and the poems he could write in those ports, watching savage dawns rise over the ocean.

There, perhaps, lay the cure for his uncertainties.

"Yes, of course, *ma chérie*," he said. "We'll go to New Caledonia together and we'll be happy."

And what of Mathilde's mother? Fully aware of the ruse, she must have been close by, huddled in some café or in another room, waiting for a sign. Perhaps she was spying through a crack and telling herself: silence is a good omen. Silence the procurer, the accomplice. She'll know how to convince him. He's a man and he'll respond to what she brings him.

But on the way to the railroad station, Verlaine began to wake from the spell and told them that before leaving he would like to say goodbye to Rimbaud. He swore he would join them in time to catch the train. Careful! The women heard these words with dismay, but Verlaine managed to persuade them and he left, nervous and inflamed.

When it was time for departure, with the train already puffing on the track, the women waited anxiously. Mathilde scanned the crowd from the running board of the railroad car. There's Paul! he's come back! she cried. Yes, he had kept his promise, but he was no longer the same person. Far from it. He was very drunk and avoided Mathilde's eyes. Getting on the train, he sat down in his place without paying any attention to what they were saying to him, muttering through his teeth. The train left and the women heaved a sigh of relief. For now, the battle was won.

When they reached the French border, the passengers had to go through customs, which forced them to get out and go to an office of the gendarmerie. Once this was over, Verlaine refused to get back on the train. He slipped away amid the bustle and when the women finally saw him, standing there motionless, they yelled at him to get on, but he did not move. Then the train pulled out and he watched impassively as they left, without making the slightest gesture.

That image was the last that Mathilde had of her husband. She never saw him again. As if it were a trivial matter, two days later Paul sent her a message insulting her: "I'm back together with Rimbaud, if he still wants to know me after the betrayal you forced me to commit."

And so she returned to Paris, finally alone. Consumed with grief, hatred, and jealousy.

But let us go back to the poem "The Spiritual Hunt".

If Rimbaud had written it in Charleville, three people might have read it, since he was in the habit of making fair copies of his work with the help of his friend Delahaye. But it is strange that Delahaye does not mention it, even though he was his first biographer. The other person, apart from Verlaine, might have been Mathilde herself, if it is true that she took the trouble to read the correspondence and sniff around in her husband's papers before destroying them. This is very possible; in fact she found various documents that helped her in her divorce petition.

It isn't hard to imagine the scene: Mathilde, filled with hate, alone and knowing that Paul was getting drunk and fornicating with the young devil, goes into Verlaine's study and, without making any noise, embarrassed at the thought of being caught by her parents, starts to open drawers, searching through the chest of drawers, the bookcase, the *secrétaire*; spying in silence, opening sealed notebooks, trying not to wake the baby in the next room. The silence of the night makes the pain more intense, the anger and jealousy more urgent. The night is a bad counsellor, and so, when she finally finds something tangible, she avidly reads these words she has been looking for, these words she prefers to see written down so that they might stop echoing in her head. She wants to put an end to that noise and there they are, there they are! She reads them again and again, in floods of tears, managing to blot out the noise.

She finds the young man's letters, yes, and she tells herself that at least they aren't her husband's, but she can imagine them, too, bathed as she is in tears of pain. Where did she go wrong? She thinks of her son and fears that one day he may read them, and she imagines the torment if she doesn't do something. She has to destroy them, to make sure they do not exist in the same world in which she wanted to be happy with him, and so, little by little, she throws the letters and papers in the fire. It is legitimate to think that "The Spiritual Hunt" took a fleeting step into the world: it was written, read with admiration and hatred by its three sole readers, and then returned to nothingness.

"The Spiritual Hunt" is thus the great nonexistent poem. The work of genius that may return one day. Such was the life of the vagabond poet, the *clochard* of letters named Rimbaud, which is why it is reasonable to ask, how many other poems disappeared? The *Illuminations* were about to meet a similar fate. Verlaine mentions them for the first time in a letter from August 1878. It seems clear today that this collection of poems—we do not know if Rimbaud conceived them as a book—only survived oblivion thanks to him. What the biographers do not know is the reason they were in the possession, not of Verlaine, but of his brother-in-law Charles de Sivry. Why? It is a mystery. The fact remains that in a letter, Verlaine tells Charles that he has read them again and will very soon return the manuscript to him. Later, he asks for it again, but to no avail.

The letters of Verlaine in which he tries to get the *Illuminations* back continue until September 1, 1884. At last, after a series of bizarre and very mysterious changes of ownership, the *Illuminations* are published in 1886 in a poetry review called *La Vogue*, edited by Gustave Kahn.

The poems were published from the fifth to the ninth issues of that year. After the ninth issue, it was announced that they would continue, but in the following issue nothing appeared. Months later, another five appeared, and at the end of that same year Verlaine himself published the first edition of the

Illuminations in book form, with an introduction by himself in which he says, among other things:

"Arthur Rimbaud is from a solid middle-class family in Charleville (Ardennes), where he was an excellent if somewhat undisciplined student. By the age of seventeen, he had already written the most beautiful verses in the world, from which not long ago I gave an extract in a little book entitled *The Cursed Poets*. He must be thirty-six by now and is traveling through Asia, where he deals in works of art. He is like the Faust of the Second *Faust*, a brilliant engineer after having been Mephistopheles' great poet and the blonde Marguerite's lord and master!

It has often been said that he is dead. Of that we have no details, but if it were true it would sadden us greatly. May he know that, if it is the case that nothing has happened to him! I was his friend and from a distance I continue to be so."

There has been a great deal of juicy theorizing about the chronology of the collections. Biographers and critics have become entangled in debate, supporting or refuting one another on the basis of the tiniest details. You could write a novel with these characters, who seem not so much critics as self-appointed guardians of Rimbaud. Some actually knew him. One of them is Paterne Berrinchon, who in 1912 published a *Complete Works* that was the basis of later twentieth-century editions. His authority comes from having been Arthur's brother-in-law, the husband of Isabelle, the youngest of the Rimbauds and her brother's favorite. This volume had an introduction by Paul Claudel, who claims to have recovered his religious faith on reading the *Illuminations*.

According to Starkie and Delahaye, the *Illuminations* date from 1872 and 1873, although Starkie goes farther and asserts that they were written over a slightly longer period, perhaps extending into 1874, since the poems reflect very different states of mind. The "Starkie theory" is that in 1874 Rimbaud decided to make a fair copy of the *Illuminations* in order to publish them, and entrusted them to Verlaine at the end of February 1875, when they met in Stuttgart. Verlaine himself says that they were written between 1873 and 1875, when Rimbaud was travelling through Europe. This theory has the support of Bouillon de Lacoste, another critic and Rimbaud scholar. Graphologists who have had access to the manuscripts assert that he wrote them in 1874, in London. But for Lacoste, the poem "Dawn" in the *Illuminations* can only date from 1875, including as it does a word in German, *wasserfall*, which, according to him, Rimbaud could only have learned during his trip to Stuttgart in 1875. Starkie counters this by saying that if Rimbaud had learned the word in Germany he would have written it correctly, in other words, with a capital letter, as it should be written in German. Lacoste also refers to the line "You are still close to the temptation of Antony," claiming he could only have written it after reading Flaubert's novel *The Temptation of Saint Anthony*, which was published in 1874. Starkie points out that Flaubert was not the only writer to treat the theme of St. Anthony, and that in any case fragments of the novel had been circulating since 1857.

Two more Rimbaud sleuths, De Graaf and Adam, in an article published in the *Revue des Sciences Humaines* in October 1950, assert that the *Illuminations* were written from 1878 to 1879. One of their arguments is that the expression *"les pays poivrés"* (lands of spices), in the poem "Democracy", can only refer to Java, which Rimbaud became familiar with during those years.

20

After the *Theory of Mutilated Bodies* operation, I moved to Spain. Here, the Far Right was closer to my ideas because it wasn't obsessed with race, like that in Germany. Yes, there had been the idea of a Spanish nation of pure and uncontaminated blood since Don Fadrique, but in practice it was only a concept, since the Spanish are very mixed and it's not easy to decree the purity of the blood without leaving out three quarters of the population, do you follow me? You can talk all you like about pure blood, you have to adapt. Queen Isabel and King Ferdinand already had that idea of purity, but ever since that time things have not been at all easy. They expelled the Moors and the Jews, which was fine, but the Moors had been living there for seven hundred years, which means they were Spanish, with descendants, and the Jews . . . They arrived in Spain before Christ was crucified! Can you imagine how mixed they were?

Not long ago, the diaries of a very interesting character from the Third Reich came to light: Alfred Rosenberg, author of the second most important book of Nazi doctrine, *The Myth of the Twentieth Century*. When he talks about Spain, Rosenberg says that Franco "preferred to turn a blind eye to the subject of anti-Semitism, out of respect for his Moroccan Jews, or because he still does not understand that Judaism is taking its revenge on Isabel and Ferdinand."

What did I tell you?

Compared with the Social Democrats or the Left, the

government of Franco was racist, but compared with the Nazis it wasn't anti-Semitic at all, which is understandable, how can you get rid of a third of your own blood? That's what happened in Spain and it's why I decided to come here, where my ideas might be better understood.

And anyway, I was getting to know the most interesting groups, and I actually encountered something very different. The subject of World War II isn't such a big thing! Franco, who was quite screwed up, sent fifty thousand Falangist volunteers to fight with Hitler in Russia, but it was his way of getting rid of a group of radicals who were stepping on his toes. Did you know that here in Spain the Fascists are called "Falangists"? Curious name, *falange*, isn't it? It means the joints of the fingers. Anyway, go read any of the novels about what they call "historical memory" and you'll understand, although you have to get to know them.

Soon after I arrived in Spain I chose Primo de Rivera, the founder of the Spanish Falange, as my point of departure. From his founding speech I took two quotations:

"Let the political parties disappear. Nobody was ever born a member of a political party; on the other hand, we are all born members of a family; we are all neighbors in a municipality; we all struggle in the exercise of a job . . . "

And the second:

"If our objectives have in some cases to be achieved by violence, then let us not hesitate before violence. [...] Dialectic is good as a first instrument of communication, but there is no more acceptable dialectic than the dialectic of fists and guns when there is an offense to justice and the Fatherland."

When I read this for the first time, it made me jump with

excitement. I realized I had found something tangible, something based in reality and not in romantic theories about tradition, which was what pissed me off a little about the guys in
Berlin. These people had their feet on the ground, I thought,
so I devoted myself to following them and understanding what
they were doing. Theirs was an eminently political struggle
against Communism and its various metamorphoses, because
the Communists were opposed to the Fatherland, which was
the most sacred thing, and that's why they had to be fought.
The other thing about the Falangists that struck me as good
was their embrace of religion; you know I'm not a believer, but
great political ideas have to be combined with great spiritual
propositions, whatever they are, otherwise they don't work.
Look at today. Without a spiritual dimension, politics has
turned into a satellite of economics and statistics.

In Spain, the unity between Fatherland and spirituality
through religion has been very natural. For God and Spain!
they used to say. The Generalísimo and the Bishop of Burgos
and the Church in Andalusia and in Galicia went hand in
hand, in procession, with the generals and the Falange and the
Civil Guard. Franco kept on his night table a piece of the thigh
bone of St. John of the Cross, and had himself called the
Caudillo, an appellation that's both religious and heroic.

When I arrived in Madrid these groups had been deci-
mated and had lost all their prestige. After three decades of
democracy, it was no time for heroic projects or great exploits.
People had other things on their minds. Prosperity changed
the Spanish, not that I knew them before, but I've read a lot
and I know that the Spaniard had a peasant or provincial
spirit, which was more restrained and austere, more cautious.
But once they joined Europe, people said, dammit, we're
Europeans now! and they caught the consumer bug. They not
only wanted to be rich, they wanted to be seen as rich, and not
only modern, but aggressively modern, and so the country

filled up with fashionable and glamorous boutiques and people started going to restaurants not just to eat but to be seen in such and such a place, and the thing you have to remember is that this is when they forgot all about Latin America. They turned their backs on us because they felt rich and European, why should they look south, to countries with political and economic problems? Spain, our Spanish brother, replaced us with a dish of goodies from Europe, which gave it money to feel beautiful and shiny, and to believe that now at last the future they'd long been waiting for was coming. And what they told us was more or less this:

"Bye-bye, poor cousins, *arrivederci*, *au revoir*, see you in the future, when you stop being small fry and can sit down at our marble table with its silk tablecloth. This is the exclusive banquet of modernity and civilization! We'll follow your lives from a cautious distance and if you need anything let us know and we'll send it to you, there's everything here so don't be too shy to ask, okay?"

That's what the newly rich Spanish seemed to be saying to a Latin American community that was stewing in its own spicy sauce. And when they went to our countries, do you remember how they arrived at the airport? Like John Wayne sitting on his horse, looking through binoculars. When they turned on the faucet to clean their teeth, they thought twice about it, did these bastards have drinkable water? In restaurants they felt uncomfortable: have they washed the lettuce with mineral water? And then they threw themselves headlong at the women, as you know, because they took it for granted that any Latin American woman was ready to kiss the hairy ass of a Spaniard in return for a promise of papers. The sad thing is that for many of them, it worked.

With things like this happening, do you think anyone was going to listen to a message of national dignity and unity? Of course not! I observed it all from a distance, because when it comes down to it what was happening in Spain was secondary. My concern is Latin America.

My rejection of democracy was growing, with increasingly good arguments and with a deeper understanding of the processes that it hides: a mockery of people, cynicism, the desire to seize control of the public purse. In a future Arcadia, in a society of fully educated and reasonable people, democracy will be the best system for living together. But not in a world like ours. Here, democracy is a process of decay, in which weakness leads to anarchy.

Look at the extreme case: Africa. Do you really believe that, just because there are elections in Africa, we can talk about democracy? In countries like Kenya or Rwanda or Burundi, people vote for the candidate of their tribe and that's why those with the largest numbers always win. What's the only way to correct this injustice? We've already seen it, the solution is to reduce the rival tribe's electoral numbers with machetes, as happened in Rwanda. Do you think the blacks are stupid?

Or take Latin America: there, it's not a question of tribes, but of financial interest. The political parties don't exist anymore, they're just power groupings; nobody believes anymore in ideas about how society should be. Or rather, those who still believe in something are either scattered in tiny parties or they're the weak part of large, already formed parties. Look at your country. There, the people who vote are something like a third of the population, am I right? And many sell their votes for fifty thousand pesos. That means that with twenty million dollars you can get yourself elected mayor, where you'll handle enormous budgets, and that's why to get into power you have to play dirty if you want to recover your investment, otherwise what kind of business would it be?

The politics I support is the work of an enlightened minority with a vision of the future, a minority that agrees to take on the task of leading the others, the great masses: those whose lights are broken or dim and who, because of the circumstances of life, don't have sufficient education to understand what the hell a community is or anything about the *res publicae*. The leader is a great father who guides with affection but can be merciless toward betrayal or laziness or theft. An energetic father who leads his children along the thorny road of life, that's what the world lacks! And such a person, begging your pardon, never emerges from a democratic process.

It moves me when a nation rises, believing in a leader strongly enough to follow him through a storm. He is a visionary who looks into the future, like the blind man in the story my father told my mother the day he met her, in that defunct Hotel Contemporáneo: someone who shows the way, sets the pace, even if that pace leads to death, it doesn't matter, you have to follow even knowing that deep down it's pointless because all that awaits us is death, but that's the fate of everything that lives and it's why we have to keep up the pace and believe, as if we weren't going to die, and it's there, are you following me? it's there that politics becomes a great art.

There is a kind of violence that I call *visionary* and that can only be exercised when we have ideals. In our future Republic the man who deceives the weak and takes advantage of other people's ignorance for his own ends, whether political or financial, will receive the death penalty!

The man who is caught using for his own good what the State placed in his custody will be sentenced to death!

The man who takes the power the State has conferred on him because of his abilities and uses it to obtain personal favors of any kind will be sentenced to death!

To serve the State will be the supreme dignity to which anyone can aspire, and that's why whoever does so must be a worshipper of the good, an altruist of the present and the future. A mystic. Someone who can also honor the vision granted by symbols, the prophetic word, the future.

That will be the great requirement of our future functionaries, a mixture of *illuminati* and legionaries, ready to die for the supreme ideal that is the greatness of the Republic, however lowly their position.

Forgive me, I've started talking to you as if I were at a meeting, I'm sorry, but I'm going to tell you something that you may like, Consul, something I repeat in my speeches:

In our Republic the works of Shakespeare will be obligatory. In them, you find all that is noblest and most profound: honor, dignity, and the ancient values of the human condition struggling against ambition, betrayal, deception, and envy. And the most serious one: ignorance, which is the mother of all evils.

Years ago I established relations with communities in Latin America and the United States. I've traveled and there's a solid network that's growing, more in some countries than in others. That's normal. In yours, everything's fine and we're strong. We're expecting things to work out. There are young leaders who aren't known yet, but believe me, they'll emerge when the time comes. People with a mystique.

Anyway, enough of that, let me continue with my life story.

When my father was elected Pope I was in a psychiatric hospital. I'd had a terrible crisis. I was on my way home, walking along Calle Fuencarral, when suddenly I knew with complete certainty that on the next corner and on all the others I had to pass, there were enemies waiting for me with saws, and one with a scalpel. They were planning to cut off my arms and take out my liver and one of my kidneys, so I stopped dead and hid in the doorway of a store.

That's how the illness is, you simply can't do anything. If my neurons were better I might be able to avoid it, but that's not the case. My masters decided to use madness to communicate, and what can I do against that? Nothing.

I was sent to the clinic just as they were about to make my father Pope. They strapped me down, they gave me hypnotic drugs, because the problem of those enemies was transferred to the corridors of the hospital: I saw them there, I heard them, I watched out for their shadows. They were behind the pillars, behind the curtains. They were waiting for me to sleep in order to perform amputations on me.

I was always a docile patient. My psychotic episodes didn't involve what in clinical terms is called "cognitive loss." In spite of the panic attacks and the hallucinations, I remained clear-headed, and of course, how could I not? My schizophrenia had a specific destination: a confessional on the other side of con-sciousness. And what was it my masters told me this time? If I were like the shepherd children of Fatima, I would go down in history recounting these conversations, but that's not the way it is. In addition to words I see sparks, glimmers of meaning.

As if the future were opening up my eyes. Suddenly a win-dow opened and I was able to contemplate what was to come. That's when I found out that the cardinals of the Vatican were going to elect my father, and that I had to prepare myself to return to my region and fight for it.

The words of my masters were: "You have to protect your land, even with more violence." And also this: "Follow your father, but not by the hand, since he cannot give it to you."

And a last one: "You will know when to do so, when the time comes to return."

Well, Consul, now I've told you almost everything. Do you still have any doubts?

21

Returning from the morning's therapies, with Pedro Ndongo pushing my wheelchair, I found the priest Ferdinand Palacios in the room. He was lying on his bed, holding up his Bible. As soon as he saw me he frowned and said:

"Quite a beating you got, isn't it? How's the other fellow? Or were you run over by a truck?"

I told him what had happened.

"Oh, yes, it's a sacred rule. You should never get involved in domestic quarrels, because in the end the two of them gang up on you. Well, may God help you with that. Thank heaven the other man didn't die because then things might have gotten out of hand. I'm going to pray for it to be resolved, did you hear that, my son?"

Pedro helped me back into bed and secured the handcuffs. I felt tired after the therapy and closed my eyes. The priest drew the curtain and devoted himself to his Bible.

"Rest, man, you're badly hurt," he said.

"Don't you also hurt, Father? With those bandages."

"Don't worry, other things hurt me. We'll talk about that when you're feeling better. Rest, there'll be plenty of time."

In the following three days he talked endlessly, as if he had been waiting years to do so. A dark (sometimes grim) torrent of words poured out of his mouth. That's how I learned his incredible story. Perhaps he was looking to confess, or to leave his mark on someone. I followed the advice of Pedro Ndongo and tried to memorize what he said.

He also wanted to know who I was, so, in an incoherent way, I told him a few details of my life.

When talking about your own life, the greatest temptation is to cop out and invent a different one. Or to talk about that lost *other* that still survives in us.

I told him I had written several novels and a couple of travel books. I had lived in a number of countries and had a whole series of occupations, namely: mechanic in Paris, student on a scholarship from the Institute of Latin American Cooperation in Madrid, correspondent and radio journalist in France, consul and cultural attaché in India, first secretary in the Colombian delegation to UNESCO.

I've traveled through Europe, Africa, Asia, and America, but dream about the Pacific islands. More than anything else, I'd like to spend time in Tonga.

I'm still a writer, I told him, although the literary world, as I had known it when I started out, has hit the skids. Almost nobody buys books anymore and as a last straw, the crisis has imposed a cruel Darwinism. It's not only the survival of the fittest, it's the survival of the most *versatile*. Some of us have taken a crash course in *versatility*, but without great results. What to do when the atmosphere in which we grew, whose air governed our intellectual metabolism, has abruptly disappeared? It's become necessary to gamble with life, believe in something, and try to survive. Like in those war movies, where in the ruins of a city after a violent bombardment something stirs amid the rubble and we see a line of tattered figures emerge. Dirty, badly wounded, but with their hearts clean and uncontaminated. Inside them there is something that protects them as they walk, perhaps to the top of a hill or even to death, with the free, confident pace of those who have lost everything. I've dreamed of being one of them. Not those who arrive unscathed from on high, but those who get up from the dust and walk, against all hope.

My antidote, I told him, was to evoke that young man of nineteen who dreamed of writing books and who is still alive inside me. But perhaps it's already too late. When the last reader dies, I added, that young writer will most likely be scribbling away in some ramshackle hotel, not knowing that nothing has a meaning anymore. I might be my own last reader, I told him. There's a kind of dignity in continuing to do things that nobody is interested in and nobody celebrates.

What else to tell?

I spent a happy childhood thanks to the books of the English writer Enid Blyton. I think I read the whole series of the Famous Five and the Secret Seven. Jules Verne and Salgari were favorites, too. At the age of eleven I read Oscar Wilde's *The Nightingale and the Rose* and Kafka's *Letter to My Father,* which I enjoyed even though my own father was good to me. I ventured into more complex territories until one day, just to emulate my older brother, I read *One Hundred Years of Solitude*. That was the start of my adult life.

At the age of twenty, I left home and went around the world reading Rimbaud. His books were always on the night tables of hotels, pensions, and hostels, before I continued my journey. I'm still reading him today, since the more I've tried to write about people who leave and return, about that flow of migrants I see circulating around the busy, noisy world, the more I feel the presence of the poet of escape, the man who turned leaving into one of the fine arts. The poet who abandoned everything and kept postponing his return, going farther every time, first to the East, like Lord Jim, and then to Africa.

Rimbaud and the art of fugue.

That, in broad terms, is what I told Ferdinand Palacios, with the slight suspicion that it was I myself who wanted to hear my own version of that life I had left outside, that life that now seemed remote. And it's quite likely that when Palacios told me the story of his life in Aguacatal, a town in the Urabá Antioquia region, in great detail, he was doing the same thing, talking to himself in order to continue believing in something, clinging to his own words as if to a burning bush. When it comes down to it, we are all hungry for something to protect us, however remote and invisible. The only thing we can do is tell stories and believe that one day we will be saved by them.

Two or three days went by. The unsatisfactory hours of calm, that cruel, monstrous mass, which is what time is when you have absolutely nothing to do. All the same, I managed to establish a certain routine. Pedro Ndongo, my friendly nurse and guard, kept me informed about what was happening in the Irish embassy siege, which had already ended its first week amid tough negotiations, and that's the reason weary voices were calling for an attack by special forces, whatever the price, to set an example. The family members of the hostages, who had gathered in Madrid, begged for calm. They feared for their loved ones.

One afternoon Pedro told me we had to go for a special checkup. I left my notebook on the table and, with effort, moved from the bed to the wheelchair.

Once out in the corridor, he said:

"There's no checkup, friend, I just wanted to give you two pieces of news. Both good: the first is that Francis Reading has at last opened his eyes. He's recovering very well."

I tried to hug Pedro, but felt a stabbing pain in my ribs.

"And the second?" I said.

"The second is quite incredible: Reading's wife has decided not to press charges against you and instead is asking her husband for a divorce! It's because of the Colombian girl. He himself confessed to her."

I felt free. It was as if the world had started turning again after a horrible stutter.

"Does that mean I can go?"

"No, not yet," Pedro said, "the judge still has to rule on a sanction for 'disturbing the peace.'"

"And in the meantime, do I still have to be handcuffed to the bed?"

"No, that's finished with. Today they'll be transferring you to another room in the hospital. And there's another thing, I almost forgot."

"Today must be my lucky day, what is it?"

"You have a visitor."

My heart skipped a beat.

"Juana Manrique?"

"No, it's the Colombian girl who hit you. She's waiting in the visiting room, do you want me to take you there?"

I recognized her from a distance. She was wearing faded jeans, sandals, and a white blouse. Seeing me, she lifted her hand to her face. My appearance was still upsetting. She came toward me, and almost got down on her knees.

"Oh, my God, look at you!"

When she recovered, she held out her hand and introduced herself.

"My name is Manuela Beltrán," she said, "how sad having to meet you like this."

She apologized for the blow. She said she'd gotten scared and hadn't known what to do.

"Don't worry, it was a bad night for everyone. I hear your friend is better?"

"Friend?" Manuela said. "No way."

"I gather he's your teacher."

"Really? How did you hear that?"

"We're sick and we can't move, all we can do is talk."

"Paco suffered a contusion from the blow you gave him. They operated on him to prevent a brain hemorrhage and possible lesions. From what I've been told, the coma was induced. After the operation they decided to wake him."

She was silent for a moment, squeezed her chin with one hand, then said:

"I came to apologize to you."

I was unable to suppress a smile.

"The blow you gave me wasn't the worst. I'm already recovering. I'm glad your friend is all right, that way we'll have fewer problems."

"He started the fight, you were trying to defend me."

"Yes, but I hit him so hard I almost killed him."

"Accidentally."

"So why did you hit me?"

Manuela did something childlike: she smiled even as her eyes expressed anguish.

"I didn't think. I had no idea who you were. When I saw Paco on the ground, bleeding and with his head cracked, I went crazy."

"Your friend's wife has withdrawn the charges."

"I really meant my apology," Manuela said.

"The main thing is to have done with it."

"I also want to thank you," she added shyly, "after all, you did it for me. If you'd been at another table nothing would have happened."

"I don't think I'll get to see your friend," I said, "but tell him from me that I'm really sorry for what happened."

Manuela's eyes filled with tears.

"It was Paco's fault and that's why I don't want to see him. He hit me in the face, in front of everyone. I was wrong about him."

"Are you in love with him?"

Manuela dried her eyes with the sleeve of her blouse. "I don't know, I was never sure," she said, "but something like that, I suppose."

"You'll get over it."

"Now that his wife has left him, he's asking that we try again. But someone who raised his hand like that dies forever."

"Was it the first time he'd hit you?"

"No, but never as hard as that. He's jealous, and he goes off the rails when he's tense. Two months ago we went to a university conference in Seville. He was nervous because he was going to meet with a specialist in medieval literature. Nobody there was supposed to know that we were together. He's my teacher and I couldn't go with him to a lot of the meetings, so I started to go out and explore the city. One evening some students invited me for a few beers and I spent a while with them, while he finished up. When I got back to the hotel he was waiting for me. He was furious. He yelled at me that I was a whore, who had I been with, I stank of men. He hit me, although without closing his hand. I ran out and went down to reception, and when he saw that I was going to make a scene, he calmed down. He started crying, he got down on his knees and begged me to forgive him. He's a fragile person."

"Are you studying literature?"

"Yes, at the Complutense. Actually, literature and linguistics; the name of the course is Hispanic Philology."

I felt a small shock.

"Really? That's exactly what I studied, also at the Complutense. Thirty years ago."

"I'd heard of you before," she said. "I've read your work. It's a bit weird telling you this now, in this situation. When I think that I smashed a chair on your head, I feel like throwing myself out the window. How could I have known who you were?"

"Fortunately, not all my readers act that way."

At last, she laughed.

Just then, Pedro Ndongo arrived, tapping his wrist with his finger. It was time to go back to my room. We had a couple of therapies. I said goodbye to Manuela and thanked her for her visit.

"I'd like to see you again, may I?"

I nodded, and she took out a card written in biro.

"These are my details, in case you leave here before I come back."

"I'll be here for a few more days. Then I'll be going to the Hotel de las Letras, on the Gran Vía."

"I hope you get better soon. And once again, my apologies."

We went along the corridor to one of the elevators and Pedro said to me:

"She's sincere, my friend. I don't know what she said to you, but you must believe her. I can recognize sincerity in people. Was she the one who hit you with a stool?"

"Yes," I said.

"Then it's a good thing she has such soft slim arms. Otherwise you'd be dead."

"She's Colombian," I said.

"Really? I swear I have to check out your country. Do they treat black people well there?"

"If they have money and a European passport, very well. If not, very badly. And if they're Colombian, worse still, unless they have money."

We reached the fifth floor, which was mine, and I noticed that Pedro was taking the longest route. I thanked him. There wasn't any therapy to attend.

"How's your roommate?"

"He insisted on telling me his life story, which turned out to be quite complicated. There were some very delicate things, I don't know why he told me. What do you know about his situation?"

Reaching my door, he went right past it. We would take another turn around the corridors, just to be able to talk.

"He's waiting for an exchange of legal files, but for now he's staying here. I only hope you took my advice."

"What advice?"

"To memorize," Pedro said.

That was exactly what I'd done.

When we finally got back to the room, the priest wasn't there. I collected my things and Pedro took me to another part of the hospital, on the third floor of the right wing. The new room looked out on a grove of trees with a parking lot in the middle.

"I'll come and say goodbye before you go," Pedro said.

I squeezed his hand.

"Thanks for your advice. Memorize. Now can I have a pencil?"

"Take my pen, I'll ask for another one in the office. Now rest."

When I was alone, I took out my notebook and started writing what I had stored in my memory. I wanted to put Ferdinand Palacios's strange story down on paper, so I started immediately. I don't know if he would have accepted this version. I like to think he would.

I'm in prison for involvement with the paramilitaries in the west of Antioquia province, but nobody can prove a thing, and even if they could what I say is this: only God can judge me. I'm a priest and in the last analysis it's only God to whom I must explain myself, because it was He who entrusted me with that task.

I sought refuge when I saw that in Colombia everyone ended up allied with the Communists. Decent people simply had to leave! Not that I admire Spain, not a bit of it. How can I admire a country where fags can marry and adopt children? And they say the government is conservative. Conservative, my ass.

They really got me with this little story, didn't they?

I don't feel any guilt because I served my fatherland and the Lord and what I had to do was on their behalf. It was a mess, and sometimes it was cruel, I don't deny it, but it has to be understood in a wider context: the struggle between Good and Evil.

It was a hard-fought battle, full of cruelty and unfair things. I wasn't the one who invented it. And as happens in all wars, anyone who wasn't there is unable to understand it and is simply judging those who actually had the balls to wage it.

Are you one of those who believe that the soldiers of the Devil go about in black uniforms, with horns and a shield on their chests that says Battalion of Lucifer? Don't think me so stupid. Those who give aid to the Communists go about as peasants, because most are Indians or country people, but also as factory workers and clerks, cooks and mechanics, volunteers for European NGOs and journalists, even members of the Congress, and of course students. Even presidents!

That's what happened in Colombia, neither more nor less.

Wherever we look there's nothing left but garbage. Most of our universities are foul brothels; instead of respecting God and their country, what young people learn there is to take drugs and offend the Lord and become Communists. That's already sufficient reason to leave this lousy world. Wasn't that what He did to his own children, Adam and Eve, His finest creation, when He saw they had disobeyed him? He kicked them out.

For me the fatherland was Aguacatal, a little town of a few thousand souls, halfway between Frontino and Dabeiba, do you know it? Everyone recognizes the name but nobody has been there, that's why they don't understand the things that go on there and the things we had to do to save it. My world was that little pinnacle. We are each given a little piece of this mysterious paradise, don't you think? I'm a priest, an educated man, but deep down I'm still just a peasant.

I was born in Santa Fe de Antioquia and when I heard the call I entered the Conciliar Seminary in Medellín. I was a studious novice, devoted to the mysteries of faith and obedience. I grew up seeing how subversion, corruption, and terrorism were dragging our country down. After God, Colombia and above all Antioquia are what I love the most. Do you believe that the Lord created those beautiful mountains, those skies, those tropical plants, and those birds with their colored plumage, that He made the hummingbirds and the butterflies, the seas and the snow-capped peaks, the rivers and the trees, only to hand it all over to the Communists and let them turn it into a sewer, a brothel, a discotheque for dopeheads and faggots? No, my friend. The Jews already killed Jesus once but they developed a taste for it: they want to continue killing him over and over again.

I arrived in Aguacatal at the end of the nineties, after having been in the diocese of Manrique and Santa Clara in Medellín. I myself asked to be transferred to a conflict zone. I did so when the Metropolitan Archbishop came to me and said:

"Ferdinand, you've finished your training here, now you have to go out and defend the Church, in the name of the archdiocese."

And that's what I did. To fight for God and to save this country from the Communists.

As I told you, Aguacatal is a town in the mountains, in Urabá de Antioquia. It stole my heart, if I can put it that way. If you could only see our church! An impressive blue and white church facing the square. The day I settled there I was overjoyed.

But you can't imagine what it's like to turn up to give mass one Sunday and find the church empty! Not a single widow, or old pensioner, not even a stupid Indian. Nobody! The central nave with the lights on, the flowers in the vases, the deacon and the altar boys in their vestments, nobody knowing what to do.

But I lost my temper and said, we're here to celebrate mass, dammit, because it's Sunday, and I went up into the pulpit and began prayers. In the name of the Father, the Son, and the Holy Spirit. The altar boys and the deacon responded: Amen.

I saw the empty pews and summoned my strength to continue with the reading of the sermon, looking at the cross and the wall fresco depicting the Resurrection.

At one point a boy put his head in the door. He looked astonished and went out again. I later learned that he had run through the streets crying: the priest is giving mass in an empty church!

The guerrillas had kidnapped my predecessor and in a

skirmish with the army he'd been wounded. Right now, he was in a hospital in Medellín, trying to recover mobility in a leg and an arm. Thank God he wasn't killed, which was what they started to do later when they ran into patrols: kill the hostages before engaging with the troops.

This was when I arrived. The priest wounded and the people terrified. That was the state of things to which the Lord led me in Aguacatal, beggars can't be choosers! But I tell it as it is, and I don't run away from things. The first thing I did, after that empty mass, was to go to the barracks and speak with the lieutenant, a young man of twenty-eight called Wilson Urrelo, who had been serving for barely six months. His predecessor had also been kidnapped, and hadn't been so lucky: one day he was found floating in the River Gualí, with his stomach ripped open. That's why Lieutenant Urrelo was taking things easy. I understood the danger, but I was angry with him: as if defending the people and protecting the church meant getting into trouble. I went to the barracks and when I arrived I saw they were being rebuilt. The front wall had bullet holes. It looked like a sieve. In back they had thrown bombs and gas canisters filled with screws. The only things still standing were the front wall and the side walls, can you imagine that?

Father, what a pleasure to meet you, Urrelo said, I haven't had time to visit the clergy house because as you can see, we're snowed under with work.

I see that, Lieutenant, I said, but for this work you don't need uniforms or rifles. You're policemen, not laborers, with all due respect, how can it be that nobody comes to mass because they're afraid of the guerrillas?

Urrelo looked at me irritably.

You see, Father, he said, you've just arrived and don't know how things are. The truth is that the guerrillas have us surrounded and if anything happens the Fourth Brigade won't even get here in time before we're all killed. We're waiting for reinforcements from headquarters. If I provoke them, the only thing that'll happen is that they'll kill the eleven officers I have, and I need them to rebuild the barracks. For now, that's all I can do.

How angry I felt hearing Urrelo! This was the enemies' work. Let them come!

The following weeks I spent going to see storekeepers, businessmen, ranchers. I realized that the guerrillas had them all over a barrel: they extorted money from them, kidnapped their relatives, took their cattle. I'd heard about self-defense groups in other parts of Antioquia and Córdoba. Decent people united in the battle.

I myself talked to some ranchers who already knew about these groups and were anxious to start one here, giving not only money, but men, ammunition, and weapons. Whatever they were asked for. The only thing they lacked was a contact and someone to organize them. That was me. In other towns in Antioquia, self-defense groups had been cleaning up the mountains for years, so it was about time.

Soon afterwards I managed to contact a priest in Yarumal, where they had been very well organized for some years now, and the good priest, whose name I don't remember, agreed to meet me in Medellín, in the cafeteria of the archdiocese. There, I told him what was happening in Aguacatal, and he said, look, I'm going to inform the people in Yarumal about the interest you have, to see if we can send you someone, so that at least you can start to organize. Just to show support, what's the name of that lieutenant? He wrote the name down in a little notebook and said, good, I'm sure he'll cooperate with us. We have to stay within the law, don't we?

A month later someone came from Yarumal and we held the meeting in the clergy house in order not to arouse suspicion, because the guerrillas had a number of informers near the barracks. Why deny it: half the town was with them. I invited some local landowners, among them the biggest of all, Don Alirio Vélez and Dr. Paredes White. A man named Piedrahíta came from Yarumal and told us about what they did there and asked us to call Lieutenant Urrelo. They'd already spoken with him and he was in agreement, because the head of the barracks in Yarumal knew him. A few minutes later he arrived in his neatly ironed uniform, and said, I'm sorry, Father, to come in here carrying a weapon, but I can't leave it anywhere. Don't worry, Lieutenant, on the contrary, I said, weapons are what we need to protect this town, aren't they?

The storekeepers gave money so that some men could come with Piedrahíta. Don Alirio and Dr. Paredes White said that training camps could be set up on their ranches. Meetings would be held in the clergy house and on Don Alirio's estate, Gaviotas. Some of the workers formed the first group and Urrelo offered to train them. The next thing to do, according to those from Yarumal, was to start with a list of people who were mixed up in it, whether they were Communists, trade unionists, or just gave aid to the guerrillas.

We got down to work. Some people had started coming to the church, especially to confession. I remember a young worker from a sugarcane factory. I questioned him without his realizing it, saying, do you feel bad about anything you've done or seen, anything that's bad? and he said, no, Father, I haven't seen bad things but I have seen people who live differently, and I said, oh, yes? and how do they live? and he said, in the mountains, Father, they have a different way of understanding life, sometimes they do things they shouldn't, but it's for an ideal, they want to help and perhaps they take the wrong path, and I asked him, how do you know them? and he said, because sometimes they come down to my farm and ask for water, they ask about things in the town, they stay for a while and then go, they don't steal my hens and they don't ask for money, but they do say they're fighting for me, so that my family can live better,

Father, they aren't bad people, and then, when the young man had gone, I took out my notebook and wrote down, Vladimir Suárez, and so, one by one, I compiled a list of twelve people who helped the guerrillas.

I took it to the first meeting and Don Alirio appeared with another list of trade unionists who were agitating on the ranches and another of idlers and dopeheads. With all that, the boys got down to work.

As it happened, the first person was the young man who had come to confession with me. Don Alirio's boys took him from his house at night, with a bag over his head, and on the road to El Alto they shot him three times. They left him outside the factory with a notice around his neck: "Helper of the guerrillas, enemy of the country."

I remember how nervous we were the next day, waiting for the guerrillas' reaction, but nothing happened, so we went on to another fellow, a trade unionist. That case was more complicated because his wife started screaming and one of the boys got nervous and shot her in front of her children, which was horrible.

They took the guy to Don Alirio's ranch and questioned him. At first he played tough and they had to soften him up with pliers until he said something, although he didn't say much. They also shot him three times and threw him in a ditch just outside town.

The people started to hear about it, and so did the guerrillas. Every night the boys took out two or three pieces of scum, most of them dopeheads and addicts. I continued questioning people and passing the information to barracks. Urrelo passed it on to the boys and bang bang. Goodbye, heartache. That's what our war was like. And suddenly the church filled up again, the congregation felt safe and returned.

Until something awful happened, which is that the guerrillas kidnapped one of Dr. Paredes White's children, Tomás, who was twenty-one. During the kidnapping there was a shootout and three bodyguards were killed. According to an eyewitness, Tomás was wounded when they took him away. That night, we met at Gaviotas. This was the guerillas' response and it showed that they were well informed. The war was starting and we had to be prepared.

Among the reinforcements sent by the people in Yarumal was a guy from Cali, Freddy Otálora, who scared even me. The kind who oozes death from his fingertips. We were told he had to hide because of a problem with the law and that he was a terrific fighter. He'd been in the Army's jungle troops and knew all about counterinsurgency. He was good at laying ambushes and especially at interrogating suspects.

Dr. Paredes White was in pieces. He swore that if anything happened to his son he would kill every guerrilla in the country with his own hands.

I understand how you feel, I said to him, your son's a soldier and I'm going to pray for him.

We're going to have to get God involved, Father, he said, because I'm quite capable of burning those fucking mountains if necessary.

Finally a plan was established. Lieutenant Urrelo suggested working on the minor go-betweens, grabbing them and interrogating them until they gave details of encampments and routes. Something like that kidnapping couldn't have been planned without the help of people in the town. We had to be very careful, and he said to me, Father, you're the one who can be the most use to us, people talk to you without reservation and nobody connects you with us.

In those towns in Antioquia the peasants are very Catholic, even if they're helpers or friends of the Communists. That's why the pulpit became a battlefront. I continued my questioning until one afternoon what we were hoping for came to pass: a good woman, a seamstress in a dress factory, confessed that her son, who worked in the café at the gas station on the road to Mutatá, hated the Paredes White family because he had been a laborer on their ranch and they had kicked him out because one day he fell asleep and arrived late and another day he showed up drunk. She'd always known that his hatred would lead him to do something stupid, and so the woman said, Father, I'm afraid my boy had something to do with the kidnapping of young Tomás, and I'm going to burst if I don't tell someone, because I can't sleep anymore! At least I can tell you, so that you can give me relief, and I said to her, you did the right thing, everything serves to understand the nature of the human soul, God is on your side. I blessed her and, when it was over, I ran to the clergy house to call Urrelo.

I have the first one, I said, this one's for certain, the son of Doña So and So, but don't grab him today in order not to arouse suspicion.

They waited two days and then went for him. They took him to Gaviotas and handed him over to that guy from Cali, that Freddy, and after just a few slaps the guy confessed: he'd given information about young Paredes White's movements and security; Freddy grabbed a machete, laid his finger on the table, and said: you have twenty seconds to tell us who you gave that information to or I'll cut this finger and go on to the next one. The boy gave up the names.

They turned out to be a worker in a sawmill and the owner of a roadside store.

Things were going well. They saved the young man's life for that night and locked him in a cellar that not even a snake could have gotten out of. He only had space to change position.

Dr. Paredes White had preferred not to be present because he said, I'll kill him, and if I kill him we won't get anything from him. Wilson arranged to go for the guys that same night.

And that's what they did, but they only managed to grab the

guy who owned the store and there was a problem because he was armed and defended himself. We had our first casualty, a good young man, a hard worker, named Farhid. It was a blow to us. There wasn't much they could have done. The terrorist had a submachine gun and mowed him down as soon as he went in.

It happened in the Espergesia motel, on the road going east, the guy was drinking rum and offending the Lord with a lady who also had to be taken away, and who turned out to be a hooker. I interceded to stop them killing her, because she had two babies, and we kept her under guard for a while, until the matter was settled. The bandit's name was Demóstenes and he was badly wounded, with three shots in the stomach. They treated him so that he could talk, but he didn't say much. He said they'd taken Tomas to Dabeiba, he didn't know where exactly, and even though Freddy put pressure on his wounds that's all he said. Then they took him to a ditch and there they shot him three times and buried him on the spot.

The next day everyone was nervous. The news of Demóstenes's disappearance spread through the town and people started saying he'd been taken by FARC. "The boys are getting angry," people said, so Wilson decided to halt operations and rely on intelligence. Demóstenes's wife went to the barracks to report her husband's kidnapping, and the officer who took her statement and made her sign it was the same one who'd shot him three times in the back of the neck the previous night. That's what this damned war was like.

Another day, Wilson called me to say: Father, be careful, the mother of the first young man told us that the only person she'd talked to about her son before he disappeared was you, so you need to take care, she may have told the guerillas the same thing. Don Aurelio sent two men to guard the clergy house and gave me a revolver, but I wasn't scared. How could I be scared? You may think a priest with a gun is a strange thing. But the archangels were militiamen, haven't you seen them in paintings, with swords, harquebuses, and spears? You have to adapt to the times. If Jesus were alive today, he'd be on our side. He'd be wearing a camouflage jacket and tramping the roads at night, looking to take out Communists.

With the kidnapping of young Tomás Paredes, other small landowners who hadn't wanted to cooperate until now made up their minds. They saw that the thing was getting serious and that a line was being drawn in the sand.

After three months the guerrillas sent a communication to the doctor in which they proposed exchanging Tomás for a group of people who had disappeared, and they appended a list of seven names. The doctor, Don Alirio, Wilson, and I analyzed it, and there was one big problem: they were all pushing up daisies!

In spite of that, we decided to answer yes, and asked for proof that Tomás was still alive. We waited for the call with tracking equipment, but the sons of bitches knew all about that and managed not to let themselves be traced.

With the help of the other landowners things were progressing well. Now we had two hundred well-armed boys, committed to serving their country and God's justice. This group started searching, making use of intelligence. They combed the mountains and gradually got a foothold.

One day Dr. Paredes White said to Lieutenant Urrelo, look, Wilson, don't attempt any rescue operation without my consent, these guys are dangerous. Before any attack I want to see what the conditions are like, I don't want him to get killed. And Wilson replied, don't worry, Doctor, you're the boss, we're clear about that. What we're doing is securing some areas and advancing into others, to see if we can find out where they have him. But you give the orders.

Time passed, and then one day Wilson called and said, Father, something terrible has happened . . . They've killed Tomás Paredes! Can I come to the clergy house?

Of course, I said, what a tragedy! Come here as quickly as you can and tell me all about it.

There had been something of an accident. A group of our people was out on reconnaissance and suddenly a guerrilla squad appeared. There were more of our boys and they were eager, so they opened fire on them, and when it was over they found nine bodies. When they checked in order to send them to the brigade they found that one of them was young Tomás Paredes. The sons of bitches had put him in camouflage gear! We don't know if the bullets he has in him are theirs or ours, they could be either, what a mess, don't you think? They're already on their way to Gaviotas with the bodies. They'll get there in the early hours of the morning. I don't know how to tell the doctor, Father.

God above, I said to Wilson, what a tragedy!

I went into the church and fell to my knees. Lord, give me some advice, a light, how can I say what cannot be said? Sometimes your ways are like deep caverns, and even I get lost in them.

I stayed there on my knees until six in the evening, I cried, and pulled myself together. Then I called Wilson and said, look, pick me up from the back door and we'll go see the doctor, let's just let it out without telling him in advance, that's best, because if I call him he's going to get ideas and then it'll be worse. I also gave instructions about what the boys should do before bringing Tomás's body.

I went to the clergy house and took a bottle of aguardiente from the closet. Not that I'm a drinker, but I'm a peasant, I like the taste, and then and there I had three glasses, and even a fourth. When Wilson arrived, I said to him, let's go.

We drove through Aguacatal. The good thing is that the barracks jeep has polarized windows and you can't see who's inside. I kept praying to God: put the right words in my mouth.

The headlights of the jeep illumined the paved surface of

the main road, then a dirt road. When we got to the gate the guards recognized Urrelo and let us pass, raising two fingers. After a while, the lights of the house appeared, on top of a low hill. I recognized the doctor from a distance, waiting in the corridor. He was smoking a small cigar, but when we got out he threw it on the ground and crushed it with the sole of his boot.

Good evening, Father. Lieutenant, good evening. What in God's name brings you here?

Let's go to your office, Doctor, I said, and have a few glasses of aguardiente.

He looked at me in surprise and said, yes, Father, right away.

At last, God, through the mediation of St. Escrivá, put the right words in my head and I said to him, Doctor, I've come to tell you something very sad, the lieutenant here told me about it a while ago.

Is there news of Tomasito? the doctor asked.

Our men encountered a squad of the guerrillas, I said, and had to confront them. After a long combat, the bandits retreated and on the path they found various bodies. Among them was Don Tomasito . . .

The doctor knocked back his aguardiente in one go and gritted his teeth. Tears welled in his eyes. I hugged him and we stayed like that for a few seconds that seemed to me an eternity. Your son fought like a hero, Doctor, I said, isn't that so, Wilson?

He acted like a man and a patriot, the lieutenant confirmed.

Dr. Paredes embraced me and said, Father, I'm going to tell his mother and the girls so that we can pray, all right? He went up to the second floor and a moment later we heard the cries of the mother and sisters. Then they came down dressed in black and we prayed in the chapel. Around nine, we called the boys and they said they'd almost arrived. We arranged to meet at Gaviotas.

After checking, the bodies of the guerillas were handed

over to the brigade. Tomás Paredes was buried with full honors in the cemetery in Aguacatal. The official version was that he had been murdered by the terrorists.

From that day on, the war intensified. Dr. Paredes White hired counterinsurgency instructors from El Salvador and brought them to his ranch. The peasants cooperated with information, but sometimes they were walls of silence, which got on the doctor's nerves. Once in El Tame, an isolated village up in the mountain, he lost it completely. He got his boys to choose fifteen youths from the village, made them kneel on a bridge, and said to them: I'm going to count to three and I want to hear names, otherwise you can tell the Lord.

And he began: one, two . . .

Everyone thought he was going to stop, that he wouldn't continue, but when he said three he fired the first shot. That gave the signal to the boys. The fifteen peasants fell to the ground. The roar of the gunfire was horrendous.

The doctor left a manager in charge of his ranch and devoted himself completely to the war. The whole thing had become personal, which is very important in view of what happened afterwards.

In Aguacatal, life improved. People walked calmly in and out of the church. That was the reward for my sacrifice. The people loved me. They greeted me on the street.

One night the boys went to pick up some dopeheads who were selling drugs. They were six of them in all. They were selling crack, pills, and cocaine in an area of Aguacatal that was a real den of corruption: there were motels and three discotheques with girls, and of course, that's where these scum multiplied, coming in on motorcycles, bringing their poison with them. The people there were apparently protecting these pushers, so one night, in two jeeps, we grabbed the six of them and took them to Gaviotas. Freddy, the guy from Cali, was in charge.

We told them, you have three options: either you tell us

who gives you the drugs and where you trade them, and then you get out of Aguacatal forever, or you work with us. And to do that you have to kick the habit and undergo training. The third option is a bullet in the ass for all of you.

As was to be expected, they preferred to save their skins. I didn't agree, because these people were scum and would continue to be scum, but that's how it went. Freddy was the one who trained them and just imagine, about six months later Don Alirio came to me and told me they'd had to shoot them. And what was it they'd done?

They'd broken into a family home, apparently saying they were with the guerrillas, and what they did was look for money, said Don Alirio. They were high on drugs. They raped two peasant women and an Indian servant.

They were tried and sentenced to death. They were made to dig a ditch and then kneel in it, and it was Freddy who shot them all, more fresh meat for the maggots.

A couple of years went by.

The group grew. There were about three hundred of us and we had a camp in Alamedas, going up toward Dabeiba. The boys trained there, they had study centers. The Salvadorean instructors, along with Freddie from Cali, gave counterinsurgency classes. I demanded that they should have regular religious services, and I went up once a month to celebrate mass.

The situation was still tense and rumors started circulating that the guerrillas were going to launch a final assault and take the town. The Agrarian Savings Bank closed, as did the schools and the Telecom office. Everybody was waiting.

The following Sunday I kept the church open and again few people came. I remember a dark-skinned boy I'd never seen before. He came in and looked around, as if taking notes, and I started to get worried. Then I saw another one, sitting in the central pews. He was kneeling and praying. And one more behind the font, who was crossing himself, although he looked out of place. I was getting nervous, I didn't know what to think, so when I finished I quickly went out to the sacristy.

At this point I saw Don Alirio and I said, how good that you've come to salute the Lord, and he said, yes, Father, in these complicated times we have to keep our souls up-to-date.

We laughed, and I gave him a hug. I walked him to the door. When he put one foot outside I heard the first shot, and some cries: fucking paramilitary! murderer! A shootout started with the bodyguards, who'd been waiting for him outside. I heard the bullets hit the door, but I resisted the impulse to throw myself on the ground. In the house of the Lord I was protected.

All at once there was a heavy silence. And a cry:

They've killed Don Alirio!

I went out and saw him on the steps, with a gun hanging from his hand. Fresh blood was pouring down the steps and seeping into the cracks and gaps in the stone.

Now the war began in earnest. That same night, Wilson asked for a meeting with Don Alirio's widow and his eldest son, whose name was Jerónimo Vélez. There were fifteen of us, landowners, storekeepers, the lieutenant, and I. There was also Freddy, the sinister man from Cali, who had gone up in rank.

Jerónimo said, gentlemen, this is a very sad day, but I'm not going to sit around and cry. I announce to you that I'm taking both the ranch and collaboration with the self-defense group in hand, are we clear?

We all said yes.

It was decided to take the boys out in various groups, and we gave the heads of squads names: Palomino, Nuche, Toribio, Familia, Bombombún, and Recocha. The coordinator would be Freddy, along with Jerónimo himself. The order was to comb each area and not stop until we found the murderers or their accomplices. I gave descriptions of the three men in the church. They had gotten away in a red Daihatsu van and one of the guys had been limping and losing blood.

Jerónimo Vélez told the boys: I'll give a reward to anyone who brings me the heads of these men, in fact, as of now I offer ten million.

Jerónimo and Freddy set off with one of the groups and Dr. Paredes White with another. The doctor's soul had been poisoned and it was well known that he liked to blow people's heads off.

In the confessional, I often said to him, Doctor, you have to seek relief, why not travel? Leave things in our hands for a while. The press is going a bit crazy, they're on the lookout.

But the doctor said, don't worry about me, Father, in this fight we're shoulder to shoulder, how can I go away now? Don't forget that the municipal elections are coming up and we have to support our candidates, organize people in the towns, raise funds. I myself have to take charge of this campaign that's starting. Don't ask me to leave now.

Two days later, Bombombún's boys found the bloodstained Daihatsu near Doradal, and so we went there. I was scared, but something told me I had to go with them. Jerónimo asked to take charge.

And what can I tell you, my friend, the thing was a mess, really cruel.

When we arrived, Jerónimo and Freddy gathered the villagers in the square, a small paved area with a flower bed and a basketball court.

Jerónimo talked to the people through a loudspeaker: we know the terrorists came to this area, and at least one of them is wounded, which means they can't get far . . . Maybe they're hidden in one of these houses. That's what I've come to ask you. You already know that hiding a terrorist and not reporting him is a crime and in this war the price you pay for it is your life, so I'm going to ask you this one question, where are they?

Freddy had a line of men and youths brought to the front. The children were taken to the edge of the square.

Nobody said anything and there was a heavy silence. Finally, an elderly woman, an Indian, said, we haven't seen them around here, Doctor, don't kill us.

Jerónimo's jaws shook with anger. He approached the line of men and shot the first one in the back of the head. The head exploded and there were screams. A woman came running up and slapped Jerónimo, but he took a step back and fired, first at her body, then at her face. The woman fell beside her husband. There was a horrible silence. A child could be heard crying from the sidewalk. He must have been about five and was covering his eyes.

Jerónimo went back to the line and grabbed another of the peasants by the hair. He dragged him to the ground and put the barrel of his gun to his bald patch.

I'll count to three and I want to hear someone say something: one, two . . . three . . .

There was a gush of blood. The peasant's body twitched a couple of times on the ground, like a snake, then lay still.

He went on to the next one and grabbed him by the hair. A young peasant who was shaking with fear. A damp patch spread on his pants.

Very well, Jerónimo said. I'll start counting again: one, two . . .

Wait, someone said, a woman.

Yes? Jerónimo said.

I saw some people going up to the mountains along the old path. They had a mule with them, with a wounded man on it. They weren't in uniform and I didn't think they were bandits.

Freddy called her to the front. She was a woman of about fifty. He asked her where she lived and she said just on the edge of the village and that she had seen them the day before. Jerónimo asked her who her husband was and she pointed to a man of sixty-five, kneeling in the line. He said to him, come, stand up, what's your name? and the old man said, Ananías

Mejía, Doctor. And did you also see them? and the old man said, no, señor, I didn't know my wife had seen that, then Jerónimo put the barrel of his gun to his neck and lifted his chin, didn't you tell him? and the woman said, no, Doctor, I saw them from a distance and I only just remembered it now that you asked.

Then the sinister Freddy said to the woman, and why didn't you tell the police? and she replied, almost crying, well, Doctor, because there are no police here, you'd have to go down to Playón or Aguacatal and go to the barracks, and Jerónimo insisted, but you know that this way you make yourself an accomplice, you know that, don't you, and the woman said, I don't know anything, Doctor, I'm illiterate, I don't have any education.

Jerónimo stroked the trigger and said, where are they? where did they hide themselves? whose mule was it? The old man was shaking and there was a dark patch on his pants. How am I supposed to know that, Doctor, if I only just heard about it? And the woman added, it was a gray mule I hadn't seen before around here, maybe they brought it with them from the mountains.

Jerónimo, blind with anger, said to her, you see a mule you don't know, with people you don't know carrying a wounded man, and you don't tell your husband? Señora, do me a favor and come over here.

Then he cried to the people, close your eyes! Anyone with their eyes open, I'll shoot them, close them and put your hands behind your heads.

He went back to the woman and said to her, now, Mother, the moment of truth has come. All you have to do is point your finger at those who are in the guerrillas, those who help that group of terrorists, and whoever owns the mule. Point them out with your finger and if you do you'll save your husband's life, how about it, Mother?

But the lady said, no, Doctor, I'm not going to kill anybody by pointing at them because nobody here is in the guerrillas, the guerrillas are in the mountains and we don't see much of them, they're dangerous people. All we do is keep our heads down and work, nothing else, Doctor.

Jerónimo started to sweat buckets. And he said to her, look, señora, if you don't talk, you're killing people, look what's going to happen if you say nothing. He made a sign to Freddy and Freddy grabbed a young man from the line and shot him in the forehead. The body jerked backwards, letting out a spurt of blood.

The people on the square got down on their knees, imploring.

No more, Doctor, you've already had your revenge and none of us are to blame, the woman's husband said, but Jerónimo again put the barrel under his jaw and pulled the trigger. The head shattered and the body fell to the ground. The woman ran to him and Bombombún mowed her down.

This was just the start.

It was now that I discovered that Jerónimo was screwed up and that he and Freddy did cocaine. I saw them go to the car to cool off and when they were there they stuck some of that powder in their nostrils. I preferred not to look at them. Then they came back to the square.

Well, my dear friends, Freddy said, we're in no hurry and I'm already getting tired of the sound of lead.

He made a sign to Bombombún and he took out a thick machete, cut in half, so that it looked like a butcher's knife.

He passed it to Freddy and Freddy walked behind the kneeling men, scraping their hair with the edge. Suddenly he stopped in front of one of them and cried, this one stinks of shit! He'd done it in his pants. Freddy made a gesture to Bombombún's men and they took the man to the corner of the square and shot him. The spurt of blood left a flower on the

wall. At this, Jerónimo lost his temper and yelled at Bombombún, dammit, I said no more noise!

And so they all had their turn, one by one, all silent, piss-
ing themselves, shitting themselves. Freddy struck one of
them so hard with the machete that his head split right down
the middle.

They left twenty-four bodies in the square. They only left
the village when they got bored and hungry. It was already
around nine in the evening. They washed their hands and faces
and wrote on a wall: "Village friendly to the terrorists." On the
way out of town they wrote another message that said: "This is
how the country punishes murderers."

"Long live Colombia!"

After that, I distanced myself from the group. It seemed to
me that these methods, although they are forms of combat and
war, were starting to be inhuman. Hate and injustice prevailed
over idealism, and once Jerónimo Vélez and Freddy Otálora
took command things really got messed up. Eventually, I
decided to leave.

Dr. Paredes White had turned vicious and no longer
acknowledged anyone else. When news got out about the massacres, it created a scandal in the press and Lieutenant Urrelo
requested a transfer. So did I. The archdiocese studied the case
and agreed to transfer me to another parish. Finally they sent
me to Guateque, in Boyacá. As far as I was concerned, it did-
n't matter where I was as long as I was serving my country and
the Church. Afterwards, things got even worse, because news
of the torture got out, and I asked the archdiocese for urgent
help to get to Spain and do a course. Or rather, I told them, get
me out of here quickly, things are getting difficult, and there's
going to be a scandal, and they helped me: I enrolled on an
introductory course on Faith last year. Then the whole thing
blew up and photographs of me were published. The
Communists started making accusations and they found out I

was here. They tracked me down and beat me up badly. I managed to defend myself. The police got them off me.

Don't think I'm trying to put you off remembering such cruel things. I'm telling them to you so that at least you know that I didn't kill anybody. I waged the fight I had to wage, that much is true, and I helped, just as others helped who now wash their hands, and nobody accuses them.

I'm not a murderer. I have clean hands. If they send me back to Colombia they're going to say I was a bloodthirsty bandit. But it's not true. The only reason I left was because sadists like Freddy ended up taking over the movement.

I know perfectly well what I did and what I didn't do.

It's a relief, at least, that someone like you should know.

That's all I have to say.

PART II
HEADING FOR THE 5TH PARALLEL
(OR THE REPUBLIC OF GOODNESS)

1

The second person to have his throat cut was a young man from Londonderry, barely twenty-two years old, named Timothy Kindelan. He was a student of political science at the University of Dublin and had been doing a six-month internship at the Irish embassy in Madrid as part of his course: in fact, he was only six days from finishing. He knew Spanish and liked Flamenco culture. He had produced a number of papers: one on the Irish in the Civil War and another, published as an article in the *Irish Political Digest*, on the legalization of the Communist Party of Spain after the death of Franco. He had been assisting the political adviser and had been doing research in the National Library in Madrid on the arrival of Islam in the Iberian Peninsula, with reference to patterns of community organization. His girlfriend, Elisabeth Hayes, had planned to arrive the day after the start of the siege to be with him in his last week and then leave for a vacation in Andalusia. Right now, she was still in Madrid.

The Kindelan killing caused genuine shock, coming as it did after a week of relative calm and intense negotiation, which had led to a hardening of positions. The TV debates were being increasingly populated by radicals, such as the Catalan pundit and political scientist Luis Bessudo, whose main argument came from what specialists call "strategic communication." In his opinion, every day the siege continued meant millions of dollars' worth of free prime-time publicity for Islamic extremism. He believed it would work out cheaper either to give them a large sum of money to get out of there for good, or to launch a concerted attack according to one of the recognized methods of antiterrorist intervention, dislodging them by force or eliminating them with the smallest possible number of casualties among the hostages.

In Bessudo's opinion, Israeli-style operations were no longer as effective as they had once been, dependent as they were on an unequal fight in which the enemy's casualties were not of the slightest importance, an impossible thing in a democratic state such as Spain, in which the rule of law prevailed. He also disdained cooperation with Russia—which had finally offered its help—because of the grim memory of its security forces' reckless actions at the Dubrovka Theater in Moscow, in October 2002, where a Chechen terrorist group had taken 912 people hostage. The strategy was an interesting and even original one, theoretically speaking, but the result was far from being a success. What they did was to pump into the auditorium through the air vents several cisterns of 3-Methylfentanyl gas, one of the active components of the main chemical weapon of the Russian army, Kolokol-1, in order to make the kidnappers dizzy and then enter by force, but the final balance sheet still makes somber reading: 129 hostages dead, as well as 39 of the terrorists. Ten years later, many of the survivors still suffer from respiratory problems. That is why the specialists prefer SWAT-type actions. Even the Colombian police's special anti-kidnapping group, the Gaula, trained to protect the lives of the hostages at all costs, was brought up in the discussion.

Naturally, the Kindelan killing marked a pivotal point in the siege, but the police and the members of the emergency cabinet kept to a policy of absolute secrecy. Rumors circulated that there had been secret negotiations between the governments of Ireland and Great Britain to reduce the number of NATO bombardments of ISIS targets, but when those in charge were questioned they denied it. Another rumor was that the payment of a large sum to Boko Haram was being considered, which would have been an illegal solution, since public funds could not be given to a terrorist group, increasing its firepower.

The TV in my new hospital room was set into the wall, between two windows. The other three beds were empty, so I was able to keep it on all the time without disturbing anybody.

I was watching it when Pedro Ndongo arrived.

"My Colombian friend! Prepare yourself, I come with news. Make an effort to relax your muscles."

"Thanks, Pedro, what happened?"

"The legal issues have been resolved. Since you're both foreigners and don't have criminal records, either in Spain or in your respective countries, it's been decided to settle the matter amicably. But I haven't said a word. In a few minutes your lawyer will be here to tell you himself and make a proposal that you must accept. I think Señor Reading has already signed."

"How did you find out?"

"Ha-ha, old Pedro Ndongo listens through walls."

At that moment, the door opened and the lawyer came in. In order not to have to leave, Pedro started diligently checking the serum in the drip bag, testing for static electricity in the stand, and monitoring the rate of drip.

The legal explanation could be summed up in this way: the best and easiest solution to this case, which did not involve Spanish nationals, was pre-judicial conciliation, in which the parties reach an agreement and manifest their satisfaction, the authority in this case being the "third party who acts or intervenes." There would only be a small sanction in the form of a fine for "disturbing the peace." To reach this conciliation, I would have to make a concession to Francis Reading that consisted of dispensing with the argument of self-defense, which might well hold up in court thanks to the profusion of witnesses, but which would inevitably lead to a long wait and the rigors of an exhausting judicial process.

"Would self-defense give me any advantages?" I asked.

"Of course," Pedro Ndongo cut in from behind the bed, "because a street fight can be avoided but not self-defense, and that works in your favor, given the circumstances."

The lawyer glared at Ndongo.

"Thank you, nurse, do you have any other legal advice to give my client?"

Pedro bowed his head. "I beg your pardon, counselor. I couldn't help it. I have a certain esteem for this gentleman. I'm going now."

He grabbed his bag with the instruments, the pressure gauge, and the case for organs, and withdrew with a bow.

I signed a few papers for the lawyer. He told me I could leave the hospital immediately, although I had to leave my passport. I could pick it up from police headquarters once I'd paid the fine at any post office.

Soon afterwards, Pedro Ndongo returned with my belongings and I was able to get dressed. The swelling on my face had gone down and the corset around my chest held my ribs in place. I got through the administrative formalities using my Italian social security card. Then I called the Hotel de las Letras, explained what had happened to me, and asked if they could give me back Room 711. I was lucky, it was free.

Then Ndongo called a taxi and, once again looking at me intensely, said: "Recover, think, and try to do something good with what you have in your mind, however murky it may seem from outside. Follow your instincts. So say I, Pedro Ndongo Ndeme."

"Subject of Teodoro Obiang," I added.

But he immediately retorted: "If I could, I'd remove Obiang's vesicle without an anesthetic, and complete the checkup with an aluminum probe in his urethra."

Finally, almost by way of farewell, he said: "Even though I studied medicine, if I had to be anyone's subject I'd choose

Frantz Fanon; plus the Négritude poets like Aimé Césaire and Léopold Sédar Senghor, Léon-Gontran Damas, Guy Tirolien, Birago Diop, and René Depestre. And of course, the black Cuban Nicolás Guillén."

When I got to the Hotel de las Letras, a bellhop helped me out of the taxi and the manager came out to greet me, very pleased at my return.

That struck me as an excellent sign, and it encouraged me to ask the fateful question.

"Are there any messages for me?"

"No, señor, we have nothing recorded."

I felt a mixture of frustration and anger. How was it possible that in all this time Juana hadn't called? I decided to wait a few days, settle the matter of the fine, and go back to Rome. The end result of the trip would be frustration.

Back in my room, I went to the armchair, from which, clearly, I should never have stood up, and called room service. It was almost three and I hadn't eaten. I ordered a chicken sandwich and a bottle of sparkling mineral water, and again switched on the TV. Two seconds later, the telephone rang. It was room service: they wanted to know if Solán de Cabras water would be okay. I said it was perfect. I hung up and they immediately rang again, which rather riled me. Now they wanted to know if I preferred a liter or half-liter bottle.

"A liter, can you bring it now?"

I hung up again, but the ringing restarted as soon as I'd put the receiver down.

"I already told you a liter bottle is fine, what more do you need to know?"

There was a silence on the line.

"It's me, Consul."

"Who . . . ?

"Me . . . Juana. It's Juana."

I was speechless.

"I'm in the lobby, can I come up?"

"Of course."

I looked around for the mirror, nervously. The bruises had gone down. With some effort, I managed to pull up my pants, which were practically around my legs, because I had lost quite a bit of weight. I felt an emptiness in my stomach.

Knock, knock.

I opened the door, but the image I'd built up of that greeting immediately shattered. On seeing me, Juana gave a cry.

"What happened to you?"

She had put on weight and there were a few gray hairs at the roots, but she still looked like a young student. I wanted to embrace her, but she was the one who leapt on me.

"What happened to you, Consul? Who did this to you?"

"It was an accident, I just left the hospital."

"But . . . who? Why?"

I told her what had happened since my arrival in Madrid the previous week. She listened attentively and in the end said:

"You can't stay in a hotel in that state. I'll pick you up tomorrow morning and take you to my place. I'm going to look after you until you recover."

"It's not necessary for me to come to your place," I said, "I don't want to be any bother. You can still help me even if I'm here."

"Don't even think about it, Consul, and besides it'd work out expensive for you. I was the one who told you to come. Let me see your diagnosis and prescriptions. Remember, I worked as a nurse in Bogotá."

I gave her the folder and she read it carefully. She wanted to know if I already had all the medicines. When she saw that some were missing, she stood up like a shot.

"I'll fetch them, I know a pharmacy around here. In the meantime, rest."

I didn't have the strength to tell her to stay and tell me

about her life, and about the child, where was Manuelito Sayeq? Why had she asked me to come to Madrid? I had a thousand questions, but Juana left in a rush. There would be time for all that.

When she came back, she spent a while organizing the medicines that she had brought, and at about ten she said she had to go.

"Why did you want to see me, Juana?" I asked her.

"It's complicated, Consul. Rest for now, and tomorrow I'll come and fetch you. Let's talk about it when you're better and we can have a drink together."

She left. I felt more anxious than before she'd arrived, and full of questions. Would she really come back? What was going on? Soon the anti-inflammatories and other pills knocked me onto the bed.

I woke at eleven in the morning, to the sound of the telephone ringing. It was Juana.

"I'm downstairs, Consul. If you aren't ready I can read the newspaper while I'm waiting for you. It's after breakfast time, but they can make an exception, would you like me to bring it up to you?"

By noon, we had arrived at her home, which was on Calle de San Cosme y San Damián. Juana asked the taxi driver to look for a parking space and help us with my suitcase, since we had to go up two tall flights of stairs before getting to the elevator. She lived on the top floor, in a three-bedroom apartment with a sloping ceiling and wooden beams.

"This is your room, Consul."

A large, welcoming room. The window looked out on an ocean of Madrid rooftops and the bright sky.

"Would you like to rest now? Are you hungry? Manuelito will be here at two."

She had on a knee-length skirt and a loose blouse. Tennis shoes and white stockings. The apartment was full of books,

Persian rugs, antique statuettes, discs, and pictures. Even a small collection of bronzes of mythological figures.

"How long have you been living here?"

"Two years, more or less."

"And what do you do? Are you studying? Do you have a job?"

"Relax a little, Consul, I'll make you some coffee and then go out to do a bit of shopping. Make yourself at home."

The guest room was clearly a study, but I didn't get the impression it was Juana's. In a corner there was a bamboo basket filled with antique canes—I've never known a single woman to collect canes—and the shelves were decorated with objects that gave the impression of having been amassed in a lifetime of world travel: jade statuettes of Buddha, small wooden carvings of African animals, two porcelain images of Mao, leather cigar cases, metal cigarette cases of different textures and sizes; on the bookshelves, many books in English and French, works of political analysis, biographies of great military figures, histories of revolutions; a sizeable bar on a table with wheels and drawers full of coasters and utensils for making cocktails. I looked in vain for a photograph. There were frames, perfectly suited to the surroundings, but the pictures seemed to have been carefully removed. Whose apartment was this? My first thought was that Juana had remarried, but if so it was strange, given that most of this stuff didn't seem to be hers, that there was no clear or specific sign of a man's presence either.

When I had finished arranging my things, Juana came in with a cup of coffee and a plate with two pills.

"Take these now, Consul. I'll be back in half an hour to make lunch. Rest. There are lots of books here, and music, too."

I wanted to ask her about the apartment, but held back. I remembered our days in Delhi. There, too, I'd waited to hear her story, and after a while, without my asking anything, she'd started to talk. And once she'd started there was no stopping her. I don't know if anyone had ever again talked to me in that way, with so much force, so much knowledge of life.

At lunch time Manuelito arrived—to me he was Manuelito Sayeq, but she didn't use his second name. A boy of about eleven, with black hair and very bright eyes. Hearing him speak was proof that they had been living in Madrid.

"Mother told me that you and she are old friends."

"That's right," I said, "and I knew you when you were only just starting to walk."

My bandages and wounds didn't upset him, or at least he didn't mention it. I assumed that Juana had lectured him about that beforehand.

"And that you're going to live with us for a while."

"For a few days anyway, while I finish recovering from all this."

"Well, I'm pleased, Consul. Welcome."

They both kept calling me "Consul," but now didn't seem the moment to change the rules and tell them I wasn't a consul anymore. Juana knew that anyway.

And that's how we spent the following four days, in an atmosphere filled with silences and questions. Nothing disturbed the routine. I devoted myself to helping Manuelito with his homework and talking to him about the great adventures of mankind. I promised him we'd go buy books by Jules Verne and albums of Tintin. I told him about the journey to the center of the earth, which you reached through a crack in the surface that connected with a descending tunnel. I told him about the Nautilus, that underwater home in which a man had decided to shut himself away, far from the world, with a submerged library. I told him the story of the five weeks in a balloon and the battles between savage tribes seen from the sky, in a dirigible, and of course about the longest and most difficult journey: the journey to the Moon.

We also talked about his history homework: about the

Mayas, their calendar and their maize, the close relationship between the two in the cycle of harvests, and how they made pyramids to see the sky more closely and to look above the trees. We drew mandalas, we made simple mathematical calculations, we studied the wars of the Cid, and what in Spanish schools is still called the reconquest, which is none other than the expulsion of the Spanish Muslims by the Spanish Catholics from the land they had shared.

Juana came in and out. In those first days I learned that she was working as a volunteer in a refugee center in Lavapiés, and had contacts with a number of NGOs. She was as active as ever. I never asked her why she'd taken so long to come to the Hotel de las Letras to keep the appointment she herself had given me.

Being in her company, I remembered Teresa, the Mexican diplomat who had helped us so much in Bangkok. I found her e-mail address and sent her a message just to tell her that I'd met Juana and her son again in Madrid, and to ask her where she was. In Mexico, I assumed.

There was a TV in my room, so I was able to follow the Irish embassy siege, which, after the terrible Kindelan killing, had calmed down again, although nobody felt really calm.

Another piece of news had started to share the front pages: the new wave of immigrants that was arriving in Europe, and its connection with the health emergency.

Because there was another human group in the middle of this tornado of fugitives, perhaps the most desperate of all: those who landed by night and early in the morning from barges, dinghies, and small ships on deserted beaches in the very same Southern Europe from which others were already starting to escape. The vast majority arrived in Italy or Spain. Exiles from Syria, Libya, and Egypt, abandoned to their fate. Fugitives from Nigeria or Mauritania, Niger or Mali. From the civil wars in Liberia and Chad, which sowed the land with hands severed by machetes. Families of immigrants from the blackest Africa ready to die to realize their dream: the dream of survival. To get to paradise alive, or what for them was still paradise. The one they saw on old TV shows, where the population had food and health and hygiene and, my God, education!

Here again, the pundits appeared on the current affairs programs, analyzing and giving their opinions.

Just with the food thrown away in the restaurants of Europe, you could feed seventy million people a year! The fugitives don't know that. They don't know the FAO malnutrition figures, of course, nor have they read *Hunger* by Martín Caparrós. But they sense it, they feel it in their guts. In fact, they can't stop thinking about it. A strange paradox: a percentage of these fugitives from hunger end up transformed into feed for the fish of the sea, or in the bellies of Mediterranean sharks. Their boats capsize, catch fire, drift. Sometimes the traffickers throw them in the water to reduce the weight. Bodies that float ashore, carried by the tide. Men, women, children, old people. The saddest drowning victims in the world. And then there's the health emergency.

Because many of those who arrive are sick and don't yet know it. They carry Ebola somewhere on their bodies. Sometimes in the pupils, in the brain, the groin. And Ebola passes from person to person, and eventually to whoever has dealings with them.

This was another source of anxiety in apocalyptic Europe: Ebola. To be black in Italy or Spain, countries less accustomed to dark skins, became a synonym of carrier, pariah. The Italian Right proposed a law that authorized the army to machine-gun those boats from the air. On political talk shows they were called "plague ships" or "Nosferatu ships," and were referred to as floating germ farms. For many people, practically speaking, this was a biological war! Nothing more, nothing less. An attack on Europe, which was why the continent's coasts had to be militarized.

More and more terrified citizens agreed with this idea. Many clung to religion and prayed on their knees: what have we done, o Lord? How many plagues are there still to come?

There are ten, a voice seemed to respond.

Ten, and we're barely on the fourth.

When at last I regained my independence and was able to go out on the street, I found that the world was still unsettled. People in Madrid were still anxious about the Boko Haram siege, although they were starting to get used to it, to see it as a macabre part of the scenery. There were even a few jokes, one particularly ironic one about "Irish vacations," which to be honest I don't dare reproduce.

I went to the post office with my ticket and paid the fine for "disturbing the peace," which came to the mysterious figure of 2,386 euros and 67 cents. I paid and, with my ticket stamped, went and collected my passport from police headquarters, where, naturally, I found a tense, nervous atmosphere that perfectly reflected what was happening in the city and the country.

On getting back to Calle de San Cosme y San Damián, I remembered Manuela Beltrán and decided to call her. Where had I left her card? It took me a while to find it, it was in my medical folder.

She was pleased to hear from me.

"How's your recovery coming along?"

"Very well," I told her, "I've just taken my first walk. How's your friend?"

"He's still in the hospital, though he's much better," and then she added, "I called you at the Hotel de las Letras and they told me you'd left, are you still in Madrid?"

"Yes, at the home of a friend, in Antón Martín."

"I'd like to see you, I still have things to tell you."

"Yes, of course. How about today?"

Juana had to work late and Manuelito had a music class until seven, so I arranged to meet with Manuela at the cafeteria of the Reina Sofía Museum. When she saw me, her face expressed a certain relief.

"Yes, you do look better, I'm really pleased; you don't have any more bruises," Manuela said.

She talked to me about the Complutense and we exchanged anecdotes about teachers who, twenty-five years later, were still there. Some of them, incredibly, with the same courses and the same reading lists as during my time there. I told her about my years as a left-wing striker, a fanatical reader of the Latin American boom, and an aspiring writer. When I asked her about Colombia, she was a little evasive. She said that she was an orphan. She was in Spain on a scholarship that the dean of literature at the Javeriana had helped her to obtain, and again I felt moved, Cristo? I remembered his incredible classes on Rulfo, and his "yellow breakfasts."

When I got home, I told Juana about my meeting with Manuela.

"Is she the girlfriend of the guy you had a fight with?"

"Well, student and lover."

"I know that combination, Consul: the teacher always on the lookout for willing female students and the nerdish girl who feels she's on cloud nine because she's sleeping with her wise teacher and getting one up on her classmates. It was a classic at the National, and I assume in every university in the world. Invite her to dinner tomorrow. I'd like to meet her."

The next day, Manuela came to San Cosme y San Damián after nine at night, bringing a bottle of Matarromera. Juana was surprised.

"You shouldn't have gone to all that trouble, it's very expensive wine!"

We sat in the living room while Manuelito played on his

mother's tablet, putting together fantastic houses and forests in a game that fascinated him and that he'd tried to teach me.

Juana put some drinks on the table. After my long convalescence, I had a strong desire to have a drink. I'd practically given up alcohol for a couple of years, but that night struck me as a good moment to start again, so I poured myself a generous gin with ice, lemon, and tonic water.

Manuela had a scholarship from the Institute of Latin American Cooperation, just as I'd had, which is why listening to her again reminded me of my student life in Spain. I noticed that, like Juana, she was very cautious about what she chose to reveal. Of her time in Cali and Bogotá she said almost nothing. Just a few very vague hints. As if her life had started when she arrived in Spain.

Then Juana asked her about Reading.

"I met Paco at the university, I took his course on the Latin American novel written in English, a course that Hispanic philology shares with English. We read Hispanic writers from the United States. I liked his teaching style. A terrific guy, relaxed with his students, and with a really cool attitude to literature. One Friday we left his class a little later than usual and walked back to Moncloa through the University City. Someone suggested going for a drink. Paco said that in the United States if a teacher went for a drink with his pupils he'd get into trouble, but they told him that in Spain it was the opposite: those who didn't go out with their pupils were considered arrogant, so we went to a little bar and then to another and another, until the whole thing turned into a binge; from there we went to a place in Malasaña that served mezcal, and by five in the morning we were all drunk, including Paco. When we got taxis, I ended up in his, and we were the last two left by the time we got to my place. I asked him if he wanted to come up and that's when everything started."

Saying this, Manuela poured herself another tequila. A Don

Julio reposado, no less, since Juana's bar was as well-stocked as that of a good hotel. Who did this very swish apartment belong to? I listened to Manuela talking and watched Juana out of the corner of my eye. Would she dare to say anything about her recent life? I really wanted Manuela to ask her about her life, just to see what she said, but she clearly felt intimidated.

We'd need to spend more time together before Manuela felt comfortable and started to trust us.

"Paco didn't tell me he was married," Manuela continued, "but I guessed it very soon, you know these things. I didn't ask myself any questions either, I liked him a lot; the fact that he was so mature and so intelligent made me feel protected."

"That's the advantage of older men," Juana said.

At about ten at night I took Manuelito to bed. He liked to read stories aloud and comment on the plot. Now he was reading a book of Norse stories with winged gods, nymphs, and dragons on the cover. That's why he asked me such strange questions.

"Is it true that an elf can't beat a small dinosaur, Consul? It's impossible, isn't it?"

"Of course it's impossible," I replied, not too sure what we were talking about.

When I got back to the living room, I noticed that Manuela and Juana had changed chairs to be closer, and they looked, from the corridor, like two old friends confessing things to each other. Seeing them, I lingered in the corridor. It was odd for three strangers and a child to be sharing a space about which I knew nothing.

Suddenly I was sure that Manuela had asked Juana about me. I could imagine the question, because Juana was shaking her head. Then they both started laughing slyly. Maybe I was imagining things. I already had three gins in me. In the end, I went back into the living room, breaking the bubble they were both in.

"Did he get to sleep?" Juana asked.

"Yes, I turned out the light."

We continued drinking and chatting. Inevitably the subject of the Irish embassy came up. Manuela said that the police should intervene, since the siege was turning into a kind of Olympic village for journalists. That day the press had identified one of the Spanish attackers as a young woman from Vallecas, the girlfriend of an African boy. Manuela had seen her Facebook page on TV, filled with images of Boko Haram, Islamic State, and the Rayo Vallecano soccer team. The news that there were Spaniards among the attackers had caused a great stir in Spain.

"I hope they don't kill them," Juana said. "I hope they can go back to Africa or wherever they came from. Nothing would be gained from killing them, and when it comes down to it they're all victims of something."

When I looked at my watch it was three in the morning and I realized why I was so tired. I excused myself and went to bed. The two women kept on chatting in the living room (I watched them for a while from the corridor), again with that same closeness as before.

The next day I woke early and a troublesome headache—the gins!—drilled into my temples. Luckily, I had dozens of painkillers, so I took one and went back to bed. What time was it? Nearly eight.

Later, I went to the kitchen to boil a little water, and to my surprise, there were the two of them, Juana and Manuela, chatting animatedly. Both in pajamas and eating cereal for breakfast.

"Good morning, Consul," Juana said, "let me make you coffee, would you like some eggs?"

I thanked her, I could make them myself.

"Let her look after you, Consul," Manuela said. "Why do they call you Consul?"

"It's a long story."

I didn't mind her adopting it, too. Some of my favorite novels had consuls as characters, and I admired them.

"Manuela stayed over and slept on the couch," Juana said. "We were thinking about going to the Retiro Park today. We'll go as soon as Manuelito gets up, would you like to come?"

I preferred to stay behind and be alone.

I read the papers calmly, in a café. Around noon, I went to the Cuesta de Moyano book market to have a look around, which may be what I most enjoy in Madrid. But it saddened me to see that they were selling books for one euro. The booksellers seemed forlorn, as if left over from another time. Three of them were gathered in one of the central kiosks, and were talking in total desperation. One asked the other:

"How do you keep count, by number of sales or by money?"

And the other replied:

"By sales. Today I've sold eighteen."

"Hell, and how much have you made?"

"Eighteen euros, of course."

I bought a French edition of a Malraux book about art, *The Metamorphoses of God*. I walked back by way of the Botanical Gardens, the Prado, and the old Palace Hotel.

They returned as it was getting dark, still together. Juana was holding a notebook, which she took to her room. I got the impression it was something very valuable. Manuela sat down beside me.

"Consul, I haven't dared tell you that I read a couple of your books. Maybe one day I'll tell you my story."

Three days later, Juana came to my room with Manuela's notebook and said:

"You should read this, it's Manuela's life up until the day she came to Spain. She wrote it for her psychologist. I asked her if I could show it to you and she said yes."

I had a strong coffee and started reading. It was midafternoon by the time I got to the end. I closed the notebook, breathing hard, my heart racing. Could it be the same person? From Manuela's first mention of Freddy Otálora, that violent man who'd become part of her household, who'd raped her and killed her mother, something had clicked in my mind. I went and checked my notes about the priest Ferdinand Palacios, and there he was, the one they called the man from Cali. It was the same name.

Manuela came back to the apartment on San Cosme y San Damián just before dinnertime. I told her that I'd read her story and had been moved by it.

"Now you know who I am, Consul."

I wasn't sure whether or not to tell her about Freddy, but it was impossible for me to talk about anything else or even to look at her knowing what it meant to her. Better make an excuse, and go out for a walk. Now that she was rebuilding her life, was it right for her to know where that man was and what he had done? Wasn't that tantamount to plunging her back into her terrible past?

That day passed, and the following one. Manuela continued coming to the apartment daily. Seeing her, my doubts and contradictions increased.

After two weeks, I decided to tell Juana. At first she looked at me incredulously, so I showed her my notes. The name wasn't a common one, and everything else matched. After discussing it, we both reached the conclusion that it was the same person. There was no more room for doubt.

"You have to tell her, Consul. These unsettled accounts grow with time. It would be the best thing for her."

"I'm worried about her reaction and what she's going to do afterwards," I said. "Let me think it over."

Two more weeks passed until one night, after a great deal of preamble, which merely increased her curiosity, I made up my mind.

"There's something I have to tell you," I said. "You remember the Colombian priest who was with me in the hospital? He told me about a group of paramilitaries operating in the western part of Antioquia. At one point in the story he mentioned a guy from Cali who was there because he had to hide, and he stayed to fight alongside them. His name was Freddy Otálora."

Manuela turned pale.

"Freddy Otálora . . . ?" she said.

"Not so long ago, he was on a ranch near Aguacatal called Gaviotas."

Manuela closed her eyes. Her face was transformed. I started to fear her reaction. She opened her eyes again and said, "I have to go back to Colombia and find him."

"Find him?" Juana said, surprised.

Manuela stood up and walked nervously to the window. A cloud promised rain. A big ugly bird, motionless on a TV aerial, looked interested in our conversation. Then she came back to the table.

"Find him and kill him," she said, biting her lip. "But not just like that, no, kill him in the cruelest way possible."

"You couldn't do a thing like that, he'd kill you first," I warned her.

"I don't care. It's him or me."

It was time for a few drinks, so I fetched a bottle of Gordon's.

"We should confirm that it's the same person," I said, "and then report him to the authorities."

Manuela took a large swig of gin. "I don't think there are two sons of bitches with the same name. Report him? Sorry, Consul, don't make me laugh. What else did the priest tell you?"

I took out my notebook and read the parts where Freddy was mentioned.

"It's the priest speaking, I wrote down what I could remember of his story."

Manuela finished her drink and crushed an ice cube with her teeth. "The man's a murderer. I'm going to get him."

We went to the kitchen and served dinner. Juana took the boy a plate so that he could eat in front of the TV set.

"It'll be much more dangerous with those people around, don't you think?" Juana said. "He'll be armed and he'll be surrounded by killers."

"I've heard that for three hundred euros you can hire a hit man in Cali," Manuela said.

"That may be so," I said, "but you'd still have to go there and find one. It's impossible."

"I'm going to do it," Manuela said. "I have to do it."

When Manuela had gone, Juana came to my room.

"I understand her. What she wants to do is a bit crazy, but I understand her. We should help her."

"She won't achieve anything except getting herself killed," I said. "And what could we do anyway?"

"I can help her," Juana said, "those killers don't scare me, I know them, I know their weak spots."

I didn't dare say anything, so we remained silent until she said: "Have you taken your pills?"

She still insisted on maintaining the role of nurse. I said good night to her.

The next day Manuela didn't come, or the day after. I started to get worried. She finally appeared on the Friday night.

"I've been looking on the Internet to find out about the paramilitaries in that area. There are articles about the massacres, but nobody mentions him."

"Maybe the priest got it wrong," I said. "Or maybe he made it all up."

"I don't think so, Consul," Manuela said. "That priest isn't stupid. Plus, I checked the other names in his story and they all exist."

"Really? That changes things. Have any been arrested?" I asked.

"No, they were all investigated, but according to the articles there was never any conclusive evidence."

"Rather than think about killing him," I said, "we should check if he's still alive. Maybe they killed him. Or maybe he's been arrested recently. After all, the police in Cali are after him, aren't they?"

Juana grabbed her cell phone and started searching through her contacts list.

"I know who can help us," she said. "Let's see if I can find him. Here he is. He's a rather strange guy, but he knows that world well and he has contacts in Colombia. He owes me a favor. If your mind is made up, I'll call him. He'll help us find him and confirm whether or not he's the same one."

Manuela replied quite calmly, "My mind is made up. Who is your friend?"

"A crazy and eccentric Argentinian," Juana said. "His name's Carlos Melinger, but they call him Tertullian."

2

After the melodramatic episode in Brussels between Mathilde and Paul Verlaine, the pair of fugitive poets headed for London. Thanks to the war the previous year, and the crushing of the Paris Commune, the city was full of French refugees: politicians, journalists, writers, deserters. Many had been sentenced to death in France.

On their arrival they were received by the artist Guillaume Regamey, who helped them to find lodgings at 35 Howland Street. The place was somewhat seedy, especially for Verlaine, who had refined tastes. And it was still summer. The fog and the cold had not yet made their appearance. Rimbaud, on the other hand, felt fine. It was his first contact with a different culture and in another language.

They soon adapted to their new life, and the truth is that, surrounded by so many exiles, the two poets felt increasingly in their element, united in the idea that they, too, were also somewhat marginal. They met Swinburne and a young English poet named Oliver Madox Brown, who was even younger than Rimbaud and was considered a poetic genius in literary circles. But Madox Brown died at the age of nineteen, which was considered a great loss. In spite of this, his works have been forgotten, as was his name.

In London, Rimbaud and Verlaine lived a life of immigrants: they learned English, they took countless walks through the city, expressed surprise at the differences, felt nostalgia for France and at the same time joy at being far from her, and discovered many things that were beautiful, along with others that were unpleasant or disappointing. Like anyone who attempts to settle in a new place, it is possible that they dreamed of another life. Of being other people.

As Rimbaud said, *Je est un autre.*

Before long, Verlaine learned of the legal proceedings that Mathilde had set in motion in Paris to gain a divorce. A bad omen. The news unsettled him, and once again his mood changed. Deep down, he didn't want a divorce, let alone to lose his son. As often happens with artists, Paul wanted to have his cake and eat it. He started writing passionate letters to Mathilde and, surprisingly, she replied.

In November 1872, Rimbaud also had a change of mind and suddenly began worrying about the fate of his manuscripts, those that had remained in Verlaine's house and, *hélàs!,* were in Mathilde's possession (or had been destroyed). The idea he had for getting them back was the strangest and most illogical imaginable: he wrote to Vitalie, his long-suffering mother, and begged her to go to Paris and talk to Verlaine's mother-in-law. Given all that had gone before, the idea was pure nonsense. But young Arthur was clever and knew which strings to pull. He told his mother that these manuscripts were valuable and that if they were published they might bring in quite a lot of money. Vitalie did as she was asked and traveled to Paris. There she met with Verlaine's mother and asked for a letter of introduction to the Meuté de Fleurys. As was to be expected, the errand was unsuccessful. Mathilde's family refused any agreement or concession, and of course didn't hand over the manuscripts (did they still exist? "The Spiritual Hunt" was among them!).

I try to imagine that encounter: on one side, Rimbaud's mother, proud and very nervous, intimidated by the luxury of the drawing room in the *hôtel privé*, and on the other, the scorn and harshness of Verlaine's parents-in-law. It was a brutal collision between the provincial bourgeoisie and Parisian nobility, made even worse by the previous experience the Meuté de Fleurys had of the Rimbaud family thanks to the young devil. The discussion must have been so tense and full of threats that Vitalie, on leaving there, immediately wrote to Arthur asking him to return to Charleville and get far away from Verlaine, or they would all be in trouble.

The incredible thing is that Rimbaud agreed.

That Christmas, after all that Verlaine had done to be with him, young Arthur returned alone to Charleville, leaving his friend to suffer the cold and drizzle of London. Verlaine, deeply depressed and feeling betrayed by his friend, wrote one of his best known poems:

> *Il pleure dans mon coeur*
> *Comme il pleut sur la ville*
> *Quelle est cette langueur*
> *Qui pénètre mon coeur?*

Then Verlaine fell sick, which allowed him to write to friends telling them what a bad condition he was in, and to his mother, begging her to come, and asking in passing that she bring Rimbaud to be with him on his deathbed. The ploy worked, and in January 1873 he was back with his beloved Lucifer and ready to resume a Bohemian lifestyle: what he himself called "our shameful life in London in 1873."

There is an important aspect that Starkie emphasizes, which is Arthur's fascination with the docks of London. "Tyre and Carthage in one!" That is what he called them, enthused by the variety of faces coming from the four corners of the world. It was something he had never seen before, and may have been an early premonition of the remote places where he would spend the rest of his life.

He was a young man watching a mass of men getting off

boats with sacks on their backs and feeling a slight tremor of anxiety, knowing that one day he would be among them, going a long way away. It is as if he recognized his destiny: to escape from a world that, with the weak body but thunderous voice of an adolescent poet, he was already cursing, already defying.

Starkie says that Rimbaud spent hours at the docks, trying to talk with the sailors coming off the ships, managing to understand them in some language known to him, and asking them about what they had seen on their travels, from which remote places they had come, and what fantastic or salacious things they had experienced. It was the first time he had seen such large boats!

He was already possessed by the tremor of travel. Once again, he heard the beating of distant drums. During that time in London, Rimbaud and Verlaine frequented the opium dens of the East End, near the dock area. It is no surprise that they were regular customers. Arthur was still searching for alternative worlds, seeing his hallucinations in a poetic light, and poor Paul, with his addictive personality, was a slave to anything that could at least offer him a little pleasure.

Rimbaud, on the other hand, even though he went to the limit, always managed to keep a clear head, and to maintain poetry at the center of his life. It is believed that it was during this time that he started to conceive *A Season in Hell*. How much in these verses derives from the hallucinations of opium? It is an irrelevant question, since, as Baudelaire said, drugs only reveal what the poet already has inside him. Rimbaud himself wrote about this in *A Season in Hell*: "Excess is stupid, vice is stupid." The young man is about to conclude a new stage and judges himself ruthlessly. He rejects his old ideas about poetry and life. In "Alchemy of the Word" he says: "Now I can assert that art is nonsense."

This is a fundamental part of young Arthur's brilliance: the speed with which he burned his bridges, the way his poetry constantly projected him forward, feeding on the ruins of his previous ideas. A process that, in other writers, might take decades, in him was a matter of months.

His poetry was heading toward either obscurity or the future at the speed of a rocket.

In April 1873, they left London. Verlaine wanted to avoid divorce from Mathilde at all costs, but he did not dare go to Paris. He was afraid he would be arrested for his participation in the Commune and his contacts with French exiles in England. That is why from London they decided to go to Brussels. Soon after arriving there, Arthur continued alone as far as Roche, in the French Ardennes, to join his mother and sisters on what had once been the farm owned by Vitalie's parents.

Green mountains, meadows, trees standing out against the twilit sky . . . And in the middle of these placid images, the ruins of war. According to his future brother-in-law, Paterne Berrinchon, Arthur showed up unexpectedly, was pleased to see his mother and sisters, but was insensible to anything else and spent the time lying half-asleep on a rickety bed, without saying a word, or else shut himself up in the barn and spent the evenings alone. This is how this period is remembered by his sister Isabelle, who was twelve at the time.

Starkie says there are two likely causes for his somber mood: either he was recovering from the drugs he had taken in London, or he was reexamining his life, prior to beginning the frenzied composition of *A Season in Hell*. In a letter to Delahaye, he tells him that he is writing some short stories in prose, which he will entitle something like *Pagan Book* or *Black Book*.

"My fate depends on that book," he says.

While passing through Brussels on his way to Roche, Rimbaud had even spoken with a printer and reached an agreement to publish it.

Again it was Verlaine who persuaded him to return to

London, and on May 27 they again set sail for England. Rimbaud already had much of *A Season in Hell* in his bag.

Here they were again, in a room at 8 Great College Street, Camden Town. But the situation was not easy. Verlaine's constant mood swings exasperated Rimbaud. Paul was racked with guilt and remorse, from which he escaped with alcohol and probably sex or drugs, which in turn engendered more guilt, and so on in a vicious circle that had no end.

Weary of all this, unable any longer to stand his sentimentality, Rimbaud began to humiliate him pitilessly. He made fun of his appearance, his mood swings. It should not be forgotten that while Verlaine was suffering these terrible psychodramas of his, Rimbaud continued writing *A Season in Hell*. In other words, Rimbaud was in a position of strength: he was creating a work of art, something he could touch with his fingers, while Paul, unhappy Paul, was only writing letters to his mother complaining of his bad luck and making an endless list of all the things he lacked.

The situation led in the end to a psychotic scene, very much in the style of Verlaine. After Arthur had made fun of him, Paul left the room and ran down the stairs. When Rimbaud reacted and ran after him, he found that he had boarded a boat on the Thames, bound for Antwerp. Arthur signaled to him to come back, but Paul, very dignified, looked away. What followed was the biggest breakdown in Paul Verlaine's life so far. From the boat he wrote a letter to Mathilde with a strange ultimatum: If she did not join him in Brussels within the next three days, he would shoot himself.

On Rimbaud's part, the drama also now became intense. What we know for certain is that after being abandoned by his lover he started drinking, and while drunk wrote him a letter begging his forgiveness and imploring him to come back. "If I don't see you again I'll enlist in the army or the navy. Come back, all I do is cry," he says.

Verlaine replied with a letter that is already the height of melodrama:

"As I have loved you intensely, I want you to know that if within three days I haven't reconciled with my wife in a satisfactory way, I'll blow my brains out. Three days in a hotel and a revolver are expensive, hence my past austerity."

Not content with this, Verlaine made the same announcement of suicide to his mother and various friends in Paris, in the hope that Mathilde would get to hear of it. He even wrote to Rimbaud's mother, and Vitalie replied, trying to dissuade him. "Do as I do, be strong and courageous in the face of suffering."

Mathilde did not go to Brussels—the letter was intercepted by her father—and when his ultimatum expired, Verlaine again changed his plan. He no longer wanted to kill himself. He wired Rimbaud and begged him to come to Brussels on July 8 to see him for the last time before he left for Spain and joined the Carlist army.

And of course, he succeeded.

But on arrival, Arthur did not find a man convinced of his destiny and packing his bags to go off to war, only the same drunken, sentimental poet as ever, now accompanied by his mother. Verlaine asked that they go back to London together, and took the matter as settled, but this time it was Rimbaud who refused. The atmosphere became heated. Sparks flew and Verlaine, now very drunk, begged and begged. Rimbaud tried to tell him that he could no longer stand this life. Verlaine drank until he lost consciousness.

Two days later the arguments continued. Verlaine wouldn't stop drinking. Finally, Rimbaud told him he was leaving. Verlaine stopped him. He locked the door and sat down in front of it. There was a struggle, insults were hurled. Then Verlaine took out the pistol with which he had been planning to kill himself and fired at Arthur three times. One bullet hit him in the wrist and the other two lodged in the wall. Seeing what he had done, Paul took fright, left the room, and ran to his mother's room—incredibly, she was still there, in the same hotel—and collapsed on the bed, weeping, saying that he had been on the verge of killing Rimbaud.

Soon afterwards, Arthur arrived, and Paul's mother, worried, bandaged his wound. Then they went to the hospital but it was not possible to extract the bullet, so Rimbaud decided to return to his family in Roche, and this upset Verlaine, who again took out the pistol in the middle of the street. A policeman who was nearby stopped him and took him to the police station, but since the crime was a serious one, they transferred him to L'Ami Prison and then to Petits Carmes Prison, accused of attempted murder.

Rimbaud was kept in the hospital for a week, because of the operation on his wrist and his bad state of nerves. In his statement for the court, he said that Verlaine had been blind drunk and had gone mad. On leaving the hospital, on July 19, he withdrew the charge and asserted that it had been an accident, but the legal process was already under way and it was not possible to stop it. To make matters worse, Mathilde now arrived in Brussels looking for evidence that would help her in the divorce proceedings. Verlaine was found guilty on August 8 and sentenced to two years' hard labor, plus a fine of two hundred francs. During the trial, the relationship between the two poets had been made public, which contributed to the judge being inflexible.

Rimbaud returned on foot to his mother's house in Roche, although others say that the Belgian police took him to the border. Whatever the case, he arrived at his mother's farm and announced to his family that he needed rest and understanding to finish a book. His mother decided to support him, so Arthur took refuge in the barn with his notebooks and pencils.

He was a young man of eighteen, alone, sick, and frail, facing a colossal task, struggling with the oceanic tide that is a great work of art. But Rimbaud lived up to the task, since that was his destiny: place himself in front of the bull and confront it. His sister Isabelle said that some nights they heard him screaming, yelling insults, and weeping. Perhaps that is how Rimbaud's work had to be written: in an old barn, howling with pain. He only came out to eat. Starkie says that on finishing *A Season in Hell*, a month later, he gave his mother the manuscript to read. Vitalie took it to her room. After a few hours she came out, brandishing the sheets of paper in her hand, and asked Arthur:

"What does it all mean?"

The young poet replied:

"It means exactly what it says, literally and point by point."

3

The plane rose into the air, took a panoramic turn over Madrid, and headed in a southwesterly direction, toward that area of the world where so many of us had unfinished business and that was now awaiting us with its best face.

A journey back to a newly pacified country.

Tertullian, with his usual humor, or his usual cynicism, said that our journey could be called *Theory of Returning Souls*. He was saying it for us, not for him. We were going to the country of peace.

Because the government and the guerrillas had finally signed an agreement that had turned Colombia into a fashionable country. Everyone wanted to come to Bogotá and stroll through Plaza de Bolívar with a Colombian friend or girlfriend, read local authors, enjoy the local food, and learn to dance their rhythms. Newspapers like Tokyo's *Asahi Shimbun*, Delhi's *Times of India*, Beijing's *Renmin Ribao*, Riyadh's *Al Riyadh*, and Jakarta's *Kompas* sent permanent correspondents and set up offices in Bogotá. Japanese, Korean, and Russian businesses opened branches in a number of cities and the new TV soap operas, focused on forgiveness and reconciliation, sold widely around the world.

In addition, Northern Europeans prepared to spend their vacations on the Caribbean coast, to buy vacation homes in the coffee-growing area, to visit the heritage sites and the wonders of nature. Dutch, French, and Norwegian left-wing intellectuals sought houses in the Candelaria district of Bogotá, in Barichara or Villa de Leyva. Others in Providencia or the Pacific islands. The Nobel Prize–winning French writer Jean-Marie Gustave Le Clézio bought a house facing the Pacific Ocean and came back to live in the Darien jungle. Widowed German pensioners sought Colombian wives between forty and fifty, preferably with grown-up children.

Real estate became big business. The price of a square meter in cities like Bogotá or Cartagena surpassed that in New York and Copenhagen.

The director Oliver Stone announced his intention of filming the story of the guerrilla leader Tirofijo, and traveled to Bogotá to meet with members of FARC in their offices in Congress. The rumor circulated that he was thinking of Willem Dafoe for the leading role.

The actor Sean Penn bought a huge colonial house in the center of Cartagena de Indias and it became common to see him out for a night on the town with Bono and Benicio del Toro. A project by the Canadian architect Frank Gehry was chosen for the Great Museum of Memory and Reconciliation in Bogotá.

Colombia was on the crest of a wave.

If Europe was on the ropes, Africa mired in poverty and a humanitarian crisis, the Middle East ablaze with wars of religion, the Caucasus and the Ukraine still confronting Putin's neo-Tsarist Russia, and other Latin American countries such as Venezuela, Mexico, or Argentina had severe problems, Colombia was the light at the end of the tunnel. With its peace process complete, it was one of the few areas of the world with a plan that looked as if it might gradually become reality.

The question was: could she do it?

Ordinary foreigners, fugitives from kingdoms shaken by the crisis, arrived to invest their meager savings, because they saw excellent opportunities and a reasonable level of security. And not only the prosperous. Even Europeans impoverished by the debacle came to seek work, which led the writer Fernando Vallejo to say—or rather, to cry—that they were very welcome, but that they had to start by cleaning toilets. Gradually, the foreigners blended into this new, optimistic, but still wary society—wary because it dreaded what might happen later. A collective psychoanalysis that might help to digest the new situation was impossible.

Rich Venezuelans, fugitives from Chavism, had crossed the border before the peace treaty was signed, but now a second and even a third wave arrived. Like the previous ones, they brought their thick checkbooks and opened businesses. They created oil companies and taught the locals how to sink diagonal extractor pipes in order to reach those huge pockets of the subsoil where the borders existing on the surface no longer matter. There was a great bonanza that later collapsed, along with the price of crude, but they had realized that if there are two countries in the world that are essentially similar, and whose differences are merely formal, they are Colombia and Venezuela.

There was another group: the millions of Colombians who had gone to live in Europe from the eighties onward and who were now returning, little by little, as the crisis reached them in their respective countries.

But not everything in Colombia smelled of roses.

The signing of the agreement made it possible to lift the great national carpet, and many terrible things that had been hidden under it jumped out like scorpions. People realized how important it was to resolve that age-old conflict before it was possible to deal with the new problems. Those of today and those of tomorrow. Those of the present.

That same present in which we were now traveling, since the plane was advancing into the semi-static sunset of those moving westward at six hundred miles an hour. But the sun is always faster and night falls in the end. Then the plane turns into a point of light that might be confused with a star.

I had asked for seat C, the aisle seat, which would allow me to go to the bathroom frequently. On my left, in A, was Carlos Melinger, alias Tertullian, and in D and E, respectively, Manuela and Juana. Manuelito Sayeq, my great companion, was in seat F, beside his mother. They had given him a child's kit and now he was drawing on a huge page full of puzzles and line drawings to be colored in.

I haven't yet said how we came to be on this plane and that's what I'm now preparing to do, as soon as I finish this gin and tonic the stewardess was kind enough to serve me, although rather low on gin and in a plastic cup, which is understandable.

I need to go back a few weeks—six perhaps?—to the moment Juana called Tertullian and asked him to come to the apartment on Calle de San Cosme y San Damián.

That's where I met him.

An immensely fat man, although not in the sense of morbid obesity, but of someone strong and at the same time voluminous. Like a rugby player or even a sumo wrestler. A solid mass of flesh. Breathing heavily and constantly sweating. Endlessly mopping his forehead with a handkerchief.

Seeing him come into Juana's apartment, I got worried. What kind of favor did he owe her? His skull was shaved on the sides, with a very short, almost monkish island of hair in the middle. It was a hairstyle a lot of soccer players adopt. There were also dozens of pendants, hanging from his ears, his neck, his wrist, even his huge waist. I later found out that each one had a meaning, which was worse. I hate symbolic people, but I didn't tell Juana.

Now, sitting next to me on the plane and ceaselessly eating, with his pockets full of M&M's, getting up more or less every half hour to go to the bathroom to clean his teeth, he provokes a certain sympathy in me. Soon after meeting him, when Juana explained the problem to him and asked if he could help us, Tertullian spent two whole days telling me his strange life story and his incredible project.

But let me go back to that first evening, when I met him.

Juana explained Manuela's situation and then she herself told him the details: the rape, the murder of her mother. Tertullian, like an FBI agent, took notes and asked questions:

"Age of the target?"

"Height? Approximate weight?"

"How dangerous, from one to ten, ten being the maximum?"

"Men under his command?"

"Possible weapons?"

Whenever he uttered a long sentence, he blinked more than usual, which is why I preferred not to look him in the eyes. It was very unpleasant. He constantly got up to go to the bathroom and I thought he was going there to take drugs, but he himself explained it.

"I have a little nervous problem with dental hygiene and that's why I clean my teeth frequently. Oh, nothing strange: weak gums that absorb germs, and we're surrounded by them!"

As proof, he took from his pocket a small bag with a brush and three medium-sized tubes of toothpaste.

"I get through three of these a day, can you imagine? It's the only way to keep it under control. It's called automysophobia: a fear of being dirty, combined with bacillophobia and dentophobia, which is a fear of dentists. Try to imagine that for a second. No, you can't, can you? It's hell, but it's *my* hell. I have to accept it. I've been through others that were far scarier."

Juana had first heard about him from a Colombian woman who told her about Tertullian's lectures and suggested they go to hear him. He gave them in second-class movie theaters that were rented for conferences or religious events. And although they were genuine political meetings, Tertullian called them "lectures." He introduced himself as a romantic philosopher, a defender of nature and his country. He was an incredible guy.

During those weeks he came a lot to the house. On each visit, he gave us news of what he called "the target."

"My people are looking for him, apparently he's moved from the Aguacatal area to the Pacific. We're trying to get close to him."

Another day he arrived and told us:

"We almost have him located, he's a very dangerous animal, isn't he, Manuelita? We've learned a few things about him."

One day I asked him:

"How far can your people in Colombia go with this?"

"As far as I tell them to go, Consul, but don't worry. I'll sort it out and take care of everything. I owe it to our friend, it's a matter of honor."

Manuela practically came to live at Juana's, the three of us forming a strange triumvirate alongside the child. It's unusual to live with two women, I think it alters your perception of time. Luckily, there were no neighbors on the same floor, but there was a doorman who asked questions and whom I decided to ignore completely.

One night something woke me. On opening my eyes, I recognized Juana. She had sat down beside me and was watching me sleep. I asked her if something was happening.

"I only wanted to be here for a while, Consul. I'm sad."

She lay down next to me. I embraced her.

"What I like about being with you is that you don't ask pointless questions," she said. "That makes me feel good."

She fell asleep without our touching. I hung on her breathing as if both our lives, both our fates were contained in it.

At dawn, with the first light of morning, I saw through her pajamas that she had a new tattoo on her lower back: a huge butterfly with a snake's head and outspread wings.

I got up cautiously, in order not to wake her, and went to have a coffee, thinking about butterflies: they change place, flutter about, seem to slide and roll through the air. Why is the goddess Psyche represented with butterfly wings? She wanders the world searching for Eros, her lost lover. I thought of the word in other languages I know: *papillon, farfalla, schmetterling, babishká, húdié, farashá* . . . A legend says that the rings on the wings—the eyespots—are the eyes through which the gods keep watch on what's happening in the world. I remembered that one day Tertullian had greeted Juana with the words: "What do you say today, Madame Butterfly?" I felt a pang in my heart; had they been lovers? You didn't have to have slept with her to see her tattoos. I knew them myself. Madame Butterfly? I don't know much about opera, so I looked for information. It's the story of an abandoned woman in Japan. She loves an absent man with whom she had a son. When they ask her about the child, she says: "His name is Sorrow."

I returned to the bedroom with the two cups in my hand. On waking, Juana saw that her pajamas had ridden up to her waist.

"Were you looking at my ass, Consul?"

I laughed. I said good morning.

"You'd never seen this tattoo," she said, touching the butterfly. "It's the latest. Do you like it?"

"I like it a lot," I said. "Madame Butterfly."

She laughed. She had a quick sip of her coffee.

"Why are you so good to me?" she asked.

I remained silent, unable to get rid of the lump in my throat, until I noticed from her anxious look that she was really waiting for an answer.

"I don't know."

The morning sun struck her face and her skin looked like porcelain. So I dared to ask her:

"Why did you want me to come to Madrid?"

She looked at me with a strangely weary expression. Then she walked to the window and said:

"I thought that if, for some reason, you'd forgotten all about me, you wouldn't come. I just wanted to know."

"Well, here I am."

She remained there with her back to me, looking at a blurry sky against which a jumble of aerials and poles, and beyond them the hazy and irregular outlines of distant buildings, stood out. I had a strong desire to embrace her and repeat in her ear, "here I am," but I restrained myself. I was afraid that something would shatter. What hung in the air was a confused mixture of the words "love" and "compassion." Or something even more unsettling: as if you could desire what the other person is and has been when he or she is alone, far from you, in that implausible world that is someone else's life, whose echo sometimes reaches us. I also realized that when we were together we were safe from harm.

From then on, she came to sleep beside me every night, although without anything that could be seen as sexual happening. I felt great desire, but she had to be the one to take the first step.

Madame Butterfly.

A week later, in the middle of the night, she said:

"Remember my story, Consul? I told you about a lawyer I worked with in Bogotá, the one who helped me to get out of Colombia."

"Yes."

"This is his apartment," she said. "He doesn't use it because he lives in Paris and doesn't often come to Spain. I've occasionally gone traveling with him, particularly to Washington or Geneva."

Then she continued:

"That's how I came to know Tertullian. Something terrible

happened at one of his lectures, one of his followers fell from the ceiling and killed himself. I never knew if it was some kind of crazy suicide, deliberately staged in public, or if he was a common drug addict who climbed up there and fell by accident. Tertullian was accused of exercising psychological control over his listeners and bending them to his will. I thought he might be useful to me at some point, so I called my friend and we found him a lawyer who didn't charge him a penny and got him off scot-free. Ever since, he's been sending me gifts and inviting me to all his lectures."

The days passed.

What was happening in Spain got in through the windows. The big news was again connected with the Irish embassy siege. One morning I switched on the TV and saw that the assault had started. The lower part of the screen kept flashing red:

BREAKING NEWS! BREAKING NEWS! POLICE ATTACK EMBASSY!

The TV cameras were broadcasting live the advance of the SWAT teams, or their Spanish equivalents. Smoke was billowing from one of the windows, and shots could be heard.

Helicopters circled overhead.

The whole of the surrounding area, considered a "war zone," had been evacuated. What the police feared was that the building might be blown up, but the assault method didn't allow the terrorists to activate the explosives.

BREAKING NEWS! BREAKING NEWS! POLICE ATTACK EMBASSY!

As it happened, three hostages died and five others were wounded. Six of the fifteen terrorists were killed in the first charge, shot very accurately and simultaneously from the other side of the avenue. Another five fell in the following minute. The snipers studied each person's moves through the windows and fired blindly, guiding themselves by sounds and voices. Two more special forces teams went in through a hole in the roof and others through the windows. They also demolished a side wall, so that by the time the terrorists realized, they were already overwhelmed. Three police officers were killed and four wounded.

BREAKING NEWS! BREAKING NEWS! EMBASSY DRAMA OVER!

Juana came to my room and we watched as the operation unfolded. She was nervous. She moved from the bed to the armchair, then to a cushion on the floor. She went for a coffee and came back. She brought a bottle of water.

According to the TV anchorman, the decision to launch the assault was taken because the police had found out through bugs placed in the walls that the terrorists planned to cut the throats of three more of the hostages that day, and that they were also considering bringing forward their own martyrdom by detonating the explosives.

"We did what we had to do," said the head of the Madrid police, "to save the greatest number of lives."

"And what do we know of the Spanish terrorists? Are they alive?" the interviewer asked.

"Four are in custody, but we cannot reveal their identities. We shall be issuing an official press release with a detailed account of what happened."

BREAKING NEWS! BREAKING NEWS! EMBASSY DRAMA OVER!

"What special forces were used to go into the embassy first?" another TV reporter asked.

"In spite of the extreme risk, the troops who went in were special antiterrorist commandos of the Spanish police," the man said proudly.

"Did police from other countries take part?"

"There was consultation, but most of the operation was ours. We have experience here."

The pundit Luis Bessudo, who had supported the idea of a police assault, was already expressing his opinion from the studio, where a panel of commentators had been assembled.

"As we know, there are several different schools of opinion on how to deal with terrorism," Bessudo said. "As far as I'm concerned they should have acted earlier, although I have to admit that by letting time pass they were able to study the terrorists' movements and get a better idea of how to deploy the special teams. In spite of the casualties, the outcome is satisfactory. We can feel proud of our police."

Another of the panelists was the former president, José Luis Rodríguez Zapatero, who said:

"It's hard to achieve peace and security when there is so much injustice in the world. Poverty, social exclusion, poor education, and failed states are all fertile ground for terrorism to gain a foothold."

He asserted that the most powerful weapon in combating terrorism was democracy and he recalled how, three days after the attacks of March 11, the Spanish came out to vote in great numbers—for him—sending a message of trust in the institutions of the State. He asserted that terrorism was the most barbaric of human reactions, and insisted on his project, formulated during a visit to the United States, to build an *alliance of civilizations,* in contrast to Samuel Huntington's idea of the *clash of civilizations.*

Another of the guests, the pro-Israeli pundit Alfonso

García Ortegón, said that we should have seen it coming and that Spain, and Europe in general, had been far too lenient toward Islamist groups.

"I've been saying it for years, dammit," García Ortegón said, "we have to take the Arabs out of the European madrassas in London, Brussels, Paris, and even in Madrid, and put them into some kind of preventive custody, and at the slightest infraction, or if we find out they are spreading Jihadist ideology, they go to prison. Europe should build something like Guantánamo to keep them locked up, or bring back the death penalty for them."

He took a sip from a small bottle of water and continued:

"Spain must put pressure on Europe and its air force should take part in the bombing, not only in Iraq and Syria, but also in Gaza and the West Bank, where Hamas operates, one of the terrorist groups that started this whole mess. Until it's eliminated, there'll continue to be conflict everywhere in the world."

These words emboldened the lawyer and international jurist Antonio Segura, who asked to speak and, even before saying anything, glared at García Ortegón and got ready to respond by reading out a text of his:

"In 2004 the Spanish had more people killed and wounded by Jihadist attacks than the Israelis," said Segura, "but that didn't mean that we started dropping bombs on the homes of the suspected terrorists. The March 11 attacks were judged by a properly constituted court of law, applying a judicial process that treats all kinds of criminals equally, and in which all criminals have the right to a fair trial, as required by the basic norms of a state governed by the rule of law. The security forces of the state arrested the suspects, investigated, and presented evidence in court, by virtue of which it was demonstrated whether or not they had taken part in the attacks, and judgment was finally passed, some of the defendants being sentenced and others acquitted. This verdict went to appeal and the Supreme Court acquitted more of the defendants, on the basis that their participation in the events under consideration had not been proved."

And he added, pointing an accusing finger at García Ortegón, who was clearly someone with physical complexes and had sunk into his chair, somewhat frightened by the lawyer's vehemence:

"That's the right way for a democracy to fight terrorism. Dropping bombs on the most densely populated area in the world or executing people without trial is another, of course, but it's not what we do in Spain!"

BREAKING NEWS! BREAKING NEWS! EMBASSY DRAMA OVER!

There was a commercial break and the usual announcement, "We'll be back with more news and comment on the police assault on the Irish embassy."

The first commercial was from a travel company: "Get away from the hustle and bustle, discover nature here, where the history of the world started," and what I saw, much to my surprise, was an image of the Amazon River, advertising a cruise.

Then a hair removal cream, with the following slogan: "Because only you know how far you want to go."

Then a make of SUVs, ideal for excursions to the mountains: "Take it to the top, where the only limit is your imagination."

The commercials seemed to be addressed to another world.

We switched off the TV and Juana went to fetch Manuelito from school. I went out to take the pulse of the street. I had assumed that tension must still be high, but the amazing thing was that people, already sitting on the café terraces, preparing for the evening with their first gin and tonics, were far from nervous. On the contrary, they seemed euphoric.

Only a group that passed me on Calle Atocha said something that seemed to correspond to the gravity of the situation.

"The four who are still alive are black, man! The three Spaniards kicked the bucket."

A young woman walked past, talking to another young woman:

"Fuck, I never thought I'd have a day like this in my life."

I pricked up my ears to catch her opinion, and what I heard was this:

"First the network was down in the office for more than two hours, then my cell phone went off and wouldn't come on again, right in the middle of a conversation with Mario! And when I got out on the street . . . my period had started! I mean, that was the last straw."

The other girl said:

"At least you're not pregnant."

The noise level on the news bulletins and the current affairs shows decreased and life resumed its normal course. The embassy siege was a thing of the past, and very soon there were new and urgent matters for the pundits to debate: the injuries of the best-loved soccer players in the West or the romance of the decade between a winner of the Nobel Prize for Literature and a woman from the jet set, when they needed something frivolous to talk about; or the boats that kept coming at night from Africa and capsizing on the high seas with hundreds of people drowned, when they opted for something more tragic. And of course financial scandals were always good for a comment, or the desires of various regions of Europe to be independent and separate from their poorer brothers: from Northern Italy to Corsica, by way, of course, of Catalonia and the Basque country.

So time passed, and all of us in the apartment on Calle San Cosme y San Damián were kept dangling, until what we were waiting for happened. Tertullian called and said he had to speak with us urgently.

"Look at these photographs, do you recognize him?"

A man in camouflage gear, getting out of a Ranger van.

Manuela tensed like a cat, swallowed, and tapped her finger on the screen.

"It's him!"

The words acted like an enzyme that unites various substances. I asked where he was.

"On a ranch near the Llorona canyon in Dabeiba, but he often goes to Cali and Medellín on drug business. It's time to go over there and launch the operation."

Manuela mentioned the savings she had. She was ready to do it. Juana looked at me and said:

"We have to go with her, Consul. It might be a good excuse to go back to the country after so many years. I've been thinking about going back and wondering if it was really possible. Is it ever possible to return? And return where? Where do we really return?"

Tertullian told Manuela to forget about the money.

"This is part of our struggle, plus there's what I owe Juana. Don't worry, we have people there who finance these things. Just stay calm."

That's what Tertullian said, "Just stay calm." And now here we all were, traveling to the 5th parallel.

The plane had already plunged into the night. There was no difference between above and below. The cabin lights were off, and the passengers sleeping peacefully.

Tertullian had his head against the window, snoring to the point of apnea. Whenever he woke, he would put his hand in his pocket, take out a chocolate bar, and gobble it down. Then he would go to the bathroom to clean his teeth and come back to sleep.

I was trying to forget that, when it came down to it, the reason we were going to Colombia was to kill someone; Manuela stood up and went to the back, where the flight attendants were. I decided to stretch my legs a little.

"You can change your mind anytime," I said to her. "Nobody should feel obliged to do something like that."

"I have to do it, Consul. Nothing I've done in my life means anything while that man is still at large. I tried to build a house on top of a volcano, but the volcano is still active. When you told me about him, it made me realize that I have to resolve this if I ever want to have a real life, a clean life. Where I came from was hell, Consul. You have to understand me."

"I do understand you."

"I'd like you to read something of mine," she said suddenly.

"Of course."

"When we get out of this, I'll show you some poems."

I went back to my seat and she remained standing beside the bathroom door, eating potato chips and candies provided by the cabin staff.

I was curious to see Bogotá. It was seven years since I'd last been there, ten since I'd stayed there for any length of time. I assumed that a number of old ghosts from my adolescence might reemerge.

4

As I've said before, I've devoted a substantial amount of time to reading and rereading the poetry of Rimbaud and fantasizing about his strange life, asking myself the questions that all those who approach his poetry ask themselves, namely: how can someone with so much talent, a true genius, give up writing? Is it really possible to abandon it? Could he have continued writing for himself in a kind of poetic hermaphroditism? Is it possible to be a poet in such a radical and even violent way and then, one fine day, just stop? What, then, does it mean to be a poet? Was young Arthur aware at any time of how powerfully he had changed the history, not only of poetry but of all Western literature? Could there be a suitcase in some attic in Charleville, Harar, or Aden, containing manuscripts from his Ethiopian period, and will anyone ever find it?

Rimbaud embodied a movement that began in the Stone Age, when man, alone, crossed the mountains and peaks and lakes, wondering what was beyond them. He was the embodiment of the fugitive, obliged to go a long way to fulfil his destiny, to meet it and embrace it. Even to interrogate it, to place himself in front of it and look it in the eyes. To go a long way, farther and farther, because any journey, deep down, is a search for meaning. I remember Lezama Lima's words: "The idea of destiny is a phrase that says *they are coming to get us*, but it is completed by another: *go out to meet them.*"

Humanity, by and large, can be divided into these two

complementary categories: those who go out to conquer some-thing, usually alone, and those who stay behind and found nations.

Both have been fundamental.

The African *Homo sapiens* of the plains, relatives of Lucy, fled north twenty thousand years ago and encountered the Neanderthal. That encounter was to provoke a major clash, and the one thing we know is who the winners were: the Africans, the fathers of today's humans. Apparently, the exten-sive European plains were not sufficiently large for both groups to live together, one on each side of the river, perhaps. This may have been a clash between two ways of conceiving life: the nomad versus the settler. The former is more skillful, has cold blood, and can be cynical and murderous. The settler is good and happy. He is in harmony with his surroundings. He loves the plants and the mountains and the clouds. That's why he is weaker. He has warm blood. He feels homesickness and understands other people.

The history of humanity was spurred on by nomads. Like Odysseus, who roamed the Mediterranean for twenty years before returning home, or Aeneas, who would never return and, with his exile, ended up founding a country that centuries later built the first great Empire of the West. The will to leave is governed by many demons and ghosts, not only that of necessity. That is why on occasion the nomad returns, but it's obvious to everyone, including himself, that what he is doing is studying new routes, mental maps, further escapes.

A high percentage of poets and artists were great nomads, as were the philosophers. Jesus, the son of Mary, spent a third of his life away from his land: where did he go? In Kashmir, in the north of India, they say that he was there, in a Buddhist monastery. That has its logic. It was from the monks that he learned piety and forgiveness, impossible ideas in the pitiless Judea of his time. Returning to his brutal land, he ordered his people to love their enemies and turn the other cheek, and before long was crucified. On rising from the tomb where they left him for dead, he set off again and apparently retraced his steps to Kashmir. And there they show you his tomb.

The tomb of Jesus.

Joyce escaped. Van Gogh was a fugitive, as was Gauguin; Nietzsche and Cioran left their homes to confront the coldness of the world. The desire to look into themselves from the opposite shore has driven travel writers increasingly far: Conrad, Bowles, Greene, Neruda, Henry Miller, Octavio Paz, Lawrence Durrell. To go looking for stories or, as Bowles says, to see oneself changed by other landscapes and worlds, in such a way that the book that is written is the result of that change. But they all seem to follow a command of Rimbaud's, the one he gives in that powerful line from "Farewell," at the end of *A Season in Hell*, pointing the direction that literature after him should take.

> À l'aurore, armés d'une ardente patience, nous entrerons aux splendides Villes.

In his Nobel Prize lecture in 1973, Pablo Neruda read a text entitled *Toward the Splendid City,* based on that line. Loyal to his militant past, he gave it a political content:

> *Today it is exactly one hundred years since an unhappy and brilliant poet, the most awesome of all despairing souls, wrote down this prophecy:* "À l'aurore, armés d'une ardente patience, nous entrerons aux splendides Villes." *"In the dawn, armed with a burning patience, we shall enter the splendid Cities."*
>
> *I wish to say to the people of goodwill, to the workers, to the poets, that the whole future has been expressed in this line by Rimbaud: only with a burning patience can we*

*conquer the splendid City that will give light, justice, and
dignity to all mankind.*
  In this way the song will not have been sung in vain.

Arthur Rimbaud is ready to leave after writing and publishing his great work, the only one he saw with his own eyes in the
form of a book: *A Season in Hell.* It is August 1873, in Roche.
But let us go back a little: the young man had just emerged
from the barn with the manuscript in his hand. His mother had
paid for the cost of publication in Brussels, and when the
copies were ready, in October, he went to pick them up to send
to his friends.

Then he traveled to Paris to await the reactions, but things
did not go well. Oh, young Arthur, what did you expect? Every
poet dreams of being acclaimed, which is why the first book is
a terrifying moment: to give it over, not to patient and charita-
ble friends, but to the eyes of strangers; a specific and very
fragile order of words that has to give way, alone, to . . . To
what? The young man wants his voice to be heard, wants
someone to understand him. That is the sublime ambition of
anyone who publishes a book and huddles in fear to await a
reaction. The anonymous reader is cruel and unfair because
that is how literature is; only he who is prepared to take the
blows can enter it.

Arthur hoped for that attentive reading, but received a pail
of cold water. The atmosphere was not propitious for a book
from him, since everyone remembered him as the little Lucifer
who had brought misfortune on Paul Verlaine. One evening, at
the beginning of November, Rimbaud went to one of the
Parisian cafés most frequented by poets and intellectuals, but
nobody said a word to him. He waited in vain until closing
hour and then, despondent, went straight back to Charleville.
When he arrived, he threw his remaining copies of *A Season in
Hell* on the fire.

Poetic revenge on those who had ignored him!

Having done this, he returned to London, accompanied by a new friend, the poet and bohemian Germain Nouveau, a contributor to the review *La Renaissance Littéraire et Artistique*, with whom he shared lodgings at 178 Stanford Street.

Little is known of those months, until April 1874. Rimbaud devoted himself to reading—and perhaps writing—in the reading room of the British Museum. The libraries of the world are the hospices of poor poets; it is where they find warmth and nourishment. There is speculation that he had a girlfriend, Henrika. He mentions her in the poem "Workers," in the *Illuminations*. But it is just a hypothesis. The truth is that he felt alone and soon asked his mother for help. And so Vitalie, with her eldest daughter—also called Vitalie—decided to pay her son a visit. Arthur went to greet them at Charing Cross Station and took them around London, showed them the city, and felt proud when they noticed his good English. The diaries of young Vitalie II describe this visit and the care and attention her brother lavished on them. She emphasizes that, in spite of spending a lot of time with them, he went every day to the reading room of the British Museum.

What was he reading?

It is highly likely that he paid particular attention to *First Footsteps in East Africa or, An Exploration of Harar*, published in 1856, by the explorer Richard F. Burton, which contains a description of the Abyssinian city of Harar. Burton points out that it is a place forbidden to Europeans. He himself was able to enter in a caravan disguised as an Afghan sheikh, named *hayi* Abdullah, and remained long enough for the emir of the city to beg to be taken by him as a disciple.

That region of East Africa clearly attracted young Arthur, since one of the things he showed his mother and sister was the collection of Emperor Theodor of Abyssinia in the British

Museum, a visit that Vitalie II recorded enthusiastically in her diary, fascinated by the tunics, the diamonds, and the silver utensils.

Travel, the desire to leave.

The young man was on the verge of spreading his wings.

One of the elder Vitalie's tasks was to help her son in his search for a job, which had become a real obsession. They sent letters, presented themselves for many interviews, and finally, on July 29, Arthur announced that he had found something.

He left London on July 31 at 4:30 A.M.

For where?

Many biographers say he went to Scotland, but Starkie states that he traveled to Reading, halfway between London and Oxford, and worked in a school, perhaps as a French teacher. Twenty years later that city's prison would house another writer and poet, Oscar Wilde, born just four days before Rimbaud, on October 16, 1854. A curious proximity between two people so different, but both geniuses.

It is from this period that "Democracy," one of the last of the *Illuminations*, must date. In it, he announces his imminent departure:

> Goodbye to here, anywhere will do. Conscripts of good will, we will have a fierce philosophy; ignorant of science, cunning for comfort. Let the world go hang. This is the true way. Forward march!

And at the beginning of 1875 he begins his wanderings around the world. A pilgrimage that would take him about five years.

The first port of call was Stuttgart, Germany, where he came with the aim of learning German. He lived in a pension, worked on his physical strength, and spent hours in libraries. His German period was marked by a reunion with his old friend and lover Verlaine, who in January 1875 had left prison a fervent Catholic. Verlaine's faith had exploded like lava from a volcano, forcing him to his knees. He renounced his irresponsible past, the mistakes he had made through his lack of character, such as losing his family. His first impulse was to seek out not Rimbaud, but Mathilde, and beg her to forgive him. An incredible wish in someone who had systematically destroyed every one of the opportunities she had given him, including waiting for him naked and perfumed in a Brussels hotel.

Of course, Mathilde did not even allow him to come near. In his desperation, Verlaine turned to Rimbaud's loyal friend Delahaye and begged him for the younger poet's new address. Oh, illustrious Verlaine: we can see the problems coming a mile off! Apparently, faith and religion were not so definitive as to put a lid on what really mattered.

One day, in Stuttgart, Rimbaud was surprised to receive in the mail a letter from Verlaine in which he asked to meet with him and begged him to convert to religion. Young Arthur, who was no longer so young—he was already twenty—must have been both amused and curious. He replied, telling Paul to come see him, he was waiting.

Verlaine arrived the next day.

How was that rash encounter?

A letter from Rimbaud, quoted by Starkie, gives us a rough idea: "Verlaine arrived in Stuttgart with a rosary in his paws, but within three hours had rejected his God and made the ninety-six wounds of our Lord bleed again."

Far from converting him, he was again, for the umpteenth time, converted by the Satan of Charleville. The scene, as usual, was a pathetic one.

Already very drunk, walking by the banks of the Neckar, they came to blows and Verlaine was knocked out. Rimbaud was strong. The next day, Arthur persuaded him to go, for the good of their friendship and to avoid more violence. Verlaine returned to Paris.

This was the last time the two great poets of France saw each other.

Rimbaud's wanderings continued: he walked across the Alps and reached Milan. From there he went to Brindisi, also on foot, with the idea of sailing to the Greek island of Paros, but he got heatstroke and had to be hospitalized immediately. Once he had recovered, the French consulate repatriated him to Marseilles. He spent the summer in Paris and at the end of August walked back to Charleville.

Decidedly, Rimbaud's feet were his best and safest means of transport!

In October 1875 he contacted Verlaine again and asked him for a loan to study the piano. But Verlaine, filled with resentment, refused, and wrote in a humorous manner that "the goose that laid the golden eggs has died" for young Arthur, referring to the fact that he was no longer writing poetry. "Where would my money go?" he asks him. "Into the hands of innkeepers and ladies of easy virtue! Piano lessons? Who would ever believe that?" Now he had to look to his son's economic security, which had been jeopardized by "the gaps opened in my small capital by our absurd and shameful life of three years ago."

Rimbaud did not reply.

By the end of 1875, still in Charleville, the young genius is said to have learned three more languages: Arabic, Hindi, and Russian. If we add German and English, Greek and Latin, that makes seven by the time he was twenty. And what's more, offended perhaps by Verlaine's letter, he began studying music and piano. It is said that he drew a keyboard on the table of the house and practiced there, in silence, while he corrected his language pupils' homework.

But very soon young Arthur again had itchy feet. He had "wind in his soles," as Verlaine said. He hoped to go to Russia with the money he had saved, but ran into problems when someone stole his money and baggage in Vienna and he had to beg in order to eat. Back at the starting point, he was more ambitious when next he looked for a way out of Europe.

The answer came from Holland, which had colonies in Indonesia: far-off Batavia, the land of tobacco and spices. Young Arthur had not the slightest problem in enlisting in the Dutch army in order to go to the island of Java, committing himself to remain in the army for a period of six years.

He set sail on June 10, 1876.

He landed in Batavia on July 23.

The Dutch colonies in the Far East were known as the East Indies, a place of tropical temperatures and dense jungles. A new world for someone desirous of fleeing Europe. That was what young Arthur wanted, but the rigors of military life soon bored him. What was he doing here, surrounded by soldiers? He wanted to go and discover the jungles and the little towns and imbibe the smells of those colossal trees!

Three weeks after his arrival, he deserted. He had the money he was given when he was recruited and, we assume, some more pay. That was sufficient for him to spend a month in the jungles and towns. But the East did not seduce him. He wrote nothing about what he saw, nor did he try to stay; before long, he was looking for a ship to take him back to Europe.

I like to imagine that in the exotic port of Samarang, from where he set sail for France on August 30—there are various hypotheses—he discovered a boat with a French flag loading spices and tobacco, the *Mont-Blanc*. Arthur watched it for a long time, sitting near the quay. Attentively, he followed the work of the sailors preparing the stowage and the crew moving with agility on the bridge. Perhaps he thought he could sail on her.

As darkness fell, one of the sailors approached the tavern where he was sitting. He was even younger than Arthur! That struck him as a good omen, so he tried to talk to him. He greeted him in English, but the sailor, although he understood, could not express himself fluently. Rimbaud recognized a Slavic accent and spoke to him in Russian, which improved things. In the end they managed to understand each other in French.

The sailor turned out to be Polish. His name was Józef Teodor Konrad Korzeniowski, a name that Arthur made him repeat several times. They drank together. Rimbaud asked about the crew of the *Mont-Blanc*, the pay, and the conditions on board. Józef told him that from Batavia they were going to the north of the Malay peninsula and then to Formosa, before returning to France. The *Mont-Blanc* had originally been due to go to Martinique, which was the destination he had chosen, but at the last minute the company sent her east, because another cargo ship had sunk.

The conditions on board were normal. A sailor had died crossing the Arabian Sea, although not because of a contagious disease. The shifts had been hard, but fair. They were leaving the following day, it was his last night in Batavia.

Rimbaud asked why he had gone to sea so young and Józef told him, in brief, that he was an orphan: his mother had died of tuberculosis and his father, arrested for some mysterious crime, died in prison. That had forced him to live with his aunt and uncle, from the age of twelve. When he had finished his studies, at seventeen, he had decided to go to Italy and then to Marseilles, where he'd signed on as a sailor on the *Mont-Blanc*.

Rimbaud told him that he had been in Italy not so long before. They talked about the Alps and the tranquil roads and the unexpected corners of Italian cities. Józef talked about Venice and Trieste. Rimbaud mentioned his intention to reach Rhodes, and his unrealized wish to get as far as Russia. The Pole heard the word Russia and went on the alert. Are you interested in Russia? For him, Russia was the embodiment of evil and danger. Then Józef suggested he try the rice liquor from China that was sold in another local tavern, so they moved on.

Young Konrad was a good drinker, and Rimbaud was not far behind.

The young men kept talking about journeys and adventures. Then the spirit of Rimbaud, swayed by the liquor, started to emerge; he told him about his decadent bourgeois life in Paris, the incredible docks in London, and his adventures during the war with Prussia, exaggerating the number of dead German soldiers he had encountered in the fields.

Konrad talked about his escapades in Munich, Vienna, and Lucerne. Rimbaud told him that a wicked coachman had stolen his money and baggage in Vienna, which was why he was here now instead of Moscow. They continued drinking until the hour when the young Pole had to go back to his berth. Day was already breaking. Before parting, he said to Rimbaud:

"You should sign onto a boat that will take you to America, to the Caribbean islands. It's a new world. That's where I'll be."

"My hope for now is in Africa," Rimbaud replied.

"Then I'll look for you in Africa. Good luck, Frenchman."

Saying this, Józef Konrad paid the check and headed for his boat. A serving girl came running after Arthur, holding in her hand a polished wooden pipe. His Polish friend had left it on the table. Arthur took it, shrugged, and put it in his pocket.

I'll give it back to him in Africa, he thought.

The return to Europe was on a British ship, the *Wandering Chief*, which set off from Batavia with a cargo of sugar on August 30. In this hypothesis, Rimbaud had been in Java just thirty-six days, and took four months to go there and come back, since he did not return to Le Havre until December 17 of that same year. From there, he went to Paris and was already in Charleville for the Christmas dinner.

The attempts to leave Europe continued, this time with another goal: Africa.

Why Africa?

It is in North Africa, in remote garrisons, that his father's shadow lies. Young Arthur wants to know what is there, in those sun-drenched lands, in those sad, silent dunes that have so dazzled him.

It is nothing new for the disappearance of, or separation from, a father to be a trigger for literary creation. The works of Joyce, Dostoevsky, and Proust are marked by that absence.

In his book *Le Génie et la folie,* the French psychiatrist Philippe Brenot also mentions something that might tally with the case of Rimbaud: the absence of the father pushing forward the figure of the mother. As Brenot says:

"The frequency of male homosexuality in writers can be explained by the Oedipal relationship with that Jocastian mother, with all sexual drives focused exclusively on the bond between them. Women are pallid figures compared with the mother and none can equal her. Only homosexuality and the role of sublimation can protect against the forbidden temptation. Proust, Genet, Jouhandeau, Verlaine, Roussel, Wilde, Byron, and Montaigne eulogize the homonymous virtues. Not to mention Socrates, Aristotle, Caesar, Botticelli, Leonardo, Francis Bacon, Lully, Rimbaud, Gide, Max Jacob, Jean Cocteau, Montherlant, Nijinsky, Pasolini . . . And the same thing happens with women, protected by homosexuality from incestuous tendencies: Ninon de Lenclos, George Sand, Sarah Bernhardt, Colette, Virginia Woolf . . . "

In the spring of 1877, Rimbaud made another attempt and traveled to Hamburg, hoping to sign on as a sailor to the Middle East. He failed in this and ended up in Scandinavia, working as an interpreter in a French circus. His great asset in those years, as we have seen, was his knowledge of languages. But the northern cold was too much for his constitution and very soon he realized that he had to leave. Early in the fall, he set sail for Alexandria, but fell sick on the high seas and had to disembark on the Italian coast.

Once again, back to Charleville.

A year later, in 1878, he tried again in Hamburg and at last found an offer of work in Alexandria. He had to set sail from Genoa. The roads through the Alps were closed in winter and he had to cross them on foot, with the snow up to his waist. He reached Genoa and set off for Egypt. The job awaiting him in Alexandria was on a farm, but he soon left. Now he wanted to go to Cyprus, but before that he agreed to go to Suez to work in a strange job that consisted of collecting the loot from boats that had sunk or broken apart off Cape Guardafui. From there he went to Cyprus, to be foreman in a quarry in the desert. It was hard, solitary work. He remained there until June 1879, when typhoid fever forced him to return to France. Perhaps he had by now resigned himself to his fate and was content to watch life go by, without any expectations.

What happened next was the death of his father, in that same year of 1879. Farewell to Captain Frédéric Rimbaud, who took his leave of the world in Dijon, surrounded by his second family. Vitalie and her children did not attend the funeral.

According to Starkie, Delahaye, his most loyal friend, once asked him what had happened to his poetry. Rimbaud grimaced and replied:

"I never think about it."

On his twenty-fifth birthday, he announced in Charleville that he was going away for a long time. A group of friends gathered to say goodbye to him in a café on Place Ducal. When Rimbaud arrived, looking very elegant, he solemnly announced that his years of wandering were now over and that he was preparing himself for great tasks. His poetic ravings had been left behind. From now on, he would live like a normal person, climbing as high as he could and building a huge fortune.

None of these friends ever saw him again.

5

We arrived in Bogotá just before eight in the morning. It was cold and foggy, which, to tell the truth, was not a good omen, although the streets were already swarming with activity.

This glimpse of the city, with its black storm clouds and its murky air obscuring the mountains, was not the best incentive for feeling cheerful, not even moderately. Quite the contrary. Nor did a glance at the other passengers suggest anything happy: sleepy and yawning, with their stuck-down hair and their rumpled clothes, they walked like zombies along the central aisle to the door of the aircraft and then along the mechanical arm that leads to the terminal, whose icy tiled floors and large windows did nothing but increase the cold and the desolation, that lack of warmth and affection that seemed to descend from the dark clouds.

You have to be very well adjusted to arrive in Bogotá without feeling a pang of anxiety, a tightening in the chest that restricts your breathing and transforms the lack of air into a kind of moral sanction. Whenever I've landed here, ever since I was a child, I've felt again that terrible dread and a strong sense of guilt, however unfounded. As if I were one of the brothers Karamazov, Alyosha for example.

Is it the thickness of the air or the quality of the light or the combination of all that with my own past? Maybe that's the key: the past.

There he is, that boy to whom nothing ever happened, who

wanted things to happen, and who looked at the sky and the mountains, wondering time and time again when it would be his turn. I could extend this to my adolescence, and to an extent I still feel it. Whenever someone has the spotlight in their face there is always someone else just outside the light, standing in the shadows, waving his hands nervously, feeling slightly sad and very anxious. That was me. The things I longed for happened to other people, people close to me, and I could do nothing but resign myself to occupying a modest place. By the time life at last started to give me something, my skin was already so sensitive that the spotlight hurt me and what I had so much yearned for did me harm in the end. All that anxiety was there, in the thick cold air of Bogotá, that low-intensity earth tremor from which I had sometimes had to distance myself in order to aspire to a life of my own.

I was one more in the stream of gray, yawning zombies expelled from the bowels of the plane, walking now with a traveling bag on my back along the endless corridors lined with advertising, bright images, colors, notices saying: Welcome to Colombia! To nature, to birds and orchids, to the five thermal strata!, "the country where the only thing you risk is wanting to stay," the condor and the anaconda, the jaguar, the precious hummingbird and the transparent waters of Caño Cristales, the green Amazon forest and the mysterious desert of the Guajira with its indigenous Wayuu people, the fertile coffee-growing area, the birds of Malpelo, "The answer is . . . Colombia!", the mysteries of San Agustín and Tierradentro, not to mention the Chiribiquete mountains, with the oldest cave paintings and the largest number of successive eras in the world, plus *cumbia* and *joropo* and *mapalé* . . .

All very happy, ready to greet those who had left expelled by war and poverty—which wasn't my case—in a fraternal embrace of welcome, since thanks to the peace the country had stopped being what it had been for half a century: an execution yard some 450,000 square miles in area, whose rivers and lagoons had been turned into dumping grounds for dead bodies and from which they were now gradually exhuming the millions of bones buried under the green layer of vegetation, which had turned the country, for decades, into the most beautiful and flower-bedecked mass grave in Latin America.

The slogans piled up along the corridors of the international arrivals terminal: "Thank you for coming back!" "Your country has never forgotten you!" "Happy to see you again!" "With you we are better!"

And on we trudged, wearily. Others, who didn't want to walk, advanced along the moving walkway. Men and women, children. All the returnees.

That joy was addressed entirely to them, but to tell the truth, they didn't look very joyful, but rather tense and expectant; they didn't yet dare lower their guard, perhaps because of that dark sky and the persistent drizzle, which filled them with foreboding.

The corridor seemed never to end and the tightness in my chest was getting worse. But then we got to the baggage claim, and the waiting, the assembly of the various items, the hiring of porters, all the things we might consider part of the "ontology" of airport life, gradually dispelled the nightmare.

At last we were outside, in the drizzle.

Tertullian stepped forward to announce that as of now he was going into "operational mode." Naturally, he wouldn't be able to spend the night with us, although he would be in "permanent contact through different means." Then he said to Juana:

"While we are here, stop using social networks, all right? And the same goes for you, Manuela. Consul, do you use them?"

I told him I didn't. I offered to take him wherever he wanted to go in the city and he looked at me with a twitch of the eye:

"Do you think I can locate a bandit all the way from Spain and I have nobody to pick me up at the airport? Thanks, I appreciate it. You're a good man, Consul. But it's better this way, for everyone's security. We each go our own way. Get settled in, Juana has given me the details. As soon as I've sorted out a couple of things I'll be in touch. Ciao."

We took a taxi to the Nogal Apartments on Seventh and 81st. It was another of the luxurious homes belonging to Juana's lawyer friend, Alfredo Conde—to tell the truth, by now I was eager to meet him.

On the way, I looked out at my old hometown, trying to recognize it amid all this institutionalized cheerfulness.

And of course I saw it.

There were the congested Avenida Caracas and its dusty urapan trees; the horrible 63rd Street with its seedy park and its church, which struck me as small and pretentious; around it I saw people sleeping on the streets, just like in Delhi, although with less filth and garbage; a number of shaggy characters sucking from plastic bottles and dodging cars, ugly, toothless people who seemed to be indifferent to the ice-cold morning. And at the Transmilenio stops, crowds of disgruntled citizens, huddled in their horrible sweaters and jackets.

I was starting to feel sick again. My heart was beating rapidly and I thought I should buy an extra dose of Losartan. I hoped and prayed there was coca tea in the lawyer's apartment, because I was already beginning to feel a throbbing in my temples.

The heights of Bogotá.

Crossing the border into the north of the city, everything was so different that I couldn't believe my eyes. Like day and night. Avenida Chile was the new financial center and its buildings, like fountain pens erect against the gray sky, proclaimed the economic boom and the longed-for growth in GDP spurred by the new era of peace. This was the Colombia of *The*

Economist, the Colombia of sustained growth, but also, by contrast, of the great disparity between salaries and national wealth that made it, in spite of the good news, one of the unfairest countries in Latin America.

Juana was showing the city to Manuelito, whose face was glued to the window and who seemed to want to swallow it all with his eyes.

"And are all these people Colombians?" he asked.

"All of them," I said.

The apartment was large and comfortable, decorated with taste, filled with books and antiques. I settled into a room at the back, facing the mountains, from where I could gaze, not only at the dawn, but at the great landscape of the capital's aristocracy. Manuela occupied the room next to mine, and Juana the one after that, with a double bed for her and the child.

"Haven't you been back to Bogotá in all these years?" I asked Juana.

"No," she said.

"But doesn't your family live here?" Manuela asked. "Aren't you going to see them?"

"I have to think about it," Juana said, somewhat curtly. "Maybe I should go with Manuelito, I don't know if they're still living in the same place."

"That can easily be found out," I replied.

Manuela said the only person she wanted to see was in Cali. The mother of one of her classmates from the convent school. I remembered the story, her name was Gloria Isabel.

"But I don't think anyone should know I'm here," Manuela said. "Don't forget I came here to settle something, not for a vacation. When it's all over I'll leave and never come back to this foul country."

The smell of Bogotá was the same as thirty years ago. A cold wind from the mountains, mixed with fuel and gases. The noises, too.

I walked to Avenida Chile, looking for a drugstore. I took a Losartan right then and there and felt better. People crossed the street without letting go of their telephones, as if to demonstrate how busy and industrious they were. I turned onto Ninth and headed south. The English houses in this neighborhood were the same, although I couldn't recognize any of the stores. Nor did I remember anything specific, so I went on and when I got to 67th the surroundings changed.

Crossing the street, I found myself in a middle-class area. There were eateries selling lunches, with plastic tables and chairs out on the sidewalk, laborers drinking soda or beer, students, office workers. Farther on, I saw the Paraíso Turkish Baths, which I'd often frequented in my teenage years. The building was the same as ever. I felt tempted but it was too early. Then I came to Lourdes Park and saw again how deteriorated it was. When I was young, that church had a certain prestige. Now it was in an obvious state of decay. I saw card players, shoeshine boys—yes, they were still there—candy sellers, sellers of *minutos*, and an incredible number of moochers of all kinds, from strange creatures with blackened skin and rags to displaced people. The forgotten ones of the post-conflict period. There was poverty and need, but people were smiling, even though these smiles didn't seem to correspond to anything cheerful.

I went into the church and was surprised by what I saw.

The Colombian episcopate had abandoned its old concepts and adopted Pope Francis's idea of a free, modern Church. They too, in a way, were possessed by the spirit of reconciliation and the new climate of national goodness. In an age of harsh competition with the Evangelical churches, it meant an opportunity to communicate with people by providing spiritual aid. But you had to be bold and imaginative.

One of the current projects was to install Wi-Fi in all the churches in the country. At the beginning of mass, the priest would give the congregation the access code, so that as they followed the sermon they could use hyperlinks in real time. Another new service was the establishment of a confession hour via Skype through the program Parish Online, which ensured strict confidentiality and the same warm, human treatment as had been available in the old wooden confessional.

In their adaptation to the changing times, they had also installed toilets in the side aisles, to avoid the congregation having to leave the church to satisfy the call of nature, during which they might have become distracted and not returned. The new training courses for young seminarists in Catholic universities already included subjects like marketing and strategic communication.

The dark nave of Lourdes incorporated some of these changes.

On the side walls were screens repeating the last mass with some important passages emphasized between quotation marks and in size 46 Garamond font. I moved into the darkest part of the church, hoping to see the altar, which was shrouded in darkness, at close quarters, and it was only when I got there that I saw a young sacristan tapping away at a computer embedded in the pulpit. He wasn't at all disturbed by my presence. Passing him, I noticed out of the corner of my eye that he had a Facebook page open and was chatting happily away with someone called Wildwolf. There was a thin thread of music, a melody by Bach. Although the doors were open, there was nobody else in the church apart from that young sacristan and me.

Suddenly I heard a moan, a very thin voice coming from the darkness of one of the side chapels. I groped my way forward and someone said my name. How strange. I was a little dizzy, so I sat down on a pew. I saw some figures of saints in the shadows, but didn't recognize any of them. They all looked stern. My temples began throbbing again, and I again heard that distant voice: "Who are you? What are you looking for?"

I thought about the enthusiasm that was out there and about how uncertainty, any uncertainty, was eventually dispelled by the force of that faith in a near future everyone assumed would be beneficial. Maybe whoever was talking to me was right: this was no longer my country, or even my city, what was I doing here? The arrogant small town of the seventies in which I'd been a teenager only existed in my memory. Return? Where was I to return to?

I got back in midafternoon to find the two women and the boy asleep in their respective rooms, jetlagged. I devoted myself to reading and correcting my biographical essay on Rimbaud. We would have to wait for Tertullian to give us a signal. That might take a few days.

The next morning I went with Juana to Santa Ana Baja, in the north of the city, to look for her parents' house. Everything looked very different. The taxi dropped us on Seventh and she led the way, but when we got to the block she grew nervous.

"Let's go slowly," she said, "I don't want them to see me."

I looked at her in surprise, was she sure she wanted to meet with them?

"To be honest, I only want to know where my brother is buried, nothing else. When they tell me that, I'll never see them again. I want to visit his grave, I want Manuelito to pay his respects."

We stood across the street from their house and she looked at the windows to see if she could see anyone moving. I offered to go and ring the doorbell. After all, they didn't know me. She was fine with that, but preferred to wait a while. We sat down on a bench at the end of the street, diagonally across from the house. She was hoping to see them without going inside and confronting her memories.

"I can introduce myself as a consul and ask them for your brother's grave," I insisted.

"Would you do that for me?"

I walked up to the door and rang the bell. I waited a moment or two, but nothing happened. I rang again and only then did I hear a very low voice arriving from the back of the house.

"Yeeees . . . ? Who is it?"

"A friend of Manuel Manrique."

There was a strange silence. I was about to ring the door-bell again when I saw someone open a kind of hatch.

"Yes? How can I help you?"

"Good afternoon," I said, "is this the Manrique family?"

The woman looked me up and down. Something in her mind must have approved of me, because she replied politely:

"No, señor. The Manriques moved away two years ago. I can give you their new address if you'd like."

"Yes, I would, señora."

They had gone to live in a neighborhood called Villa Magdala in the north of the city, near the freeway. We took a taxi, and counted the streets as we went. It was an apartment block. Their apartment was number 308.

"Would you like me to go again?"

Juana thought about this for a moment. I remembered the tattoo on her hip, Madame Butterfly.

"Yes, Consul. You go."

I announced myself with my name and said I was consul in India, which was false.

"Go on up," the doorman said.

It was the mother who opened the door to me, a skinny, gray-haired woman. Deep down in her expression, I thought I saw something of Juana's hardness. Behind her was the father, who invited me in.

"It's good of you to remember us, Consul," he said.

The living room was a small rectangle with barely enough room for a couch, a coffee table, and a stand for the TV. It was a sad place.

The mother brought coffee and sat down at the table.

"I went to your old address, in Santa Ana. The new tenant told me you had moved and gave me your details."

"Yes," the mother said, "she's a very nice lady."

"I still remember your phone call asking about Manuelito," the father said. "I was very grateful for that. I can imagine what it must have cost you."

"I don't want to disturb you or revive bad memories," I said, "I just wanted to say hello to you in person and, if you don't mind, ask you where Manuel is buried. Over the last few years I haven't been able to forget what happened. I'd like to see his grave."

The two old people looked at each other in surprise, but there were no tears. The father was about to say something and then couldn't, it was as if he was paralyzed. Then the mother said:

"He's in the Gardens of Remembrance, not far from here, following the freeway until 207th. It's plot 839-F. We wanted the Gardens of Peace, but there was no way, the prices were too high. This one we got on an installment plan. We're still paying for it."

The father looked at her uncomfortably. Why say that?

"Manuel told me you used to work in a bank," I said, looking at the father.

"Yes, years ago . . . But with the political unrest in those days, they transferred me to Cedritos, to a horrible place. I asked for early retirement in order not to have to deal with those lowlife customers."

The mother offered me some cookies on a plate.

"Of course that way the pension was halved, wasn't it?" she said. "Anyway. You have to be optimistic. God knows why he does what he does."

The father gave a strange smile that was more like a grimace, although not addressed either to me or to his wife but to something situated outside the window.

"Now that I've seen something of the peace, I'm happy," he said, "but I'm happy for other people, because the violence took everything from us. It took our two children, can you imagine?"

I wanted to tell them that their daughter was outside and that they had a grandchild, but I restrained myself. I had to respect Juana's wishes. As if reading my mind, the mother said:

"Same with the girl; who knows where she's buried, poor thing. Always so hard, so argumentative. She wasn't like the boy at all, he was sweet and shy."

I finished my coffee and stood up.

"Thank you so much," I said to them.

"Thank *you* for wanting to see Manuelito," the father said. "You're probably the only person, apart from us, who remembers him."

"No, that's not true," I said.

He looked at me questioningly. I didn't know what to say.

"We're all going to die and be forgotten."

I left the apartment and walked quickly downstairs, in the hope that the cold air would dry my tears.

Juana was waiting for me in a café.

"Did you get a chance to talk with them?"

I passed her a piece of paper with the information.

"That's where Manuel is. Gardens of Remembrance."

"Thank you, Consul," she said.

She didn't ask anything more, she didn't want to know anything about her parents. I remembered her mother's words: "Always so hard, so argumentative."

It was already after five when we got in a taxi. Getting back to the Nogal Apartments at that hour was a titanic undertaking. The city was dense with traffic, as if shaken by a small tremor caused by the brief displacement of millions of tires on the asphalt. The people, weary, red-eyed, looked around them with resignation. The taxi driver tried to get onto the freeway, but the avenue was blocked. Then he thought to take Ninth, and that's where we were, unable to move. Juana avoided looking at me, taking refuge in the earphones connected to her cell phone.

The cell phone networks were the great beneficiaries of the blocked and motionless city. Everyone was chatting and gesticulating in their cars, some on "hands-free," others with Bluetooth speakers, and the most disobedient with the apparatus in their hands or wedged into their shoulders. The women, statistically more devoted to messages, were all on WhatsApp. Passing 127th Street, I tried to recognize the neighborhood where I'd spent my teenage years, but it had changed a lot. The bakery, the house of the Pintos, my own house on the corner of the park, where had they gone?

Unlike cities such as Paris or Rome, Bogotá is a city of memory. Anyone looking at a corner is seeing something else: what was there before, what was demolished to give way to something new.

It was very late when we got to the Nogal.

Manuela was looking after the boy, who was having fun playing that game that consists of building islands and shelters. She herself was reading one of the many books there were in the apartment. I looked at the spine and felt something: *A Season in Hell* by Arthur Rimbaud.

"Do you like it?" I asked.

"Yes," Manuela said, "I read it years ago."

"Doesn't it make you want to write when you read it?"

She looked in the air for a few seconds. "I feel betrayed, so right now I can't even think about continuing. Sorry to talk like this, Consul."

"You were betrayed by a friend, not by poetry."

"The old bitch. I hope she rots and turns really ugly."

My situation in that apartment was increasingly strange, but even so I didn't want to call any of my old friends. I liked the idea of being incognito in my own city. In addition, it was essential I didn't lose sight of the fundamental point, which was that we had come on a mission of revenge. Although I still hoped that Manuela would change her mind. I still thought she would when the time came.

Watching television and reading a little of the press, I realized that in post-conflict Colombia, the new hero was the man who opened his arms and found someone to reconcile with. The ethic of forgiveness had replaced the old local Darwinism and become a kind of policy. Rather than receiving forgiveness, everyone wanted to give it. That's what taking action meant. The new aspirational prototype was the status of victim, real or symbolic. Never before had the fact that you had suffered terrible things brought so much prestige.

The Colombians were inundated with these feelings, caught up in a vortex of kindness and tolerance. That's why the TV program makers had drastically changed the formats of their reality shows. They were looking for the new man, the new woman. The models with their sinuous curves, the boys with their gym-toned muscles, now had another project, a new aspiration in life: to be tremendously understanding and tolerant.

The new national capitalism tended to reward the paradigm of a responsible, caring *agent*, in opposition to the previous model of a successful, misanthropic metrosexual who abstained in elections. These were the new social codes you needed in order to accede to respectability. The advertising agencies understood that the change of model involved modifying the old parameters, and instead of the strong young white Caucasian male of Blumenbach's craniology, they now looked for a male of mixed features, a somewhat bigger body structure and a round face, more *Homo familiaris* than *Homo faber*, who, according to studies, corresponded to the modern image and psychosocial brand.

Everywhere, this strange hurricane of goodness blew,

although if you opened your eyes on the street, on certain corners of the city, you again encountered the baleful looks there had always been and the sensation that at any moment, without warning, horror could be unleashed. Bogotá had always been like that, which made it a perfect reflection of the country, in its capacity for indifference and its occasional cruelty, even though this was currently concealed by the joy and the desire for redemption.

It was strange. We had come from another atmosphere, unbreathable and sick, with the aim of eliminating someone in the very place where humanity seemed most cheerful and reconciled. When it came down to it, Manuela was the only one who could really forgive, but . . . was she ready to do that?

The next day, halfway through the morning, Manuela arrived from the street with a book.

"These are my poems, Consul."

The title was *Songs of the Equinox*, and the author, Araceli Cielo.

I knew her. We had met at a conference some years ago. Perhaps in Puerto Rico or México, I couldn't remember, but of course I remembered her: proud, oracular, elegant, every phrase laced with an enigma or a metaphorical perception. On the cover of the book there was a sticker that said "Third Edition," which wasn't common with poetry books.

I started to read and discovered a very powerful voice, so much so that I doubted it could really be Manuela. Was her story of plagiarism true? I have learned that people without parents have a marked tendency to invent lives that, over time, stop being parallel and get confused with their own until they replace them. As if the biography truncated by the absence of a father or a mother created a void that can only be filled with words.

Many writers, like Rimbaud, have looked untiringly for their father: they have created nets to trap that figure that abandoned them, or they have run away themselves, in search of something still without a face or substance, perhaps hoping themselves to personify the absent one. Manuela's poems showed that wound at the center of her life, a scar that reopened several times. Absent father, treacherous mother, aggression. Pain was the origin of her creativity, but she could not continue until she had taken her revenge.

That's what she believed.

Reading the book, I became convinced that the author could only be Manuela. Everything corresponded to her life. The strange thing is that nobody in Araceli Cielo's poetic circle had suspected a thing; after all, the references in the poems didn't have much to do with her, a poet who was more whimsical and frivolous, her women halfway between objects and symbols. That's what I remembered, although it's possible that the image derived from the harsh portrait that Manuela drew of her in her memoir. I don't know.

Tertullian appeared at last. He spoke with Juana and said that things were almost ready. He brought news.

When he came in, I didn't recognize him. He was wearing a diamond-patterned sweater, a high-necked shirt, a coffee-colored jacket, corduroy pants, and Clarks chukkas. He looked like an architect. A silk scarf around his neck and a hat completed the image. As if straight out of the Gun Club.

"How elegant," I said.

"It's a mimetic disguise. You know, the best way for nobody to see you, here in Bogotá, is to dress like a bourgeois preppy from the Center-Left, or as a Francophile intellectual. I chose a mixture of the two. Does it suit me?"

"You look like an executive from Canal Capital," Manuela said.

Tertullian didn't laugh. He went straight to the dining room table, looked up at the ceiling, checked the corners, then went over to the window and looked out.

"Are we safe here? There's nobody listening to us?"

Juana assured him the apartment was completely safe.

"Look, this is a very complex thing, right?"

"It's one hundred percent safe," Juana insisted, "let's cut to the chase."

Tertullian left his jacket, scarf, and hat on hangers, took some folded sheets of paper from his pocket, and spread them on the table.

"Good, we have something concrete. Look here, it's a house on the outskirts of Cali, in the Pance area. A swish neighborhood. In ten days' time, they're holding a meeting, followed by a party, and Freddy's invited. The aim of the meeting is to divide up the sale and distribution of pink cocaine, practically throughout the country, with two other bosses."

"Pink cocaine?" Juana said.

"It's an alkaloid," Tertullian said, "a recreational drug, I mean, I'm not sure what the hell it is, but it's not the usual cocaine. What I do know is that it's more expensive. It's worth a hundred fifty thousand Colombian pesos, and outside, something like seventy-five dollars a dose. It's for yuppies and daddy's boys, for rich and androgynous young men who still haven't discovered their true sexuality; also for the young second wives of elderly tycoons, you know? The kind who spend the morning fucking their Pilates instructor, half the afternoon fucking their tennis instructor, early evening sucking their yoga instructor's cock, and at night tell their husbands they prefer not to fuck because they don't want to feel they're being treated like objects, do you copy me? I'm sorry, Juana, and you too, Manuela, you already know I'm politically incorrect."

Tertullian took out a handkerchief and wiped the sweat already appearing on his bare cranium.

"Right, there are two options. We have an infiltrator in the group that's organized the party, the one in charge of getting hold of girls. You know what I mean, right, Consul?"

"I get you," I said.

"Right. Those parties always end up the same way, with the guys drunk, doing coke or amphetamines or crack, until each of them goes to a room with two or three bitches to fuck. That's how it works."

He pointed to the second sheet, which had a sketch of the house.

"This is how it is: we have to put a girl in there who, when the time comes and the guy has his pants down, neutralizes him, gives him a substance that knocks him out. Then that girl will open a window and let in my team to get the target out of the house and put him in the van."

He placed his finger on the map and moved it across the sketch of the house.

"All of the rooms, including those on the upper floor, have big windows that look out on the inner garden, but since we can't know which room he'll use we'll need the girl to tell us. Once we get him, everything's arranged. There's a place ready where Manuela can be with him and do whatever she wants to do: a soundproof cellar in the middle of the countryside."

"And what's the second option?" I asked.

"Well, the second is a bit more like in a movie, if you like. It consists of intercepting him on the way and opening fire on him. He always takes two cars, with escorts, but we can have long-range weapons ready on the road. Of course, this has the disadvantage of noise, plus it's risky. If the police happen to pass by, we're screwed. And if he realizes that someone's after him, he'll hide and we won't be able to grab him for God knows how long."

"So you're inclined to the first option," I said.

Tertullian again hit the table with his thumbs.

"Yes, I am. It's the kind of plan I like because the risk is contained within relatively calculable vectors, and the operation depends entirely on the talent of those involved, not on fire-power or other variables. Even intelligence plays a role. It's like microsurgery, while the other way is like fumigating from above or fishing with dynamite, know what I mean?"

All eyes, naturally, turned to Manuela.

"Let's do it the first way," she said, "I'll get myself into the party."

Tertullian was surprised.

"Look, I don't know if you'll be able to, because if he recognizes you, you won't get out alive. You're not only a witness, but from what you told me, you gave his name to the police. You're an enemy. However much we change you, he can still recognize you, and everything will go to hell."

"Before he can kill me I'll knock him out."

Tertullian scratched his chin and neck.

"In those parties, they give the girls a thorough inspection, they check their vaginas and their colons, you understand? You won't be able to sneak in even a pin. That's the problem. It's better if you stay in the house and when we have him you go into action."

Juana had been watching all this from the back. She took a step toward the table and said:

"I'll do it, I'll go."

I'd imagined she might suggest this. I thought it was madness, but I preferred Tertullian to be the one to tell her so.

"Are you crazy? You have a kid, and this is a dangerous game. Right now my contacts are looking for women to train."

"I know these guys, I can do it," Juana said. "I've been a hooker, and in worse situations than this. Only the consul knew that, but now you know. I know what to do to get him to come with me to the room. I'll do it."

The coldness and conviction in her voice left us speechless. And it left me scared, powerless, desperate. How could she want to do something like that? How to dissuade her? Juana liked putting herself to the test. The idea of taking part in a revenge attack on a murderer and rapist excited her. I was afraid for her and the child, but saying something would be like screaming underwater.

Manuela looked at her in surprise.

"You were a hooker?" she said.

"For revenge, not for money," Juana said. "And this is the same thing, isn't it? I also have plenty of reasons."

Tertullian looked at her admiringly, grabbed her by the arm, and said:

"So are we all on the same page here? Idealism is important. Believing in things out of principle, not out of self-interest. Great. All right, Juanita, if your mind is made up, the mission is yours. Taking those human containers of radioactive garbage out of circulation is my mission on earth. But first of all we have to give you training, are you sure?"

Juana looked at me. "Consul, what do you say?"

I said nothing for a moment, my heart racing slightly. I thought about Manuelito Sayeq playing with the tablet in his room. About Juana's parents, alone in that sad house. I even thought about myself. In a way I had caused all this.

"If anything happens to you, I'll never forgive myself."

"Of course you will," Juana said, "this is the country of forgiveness."

"The only thing I ask is that afterwards, when this is over, we go to see your parents. Could you do that?"

Juana's cheeks tinged with scarlet. She was about to say something and stopped. She walked to the window. Finally she returned to the table and said:

"All right, Consul, I promise."

The next day, Tertullian came for Juana very early, to begin what he called *pre-operational training*, starting with a series of physical exercises.

When they had left, I spent a while looking at the rain. Its strange capacity to distance us from reality, to make it lighter, less uncontrollable.

It occurred to me that I should do some research of my own on the guy we were supposed to be removing from circulation, and about his business, so I made an exception and called someone I trusted absolutely.

He was an old journalist from the same generation as me, who had worked as a crime reporter for a number of national dailies and for some years now had been the correspondent for a Mexican newspaper group. I opened an old file on my computer and found his details. I sent him a message saying that I'd like to speak with him and to my surprise he replied within ten minutes.

"This is my number: 317 . . . Call me."

I called him immediately.

"Víctor?" I said.

"Yes, speaking," he replied at the other end. "What a fantastic surprise, when did you get back?"

"I'm passing through," I said.

"Right now everybody's coming back," Victor said, like in the song by Rubén Blades. "Are you still a diplomat?"

"No," I said, "I gave that up more than five years ago."

"And are you writing? Are you here for a book?"

"More or less," I said. "I'm doing some research and that's why I called you, can we meet?"

"Sure, how about the Juan Valdez on Seventh and Sixty-first?"

"I'd rather go somewhere we can be sure we won't see anybody we know. I'll explain later."

"Perfect, tell me where I can pick you up and we'll go to a *non-place* that I know."

An hour later he picked me up on the corner of Avenida Chile and Seventh. Víctor had changed a lot. His hair and beard were white. He hadn't put on weight. He was doing well judging by his car, a black Jeep. He leaned back in his seat and gave me a hug.

"It's great to see you, brother!" he said. "Let's go."

He turned a couple of corners onto what, I later realized, was Avenida Suba, and finally drove into the garage of one of those houses in the old residential area of Niza IV.

"This is my house," he said, "*bienvenu!*"

We sat down on a wicker couch in the inner garden, beside a grill and a barbecue. Víctor went for an ashtray and came back pushing a little table on casters on which were various bottles: whiskey, gin, vodka, aguardiente, tequila, Kahlúa, Bailey's, Havana Club.

"Hell, the bar of the Ritz," I said.

"With ice or without?

"Two cubes, double gin, tonic," I said.

We toasted, then Víctor said:

"All right, maestro, now tell me, how can I help you?"

"You can ask questions that I can't and you have the contacts, but let's take it one bit at a time."

My first question was about pink cocaine. What the hell was it, where did it come from, and who sold it in Colombia?

Víctor made a few calls to journalists he trusted and then explained. This is how I recorded it in my notebook:

The chemical name is 2C-B, which explains the other generic name TwoCB, or in the vernacular: *tusibí*.

Formula: *4-bromo-2,5-dimethoxyphenethylamine* of the family 2C.

The effects of *tusibí*? Halfway between LSD and ecstasy, but not equal to the mixture of those two substances. Not as intense as LSD and less stimulating and euphoric than ecstasy.

It is called "pink cocaine" because of its synthetic color, produced by aniline, and its presentation in powdered form. Why that color and not another? A marketing ploy. There's a clear sexual metaphor, in that it disinhibits and powers the stimuli. It also suggests "pink Viagra." It's inhaled as powder; it can also be smoked, taken in tablet form, or injected. When it reaches the brain it attaches itself to the dopamine, adrenaline and noradrenaline receptors. It produces dizziness, a feeling of flight, hyper-confidence, a love of oneself and others, and overestimation of one's own ideas.

A dose costs 150,000 pesos, 75 dollars in the United States. When it is sold to the public, it is mixed with amphetamines. Pure, it would be very powerful—and dangerous.

In Colombia it's not easy to get hold of the ingredients. They are extracted from pills like Rivotril, which contains clonazepam, an anxiolytic and anticonvulsive used in neurological treatment.

We served ourselves another round of drinks. The Bombay gin coursed pleasantly through my body.

I told Víctor the story the priest Ferdinand Palacios had told me in the police hospital in Madrid and his connection with the paramilitary Freddy Otálora. What role did Freddy play in the pink cocaine trade?

Víctor looked in his files and couldn't find the name, which meant he wasn't one of the big bosses. He called a friend who worked in the crime and narcotics section of a weekly paper, who confirmed to him that yes, he was a rising drug trafficker, with quite a long criminal past behind him, a whole series of previous crimes as a paramilitary. He operated between Antioquia, Caldas, and Cauca. He was indeed involved with pink cocaine and had made a deal with the bigger bosses to keep part of the trade for himself. He was close to various families who managed the retail side. He had good contacts and although he was still in the category of "local mafioso," he was considered a key element of the Mexican cartels in Colombia. That's what gave him his power of negotiation.

"Do you know Quitzé Fernández?" Víctor asked.

"No," I said, "who is he?"

"A journalist from the *Diario de Sinaloa*. The cartel kidnapped him last year and almost killed him for something he'd written. They kept him for about a month and eventually let him go, but in pretty bad shape. He was considered a survivor, and the Mexican government and the newspaper wanted to send him to Europe, but he refused. He didn't want to give up writing about secret tunnels and throat cuttings to write about Aztec ceramics in the Louvre. They offered him the United States and he refused again. 'Stupid gringos,' he said, 'I wouldn't be seen dead there for how they treat Mexicans.' The only thing he accepted was Colombia, to study the cartels' branches and alliances here."

"That's the guy for me," I said.

Víctor took out his phone and called him. He spoke for a while, and finally said to me:

"He's coming here."

When he saw me, Quitzé hit his forehead with the palm of his hand and said:

"I know you, man, a friend of mine gave a seminar on you at Ibero University in Mexico City. And I went to see you when you came to the Book Fair in Sinaloa two years ago."

He poured himself a long glass of whiskey and came and sat down. Without beating about the bush, Víctor brought him up-to-date and asked him about Freddy Otálora.

"Well, he's starting to make a name for himself. The Mexicans trust him because he finds them good suppliers of coke and crack. What the cartels are trying to do is control the whole chain, from production through to retail. It's one of the most obvious expressions of capitalism, except that it's illegal; no restrictions placed on it by the State. That's why they need to have people here. They know that those who have the best contacts in Colombia will be the strongest here. It's a matter of time. The cartels were working with some elements of FARC, especially in Putumayo, but the peace process has screwed that up: the rules changed, they lost control of the territory, and the guerrillas who continued in the business had one big problem:

the others, the ones who agreed to the amnesty, knew where the labs were, knew the routes, knew how they worked with the growers and pickers. Obvious, right? After the process, a lot of people were arrested and a lot of fields bombed. The very same people who were demobilized showed the army where to go. The amount sent to México fell by forty percent, and on the border things started to heat up, not because of the shortage of coke, but because of the prices, which started rising. And then came the disaster: what they received was already very cut, inflated with all kinds of crap, and so by the time they sold it, which is when they cut it again, there was nothing left. It was chaos! And chaos causes a standard reaction, which is that heads roll, and not in a figurative sense. It's our way of killing. The Mexican Revolution was made by cutting heads, like with the Aztecs."

Quitzé knocked back what remained in his glass and poured himself another drink. Víctor handed him a bowl of potato chips and peanuts.

"That's why the cartels started working with the ex-paramilitaries. As exporters say: you have to make sure of the supply in the off-season. They didn't give a damn that they were the enemies of their previous partners in FARC. Their motto is: 'Don't get involved in other people's problems.' They do their own thing, they pay, they transport. If you have problems with your mother that's your business, and as they say: as long as you give us what we want, fine, if later you want to kill each other, you're perfectly within your rights, but first things first, okay? It's the morality of capitalism. Colombia is their promised land! The term they use for this practice is 'disintermediation,' an aggressive modern management model; it's a strange word, and I hate to write it, but it means exactly what it says: do away with external intermediaries and keep the whole chain under your control. They use the same system with arms: they don't buy from a Mexican gang that brings the arms in from the

United States, they have people themselves who do the job. It's a very sophisticated business model, unlike other organizations like the Zetas, who still control the Caribbean area around Veracruz, while Sinaloa is stronger on the Pacific."

Quitzé drew long lines in the air with his fingers as he spoke. He was a short man, and slightly overweight; he had a slight limp I didn't feel like asking about.

"They had and still have ex-FARC people around Caquetá and Meta," he continued, "and especially around Catatumbo, to pass it to Venezuela through Táchira, and from there, with the help of the guys in red caps, get it out to the north. Then the army took out Megateo, who was their ally in the area, and they had to reorganize. And every setback like that costs them millions! Around Cauca they worked with Macaco, the paramilitary who was extradited, but that was a few years ago. Since then the Sinaloa boys have started to take over Lower Cauca. Their people buy cocaine from the highest bidder, make half-ton bundles, and launch them on the Pacific in fast boats. Then once out at sea, a ship picks them up and takes them to Central America or straight to Mexico. Doing it all themselves triples their profits, and they don't have to give a cut to any of the Colombian cartels, who would end up being their competitors. I've calculated that here in Colombia a kilo of cocaine is worth twenty-four hundred dollars, but once over the border with the United States it goes up to thirty-three thousand, three hundred dollars. And then, divided into small doses in New York or Houston, it produces a hundred twenty thousand dollars. Do you know any other business in the world where there's such a huge gap between the cost of production and the selling price?

"That's where Freddy Otálora comes in, because he runs the Urabá area and has contacts in Cauca. In addition, he serves them as a double agent, because the Sinaloa boys are in the middle of a *narco-revolution*, successfully diversifying into synthetic drugs. They have labs in Culiacán, where they do the synthesizing on an industrial scale and from there distribute around the country and across the border. Being well established in the ports, they bring in the ingredients really cheaply from China or India. Here in Colombia it's more difficult, and that's why Freddy is winning the game of pink cocaine against his competitors in Cauca. The Sinaloa boys pay him in chemical supplies or even give it to him and then charge him a percentage on the sales. The other groups have to find the ingredients in medicines whose sale is reserved for psychiatric patients. That's not so easy, and the profit margins are small."

The doorbell rang and Víctor said, ah, that's the delivery, I ordered us some takeout food. He soon returned with a tray of barbecued chicken wings and spicy sauce in plastic cups.

"What about the tortillas, you lousy Colombians, when are you going to learn how to eat?"

Víctor wagged a finger in his face. "If you don't shut up about the food, I'll tell your paper you're drinking whiskey, not tequila."

"For your information, my favorite drink isn't tequila, or even mezcal. Don't you know sotol, from Coahuila? The indigenous people drink it in rituals and celebrations. The tequila you get here is very bad, and the good stuff is very expensive."

We ate the chicken wings with our hands. To be honest, the gin we'd been drinking had been begging for company. Quitzé continued with his story:

"Because of that advantage he has with the Sinaloa boys, Freddy Otálora has carved out a space for himself and is growing, and now what he's looking for is a larger structure. He comes from the paramilitaries in Urabá. Since that organization was financed by ranchers and landowners, when demobilization happened most of the fighters, the foot soldiers, either went back to their lands or continued the fight as criminal gangs. Some even joined the guerrillas. Having learned to get what you want with a gun spoils you, and then it's not so easy to get out. That's why Freddy was left alone, he didn't even have money to maintain all those people. And that's why he's looking for alliances with larger groups. That's where he is now. The Sinaloa boys give him a free hand to do as he pleases, as long as his schemes work, because the day he makes a mistake he'll show up in a barrel of cement or with his skull in such a bad state that only his lousy dentist will be able to recognize him."

I felt dizzy from the gin and called a taxi. The information I'd learned from Quitzé made me realize that I had to persuade Manuela, at all costs, to go back to Madrid, finish her psychoanalysis, and get on with her life. It was too dangerous a game for a young literature student. And the first victim could well be Juana. I didn't want to lose her again.

6

His African period began in 1880, with a prologue on the island of Cyprus, where he returned to work as a foreman in a construction company in the great port of Limassol. Ever since the British had taken the island, there had been a great deal of public building, and it was easy to find work. He could have stayed and progressed in that position, but young Arthur already belonged to that anxious legion of those who dream every day of being rich the next day. Where did that ambition come from? Perhaps from his mother's social expectations.

Rimbaud had a somewhat messy relationship with money. For several years, he was maintained by Verlaine and didn't have to worry; his drinking bouts were paid for, as was his food. Both important things for a poet! When he was left alone, he managed to find small jobs that allowed him to get by, but he did not persevere in any of them. Two weeks, a month, two months at the most. His longing for financial success was such that he saw the passing of time as a prison sentence.

He had to be rich now, this minute!

It was an obsession that led him to hate his employers, who never paid him what he thought he deserved. Because another characteristic of this legion of the anxious is to consider themselves eternally undervalued. Their own estimation of themselves is, alas, never shared by anyone else. Their rebellious dignity conspires against them and leads them to make disastrous decisions. Rimbaud would always end up insulting those above him and slamming the door.

So Rimbaud left Cyprus, with his head held high, but without a cent in his pocket. He crossed the Red Sea and looked for work in a number of ports, eventually arriving in Aden, which today belongs to Yemen, where he found work as a commercial agent for a French coffee exporter named Pierre Bardey.

He settled in the city.

"Aden is the crater of an extinct volcano with the bottom covered in sea sand. Nothing can be seen but sand and lava, incapable of producing any vegetation. The surroundings are a desert of sand, absolutely arid. And inside, the walls of the crater stop the air from coming in so that we roast at the bottom of this hole as if we were in a lime kiln." (Letter of August 25, 1880.)

This is the fearful description he sends his mother, since even though he wanted to leave Europe forever, excoriating it in his poetry, the truth is that he felt no great love for the places he visited, or at least never expressed it. Perhaps he did not do so in his letters to his mother in order to keep her anxious and on his side.

His modest job in Aden got him a little closer to Abyssinia. Years earlier, in the reading room of the British Museum, he had read Burton's writings about Harar, the sacred city of Islam, with its eighty-two mosques, walled and shut off from Europeans for decades and opened to trade only since 1875, when it was conquered by Egypt.

I can imagine Rimbaud's surprise on hearing his employer mention Harar. It was a key city on the trade route from the interior of Abyssinia, and through it coffee, ivory, hides, and rubber circulated. Indeed, Bardey decided to go there and investigate for himself. Enthused by the possibilities, he rented a huge building and transformed it into a store and warehouse.

And in November 1880, he sent Rimbaud to take charge of the branch.

The young poet—no longer so young and no longer a poet, as far as he himself was concerned, even though he was already the greatest poet in France—set off.

Harar! Passing through the gates of the walled city and entering that maze of dark streets, Rimbaud once again let himself be carried away by his own dreams of greatness. He was the only Frenchman in the city and had to take advantage of the situation. He could establish a monopoly over what was produced in the area. This fired his imagination, and he asked his mother to send him books about the strangest professions. He wanted to learn it all, to be a merchant and at the same time a builder. But as usual, this sudden enthusiasm faded, and young Rimbaud was left to face reality, which is that he was merely an agent for someone else's business, while life in Harar was unbearably tedious as soon as darkness fell.

In a letter to Vitalie from February 1881 he says that he is dying of boredom and that he will be leaving very soon, when he has saved enough money, because he has already realized that life in Harar will not lead him to the wealth he longs for. Looking for alternatives, and a place that would allow him to realize his dreams, he remembered that strange Polish sailor with whom he drank Chinese rice liquor in the harbor of Samarang before leaving for Java. Could America be the continent where he would be able to achieve his ambition? Could that young man named Józef Konrad have been right when he told him that it was the "new world?" What is certain is that in the same letter in which he complains about the lack of opportunities offered him by Harar, he asks his mother the following:

"Send me news of the works in Panama. As soon as they begin I'll go there. I'd like to leave immediately."

He is referring to the Compagnie Universelle du Canal

Interocéanique in Panama, a French company that had bought the concession and was getting ready to execute the plans conceived by Ferdinand de Lesseps, the engineer of the Suez Canal, who had been in the isthmus since 1879, preparing to start.

This is how Rimbaud learned of the project. Lesseps was to take to Panama many of those who had worked on the Suez Canal, and throughout the region, including in Aden, rumors must have been circulating widely about this new enterprise, which was due to get under way in 1881.

But Rimbaud was incapable of maintaining the morning's enthusiasms until evening, and the idea was quickly forgotten and replaced by new delusions.

After contracting syphilis—how? from whom?—he again spent some time in Aden. He was already anxious to leave Bardey's company, but unable to settle on anything else, he found himself reluctantly obliged to continue in his current job.

One of his intentions was to work for the Société de Géographie de France, sending accounts of his travels through as yet unexplored areas. The Société showed no interest in him for the moment, although some years later, in 1884, they did publish a report on his journey to the province of Ogaden, as far as the river Web, on the southern outskirts of Harar.

According to Starkie, the report was very well received and the Société wrote to him asking for biographical information and some photographs to be included in an album of famous explorers, but Rimbaud did not deign to reply. Rather than lack of interest, his attitude concealed something deeper. He was still smarting from the contemptuous reception of *A Season in Hell* and did not want to be seen as a mere travel writer. He imagined one of the Parisian poets he detested saying sarcastically: "Well, well, look at this, young Rimbaud is now busy writing travel reports!"

His life in Harar continued, although he would never stop complaining and conveying to his mother and sister his feelings of being abandoned, of being the victim of something he did not know. As if he were threatened by some strange, uncontrollable metaphysical conspiracy.

On May 6, he writes to them:

"I am sorry I never married and had a family. (. . .) What is the point of all these comings and goings, all this weariness, all these adventures among strange races, all the languages that have accumulated in my memory? What is the point of all these nameless sufferings if it is not going to be possible for me, after a few years, to rest in a place I like, have a family and bear at least one child? (. . .) Who knows how long my days in these mountains will continue? I could disappear, in the middle of these tribes, without the news ever reaching the outside world."

It is far from certain that Rimbaud was sincere in writing this about the place where he lived for ten years and was reasonably happy, but he liked to keep his mother feeling sorry enough for him to help him in his wild schemes. Vitalie continued sending him books on the most varied subjects: not a small expense if one adds in the shipping costs. Curiously, we know the lists of the books he asked for and not one is a literary work. Does that mean that he not only abandoned the writing of literature, but also the reading of it?

This has still to be demonstrated.

He may have come across books in Aden, in the Grand Hôtel de l'Univers, through which many foreigners passed; he might have had a personal library. It is hardly credible that someone like him could really have abandoned literature to the point of no longer reading it. Stopping writing is possible, but stopping reading?

That is more difficult.

On this subject there are, as far as I know, no precedents.

Readers who abandon reading? Someone who has read and loved books is like someone who has tried the coolness of water or the pleasures of sex or good food. He may stop cooking, but not eating. A chef may stop inventing delicious and sophisticated dishes, but I doubt he can do without decent food and willingly decide to spend the rest of his life on bread and water.

For now, his great objective, the telltale heart that never stopped beating, was his desire to become rich, perhaps with the idea of returning to Charleville or Paris surrounded with luxuries; repay his family; and take revenge on the Parisian intelligentsia. That must have resonated in the young man's mind or even in his guts, which was why he decided to go for broke.

The war in Abyssinia was still continuing, and in 1884 Egypt lost control of the area. The British preferred to withdraw, leaving Harar in a chaotic state. Rimbaud quickly moved to Aden, but with a surprise. On this occasion he arrived with a young Abyssinian girl! We do not know her name, just that she was tall and slim, like all Harari women, and with relatively light skin for an Abyssinian. The Europeans who saw her thought she was a slave, but it has been confirmed that Rimbaud led a conjugal life with her, although without children. They seemed happy and Rimbaud sent her to the school of the French mission. After spending some months with her in Aden, he gave her some money and sent her back to her home. Presumably when the situation had settled down in Harar.

Arthur needed all his concentration to undertake his next project, his most ambitious commercial exploit, which consisted of selling a shipment of arms from France and Belgium to King Menelik of Soa, who was at war with the emperor of Ethiopia and king of Tigré. Rimbaud calculated that he could earn five times his investment, and he threw himself headlong into this new scheme. In October 1885, he had a violent argument with his employer, Bardey, and gave up his job with the company.

As he himself told his mother:

"I have performed many services for them and it was assumed, to please them, that I would spend the rest of my life with them. They did all they could to keep me, but I told them to go to hell, with all their privileges, their trade, their awful store, and their dirty city." (Letter of October 22, 1885.)

That monstrous pride that in its various guises takes the name of "dignity" had again seized Arthur. What did a modest job as a commercial agent matter when he was on the verge of becoming rich? The idea was to buy the arms in Europe, unload them in Aden, and take them to the Somali coast, from where he himself would take them in a caravan to Menelik's kingdom. He was investing a capital of six hundred pounds. According to Starkie, that amounted to six years' savings.

No sooner had he started preparations than a thousand problems arose. First, he had to obtain a special permit from the British authorities to unload the rifles, something he managed after an enormous number of difficulties and a great deal of wasted time. Then he decided to start the expedition from the French concession of Tadjoura, an inhospitable and unhealthy little town, famous for its role in the slave trade. He had to wait a year before leaving, a time that must have seemed hellish to him. To speed things up and feel more secure in his dealings with Menelik, he joined forces with another French trader named Labatut, who had relations with Menelik and seemed to be a good ally. At the beginning of 1886, the arms were ready in Tadjoura and Rimbaud took on the task of finding camels for the caravan, but the natives of the area, the Danakils, used them in their daily chores and were not ready to rent them out. It took him several months to gather what he needed, having to incur expenses he had not reckoned with.

Time was passing and things were becoming ever more desperate.

The figures must have been dancing in his mind while the seasons turned. As well as camels, he needed to find porters prepared to make the journey, which was one of the most dangerous in the region. Other caravans had been attacked and one of them, led by the explorer Barral, ended in a bloody massacre, with mutilated bodies left to be devoured by the vultures and the beasts of the desert.

To complete the somber outlook, his partner Labatut fell ill with cancer and died before the expedition could set off. What could he do now? Labatut had been his best link with Menelik, the guarantee that the devious king would pay for the arms they were about to take him. The solution was to join forces with another French arms trafficker, named Soleillet, but once again he was out of luck: in September 1886, Soleillet suddenly died on a street in Aden!

Again, thoughts of a metaphysical conspiracy, anxiety attacks.

Then Rimbaud decided to go alone to see Menelik, and so it was that at the beginning of October 1886, the caravan set off.

I can imagine him in the convoy, on horseback, watching the silhouettes of the camels advance in a line at sunset and thinking that in that moving line lay his destiny, his immediate future. The suppositions he had made regarding these arms that were swaying on the backs of the camels! Now he had to make a final effort, to trust in luck. The most important thing was to get across Danakil territory alive, reach the kingdom of Soa, and hope that Menelik was a man of his word and would do what he had promised more than a year earlier to a partner who was now dead.

No, young Arthur, it wasn't going to be easy.

The terrain was almost impassible, most of it black volcanic lava. They could only count on the water they carried in their goatskin flasks, which, when warmed up, became poisonous. And then there was the danger of attacks by the Danakil or other tribes considered "savage." Starkie says that for one of these tribes the greatest reward of war was to cut off the enemy's genitals, which must have been somewhat unsettling.

Among the curiosities of the journey, which Rimbaud later wrote about, was the crossing of the saltwater Lake Assal, a kind of Dead Sea in Abyssinian—or *habesha*—territory surrounded by basalt stone and lava. Reaching the river Hawache, Rimbaud already felt close to success, since on coming down from the mountains they again encountered fertile land and greenery. They floated the camels across the river and soon arrived in Ankober, capital of the kingdom of Soa. The journey had lasted four months!

But when they arrived, King Menelik was not there.

A new setback, a new feeling that fate was playing him dirty tricks. Could he not hear the strange language of fate? For some years now, a voice had been pursuing him, telling him: keep calm, take deep breaths, stay in one place.

But nothing could stop this restless young man, so he urged the caravan on to the town of Entoto, where the king now was. When he got there he still had to wait several days to see him. So far, the entire undertaking had consumed a year and a half. And he still didn't have the money in his bag!

His interview with the king saw his tribulations enter a new phase. The hard journey through Danakil territory had been the easiest part. Menelik proved to be a tough character, a quick-witted and demanding negotiator. Plus, he had an excellent memory. The first thing he did was to confiscate the arms and tell young Arthur that he would not pay for them per unit but would pay an overall price, which reduced the total amount. Then he pointed out that Rimbaud's first partner, Labatut, had an outstanding debt toward him, which he now deducted from the payment. In fact, Arthur's ex-partner had contracted debts toward many other people, and he soon found himself besieged by creditors. Even Labatut's widow demanded her share of the profits. Rimbaud did not know what to do. The final straw came when Menelik told him that he had no cash, but would have to pay in kind, particularly in ivory.

Rimbaud could not accept this and so Menelik told him to go to Harar, since the new governor, *Ras* Makonen, did have cash available and would be able to pay the balance of what was owed.

This was the sad end of his dreams of wealth. After deducting the countless debts and sharing out the profits, the net earnings were quite meager. He recouped his investment, but had obtained little for the two years of hard work, expense, and red tape.

One fine day, in Aden, Rimbaud woke up to the fact that he had spent seven years in the Red Sea area and his financial situation wasn't getting any better.

The laconic letter he sent his mother says:

"My life is drawing to a close. Enough of how you'd imagine a person should be after exploits like the following: journeys by land, on horseback, in a rowing boat, without a change of clothes, without food, without water, etc.

"I'm terribly weary. I have no job and it terrifies me to lose the little I have left." (Letter of August 23, 1887.)

Thanks to his recklessness and his constant abuse of his physical strength Rimbaud was physically weary. There is a testimony about him from the beginning of 1888, provided by Ato Joseph, the consul of Ethiopia in Djibouti, and quoted by the researcher Charles Nicholl: the impressions of a number of travelers and of a French couple named Dufaud who ran a hotel in Obock and knew Rimbaud as a guest.

"Physically, Rimbaud was quite a thin man, of slightly

above average height, with an emaciated and not very attractive, even ugly face, which made his *hoteliers* say: 'Abyssinia won't form a very good impression of the French race through him.'"

This was what remained, three years before his death, of that angelic young man with blue eyes and golden curls who had charmed everyone with his intelligence and beauty. The only beneficial result of that crazy expedition was that between August 25 and 27, 1887 the Egyptian French language newspaper, *Le Bosphore Egyptien*, published his report on the journey from Tadjoura, advising against the route described. That autumn, from Aden, his articles were submitted to newspapers in Paris, such as *Le Temps* and *Le Figaro*. Nothing came of it. He also offered his services as a war correspondent—on the conflict between Italy and Abyssinia—but *Le Temps* did not consider him, even though Rimbaud was already well known in literary circles in Paris. It is worth remembering that one year earlier, in 1886, Verlaine had published the *Illuminations* with that famous introduction in which he says he does not know if "Monsieur A. Rimbaud is still alive."

Arthur's dreams of grandeur did not end there. Something told him that, because of the instability in the region and the growing European military involvement, arms would continue to be a good business. And once again he threw himself into it. He obtained something that was quite difficult to get: a license to import arms to the Kingdom of Soa, in other words, Menelik's territory, and with this valuable document he went and knocked at the door of the two biggest arms traffickers in Aden. Two Frenchmen named Tian and Savouré.

He now returned to Harar to run a branch of Tian and Savouré's business in terms very similar to those of his former boss Bardey.

This cheered Rimbaud. After all, Harar had been the place where he had created something, where he'd had a lover, and where the wind from the mountains cooled the air, far from the ferocious heat of the coastal towns in which he'd been forced to spend a large part of those years. In the new Harar there was already trade, alcohol could be obtained, and something he might have considered a sign of a civilized life: brothels. Rimbaud had already contracted syphilis, so he must have been an assiduous visitor. There may have been a great deal of the mystic and the dreamer in him, but when it came down to it, he was a poet.

7

The hurricane of national goodness completely enveloped reality, disguising it. The enjoyment of that longed-for peace was too big a phenomenon to be disturbed by the daily evidence that, here and there, serious new conflicts were emerging.

It was hardly normal. Nations are populated by human beings who are dreamers, egotists, highly-strung people aware of their finite nature and their problematic claims to happiness. And there is nothing more likely to generate conflict, socially speaking, than the pursuit of happiness. Many people didn't see it because they didn't want to see it, but the world was still substantially the same.

All the same, the index of self-esteem had never been as high as it was during those months. It was as if the whole population was experiencing the artificial high caused by certain recreational drugs, like Freddy Otálora's famous pink cocaine. People were happy because they wanted to be happy, and would never allow anything to hinder this induced and, for that very reason, precarious joy.

Displaying great patriotism, and respecting their constitutional duty to support the evolution of the nation, the Armed Forces joined in the construction of a new, happy, active, and healthy society. Their contribution consisted of channeling the excess of collective love toward physical disciplines, establishing sports routines to build healthy minds and consecrating exercise as a way of forging a bond between the current self-esteem and faith in the future. Their motto might have been: "The passing of time will not weaken our convictions!"

That was why, from very early, the sports fields and gymnasiums of the various battalions were opened to the public, providing opportunities for citizens to exercise alongside the soldiers of the Fatherland, with military instructors providing guidance in all kinds of activities: racing, high jump, weightlifting, team sports such as basketball and soccer, and even riding in some cases (insofar as this activity, in which it is the horse that moves its muscles, can be called a sport).

Everything began at six in the morning, when the country's radio stations broadcast the national anthem. In every barracks, the sporting day opened with the soldiers singing Rafael Núñez's words at the tops of their voices, with their hands on their chests, feeling proud of that music and those lines in every fiber of their being. The army also felt proud of seeing the population increasingly healthy, unreservedly expressing its love for its country. A joy so unexpected and pure that it produced vigor.

Returning from my morning walk, a little shaken by the previous night's gins—Víctor and Quitzé, as far as I knew, had embarked on a complete blinder, which consists of drinking until you're dead drunk, then going to La Piscina and ending up in the arms of some murky beauty—I had a coffee in the kitchen with Manuela.

"Are you still determined?"

"I haven't thought any more about it, Consul. It's what I have to do, and that's it."

"I found out a few things about Freddy last night," I said. "He really is a very dangerous guy. I respect your views, but just remember, there is another possibility, which is to go back to Madrid, continue building something that's yours and yours alone, and get away from the sickness of the past. Your poetry is good, you should continue with it. I think that's the way forward."

"I can't," Manuela said. "This is something that hurts me every day. It won't let me breathe. Knowing he's at large chokes the air in me. The thought that he's alive is so invasive it obscures any other thoughts, I don't know if you understand what I mean. I'm sorry that Juana is going to take such a risk for me, and believe me, I'm asking her every way I can not to do it."

"I know her and she's going to do it. Let's hope nothing happens to her."

The boy was still asleep and Juana hadn't come back during the night. The training must have gone on until very late. It wasn't until midmorning that she called and told us to get ready, we were traveling to Cali that very night.

"Well, it's starting," I said to Manuela, "we're going tonight."

"To Cali?"

"Yes."

I saw her give a strange, complex smile. Cali was the realm of her nightmare, but also of her childhood. And we are all of us products of where we were children, even if we weren't happy there.

Juana and Tertullian arrived at noon for the preparations. Manuelito Sayeq was ready with his satchel and his tablet. We would travel separately. Tertullian under his own steam. Manuela on one plane and Juana, the boy, and I on another.

"It's better to be compartmentalized, you do understand that, don't you, Consul?" Tertullian said.

"Yes, I do," I said.

When we got to El Dorado airport, I saw our image reflected in one of the glass doors: the child, Juana, and I, holding hands. The flight was very short, and at Bonilla Aragón airport we were aware of a different smell and the warmth of the air. Immediately, Manuelito cheered up.

"Summer is coming."

"Here, it's summer all year round," his mother said.

We took a taxi to a place in the west of the city, an old house in the hills. From the street, all that could be seen was a stone wall reached through a side gate. The house was farther up, covered by trees, only visible from the upper floors of the neighboring buildings. It had a garden and a terrace with a swimming pool. It was a solid middle-class house from the 1940s. Soon afterwards Manuela arrived, and we awaited instructions. Tertullian came after nightfall.

"Is it all right? Do you like it? Are you comfortable?" Tertullian asked, bowing. "It's just for you. I'm not going to stay here. You, Juanita, come with me. There are things we have to prepare, and you'll need to get into the swing of things beforehand. The party is in eight days' time and we have to be sure of everything. Consul, Manuela, you wait here with the child. When the meat is in the sandwich, you'll go into action, Manuelita, do I make myself clear?"

Juana said goodbye to her son. It wasn't the first time she had been away from him and the child accepted it easily. They set off into the shadows. When I said goodbye to Juana, I said to her:

"Look after yourself, I'll take care of Manuel."

"If anything happens to me, protect him. But don't worry, nothing's going to happen."

"You're not obliged to do this," I said.

"Yes, I am obliged because it's the right thing to do, wasn't it you who said that? I think it was."

"When you know the right thing to do, the hard thing is not to do it. Jewish proverb."

She gave me a big hug. Her body clung fiercely to mine.

"I like your smell, Consul."

"Look after yourself and come back safely. You still haven't told me anything."

"I know you really love the boy. Keep him entertained."

"I'll be with him every second."

Then she hugged Manuela. I thought I saw a few tears, and looked away. Nothing of what we were doing was irreversible, but it didn't seem possible to change anything.

Then Tertullian came up to me and said:

"Consul, I know this is all a bit different than what you're used to, but here you are, by their side, taking responsibility. You're a good man, I say that in all seriousness. Let me hug you."

His belly forced me to twist my waist rather uncomfortably, but I managed to get to his neck. He was sweating profusely and seemed rock hard.

"Let's go, Juanita," he said. "Don't spend too much time saying goodbye, it's bad luck. We'll be back in a week, all right?"

Manuela and I watched them walk down the steps beside the swimming pool and out onto the street. In the house, silence reigned.

Cali had a pleasant smell. It reminded me of Delhi because of the trees and the unruly vegetation sprouting through the cracks in the asphalt and climbing the walls. Also because of the heat and the feeling that the temperature changes the state of your soul. There was everything we needed in the house, but I decided to take a walk and buy provisions: a little milk, bread, cheese rolls, fruit; Manuela swam in the pool with the boy.

A little later I said to Manuela:

"What do you talk about when you're waiting for something?"

She looked up for a while and said:

"I don't know, all kinds of things. Wild animals, murderous insects, one-celled organisms. How about you, Consul?"

"The same things as you. Also about frankly impossible adventures."

"Impossible?" she laughed. "Why talk about them if they're impossible? Let's see, tell me one."

 I had already imagined her question.

"For example, the idea of returning."

"Returning where?"

"Anywhere, just returning."

She looked at the city on the other side of the window and nodded. Then she said:

"And you never talk about poetry? Tell me about Rimbaud."

"Rimbaud . . . " I thought about it for a moment. "He wanted to return, except that for most of his life he didn't know where. And when he finally realized, he couldn't. They amputated his leg, he lost one arm and part of the other. He died in the attempt."

"And where did he want to return?"

"To Harar. That was his only home."

Manuela looked at me questioningly.

"It's in Ethiopia, near Somalia," I said.

"What about you, Consul, where would you like to return?"

"I don't know. I still haven't found a place."

"Then we should go there."

"Where?"

"To Harar," Manuela said, "where Rimbaud wanted to go. Maybe I'll recover the poetry that was stolen from me by that old bitch."

I shrugged. It might be so.

Outside, there was Cali.

At about five in the afternoon there's a breeze that revives the spirits. Manuela and I would go out on the terrace to feel it while the boy played with some Lego aircraft bought at the airport. The maid Tertullian had hired told us that the wind came from the sea, behind the mountains. The Pacific Ocean was there. And it was true: some dusks, we saw seagulls flying. But none of these things that excited us could dispel the fear.

"Are you writing?" I asked her one afternoon.

"No, not at all," Manuela said. "Until this is sorted, I can't. The day after the revenge will be the first day of my new life. Perhaps then I'll be able to. I've thought about it, Consul. That day I'll be free."

The date was coming closer.

I was obsessed with the news: radio, papers, TV. If Freddy was to come to Cali things might happen that would make us abort our plan. For example, the police might grab him while he was on the move. The most desirable thing of all was that the army would ambush him on the freeway, he and his body-guards would resist, and he would die riddled with machine-gun bullets fired from a military helicopter, like the trafficker Gonzalo Rodríguez Gacha. It was an unlikely idea, but possible. That way Juana and Manuela would be saved from having to do what they were planning to do.

Waiting, waiting . . .

The day is marked out with floating buoys you have to make an effort to reach: lunch, dinner, sleep, breakfast. Anyone who waits—this text is full of unbearable waits—feels the passing of time and its speed in a physical way. It is slow and laborious.

I don't know who felt the weight of this stillness most, Manuela or me; what is certain is that by always being in the house—except for my brief morning excursion for provisions, which Manuela denied herself for fear that someone might recognize her—each of us ended up marking our territory, and she practically imprisoned herself in her room.

The child was spending more time with me, which made it easier for me to endure the hours. For children, time is like an accordion, it opens and closes; their one objective is to enjoy themselves, to play and keep their minds occupied. To spend time well. That's why a child is the ideal companion for a wait. I spent hours making rockets out of Lego, strange combat vehicles and spaceships, or reading stories about fantasy characters. We watched episodes of *Animal Planet* on TV, and his great discovery in Colombia, *El Chavo del Ocho!* At first it struck him as strange, but once he got used to it he started watching it for hours on end and gradually took to repeating its catchphrases.

At night, when the child was asleep, I would go back to my Rimbaud notes and lose myself in that strange, sad life full of hopes and desires and dreams that almost never came true.

On the appointed day, Manuela and I looked like two ghosts, going out again and again to watch the street from the terrace. We barely exchanged a word.

I didn't want to leave the house in case something unusual happened, and for the first time I was grateful that a child could spend twenty-four hours engrossed in the games on his tablet. That allowed me to concentrate on the news and check what was happening in Cali.

There was no news during the day and until well into the night, so I tried to sleep, which was impossible, as it was for Manuela, who decided to sit on one of the deck chairs by the swimming pool with her cell phone beside her.

I was reading in bed when they burst into the house.

Tertullian wasn't with them, only Juana and three strange characters. It must have been about four in the morning, day hadn't broken yet. Manuela came out of her room with a T-shirt down to her navel and boxer shorts, but seeing the strangers she went back to get dressed.

Juana had a bandage on one arm.

"Did something happen to you? How did it go?" I asked anxiously.

"It's nothing, just something dumb. We have him."

"Was it difficult?"

"Difficult, no, almost impossible! Let me rest and I'll tell you tomorrow. How's Manuelito?"

"Sleeping, no problem."

"Thanks, Consul, you're a guardian angel."

"So—the plan worked?"

"Something unexpected happened . . . We'll talk when I wake up," she said, "right now I'm half drunk and a bit high. Manuela has to go with them now."

Manuela came out of her room in jeans, tennis shoes, and a black T-shirt. She gave me a hug and left with the three men.

"Take care," I said.

"Yes, Consul. Thank you," said Manuela.

She hugged Juana and said:

"You're great, I owe you my life."

"You don't yet know how it went."

"You'll tell me when I get back."

She walked around the swimming pool and went down the stairs. Juana went to look at the boy, who was still asleep; she gave him a kiss on the forehead.

"He's going to wake up in a while and I'm exhausted, Consul, I don't want him to see me like this."

"I'll take care of him, you go rest."

Before she went, she gave me a kiss on the mouth. I felt her nervous tongue. She suddenly pulled away.

"Forgive me, Consul, I told you I was drunk and high."

She went to her room and closed the door.

I touched my lip where she had kissed me. The next day she wouldn't remember, I thought. I, too, would do well to forget about it. I had to fight against another idea, which was to go into her room, kiss her, and have wild sex with her, as I had dreamed of doing so many times in the past few years.

I went back to bed and tried to sleep.

I got up after seven. I switched on the TV in the kitchen to watch the news program and at last found something. There was an item about a massacre in a luxury house to the south of Cali, "a property that was subject to judicial process because it had belonged to a person extradited to the United States," according to the reporter presenting the item.

The head of the police, speaking live, said the following:

"What we've been able to establish so far, from the first evidence and a number of testimonies, is that two criminal groups, apparently connected with the traffic in synthetic drugs, as well as normal drugs, met in that house for a party as well as to reach an agreement on the dividing up of the territory. There must have been an argument or perhaps one of the groups went in planning to cause trouble, we don't know that for sure, what we do know is that there was an exchange of gunfire among those present, resulting in six dead and three badly wounded. Among the dead bodies are two women, apparently sex workers who had been hired to liven up the party. Another woman is in serious condition. When the police entered the property, the criminals retaliated and there was a lengthy exchange of gunfire, until most of the gangsters escaped between the neighboring houses, which has made the search operation difficult. The actions of the police resulted in the capture of three men, who are currently being questioned. Rifles, automatic weapons, grenades, and ammunition of various calibers were seized. The type of wounds suggests that those killed were executed at close range, while others have gunshot wounds in various parts of their bodies. Alcohol and drugs were found on the premises, which were clearly being consumed by the guests, for their own recreation, at the time of the quarrel. Large quantities of pink and white cocaine, crack, marijuana, and ecstasy pills were seized. Our first hypotheses point to a vendetta, or a restructuring of the distribution side of the synthetic drug trade. One of those killed, Néstor Pombo Holguín, also known as Cusumbosolo, second in command in the organization of the paramilitary Freddy

Otálora, is famous in the underworld for his scientific knowledge about the crystalizing of drugs. It's worth remembering that the last of these factories destroyed in a controlled explosion by the police was on the banks of the River Cupí, on the road to El Zunjal, in the municipality of Timbiquí, Cauca, a wild area that the troops could only reach by helicopter and descend to on ropes. As for the paramilitary Freddy Otálora, who we are absolutely certain was at the party, he may have escaped and his whereabouts are unknown."

On another news channel, there were further details:

"According to information from the police, the ex-paramilitary and drug trafficker Freddy Otálora was negotiating an alliance with criminal gangs in the north of Cauca aimed at putting pink cocaine on the market and then exporting it to South American countries such as Chile, Argentina, and Uruguay, but it seems they were unable to reach an agreement, which is what caused the quarrel and the subsequent violent outcome. We are also informed that bags of white cocaine were seized on the property, which were presumably being tested with a view to future business, since there were eight different brands, which might mean that it was going to be given to eight drug cartels, including the Sinaloa cartel, of which, according to the latest reports, Freddy Otálora was a representative."

PLAYING TO KILL
(JUANA'S STORY)

When I left here, Tertullian took me to a house on the outskirts of Cali where there was a group of women, all young and very sexy, most of them from Cali or Antioquia, who are the best women in this country, some of them normal, like me, but most with huge asses and silicon boobs and with lips, Consul, that didn't look like mouths so much as vaginas they could talk and eat through. I was there one whole evening, for the others to see me. It was all under the control of Tertullian's contacts, that's what he told me we should call them, *contacts*, and without names either, just Contact A, Contact B, and I said sure. We had to talk as little as possible. From the start, I saw that they were real hookers, because almost none of them was sober after five in the afternoon and by midnight they had so much coke in their brains they could barely control their jaws and the cigarettes fell out of their mouths. You know me, Consul, I'm a warrior, so I put on a pair of low-riding shorts and a top and launched myself into that jungle; I'm not as young as I was, the calendar was having its effect on my body, bombs have exploded and there have been collapses, but I keep going, I hang in there, so I sat down with them. Contacts A and B told them that I was here to work, that I was from Bogotá, and they all looked at me a bit suspiciously, you know nobody likes us in the rest of the country, but since they're professional hookers, they know they mustn't ask questions and nobody said anything and I didn't ask anything either, except their names, because we all know they're fake names anyway, so I said, my name's Susan. Susan? the girls said, and I said, yes. There was one whose name was Stephany, another was Lady Johanna, and one was simply called Pussy. She laughed when she said this was her work name, she'd chosen a direct marketing tactic, I'm Pussy and that's it, and the girls from Antioquia said to her, did you hear that, and why didn't you just choose Cunt? or Vagina? and another said, what about Thrush, why not? and the girls laughed, you know, Consul, I know that world, I'm good at blending in, my brain is like a computer that goes into sleep mode and I go off to another place, far away; I leave just an office with the light on, just enough to stay behind and socialize with these poor girls who aren't the brightest sparks intellectually, poor things, and what brains they have go out the door with their fourth aguardiente or their second line of coke.

Somewhere around the third day Contact A came and took some photographs of me to put on a cell phone that was going to be mine; Tertullian said: it isn't credible for you not to have a cell phone, and the cell phone of a woman like you has to have photographs one way or another, and I said, of course, and he told me that when we got to the house the likeliest thing was that they would confiscate all the girls' phones for security reasons, and that meant the phone would stay there, so the photos shouldn't be of faces; they also put a whole lot of fake names on the contacts list, just so the traffickers or even the police, if they wanted to investigate, wouldn't find anything compromising; then he told me about the cyanide pills, he said that in such cases the best thing was to carry one in the gums, under the upper lip: the contents only spilled out if you bit into it or broke it with your nail, and it was the only thing that could pass the inspection, it's the only thing you can use there, he said, you take it out of your mouth, you break it and pour the powder into a glass, the person dies after twelve minutes, more or less, depending on the composition, but I'm not stupid so I asked him, isn't that a suicide pill? and he said to me, good, that's another thing I want to talk to you about, Juanita, which is that if you find yourself in a very bad situation, where they could do you a lot of harm or threaten you with things, you know you have a way out, you just have to lower it into your mouth with your tongue and bite into it, and you'll be free of everything, it's just hypothetical, the pill is coated with a layer of rubber, and nothing will happen to you just keeping it there, if you don't use it you just have to spit it out, and I said, right, got it, and then we went on to the other pill I had to hide in my mouth, on the other side, which contained an extract of diethyl ether and was for the same purpose: when I went to the room with the target, in other words, Freddy, I would have to put it in his drink to knock him out and go on with the plan, switch the light on and off three times, to signal to Contacts A, B, and C which bedroom I was in, and they could come in in their ninja costumes, get him out of there, and take him away. The plan was quite simple; if there were bodyguards or security staff it wasn't my problem, the contacts would deal with them, it was a well-trained group, better than the army's "jungle men," Tertullian said, and so we continued with the training, although sometimes all this hush-hush stuff made me laugh, he showed me various photographs of what he called Target 1 and his followers, the second and third in command, and some of the bodyguards, the guy they had in there undercover knew he was supposed to call me Susan, but he didn't know why, so I couldn't count on him, in case of problems; he didn't have any orders or instructions about protecting me, so when I went into the house I'd be on my own, he told me that a whole lot of times, and I said, yes, I know, I've known it from the first day, and then he said again that as soon as I gave the signal with the light they would come to the window, and he said, if before they went in there was any emergency

I had two options, either to switch the light on and off twice, or to cry out, "I'm coming, sexy," have you got that?

He told me that if that happened the contacts would try to figure out what was going on and would come to a decision based on their experience. And there was something else: if things got really bad, if I was in extreme danger for any reason, what I had to do was cry, "Help!" and throw myself on the floor or protect myself, because at that moment all hell would break loose from the window, the contacts would fire a volley at a minimum height of three feet, and he repeated this several times, three feet, remember that, three feet!

I trained with men who weighed the same as Freddy, especially Contact C, practicing giving him a series of blows that didn't seem very strong but had a tremendous impact in sensitive areas, the balls obviously, but not only there, the kidneys too, and that's how we spent the week, including PowerPoint presentations about the various guys, who they were and what they'd done and how dangerous they were and how old they were and what vices and what diseases they had, plus physical exercises and combat methods, and the tactics I should use to make sure Freddy ended up choosing me; they knew he liked women who stood out from the crowd for some reason; they'd deliberately selected the other girls so that I would stand out, and anyway, I had to do everything I could to trap him, make eyes at him, give him signals, the kind of thing any woman can do, right, Consul? The training was good for me, and it was funny, I had to do it wearing just a top and boxer shorts, to be in the same conditions I was going to be in when I was in the house, so when I worked with Contacts A, B, and C, they kept looking at my tattoos, probably wondering, who is this crazy woman? where did they find this walking art gallery?

At last, the day arrived.

Tertullian doesn't believe in God, but in a very strange thing he calls the Ancient Masters, and so he made us perform a ritual, grabbing handfuls of earth and kissing it. The contacts weren't very eager to do it, because they were Catholics as well as one hundred percent Nazis. Contact C, the one I practiced self-defense with a thousand times, had a swastika tattooed on his left nipple, and it struck me that they were guys who'd had military training and were used to heavy weapons, so it would have been very strange if they weren't army or paramilitaries, but I didn't ask any questions, their uniforms were very tight-fitting black outfits, bulletproof vests, black ski masks and helmets, a pretty disturbing image! If you met one of these guys in the middle of the night you'd piss your pants with fright; the traffickers we were going to attack, starting with Freddy, had no idea what was in store for them, and eventually Tertullian's undercover guy called and seven of the girls in the apartment, including me, had to go.

They took us in an SUV to a house, which wasn't the final one; there they made us change and gave us a thorough inspection, took away our cell phones, and even made us all take a shower, and then, a horrible thing that Tertullian had told us about: a security woman made sure none of us had anything in the vagina or anus, in other words, they stuck their fingers in on both sides, with a rubber glove and lubricating gel. After the shower, we were able to choose clothes from a wardrobe full of really tacky things, I put on a pair of skimpy denim shorts, and a top that left my tattoos visible, I knew that would mark me out from the others, who had really ordinary tattoos; there, they also gave us a few rounds of aguardiente to liven us up and took out pills and mirrors with lines of cocaine, white and pink, but I acted dumb and didn't do it, I thought it was best to be clearheaded when we got to the place, at least until the plan of action got going, and anyway, around nine in the evening, they put us in another van and this time they did take us to the house, after half an hour of streets and traffic lights and sudden bends, I couldn't have said where the hell we were

and I didn't once look back to see if A, B, and C were following us in a car, but obviously they weren't going to let themselves be seen, they already knew where they were going, so we
arrived and they let us in through a side door into a huge house
with a swimming pool and a walled garden, and I thought: how
are my ninjas going to get in? But if ninjas know anything, it's
how to climb walls.

The house was all lit up and before we went in they again
inspected us, making us pull down our panties and giving us
the once-over, this done by a woman who was eating a piece of
chicken with her hand and had grease stains up to her elbow.
As she talked, you could see strips of meat stuck in her teeth,
and she dribbled fat, it was disgusting, Consul, and I thought,
this is getting very strange; I moved my upper lip a little to
check the two pills, which by now I couldn't even feel, and
they made us go into a dressing room to freshen up; in it, there
was another tray with aguardiente and ashtrays filled with pills
and coke, and a kind of madam said to us, well, girls, you
already know what you're here for, right? I hope your pussies
are shaved and clean, they're going to pay you like princesses
and the only thing you have to do is forget all about the word
no, just that, just remember those guys in there are the mambo
kings, right? and if they tell you to open your legs above the
table and fart you do what they say, okay, girls? the first one to
say *no* gets kicked out of here on her butt, do you get me? and
we all said, yes, and then she grabbed one of us and said, come
here, let me test you, you're . . . Selene, wow, that's a real
hooker name you gave yourself, now let's see, if one of those
guys tells you to pee in his shirt pocket, what do you do? and
Selene, who was from Antioquia, and was dying of laughter
because of this test, said to her, that's easy, I lift my leg and piss
where the gentleman tells me, and the woman applauded and
said, good, next one, let's see, and she looked at the list and
said, which one of you is Mireya? and another girl from

Antioquia said, I am, señora, and the woman said, what do you do if one of the gentlemen tells you to put a pencil in your ass and write your social security number with it? and she turned red and said, well, I'll put in the pencil, señora, but I'll write the number of my ID card, because I'm a minor, or if he prefers, my cell phone number, and they all laughed, and the woman called another one, Virginia, wow, what a name, you're no virgin, and said to her, well, Virginia, if one of the gentlemen asks you to eat Mireya's pussy, what'll you do? and Virginia said, well, I will, but only if she lets me, and Mireya said, of course I would, you cleaned your teeth, didn't you? you aren't dirty? and they kept laughing until they opened a double door and let us through into the living room where the men were.

There were two very big white leather couches arranged in an *L* and a whole lot of chairs and armchairs: it was a big room that extended out onto the terrace and then to the swimming pool, a huge house. The woman, announcing us, said: Sorry to interrupt you, gentlemen, the girls have arrived, don't these cuties deserve a round of applause? and they all applauded and I looked over them one by one until I saw him, there he was, in the angle of the *L*, that was him, Freddy Otálora: in front of him he had a dark bottle of whiskey, and I saw that each of them had a different bottle. There were bodyguards near each of them, but it turned out they were more like waiters, one for each guest, because whenever someone wanted to light a cigarette or have another drink or snort coke all he had to do was signal and the servant would attend him, and so we launched ourselves into the room and sat down where we could, I took up a position opposite my target, without looking him in the eyes, and started talking to another guy, who offered me a vodka; they must have been going for a while because their eyes were shiny, and then one who I recognized as the host, also known as Camándula, said to us, what would this world be without women? and he raised his glass and said, well, these beauties are here for you, my guests, make yourselves at home! But someone replied, forget it, Camándula, the last thing I'd want right now is to be at home, with a wife on top it'd be a prison! and they all laughed, and another one said, I also prefer this house to mine, and they raised their glasses.

I saw that Freddy was drinking a very good whiskey, Johnnie Walker Blue Label, in an aguardiente glass, and I started doing this thing with my eyes, which is what you have to in order to make a guy look at you, and which consists of looking about four inches above his head, it never fails; I started sending him visual signals; the other guys offered me drinks and talked to me, but I avoided anyone grabbing me until I asked to go to the bathroom, which was behind Freddy's couch; when I asked the woman she said, no, girl, if you want to do coke do it here, but I said, no, I'm sorry, I really need to take a leak, and she said, oh, a leak? good, if it's like that go take a leak, it's that way, and she showed me the way, which I already knew; so I paraded in front of Freddy with all my artillery, I passed close to him and when I got to the bathroom I thought: if it works I'll take off my hat to myself; when I came out and passed him again, very slowly, he said to me, you aren't from Cali, are you? and I said, no, I'm from Bogotá, and he said, come sit with me a while, I like girls from Bogotá, and I said to myself: first phase of the plan successful, now I have to make sure of him; he offered me a glass of whiskey from his personal bottle, and when he said he liked it without ice I said me, too, you had to spend ages getting it out, and so we started talking, and when he made a place for me beside him on the couch, I realized it was in the bag, all I had to do now was wait. Men are so . . . predictable! Soon he'd suggest we go to the room, so I relaxed and continued drinking, and of course, he made me drink whiskey at his pace, and I had to do a bit of coke, too, the pure white stuff, to be strong and get through, and then he said, don't you like pink coke? and I said, I'm scared I'll freeze up, later when we're alone you can let me try it, and the guy said, sure, darling, you're the queen here, for now do the other, it's good, really good, these guys have good stuff, but the pink stuff I make myself, and so I said, acting dumb, really? so you must be a very important person, what an honor it is that you're with me, and he said, when we're alone, darling, you'll tell me all about these pictures you have on your body, and I said, you can't see the best ones because they're lower down, you'll be surprised; I put my hand around his waist and now we were bang into phase two, the bird entering the cage alone; a couple of hours passed like this, talking nonsense, dancing very close, what can you talk about with a guy like that? I saw that he was strong but that he was also nervous, and he had a gun in his boot, I noticed that when we were dancing, and I remembered that those hands had raped Manuela when she was a child and burned her mother, and I looked at him and said to him in my mind: enjoy this dance, you son of a bitch, because it may your last, your last tango even if it isn't in Paris, and anyway, the thing continued, the other girls had already been paired up, they kept giving us booze and drugs, one of the girls from Antioquia who was smoking crack with the bodyguards was already being groped in full view of the audience and she didn't notice or didn't care, she was already so far gone; others were already kissing while dancing and letting themselves be touched. I felt nervous because it struck me that I wasn't going to be capable of letting Freddy touch me, let alone fuck me, that part of the training hadn't worked, I'd thought I was colder and harder and more professional than I was; I started to feel disgust and what I did to contain it was to say to him that I'd like to do everything but when we were alone, not in front of everyone like the others, and I started criticizing my colleagues, saying that those girls doing crack and letting themselves be fondled were the worst, and then Freddy, incredibly, said, oh, darling, it's because you're special, you're not just anybody, that's obvious.

Suddenly the host said we should have a dance contest and whoever won would take away a bag with twenty-five thousand dollars. He took it out and showed us the money, and Freddy said, good, who will the judges be? and the host said, we'll all have a vote, I'll hand out papers and pencils, each of us gives a mark from one to five and at the end we add them up, whoever has the highest score gets the money, shall we start? One of the couples went out on the terrace to dance, with the guests making a circle around them, and Freddy said he was going to the bathroom for a moment. I thought: this is it. He left his whiskey on the table, so I took out the ether pill without anyone seeing me, broke it with my nail, poured it in the glass, and stirred it with my finger; I grabbed the glass and, taking advantage of the fact that everyone was distracted by the dancing, I headed for the bathroom to wait for him. But on the way there, through a door that led to the kitchen, I saw some guys passing; they were bent over and had weapons, and I thought, something bad's going to happen, they weren't my contacts A, B, and C, so I kept walking, and got to the bathroom just as Freddy came out.

You left your special whiskey behind, darling, I brought it for you, and he said, you're a princess; he knocked it back in one go and just like it was a cut in an action movie the first shots rang out. Gunfire, yells, things breaking. Freddy rushed back into the bathroom, grabbing me by the arm; we closed the door and I switched the light on and off a few times, and he said, what are you doing? And I said, nothing, switching it off so they don't see us; at that moment his head fell forward; he took his revolver from his boot and stammered: what the fuck did they give me? And he fainted. The windowpane shattered and one of the ninjas jumped inside. Come on, Susan, he said, let's get out of there, the shit's hitting the fan; in the house there were sounds of gunshots and cries of pain, and also orders. The host was saying to the hit men, this one, and that one over there! and I even heard, where the fuck is Freddy? where's that son of a bitch gone?

I went close to the window and an arm pulled me up, but just as they were hoisting Freddy up I heard pounding on the bathroom door and a number of gunshots, I don't know if the bullets came through the door. The door finally yielded and they opened it just as my ninja B was about to jump through the window, so he had to turn and mow down the hit men, who fell, but other killers arrived and a shoot-out started. Then I heard cries, *on the roof, on the roof!* And more shots. I ran over those tiles in the tennis shoes they'd brought me and the guys in the house kept yelling, who are those people on the roof? And a voice said, it must be Freddy's security people, they're getting him out! When we got to the wall I saw the van and sighed with relief. We set off at high speed, while they were still shooting at us.

Inside, the shooting was still going on, some of Freddy's bodyguards had managed to barricade themselves in and retaliate, I don't know how because supposedly they were unarmed, although they must have had concealed pistols; anyway, before we left, as part of the plan we called the police; what we hadn't reckoned with was that the people throwing the party were planning to kill Freddy, so in a way what we did was save his life; every second that man breathes from tonight on is borrowed time, but maybe he's going to be sorry he didn't die in that house.

We came out onto a big avenue and in the other lane saw a number of patrol cars with their sirens on and a special forces truck. Tertullian, who was in the van, said, look, it's worked out better than we thought, we have the sausage in the hot dog and the shooting in there will cover our tracks, it's great!

I saw Freddy trussed up like a package, with straps tying his arms and a plastic tape around his neck that held his head to the floor, in case he woke up, although one of the ninjas, I think it was C, was sitting next to him.

Tertullian patted me on the leg and said, congratulations, Juanita, you're great, was it a good party? did he enjoy himself? and I said, he wasn't aware of much, when he opens his eyes he's going to think we're from the other gang, and Tertullian said, that's good, that'll cover us. But I tell you this: right now, sleep is protecting him, because when he wakes up what's waiting for him is hell. Those minutes will be his last bearing any resemblance to life. He's going to realize that he's sitting in a frying pan with oil, and the stove is on! He'll regret ever being born and he'll probably end up cursing the bitch who gave birth to him. As I told you, I don't even consider these guys to be human: putting these humanoids out of circulation is good news for any living being, even in the vegetable kingdom. Now, let Manuelita come and we'll see what she wants to do, although I'm already starting to get a few ideas, things I haven't done in a while, Tertullian said, in the refuge there are decent surgical instruments; but I didn't even see them because when we arrived I felt terribly homesick for my son and longed to be surrounded by people and not by murderers, so I changed, burned the clothes I'd been wearing, and rushed back here, and when I saw you in the door, Consul, I swear to you, I thought you were the first good man I could embrace on the surface of the world.

8

H e remained in Harar for three more years, the last years of his life, devoted to his work as a commercial agent: the same post he had had with Bardey before his experience as an arms trafficker and had repudiated. He was back where he had started, although part of his business still involved arms, and even slaves, on the Tadjoura road, the very route he had advised against in his report for the French Geographical Society.

It was a period of great commercial activity. Menelik had finally unified the territory, proclaiming himself *negus* of the region, a word that means "king of kings" or emperor. And Harar was the hub, an obligatory staging post for the caravans traveling toward the Somali coast from inland. It was also a special place, thanks to its pleasant climate. Addis Ababa had not yet been founded, so the city where Rimbaud lived seemed the best place for someone with good business sense and the desire to strike good deals. And this, according to Starkie, was precisely what Rimbaud lacked: business sense. Which is why he never managed to amass a solid enough fortune to allow him to change his life. It might be asked: what kind of life did he want, and for what purpose? Although an experienced traveler, he was hopeless when it came to solving practical problems, and at the same time he was too proud to lower himself to negotiating with certain people or reaching agreements that would make his life easier to survive; he wasn't very skillful at obtaining favorable conditions in negotiations, as we saw with

Menelik in the matter of the rifles and with the creditors of his dead partner, Labatut.

His dreams of wealth were becoming so remote from his real life that, with time, Rimbaud started to content himself with amassing at least a small amount of money. He became enormously thrifty and austere. He ate little and badly. He stopped frequenting the cafés and taverns of Harar. He moved about on foot. A French priest in Harar, Monsignor Jarosseau, quoted by Starkie, says that he lived "soberly and chastely, like a Benedictine monk, and should, by rights, have been a Trappist." He was a hard worker, he got up early to open the store and was already very busy by the time his staff arrived. This priest gives us a key testimony about Rimbaud. He says that he often went to see him for a chat: "We talked about serious things and never about him. *He read a lot* and always appeared distant."

He read a lot.

When it is said of someone that *he reads a lot* it never refers to practical manuals about field irrigation or the maintenance of canals. It is said of those who read literature and the humanities. In a letter to Paterne Berrinchon—the husband of Isabelle Rimbaud—his former employer, Bardey, said that Rimbaud wrote constantly. It is possible that with the passing years and the tranquility that age brings, Rimbaud took stock of his life and went back to certain things that had been important to him, such as reading and writing.

There was another new, and apparently contradictory, attitude: during his last years, according to those who had dealings with him, including his employers and associates, he became extremely generous. Perhaps the realization that the fortune he had dreamed of was completely out of his reach had liberated him and helped him put his feet back on the ground. He was now surrounded by normal people, with whom he had to get along. That angry young man who hadn't cared what he did or said to satisfy his whims; that young man who had been kept by Verlaine or by his mother, whom he blackmailed emotionally; that young man whose poetic ideas had to be carried out to the letter now gave way to an adult somewhat more accustomed—thanks to the repeated blows he had received—to the painful contradictions of life, which may be why he started to be good-natured and loyal.

His biographers say that not only was he generous in material matters, but also in words and gestures. He helped everyone; he received in his house whatever explorer or trader happened to pass through Harar and offered his advice. These visitors commented on Rimbaud's friendliness and his verbal brilliance and inventiveness.

"I've never hurt anybody. I try, on the other hand, to do what little good I am able and that, in fact, is my one satisfaction." He wrote this to his mother and sisters in 1890, during his last year in Harar.

There is an episode that is very revealing about who Rimbaud was in those last years, and the way he evaluated his past. It is a letter that he preserved and always had with him, in which the editor of the review *La France moderne*, Laurent de Gavoty, praised his poetry and suggested he become a contributor. In February 1891, the review announced that it had located the whereabouts of the young genius. "We know where Rimbaud is, the great Rimbaud, the one true Rimbaud, the Rimbaud of the *Illuminations*."

That means many things, but the most important of them is that this little book, *Illuminations*, published by Verlaine in 1886, had been received as Rimbaud would have liked *A Season in Hell* to be received. What a strange destiny, for poetry and for life. While he was trying to make his fortune in Abyssinia and Somalia, his poems, circulating far from him, had carved out a huge reputation for him, and he was now acclaimed in his absence. The fact that he kept this letter means that, deep down, he had been touched. No poet, however arrogant or implacable, can ignore praise. Rimbaud may even have thought of using that contact later, but this plan was cut short by illness and sudden death.

His life in Harar, the fact that he had settled in a house of his own—a place in the world—led him again to think about marriage. Apart from the young woman he had taken to Aden he is known to have had relationships with other local women, but none became established, as far as is known.

On August 10, 1890, he wrote to ask his mother if she thought it possible he might marry the following year, and in particular if there was any woman in Charleville or Roche willing to follow him to Abyssinia: he recognized that he could not stay in France because of his work. This hypothetical woman would have to accustom herself to his constant wanderings. Does anyone like that exist? That is what he wondered. Rimbaud was an unrepentant traveler, who associated travel with freedom and fulfilment.

To travel, to live, to be free.

He had already written that on his departure, in the final text of *A Season in Hell*. "*At dawn, armed with a burning patience, we shall enter the splendid Cities.*" What are these cities?

I have wondered that a thousand times. In her analysis, Starkie speaks of magic and alchemy, the struggle between Satan and Merlin that would mark the end of his claim to equal God. Others mention the cities of God, whose gates had suddenly closed to him but would now open, which is a cause for joy.

But I think he is referring to something much simpler. The desire to mark out a literary path: the path of mysterious cities. It is here that the best stories happen and unknown people live. Much of the twentieth-century novel followed that line. With that phrase, Rimbaud sealed forever the union between writing and traveling, between freedom and the mystery of creation, that particular solitude that is only found in hotels and at border posts.

To travel, and to go farther each time.

And occasionally, to return.

Rimbaud's life in Harar was peaceful, for all his constant complaints. One of his best friends was none other than *Ras* Makonen, the king or governor of Harar, who was Menelik's nephew. There was also his servant Djami, of whom Rimbaud was very fond. He was a young man of twenty, a constant companion in his adventures. According to his sister Isabelle, when Arthur was dying, Djami was one of the few people the poet remembered with affection.

In 1891, fate took a hand and forced him to return to France. Not definitively, of course. Nothing is definitive at the age of thirty-seven, especially considering young Arthur's dreams and desires. A volcano that any little spark could reignite.

Around February, he started to feel discomfort in his right kneecap. What was it? A man of action like him, accustomed to walking twelve miles a day, could find a thousand explanations before considering the possibility of serious illness. Let alone that it might be anything fatal!

Oh, young Arthur, you have defied death for so long.

The pain in his knee persisted, so he resorted to home cures. He put on a tight bandage, thinking it was a question of circulation, varicose veins, and continued with his normal life. But it kept getting worse: now his thigh and shin were swollen. The swelling went all the way down to his calf. He developed a fever.

His commercial duties kept him busy and he put off seeking medical attention. In Harar, the last doctor had left a couple of years earlier. His leg got worse. He could no longer bend it, and it was very swollen. In spite of this, it was two months before he made up his mind to go to Aden. He had to close the store, which of course meant incurring substantial losses. The journey to the port of Zeila, in a litter with a canopy and six-teen porters, was agonizing.

He left Harar on April 7, 1891.

He would never return.

Starkie reconstructs the journey: the rain, the camels scattering because of the storms, the lack of food, the heat, the swaying of the litter, the unbearable pain. All this for three agonizing weeks, until he got to Zeila and embarked for Aden, suffering another three days of torture on deck.

In the hospital in Aden, the doctor's first thought on seeing the leg was to amputate it, but then, afraid the patient would die, he had second thoughts and decided to treat him in the hope of achieving some improvement. Another week of suffering without any result. When it was finally decided to repatriate him, Rimbaud liquidated his remaining assets. He was sent on the next boat to Marseilles, where he was immediately admitted to the Hospital of the Conception and given the registration number 1427. After being seen by the doctors, on May 22, he sent the following telegram to his mother:

> *One of you must come to Marseilles today by express train. On Monday morning they amputate my leg. Risk I might die. Very important matters to settle. Hospital Conception. Reply promptly.*
>
> *Rimbaud*

The die was cast by the time Vitalie got to him. The leg was amputated, but very soon he began to feel stabbing pains in the other leg. His mother had to go back to the farm in Roche, because her younger daughter, Isabelle, had fallen ill. The pain and desolation she must have felt, having lost her elder daughter and now having her son in hospital, one leg gone, and her younger daughter suffering health problems! The sad journeys she must have taken, alone, traveling up and down France!

Rimbaud tried to overcome the pain of the amputation and come to terms with the fact that it was forever. Alas, he did not know that the only "forever" he could count on was a few months. Death was already sitting at the foot of his bed, watching over him and passing its icy fingers through his hair as he slept. Caressing him. That painful amputation was a defeat, pure and simple. He himself had led his life down that strange path that, after many vicissitudes, had driven him to that sad hospital in Marseilles.

"My life is over, I am nothing now but an immovable trunk," he wrote his sister Isabelle.

At the end of July Arthur left the hospital and, a convalescent on crutches, returned to the farm in Roche to rejoin his mother and his sister. Twelve years had passed and now he returned prematurely aged, without a leg and without wealth. He was not unaware that in Paris he was acclaimed, but he bypassed it and hid on the family farm. He did not want to see anyone, not even Delahaye, to whom he had written so many letters.

For Isabelle, her brother's arrival was the central event of her life. She had been just nineteen when Arthur had left, which means she was a woman of thirty-one when he returned. She went to a lot of effort to arrange the best room on the farm, adorning it with flowers, sprucing it up with intense love. If we could look inside her head we would see a young woman burdened by the death of her sister when she was in her adolescence, with an older brother, Frédéric, who was the idiot of the family, and with this other strange, remote creature, a poet and a rebel, whom she had heard from in letters that turned him into a myth, a palpable extension of that distant father, the other Frédéric, whom she had barely known and who had abandoned her.

That is why it was she and not the strict, severe Vitalie, hardened by life, who took it upon herself to look after Arthur in Roche. Isabelle became his shadow and his nurse. And more important still: his friend. They talked endlessly and he told her all about his adventures in Abyssinia. With the passing of the days, it was to her that he confided his desire to return to Harar, which was his true home. In spite of being on the verge of death, when he had left Abyssinia he had thought to take with him a collection of rugs and objects that he considered special and that would remind him of his home wherever he was. These things were now spread about his room.

The pain continued, as did the fevers and the insomnia. His right arm, on the same side as the amputation, was frequently numb. Something strange was eating away at him from inside. His only relief from the pain and the fevers was to shut himself up in his room, lower the blinds to shut out the sun, and play an Abyssinian harp in a melancholy fashion while he told stories to Isabelle.

In Paris, his fame was growing and many already considered him the greatest poet of the century, but nobody knew that he was so close, recovering from an operation. If the poets of Paris had known, they would have come to acclaim him, which might have given him a new lease on life. We cannot know that. His presence was a little secret in Roche, although an open secret, since Starkie says that some inhabitants of the town came to his window at night to hear him playing and singing, as if he were an Eastern holy man.

But it was a cold summer and his health deteriorated. By now, he could barely move his right arm and the fevers and discomfort continued. He was horrified to think that he would remain paralyzed for life, and despite the care of his sister Isabelle, who fed him as if he were a baby, he decided he had to go. Where was his beloved Harar? Why so far? The cold of the north made him feel that he was in danger and he devoted his remaining strength to the dream of returning.

In Abyssinia the sun would give him back his life!

Against the better judgement of Vitalie, who could stand it no longer, Arthur decided to return to Marseilles. There were hesitations and tears. His insomnia had made him irascible, unable to make up his mind. But about one thing he never wavered: he had to get close to Africa. On August 23, he and his sister took the train. He was in unbearable pain. Reaching Paris, they transferred in a horse-drawn carriage to the Gare de Lyon to continue the journey south.

It was raining in Paris.

The images of that damp, half-deserted city at nightfall were his last of the great capital. None of those who saw the carriage passing in the rain could have suspected that inside it was France's greatest poet, let alone that he was on his way to an appointment with the Grim Reaper, who was sitting waiting for him in a bed in the Hospital of the Conception in Marseilles.

On his arrival, the doctors told him he had a carcinoma. It was thought that the illness might be related to the syphilis he had suffered years earlier. With the passing of the days his body became more paralyzed. He was incapable of getting out of bed alone. For Isabelle, this time by her brother's side was a strange mystical journey. The doctors gave him morphine for the pain and he indulged in profound daydreams.

When Arthur was delirious, he talked about Harar.

About Djami and the caravans, the cool air of the mountains, the indigenous Hararis. He would say words in Amharic that she did not understand. Isabelle's final struggle was to convert him, to save his soul. Arthur, paralyzed and stuffed full of morphine, agreed to receive the last rites and apparently, according to Isabelle, converted at the last minute. It was her greatest joy. The letter in which she tells her mother is euphoric. I saved him! she seems to scream. But immediately, in a flash of lucidity, Rimbaud again cursed religion.

He tried to escape death one last time, on November 9, 1891. He asked his sister to write a letter to the shipping company in Marseilles, asking them to take him immediately to Aden, insisting even on the hour when they could move him on board, taking into account the fact that he was sick and paralyzed.

It was his last attempt at escape, but it was futile.

He died the following day, November 10.

His supreme and final escape was death, distancing himself from the life he could not keep hold of, the life that slipped through his fingers.

He never fully returned, because coming back to France, getting to his family home in Roche, passing briefly through Paris, he realized that his only possible return was to Harar.

That remote valley was his only place in the world.

> *That Man should Labour & sorrow,*
> *& learn & forget, & return*
> *To the dark valley whence he came,*
> *to begin his labours anew.*

It is possible that before dying, still harboring hopes of returning, he recalled these lines from Blake, which he had read in the reading room of the British Museum. This clinging to life with all his might concealed the same words: return, sorrow, forget. To start all over the following day, doubtless at dawn.

In Harar, only in Harar . . .

There, in his dark valley.

9

The newspapers the following day carried photographs of the "slaughterhouse," as they called it, to the south of Cali and in their digital editions showed a detailed galley of images with the legal warning "not for those of a sensitive disposition."

Juana and I looked through them, and as we did so she told me who was who. Some, in addition to being wounded in the chest, had received the coup de grâce in the back of the neck. The explanation that was given for what had happened can be summed up in this press cutting:

"A revenge attack, a settling of accounts, or a turf war: these are the hypotheses offered by the criminologists of the Prosecutor's Department's technical investigation team, in collaboration with technical units of the Criminal Investigation Department, after inspecting the property in this exclusive area to the south of Cali in which early yesterday morning, during a party, a gun battle took place that left six dead and three seriously wounded. Among the bodies found was that of Néstor Pombo Holguín, also known as Cusumbosolo, second in command in the organization led by Freddy Otálora, the ex-paramilitary and head of an organization specializing in the production and sale of pink cocaine, who may have escaped. Among the dead are other members of the criminal gang, such as Belisario Córdoba Garcés, also known as Maluco, Andrés Felipe Arias Carvajal, also known as Palmasoya, Enrique

Gómez, also known as Pelaíto (a minor), and the women Esperanza Echeverri Santamaría (from Medellín), also known as Mireya, and Martina Vélez Uribe (a minor, also from Antioquia), also known as Pussy.

The place has been cordoned off and surrounded by police cars. A special prosecutor has been coordinating the investigation into these multiple murders."

Now we had to wait for Manuela. Another long wait.

I felt guilty for not being like most of my compatriots: optimistic, energetic, looking to the future, hoping to contribute in my own way to the construction of the new man.

When my phone vibrated, indicating another message, I immediately thought of Manuela. Maybe she was trying to communicate this way, but it wasn't her.

It was Teresa, the Mexican diplomat!

"How's it going, my dear Consul, and how wonderful that you managed to find Juana. How is she? And the child? Maybe you can send me some photographs. I left Thailand for Mexico City in 2010, but last year I was sent abroad again. I'm an ambassador now! Don't go thinking they sent me to Washington or Paris. No, I'm in Addis Ababa, Ethiopia. Mexico has just opened an embassy because this is the headquarters of the African Union and you can talk directly with fifty-four countries, it's just like the Brussels of Africa. You should come and see me, I have a nicer house than the one in Bangkok and much bigger. Why don't you come and spend a few days with Juana? Where are you both now? From Rome there's a direct flight on Ethiopian. Let me know if you like the idea. Affectionately, Teresa."

What a surprise: Ethiopia, Ethiopia.

I went back to my guard post in front of the TV, waiting for new revelations. The news may be the only drug that can make waiting more bearable. All the same, I was surprised by the amount of unimportant news that was produced daily.

"Two trucks were involved in a head-on collision on the way out of the Unicentro shopping mall in the city of Pereira, leaving one person injured and losses of several million. Since one of the trucks was transporting foodstuffs from Venezuela, it is believed that this may have been a premeditated act."

"An Italian citizen named Rocco Dozzino, a promoter of young Colombian soccer players to European clubs, reappeared yesterday in the city of Cartagena de Indias, where he was presumed to have been kidnapped two weeks ago. The supposed disappearance had alarmed the consulate of his country, which informed the authorities. On boarding the plane back to Bogotá, Señor Dozzino expressed surprise that he was the object of a search and explained that he had withdrawn to an isolated hotel on one of the Barú islands with his new partner, the Afro-Colombian Luis Pupo, thirty-six years old, former goalkeeper of Cortuluá soccer club. In any case"— and this was the other news—"Señor Dozzino will have to face a number of accusations of fraud."

And of course, the slow and laborious construction of the Republic of Goodness continued.

One of the principal changes in the legal system was the "legal jubilee," in which one day every two months the Public Prosecutor's offices were opened to all those who wanted to confess a crime, in this way obtaining a substantial reduction in the sentence, provided it did not involve a murder or a crime against humanity. The aim was to institutionalize forgiveness and provide incentives that could heal the wounds left behind by the conflict.

In a similar vein, the Union of Prosecutors' Departments and the Ministry of Defense created a show on the educational channel called *The Forgiveness Hour*, which knocked the most popular soap operas, and in some cases even soccer matches involving our beloved national team, off the top ratings slots. The format of the show was to confront former combatants, from whichever sides, with their victims. It was recorded in the open air in front of a large audience. In most of the episodes, the perpetrator would present his case in front of the victim, who watched him from one of the seats on the improvised set. When he had finished, the perpetrator would approach with a wireless microphone and beg forgiveness, sometimes even getting down on his knees. This was the most emotional part of the show, since the victim, generally in tears and clenching his teeth, ended up by agreeing and saying, "Yes, I forgive you," which would lead to thunderous applause, cries of congratulations, and whoops of joy from the audience. In some cases, the perpetrator and the victim embraced.

This program of reconciliation had been imported from the experience of the Republic of Rwanda, where the Hutu population had exterminated a million ethnic Tutsis in the space of two or three months in 1994.

Many hours passed before Manuela returned. Tertullian told us we had to go back to Bogotá immediately. He would travel that same night to Amsterdam. My attention was drawn to his strange golfer's outfit: a pair of plaid pants and a light jacket.

"Well, my dear friends, it was a pleasure," he said, bowing, "nature can feel proud of us. Mother Earth is a little better than she was a while ago, and that's something our ancestors will thank us for; anyway, Manuelita will tell you the ending of this story. I just want to repeat two instructions: stay together, but keep out of sight, am I making myself clear? Juanita: you and I are quits. It was a pleasure being able to help you. Consul, the honor was all mine."

Having said this, he left.

Two hours later we were on a flight to Bogotá. Manuela maintained her silence during the flight and when we got to the apartment in the Nogal she shut herself in her room. When

Juana went to ask her if she would like a cup of tea, she found her on the floor, in a fetal position, hugging her legs.

That night, watching the news, Juana and I found out what had happened.

THEORY OF ACIDS
(MANUELA'S STORY)

When we got to the house they took off the eye mask they'd put on me because Tertullian said, if anything happens, it's best you don't know where we went, and that's why I was only able to see when I was already inside, although of course thanks to the clouds and the air and the smell and what was visible in the distance I knew we were somewhere between Cali and Palmira, how could I not know where we were when this is my land? He said to me, Manuelita, think carefully about what's going to happen now, all right? when you see him, he'll be unconscious because we gave him a very powerful soporific; he's also tied up in case he wakes up, but I want you to internalize whatever it is you're going to do, all right? I don't want you to get cold feet, and I said, cold feet? forget it, this is the moment I've been waiting for my whole life, how can I turn back now?

Revenge is the great orgasm of hate, I thought, it's when you can at last give shape to what you've been feeling and harboring inside you, like the fetus of an unborn child, because you devote energy and imagination to hate, almost as much as or even more than to love; and of course, they've both done me a lot of harm, but life is like that, we steal from each other, although this is different because Freddy stole my childhood and you know that childhood is the only true country, and as far as I'm concerned that man kicked me out of mine, tore it to pieces, and then killed my mother, who was an idiot who first let my father go and then got involved with a thug like that, out of pure stupidity, and that's why she had to die, by the law of female ignorance and stupidity, but in spite of that she was my mother and the guy killed her.

He humiliated her and killed her.

Tertullian led me down some steps to the basement, asked if I was ready, and said that they had him behind the door he was going to open. I told him not to worry, I was ready, and then, being a man who loves rituals, he had a servant bring him an urn filled with earth and explained that before seeing him we had to honor it, that I should grab a few handfuls and kiss it, and he did the same and even rubbed it on his cheeks, and when he finished he opened the door and fortunately Freddy was still asleep, because when I saw him, my knees started shaking, it was as if I'd been hit but I stood there and took it.

We went in.

They had him on a metal bed, like a hospital bed, with the floor covered in plastic that was stuck to the wall with tape and there I saw his face, that cursed face I remembered so well. The bastard was well preserved, life in the paramilitaries had kept him in good shape. He was going to make a slim corpse. He had lost weight and his face was thinner, but the rest was the same, with that expression of someone who's about to do something terrible or explode with rage; then I focused on his hands, which lay rigid on the bedspread, and looked at his fingers: I couldn't avoid the image of those foul meat hooks taking down my panties, parting my legs, touching me with his filth; it was those fingers that raped me, and I thought, how many people have those short, thick, hairy fingers killed, how many women have they beaten or hurt; I was struck by how well tended his nails were, but of course, since he was going to a party he probably had a manicure; what a good thing it was to appear before the judges looking so good, because this would be a premature final judgment.

Suddenly I noticed something imperceptible, a reflex, so I

raised my eyes and I saw him looking at me: there were his horrible eyes; a wide surgical bandage covered his mouth and he couldn't speak, but the way he looked at me showed what was going through his head, or what he was trying to understand, because I think he recognized me: I saw it in the cold intense way he was looking at me; I felt a tear in the stomach so strong that I even started my period because of the nerves, but I didn't cry out or say anything, and when Tertullian said to him, hey, what have we here? a little angel opening his eyes! hello, I have some so-so news for you that has to do with your immediate future, isn't that right?, Freddy moved and tried to free himself but the straps kept him tied to the bed, and then Tertullian said to me, well, what do you want to do? this sack of garbage is all yours, I've put out a few things to give you some ideas, I don't know, for example we have a nice bottle of sulfuric acid, which corrodes the tissues, sometimes it even gets down to the bone, and maybe even reaches the trachea, do you see? I know a lot about this because, I have to confess, I love acid, I have a weakness for acids, if you know how to do things you can achieve a gastric perforation and cause peritonitis, and when you get to that point the die is cast, it's one step from circulatory collapse; the likeliest thing is that eternal sleep follows, but I don't know, you choose, Tertullian said to me. My tongue was stuck to my palate, my mouth was dry, I couldn't utter a sound.

I asked him to excuse me, left the room for a moment, and threw up in the bathroom, crouching, while one of Tertullian's colleagues held my hair away from my face; when it was over I wiped my mouth and went back, already recovered, and said to him: I'm not going to be capable of killing him, I know you've taken risks to help me, this world disgusts me completely, but killing him would be going over to the other side, so Tertullian said, don't worry, Manuelita, you don't have to do anything, just tell me what you want and that's it, this man is a mistake of nature, a tumor to be cut out of the human race, a humanoid and a piece of scum, you know nothing is going to change under the stars when this piece of shit goes, bye-bye, you know that, don't you? and I said, of course I do, I leave him in your hands, he's yours, I can't forgive him; and I confess, Consul, that I actually made an effort to forgive him, but I couldn't.

I had more than two years of psychoanalysis in Madrid, I devoted myself to studying Indian gurus, like Osho, who teach you to control "associative thinking," but it made no difference. In the end I realized, or thought I realized, that forgiveness can only be collective and form part of a project; that's the only way to be human again and maybe some people can accept it, but realizing this distanced me even more because nobody was going to rebuild anything with my forgiveness, not even myself; in my case, it would be tantamount to keeping the past fresh and not allowing the future to occupy my life; to leaving the scar open and bleeding, as it has been since the day that man mutilated me.

I can't kill him, I said to Tertullian, but he has to undergo a terrible punishment. My hate rose again and overcame the fear, and so I said to Tertullian, killing him would be a gift. He has to suffer for as long as he lives, he has to yearn for death, he has to be marked by this.

Then Tertullian said, I like that idea, Manuelita, I was always amenable conceptually to what I call partial removals, and for the same reason that you say, it's a truly educational task! And anyway, don't worry: this gentleman, or what'll be left of him, will go to prison as soon as they find him; they may not recognize him at first, you can be sure of that, but with the criminal record he has I don't think he'll ever again spend a single free day in his life. He'll think that what we're going to do to him was the work of the rival gang. He saw you, of course, but when he opens his eyes again he'll think it was a dream.

Then Tertullian said, now let's get down to action, I'm very fond of amputations, what would you like us to take off him?

He suggested making two large cuts, one arm and one leg, on opposite sides, and because he was a rapist emasculation was almost obligatory; if in addition I wanted to do something in my mother's name, we could think about a controlled sprinkling of acid on the cheeks, enough to burn his skin and some cartilage in such a way that even his fucking mother wouldn't recognize him, that's what Tertullian said, Consul, how embarrassing to repeat these things to you, and I replied yes, I liked that idea, although I hated his fingers, especially his rapist's fingers, and he said that with the arm we were thinking to leave him we could do another small amputation and leave him only the thumb.

I went in to look at him for the last time and again felt that stabbing sensation in the stomach, so I went back out again and looked through the hole in the door. Tertullian and his assistants got down to work. They moved some small metal tables close to the bed, with surgical instruments on them: dividers and forceps, scissors and scalpels, three sizes of metal saw, a precision hammer and a millimetric aluminum ruler; seeing all that, Freddy started writhing and struggling. I saw the panic in his eyes when he lifted his head a little and discovered that the floor was covered in plastic sheeting.

I sat down in the corridor and saw them putting on white coats and gloves. Tertullian seemed excited; when they were about to start I heard him say to Freddy: well now, my dear friend, we're going to give you one last surprise gift, a cocktail of ether and two other anesthetics, courtesy of the house, of course, so that your muscles are relaxed while we remove a few things you're really not going to need anymore, just wait and see how relaxed and light you feel when you wake up, but for now, take this moment to have a last look, because soon you're going to lose approximately thirty percent of your body mass; the first thing we're going to remove is your cock, nip and stitch, and be grateful I'm not such a good surgeon because if I was I'd give you an artificial cunt, so they can fuck you that way in prison. The most likely thing, my friend, is that they'll use you as an inflatable doll and break your ass, I hope you like that, they say it only hurts the first time, and it's better late than never; anyway, my dear Freddy, what you see around you is both a mausoleum and a delivery room, one goes and another is born, a metaphor for life, don't you think? You'll have plenty of time later to think about existence and the painful dominance of the flesh.

Okay, enough of the induction speech, boys, let's get on with it!

I heard gasping and struggling.

I realized they'd given him the anesthetics when he stopped moving and emitting noises. I dared to look and they were already operating on him. Tertullian was whistling and saying incoherent things. A kind of antiphonal chant to which the others responded, as if in chorus. I listened to them for a while and felt my heart beat faster, I was sweating and dizzy. I asked one of the men, the one who'd held my hair while I was throwing up, to take me out of there. He took me to a servant's room where there was a TV and a bed. I tried to distract myself for a while and fell asleep. When I woke, someone was looking at me from the door and signaling to me. It was still night, or maybe I was in a part of the house that the light didn't reach. I had no way of knowing.

The master wants to see you, he said, so I went along the corridor again and got to the door of the room, thinking I'd never heard him called "master" before. Tertullian came out looking tired and sweaty and said, my dear, the operation was a success, we've already removed quite a lot of the body, including the fingers you wanted, and we gave him a face mask of sulfuric acid, nothing very deep, just enough for him to be disfigured without it eating into the bones. It was difficult to keep control of the nose and in the end almost all the cartilage got burned away, I was tired, but we managed to save half. Oh, I almost forgot: I also removed his cock. With his face all burned and disfigured like that, he isn't likely to be using it much, don't you think?

His colleagues finished taking off the plastic sheets. They dissolved the amputated limbs in a five-liter earthenware bottle of acid then threw them on the fire. I looked at what was left of Freddy. There wasn't much to see. His face was covered with a bandage and there was a blue sheet over his body. I asked how long he would be like that, and Tertullian said, he'll wake up in six hours. They would leave him connected to a drip containing serum and a carefully measured dose of morphine. Because we're going now, he said, but before that we'll call the ambulance service and the police and ask them to come for him.

I want you to know something, Tertullian said as he left: when he opens his eyes and sees the hell he's in he may think of you, although it's unlikely he'll remember what he saw. The dose of anesthetics we gave him cuts out short-term memory. Gradually he'll remember the party in the other house, where they would have killed him if we hadn't gotten him out of there.

* * *

What I saw on the TV news that night left me astonished. It was in all the main headlines: the discovery of Freddy Otálora abandoned in an old house in the country, alive but with horrible amputations and his face dissolved by acid. After the massacre in the house to the south of Cali, it seemed like an even more macabre sequel; nobody had the slightest doubt that both events were connected, that the second was a consequence of the massacre, which had been interrupted by the police. That kind of torture and amputation led them to think of the Mexican cartels, which were famous for their horrendous crimes.

One of the main commentators said the following: "These internecine wars between drug gangs are an example of how the new actions of the police and the army, which in this new country can be devoted exclusively to public order, are having a devastating effect on crime, generating such nervousness and insecurity among the gangs that they end up destroying each other."

When Manuela finished telling us her story, I asked:

"Do you feel better now?"

"No, Consul," she said. "I have to let a little more time pass. I look through the window and feel scared."

Two days later, on the Sunday, I went with Juana and the boy to visit her brother's grave. Juana kept her promise and paid her parents a visit, but she insisted on going to the cemetery first. I assumed we would meet them there, by Manuel's grave, and I wasn't wrong. I had the boy by the hand when I saw them from a distance. Juana also saw them.

"Wait for me here a moment, Consul, stay with Manuelito. Let me go first."

I took the boy over to some vases of flowers, where a hummingbird was flying, and watched her approach them. She didn't slow down until she was very close to them. The two old people were facing the stone, and the mother was trimming the grass that had grown around the grave with a pair of garden scissors.

The mother was the first to see her. She dropped the scissors and raised a hand to her mouth. Then the father saw her. He gave her a hug and looked at her and again hugged her and the mother also joined in the hug. My heart skipped a beat. I followed them with my eyes while the boy imitated the hummingbird with his fingers. What were they saying to each other? The scene was too intimate for me to get any closer, but that was fine. Suddenly Juana turned and looked for her son. I pointed to his mother and said:

"You see your mother over there? Run very quickly, she has a surprise for you."

The boy ran off like a shot, jumping over rows of flowers and stone paths. He ran and ran with pure, unpolluted joy. In that movement of the child toward her and his new grandparents I thought I finally recognized something lasting, something fundamental.

It was rather more than I had been looking for, so I walked away toward the avenue. Before leaving, I turned to look at them from a distance. From where I stood, they looked happy. When I hailed a taxi, it was starting to rain.

That night she got back to the house quite late.

"Thank you, Consul," she said. "I'll never forget all you've done for me."

Manuela remained glued to the news, hungry to hear the outcome. She thought Freddy might die of his wounds, but that news didn't come.

From that day on, Juana started going to see her parents every afternoon, with the boy. On the fourth day, though, she said to me:

"Tertullian says we should be on the alert, there might be security problems."

I thought we should go, postpone once more the final return, although again I wondered where. I wasn't Ulysses, returning to a woman's side. There were no islands for me in the world. The only return possible, I told myself, would be to a place devoid of uncomfortable and obsolete experiences. To return where I had dreamed of going and couldn't. But what place was that? I thought about Manuela's words and about Teresa, the Mexican woman: perhaps the same place Rimbaud had wanted to return to.

EPILOGUE
RETURNING WHERE RIMBAUD WANTED TO RETURN

S een from the plane, Addis Ababa looks like a sloping table. A green table that rises and disappears into the Entoto Mountains, whose peaks can be seen in the distance. In Amharic, the principal language of the country, Addis Ababa means "new flower," a flower in a land that slopes. These are the highlands of Africa, no mosquitos, no malaria. The sun is bright but harmless and the wind dries the skin. What does this "new flower" smell of? Early in the morning, apart from the dense aroma of coffee, it smells of the cold wind from the mountains and of motor fuel without much oil, the smell of bonfires and carbon monoxide: the exhaust fumes from taxis and buses laboriously climbing Bole Avenue to Meskel Square.

*

It had been a long flight, and we were tired when we arrived at Bole International Airport.

Teresa was waiting for us with two officials from her embassy. As a diplomat, she was able to come right up to the door of the plane. We gave each other a big hug. She looked exactly the same, not a single white hair.

"Welcome!" she said.

We were helped to fill out the forms and get through the immigration formalities. Teresa gave Juana a big hug and lifted the boy.

"And this cutie pie?"

She had brought a box of Lego as a gift for him.

I introduced her to Manuela and we went straight to her residence. It was a beautiful day.

The diplomats in Addis live in the Turkish Compound, which is near the airport, an elegant area of mansions and bungalows surrounded by gardens. Uniformed servants cut the grass and take care of the plants, and others collect dead leaves from the ground. There are palms, shady trees. At the far end is a river whose waters, strangely, accumulate foam.

When we got there, Teresa showed us around the house, including the three rooms she had prepared for us: Juana and the boy in one, another for Manuela, and the third for me.

*

I looked through the window of my room: on the other side of the wooden fences and the gardens are the Brazilian and Portuguese residences. In the sky fly a dozen marabou storks, those huge ugly birds that look like frock coats, with curved beaks that sink into carrion like scalpels. They circle, waiting to home in on garbage dumps or the rib cages of dead animals. There are also falcons and eagles, perhaps the true masters of the city.

Teresa was impatient to hear our story, but said:

"I have to go to the office, but you all make yourselves comfortable and relax. This Mexican house is yours."

And she added, for my sake:

"If you want to have a look around the city, Tibabu will take you. We can catch up tonight."

Tibabu was her driver.

*

The women and the boy decided to stay. I needed to be alone and lose myself a little, try to forget what we had left behind. That's what traveling is, too: starting over again, purifying yourself amid the anonymous crowd.

The driver left me near a place called Africa Hall, on Avenue Menelik II. The air pollution made my eyes water. The headquarters of the African Union was there. I kept going, toward the center, and soon afterwards the sidewalks stopped. People walked on the edges of the roadway, but the drivers were friendly. After a while I came to something that, from what I could see, was the central point of the city. They call it Piazza. Despite the grime on the walls and the powdery air it still had a kind of nobility, especially in the high doorways and balconies. Farther on, I saw the Hotel Taitu, the oldest in Addis. The sun was already going down and there was a great deal of bustle.

On the street there was a small flea market that didn't seem improvised. What were they selling? Old illustrated Bibles in Amharic, silver Orthodox crosses, icons, amber beads, horn spoons, wooden animals. At the end of the street I saw a pharmacy. Farther on, an auto repair shop. A pair of legs stuck out from beneath the engine of a Peugeot 404.

*

I observed the people. Ethiopians are physically beautiful. Very dark eyes, fine features. They are tall and thin, like the Masai. The women smile and their teeth glisten. In the café of the hotel I asked for a beer and chatted with the manager, a man in a white shirt and tie who strolled back and forth between the tables and the reception desk.

"There are three kinds of people in the world," he said, "the *faranyis*, the negroes, and the *abeshás* (Abyssinians)."

I remembered children on the street calling me: *"Faranyi,*

faranyi, faranyi!" which means "white foreigner." That word is an old acquaintance. In Thailand they pronounce it *farang* and in Malaysia, *feringui.* It's a corruption of the word "Frank" that, since the crusades of the twelfth century, has traveled with Islam from North Africa to Asia and is used, by extension, for every white Westerner.

*

After a while I decide to go back to the residence. Night is falling, and I don't know the city. The streets of Addis are dark and full of half-constructed buildings, some just raw shells. The scaffolding is made of long bamboo poles and looks fragile. It makes you dizzy just imagining the workers up there, swaying in the wind.

I take a taxi from the Taitu. On the ride back, I see stores with merchandise in the doorway, kiosks, and dusty stands, but also, farther on, shopping malls with lavish neon lighting. I write down in my notebook the name of one of them, the most extravagant: Bole Dembel Shopping Center.

*

"Where have you been, Consul?" Juana asked me when I got back.

"I had a look around Addis."

"Is it nice?"

"Yes."

"What I saw from the car looked sad and poor," Manuela said.

"It's Africa," I said.

None of the three wanted to look in the online papers for the latest developments from Cali. The last thing I'd heard, at the airport in Rome—we came to Addis on Ethiopian—was a description of Freddy Otálora's body, "disfigured by acid and with extraordinary macabre amputations." That was what a newspaper said. Everything was still being blamed on a rival gang.

*

When Teresa arrived, we sat down to a delicious dinner. The calm, orderly atmosphere of that luxurious residence was in marked contrast to our devastating memories, but nobody said anything. I still felt as if my soul was dirty. After dinner, we went out on the terrace and Teresa opened the bar. Tequila, gin and tonic, whiskey. For the first time, Juana talked about her life.

"I was in Paris for a while with a Colombian friend," she said in response to Teresa, who had no problem asking her questions, something I hadn't dared to do. "I learned French, worked with political exiles, traveled a little. The boy started school and we led a normal life. I started working with an NGO investigating human rights violations in Colombia, but I kept away from the country. Then I went to Madrid, still working for that same French NGO. I spent a long time looking at the windows of the houses. A simple life, the life that so many other people led. Nothing heroic."

*

Three days went by and Teresa took us to see some of the sights of the city, such as the Merkato, the great open-air market, with alleys of spices, baskets and vegetables, fabrics and leather, workshops of wood and ironwork. In the antiquarians' area we saw Orthodox crosses, reliquaries, rosaries, amber, and the curious funerary images of the Konso people, which depict their dead on posts with penises carved in the front. I took notes, reviving the travel writer who had lain dormant in me in the past few years, but I never forgot that our true destination was Harar, Rimbaud's home. I didn't want to tell Teresa yet.

*

Another day, she took us to the Memorial of the Red Terror, dedicated to Mengistu's great repression of 1974.[1] We saw photographs of massacred students, lists of names, and something particularly shocking: life-size dolls in strange positions, illustrating the torture methods. Manuela started to feel bad and I hurried us on. Another of the rooms was filled with skulls and bones taken from mass graves. I copied the names of two young people: Walelegne Mebratu and Marta Mebratu, two siblings who were students, brutally tortured and murdered. Suddenly Manuela ran to the exit. I saw that she was crying.

We left.

*

Tibabu is a retired teacher from the National University in Addis and decided to lecture us about his culture:

"We have our own alphabet, our own languages, which nobody understands anymore, and even our own system of hours and a calendar that's four years behind the Gregorian.

[1] In 1974 Lieutenant-Colonel Mengistu Haile Mariam seized power in a coup and assassinated Selassie, Tibabu tells me. He was the leader of a military junta known as the Derg. In 1987, he established the People's Democratic Republic of Ethiopia, allied with Moscow. It lasted until 1991. Mengistu escaped in a plane filled with gold, sacks of dollars, and jewelry. Today he lives in Zimbabwe, protected by his friend Robert Mugabe. He is accused of genocide and has already been sentenced to death. He cannot return to Ethiopia.

Amharic is a Semitic language, and is the most widely spoken, but there are also Oromo, Tigrinya, and Harari."

*

When we get back to the house I tell Teresa that we want to go to Harar and of course she offers to arrange everything and find us a van. I tell her no: I feel we have to travel alone, under our own steam. Get there in the simplest possible way.

*

The next day I went to buy tickets from the Salam bus company and we prepared for an eleven-hour journey. The old French railroad line that joins Addis with Dire Dawa and the Red Sea, on the coast of Djibouti, has been abandoned. There was no choice. We could go in a ramshackle Canadair plane of Ethiopian Airlines, but we wanted to approach it more slowly, see the mountains and the rivers.

So now, off to Harar.

*

It's still dark when we get to Meskel Square to take the bus. It's cold. A woman drags a cart filled with thermos flasks. We have coffee and wait. Manuelito Sayeq is sleepy, and seems very quiet. I realize that he's used to the company of adults and to strange situations. He plays with a doll and carries a bag of Lego pieces in his hand. We are a strange quartet, but the faces watching us from the darkness are friendly.

At last the bus appears, a modern lime-green vehicle, and a silent group of travelers, frozen stiff, starts to board. The dawn rises behind the roofs of the outskirts of Addis until, ahead of our bus, the highway appears: two wide lanes, with asphalt that looks to have been renovated not long ago. "The Chinese did that," someone tells me. Harar is in the east, near the border with Somalia. We exit on the eastern side of the sloping table.

I'm nervous.

*

The vegetation continues to be green, although it's mostly dry, prickly shrubs. And the ground is as black as volcanic clay. Everything is very dry in spite of the altitude. "It's because of the wind," says one of the people sitting near us. Strange hillocks appear, looking like huge tortoiseshells that have fallen on the plain. The bus driver toots his horn to disperse flocks of goats. On the sides of the road donkeys appear, with loads of wood tied to their backs, barefoot children urging on cows with wooden rattles, a few camels. We see small villages of circular huts with straw roofs. The temperature rises. With the animals are peasants, young girls carry their younger brothers on their shoulders. A little farther on—it's almost noon—I see a child sitting beside a brown puddle. God above, he's drinking the water! In the background, between the dunes and the prickly brambles, a woman walks very upright, carrying a huge teapot on her head. It's like a painting by Dalí.

My three companions are asleep. I can't stop looking through the window and writing in my notebook. I feel that we are leaving one world behind and advancing into another, a new one, only recently discovered.

*

As the road descends, cultivated fields appear and the earth becomes more fertile, this is the red earth of Africa. I see fields of corn, small vegetable gardens, banana shoots. The conditions of the peasants improve: the temperate climate makes poverty more bearable. In the villages there are square shacks with zinc roofs, mixed with the circular ones of straw. The walls are of beaten earth and wood.

All life is on the road. Children approach the bus, asking for empty packaging, plastic bottles. They're recyclers. Some stare longingly at the vehicle. Maybe they dream of leaving, some day, on one of those buses. The women sell bundles of fruit. Mandarins and bananas. Inside, a television is showing a Jean-Claude Van Damme movie. The people are supportive of each other. Someone behind me opens a pack of potato chips and offers it to his neighbors. Another shares the mandarins he has just bought.

Soon afterwards we stop in a village, it's lunchtime. We sit down in a kind of canteen and Juana takes out a bag with fruit and sandwiches prepared by Teresa's cooks. I ask for a beer. One of our neighbors orders *inyera* with spicy chicken sauce. We have half an hour.

*

The journey continues. The road rolls on along a steep precipice. These are the highlands. On our left are endless plains, a horizon that could be hundreds of miles away. It is a majestic sight, dotted with falcons and marabou storks. Now Manuelito is beside me and together we look at the landscape. We see some trees that look like birds with their arms bent, like the *ashok* in India. What is it? he asks. "It's called a *ziqba*," someone says, "and the one over there is a *wanza*, it has brighter leaves."

Many hours later we reach Dira Dawa, the poor one-horse town where the airport is. "From here to Harar it's only fifty minutes," they tell us. And again the bus ascends to the mountains.

*

How long have I been dreaming of going to Harar? Is this the final return? Manuela sits with me on the terrace of the Ras Hotel and from there we look down at the old walled city. We recover from the journey with a Harari beer. When Juana and Manuelito are ready we leave for the encounter.

"At dawn, armed with a burning patience, we shall enter the splendid Cities," wrote Rimbaud.

We, too, were about to enter this old city. Passing through the wall, I felt a strange, inexplicable nostalgia.

*

Rimbaud came through that arch just over a hundred and thirty years ago, but the walls and the stones massed on the sides seem to be the same. The city within the walls is called the *Jegol.*

*

We enter the *Jegol* through the eastern arch, the Asmaddin Beri. In this section the walls have Arab-style minarets, the wall is of earth and dry stone. The gate is a brick turret with a pointed arch, decorated with a brief piece of Islamic calligraphy and two lines of yellow tiles. There is a poor market in which people display their offerings on rags or mats. Everything looks quite dusty. There are beggars and lepers. *"Faranyi, faranyi!"* the children yell at us. A crazy-looking woman approaches Manuelito and he isn't scared, he just looks at her with curiosity.

*

Within the *Jegol*, walking along the main street, the Andegna Menguet, which leads to the square. On either side are two-story buildings with shops in every doorway: sellers of fabrics, jewelry, dresses and gifts, grocery stores. Also butchers' shops where camels and goats are cut up and the pieces hung on the door. This is purely local trade. There are no souvenir shops or anything like that.

On the ground are people chewing *qat*, the green leaf with natural amphetamine properties. Old women, squatting, sell bundles of it for a dollar fifty. There are skeletal men, with leafless branches all around, sleeping on the dusty sidewalks. *Qat* relieves pain and replaces food. Those who are not asleep look up at the sky and drink water, their red eyes fixed on a point in the air: it isn't clear if they are trying to see into the future or simply watching insects swarming round a streetlamp.

*

Harar is a succession of narrow alleys lined with one-story houses, built of earth and stone, with painted walls of colored stucco. There are eighty-two mosques, most of wood. The tutelary fathers of the city are Sheik Abadir, who arrived from Arabia in the tenth century, and the sixteenth-century Emir Nur, who built the wall.

But our strange quartet, including a child who knows nothing but understands everything, is here because of a poet.

*

Rimbaud's original house was demolished. Today it is a modest hotel called Wesen Seged, on Feres Megala Square. A two-story building, with two blue windows.

There it is, although the building is different.

Up there, in the blue windows! (I point it out to Manuelito.)

There is a very dark bar on the first floor. The day drinkers look at us and are upset. What their reddened eyes see has to advance through the optic nerve and cross a dense layer of lukewarm beer before reaching the brain. I go to the back of the room, where a rotted wooden staircase leads to the rooms on the second floor. There is a smell of urine. Standing by the ramshackle staircase, I think of Rimbaud's desire to distance himself from Europe and live forever in sordid places, where the only memorable thing is the smile of the people. It is not a small thing.

People make the dirtiest and most remote places seem beautiful, that's why there is a great beauty in the ugliness of these impoverished cities.

*

Dusty cities, dark at night; cities of the red night inhabited by crazed creatures who chew *qat* and drink water, foul-smelling beggars, crazy, toothless old women, lepers. This is what cities must have been like in the Middle Ages. To return to Harar is to return to the past, to something basic that hasn't changed with time. Rimbaud had been dreaming of it since he was young and had already written before coming: "I liked the desert, the scorched earth, the shriveled bars, the warm drinks. I crawled through foul-smelling alleys, with closed eyes, and offered myself to the sun, to the God of fire."

An ideal place for people haunted by dark memories. It was only in that atmosphere that we could heal.

*

The Ras Hotel has a small bar at the entrance. After dinner, the women went to sleep and I stayed there for a while, drinking a gin in silence. Then I went up to my room. I was about to switch off the light when I heard knocking at the door. It was Juana.

"Can I come in?"

"Of course."

She walked across the room to the bed, without looking at me. She lifted the counterpane and got in, but before doing that she dropped her robe and her very white panties on the floor.

"Enough of this, Consul," she said sadly. "I'm tired of waiting for you to make the first move. I'll give you thirty seconds to tell me you don't want it, otherwise take off your clothes and come here."

I hadn't kissed anyone with such pleasure and desire since my teenage years. I licked her lips and neck, passed my tongue over her tattoos, sucked her breasts and the lined skin below her navel; I parted her legs and filled myself with her smell and her juices. Her body was starting to slacken, but it was full of a life I longed for. In a moment I had the butterfly tattoo in front of me.

Madame Butterfly.

I could swear it was beating its wings.

*

Rimbaud lived with Oromo or Harari women, mostly Muslim, dressed in wide skirts of printed cotton and colored veils, with fine features. He saw slender youths, the *abeshás*, as thin as sculptures by Giacometti, strolling in the darkness with their linen hoods, looking at him with curiosity and doubtless calling him *faranyi*. Tichaka, the young man at the bar, says to me: "Rimbaud stayed with us because he found a life that was rough and wild." He pronounces it *Rambo* and only knows "The Drunken Boat," which is printed on a banner in the cultural center that bears his name: a three-story wooden house that used to belong to an Indian merchant and has been restored.

*

Rimbaud spoke Amharic and Arabic and had friends among the local population, even lived with a woman for just over a year, and traveled, finding in this dusty, rocky place the perfect setting for his restless soul. Perhaps he was searching in this remoteness and solitude for a chimerical encounter with his father, who had always been far from him in his childhood, always there in the deserts, in distant garrisons. Simply, Rimbaud opted to leave.

As the writer and traveler Paul Theroux says, Rimbaud is the patron saint of all of us, the travelers who throughout the world have repeated over and over his unanswerable question, the one he uttered for the first time in Harar: what am I doing here?

*

One morning, at breakfast, Manuela said to me:

"Last night, hearing the cries of the wild animals, I felt that the revenge hurt me, too, although in a different way. My anger is still there, but I've stopped crying: now I can read and remember. Very soon I'll be able to write."

It struck me that I should be grateful to the beasts of the night and the remoteness of the world.

*

Outside the hotel we can hear the howling of the hyenas and the barking of the dogs. It's an infernal din that comes from the mountains around Harar, which are full of animals. A strange madness overcomes this city at night. The wild hyenas approach the walls and a man feeds them ("the son of Yusuf," Tichaka tells me), gives them bones and pieces of meat he collects during the day from the butchers' shops. There is a legend of a hyena man who comes to destroy the city. Giving them food is a way of preventing them from attacking the peasants. That rough night concert of dogs and hyenas makes us feel protected.

*

Juana searched for a while on her computer and finally gave me a strange text to read.

"Look," she said to me, "this is from when I also read Rimbaud. A crazy invention. Let's see if you like it."

Today, Death paid me a visit.

Before, my life was a feast at which all hearts opened, and all wines flowed from glass to glass, from mouth to mouth.

One of those nights, I felt Death on my knees and found him bitter. I cursed him.

"Oh, Death, come and take away the thought of Death," I read in an old book.

"When me they fly, I am the wings," he replied, from another poem.

I summoned all my strength. I planted myself in front of him and rejected his terrifying fury. Then I escaped.

Death had a thousand faces.

Sometimes, he had blue eyes and was a young poet gazing at the twilight, in the port of Aden.

Death is here, and oh so punctual. Lord, your guest is waiting for you in the drawing room. Entrust my most precious treasures to the witches, to the spirits of poverty, to hate. I have succeeded in banishing any human hope from my soul.

As I already said: today, Death paid me a visit. Death, the Grim Reaper. Death who never rests from his labors, from his sleeplessness. Who loves us and passes between us like a wind, a *venticello*, a slow, dense music, a dark cloud.

I called to my executioners to raise their rifles, I summoned all the plagues to drown me in their sand or their blood.

Everything is merely proof that I can still dream.

Then I lay down on the dusty soil of Harar and saw the young poet again.

He was writing letters, looking southward. Every now and again he sank his hand into the red earth and let it run between his fingers.

We played with madness (were we fantasizing?) until the afternoon gave my mouth the terrifying smile of the idiot.

But I recovered my appetite, and went back to the parties, to the wine. Death was still there, I couldn't ignore him.

Everything is merely proof that I can still dream.

I read it twice, surprised.

"Did you write this? I mean, did you . . . ?"

"Don't ask me these questions, Consul."

*

Listening to the howling of the hyenas on the terrace of the Ras Hotel, I go over the correspondence linked to Rimbaud and find a letter from 1887 written by the French vice-consul in Aden, in which he asks for information about a fellow countryman named "Raimbeaux, or something similar," who has been handed over to him by the police. The individual has no papers, his appearance is slovenly, and he is unsteady when he walks. I feel envious of that description, and hope that one day I can live up to it.

*

Manuela prefers not to leave the hotel at night and stays with the boy. She writes and writes. Juana and I go for a drink at the National Bar, an old, dark, and, above all, empty place. Once my eyes get accustomed to the darkness, I see the music is coming from a humble duo: a female singer and her organist. They perform romantic songs and, in the darkness, she waves her arms, moved by her own words, trying to enliven an audience of ghosts. We ask for two beers. When they finish the song, there is no applause at all, of course, but the woman, in her evening dress, makes a solemn bow to the gallery.

I think it's the saddest, most heartbreaking, but also most beautiful gesture I have seen in my life.

*

The next day we return to Addis.

ABOUT THE AUTHOR

Novelist, short story writer, and journalist, Santiago Gamboa was born in Colombia in 1965. His American debut, published by Europa in 2012, was the novel *Necropolis*, winner of the Otra Orilla Literary Prize. He is also the author of *Night Prayers* (Europa, 2016).